ALSO BY PATRICIA O'BRIEN

Staying Together: Marriages That Work
The Woman Alone

THE CANDI

PATRICIA

SIMON & SCHUSTER

DATE'S WIFE

A NOVEL

O'BRIEN

New York   London   Toronto   Sydney   Tokyo   Singapore

SIMON & SCHUSTER
Simon & Schuster Building
Rockefeller Center
1230 Avenue of the Americas
New York, New York 10020

Designed by Deirdre C. Amthor

Manufactured in the United States of America

10 9 8 7 6 5 4 3 2

Library of Congress Cataloging in Publication Data

O'Brien, Patricia.
    The candidate's wife : a novel / Patricia O'Brien.
        p.   cm.
    I. Title.
PS3565.B73C36   1992
813'.54—dc20   91-36109
ISBN 0-671-73447-4   CIP

Acknowledgments

First of all I must thank my daughters Marianna and Margaret for their early readings of this manuscript, and Maureen and Monica for their encouragement and loyal support. Special thanks also to my good friends Ellen Goodman and Irene Wurtzel for their patient reading of endless drafts, to Laurel Laidlaw for helping me meet crucial deadlines, and to Everette Dennis, Executive Director, and the staff of the Freedom Forum Media Studies Center at Columbia University, for their help and support during my fellowship year.

To Michael Korda and Chuck Adams, my gratitude for their suggestions and astute editing. And a grateful tip of the hat to Esther Newberg, a generous guide to a new world.

Finally, love and thanks to Frank Mankiewicz, husband and best friend, for everything.

FOR FRANK

Prologue

Even with the sound of the television set in the background, the room seemed almost eerily quiet. Kate Goodspeed stared at the telephone resting on its stand. That's it, she thought. The phone isn't ringing. She was alone, nobody was trying to reach her, there was nothing she had to do, nothing but watch the changing presidential vote tallies flashing on the TV screen and try to figure out what came next in her life.

Slowly she moved around the room, touching familiar objects, remembering all the little automatic tricks she had used for so long to make the sterile confines of hundreds of hotels feel a little bit like home: turning on the lamps, propping the silver-framed photograph of the kids on the dresser. None of that was necessary anymore. It's over, she thought in dull surprise. It's really over. And then the exhaustion was complete. She felt as if she were floating in warm water, all muscles, all nerves inert. Wandering aimlessly, she picked up a book she had never finished and found herself wondering if now, perhaps, she might have time to read it to the end. A flash of white paper tucked inside caught her eye. It was an old schedule, dog-eared, grimy with smeared pencil scribbles in the margins. Kate smoothed it out and read, curiously.

Dallas, 8:00 A.M. Hispanic leaders breakfast meeting; Phoenix, 11:00 A.M. tour of children's hospital; fly to Los Angeles, four interviews on the plane; a helicopter tour of the fire-ravaged Hollywood Hills; airport stop in Eugene, Oregon; then on to Seattle to "rest" overnight, which was a joke. Nobody, especially the candidate and his wife, rested on a presidential campaign.

How did I do all this? She stared at the schedule in disbelief. How could any normal human being live this way? She felt numb, totally without connection to the evidence of her frenetic life. Suddenly the piece of paper in her hands felt too heavy to hold. Wearily she put it back inside the book and glanced over at a tray by her chair. I ate a chicken sandwich for dinner, she thought, staring at the remains lying on a plate. How strange. This evening, unlike all the others, I am actually noticing what I ate.

Then, inevitably, almost reluctantly, she walked over to the television set and forced herself to focus: to pick up information; to track these final moments of Luke Goodspeed's race for the presidency of the United States. She couldn't do it. There were suddenly tears in her eyes, and all she could see was a blur of color. I've got to stay calm, she decided, and wait this out. It'll be over soon. So much is over. But at least the telephone wasn't ringing—she could be grateful for that.

Resolutely, she stared at the images on the screen. It seemed such a long time since it all began . . .

1

Kate was already sinking back into the couch and wiggling her toes free of her shoes when she spied the reporter in the red skirt heading her way.

"Hi, Mrs. Goodspeed," trilled a confident voice that easily pierced the noisy din of the crowded convention suite at New Orleans' Hyatt Regency Hotel. "I know I'm going to be thrown out of here in a couple of minutes, but can I ask you a couple of questions? Please?"

Damn, Kate thought. "Sure," she said with a smile, shoving her swollen feet back into her shoes. Don't be a martyr, she scolded herself, just because you're hoarse from talking nonstop all day. Anyhow, on this wonderful night, why would she want to brush off a home-state reporter? Particularly Annie Marshall of the *Chicago Tribune*.

"What a moment this must be for you," said Annie, flashing a triumphant grin as she sat down and clicked on her tape recorder. "In less than an hour, Senator Goodspeed becomes the Democratic nominee for president. How do you feel?"

"Like I've won a Pulitzer and the world's biggest lottery, I guess," Kate said with a quick laugh. Her voice was cracking slightly from fatigue, but her gray eyes were steady. They were large eyes, framed with thick lashes, and always expressive; never more so than now. How could she ever describe how she felt? This was the most exciting, electrifying night of her life. I'm dazzled, she thought; flat-out dazzled.

"Have you put much thought into what happens to you if Senator

Goodspeed really does win?" Annie asked eagerly. "I mean—you'll be First Lady, but the White House can be a trap for women, don't you think? Either that, or they get crucified; some people say that's what happened to Nancy Reagan. Now you, you're different. You're independent, you do what you want to do."

Thank you for the invitation to get myself into hot water, thought Kate with amusement. "No, Annie, I won't be trapped," she said lightly. "Or crucified. And I intend to stay active on the things I care deeply about."

"How about the kids? Can they handle the White House?"

"Nat's not terribly impressed," Kate said. "At least, he says he isn't; you know how eleven-year-olds are. But Abby has big plans. She wants to celebrate her sixteenth birthday with a party in the East Room." Kate paused to push back the full, dark hair that was always falling in her eyes, thinking about her children. "They're great kids," she said feelingly.

"How come you weren't interested in politics at Indiana University? Too boring?"

"Oh, I was interested," Kate said, wondering when Annie would get to the point. She knew all this stuff; she was after something else. "I was just too busy taking history courses—until I got a summer reporting job and found that was more fun than studying the Civil War."

"So you worked for a local newspaper, then you headed for Washington and met the young, dashing Congressman—"

"Not for the first time," Kate corrected.

Annie nodded. "Oh yeah, first time, he was the young, dashing senior class president at Notre Dame. More interested in law than romance."

Kate laughed again. "You could put it that way." Her feet were itching now; she wasn't waiting any longer. With undisguised relief, she again pushed off her hot patent-leather shoes, and sighed. Come on, Annie, she thought, wrap it up.

Annie glanced quickly at her watch. "Is it true you and Marty Apple aren't seeing eye to eye on running the campaign?" she said abruptly, her pen suddenly poised to write. "And is Steve Feldon going to be fired?"

Kate paused. Even if he was considered the campaign's orches-trating genius, Marty Apple was not one of her favorite people, and

Annie knew it. And Steve was Luke's old friend and closest Senate aide. It felt disloyal to talk about him.

"Marty runs the campaign, not me," she said, hoping she didn't sound too brusque. "As far as Steve is concerned, he's up to his elbows in work in Luke's Senate office. Absolutely invaluable."

"Not going anywhere, though," Annie said briskly. "But, hey, that's politics." She flipped her notebook closed, but did not turn off the tape recorder. "About Marty—" she continued—"is it true he's trying to force you into the back seat? You know, making you the plastic lady, the old-fashioned candidate's wife?"

Kate's voice was firm. "Nobody forces me to do anything, Annie," she said.

"I'm not saying he is," Annie said, a little too quickly. "I'm just repeating a rumor, Mrs. Goodspeed."

This time Kate kept a pleasant look on her face and said nothing.

Annie gave up. "Okay, forget that," she said with a small sigh. "Tell me, what have you learned about your husband during the campaign?"

"Luke isn't afraid of anything," Kate said. She liked this question. "He'll stand up for what he believes in, and he'll do it from his heart as well as his head."

"What does he believe in?"

"His country. A strong sense of what's right and wrong. And his family—Nat and Abby and me." The words came quickly and easily; she hoped they didn't sound corny.

"Some people say you have the perfect American political family," Annie began, just as a campaign aide materialized and tapped her authoritatively on the shoulder. Irritated, she shook him off. "Do you?"

Annie's getting a bit desperate for a story, Kate thought. "Oh, come on, Annie," she said with a smile, hitting what she hoped was just the right self-deprecating note. "We're not perfect. I'm a lousy cook and Luke won't empty the dishwasher. We have our moments. Doesn't everyone?"

"But—" Annie started to ask something else, but the aide had grabbed her firmly and was guiding her up from her chair and toward the door. The room was being cleared of reporters. Kate shrugged and smiled and waved, keeping eye contact for five critical seconds. Then she stretched her legs and looked around. Finally she could

15

relax. The crowd of aides and supporters was growing noisier and more excited; all the outsiders were gone now. She spied Harry Hillman, one of her favorite Secret Service agents, working his way through the crowd in her direction.

"Nat's watching television in the other room," Harry whispered, the gun in his jacket bulging forward as he bent toward her ear. He paused, looking for a moment like the quintessential farm boy he was. "Mrs. Goodspeed, he's a good kid. He didn't mean to worry us by wandering off. Hope it didn't scare you too much."

Kate gave him her warmest smile. Scare her too much? Nat's fifteen-minute disappearance from the protection of the Secret Service this morning had totally petrified her. Wandering off to inspect bikes in a bike shop was not something he could do anymore; he had to understand that.

"No, no," she said, keeping her voice light, trying to erase the anxious look from Harry's face. She knew how responsible he felt. "I knew you'd find him fast. Look, call me Kate from now on, will you? Nat thinks the world of you, and so do we."

"Okay," he said, this time with a tentative grin. "Kate it is."

"What's happening downstairs?" she asked curiously.

"Looks like forty thousand people roaming the lobby," Hillman replied. "They closed the doors at the Superdome, so the overflow is everywhere—even the elevators are getting stuck."

"Any demonstrations?"

"Bad, good, or interesting?"

She laughed. "Tell me about the interesting ones."

Hillman's demeanor was loosening quickly. "Well, the Coalition to Legalize Cocaine had a fight with a bunch of Scientologists for space under a shade tree this afternoon," he said. "No bloodshed. Still could be some over the survival kits, though."

"Why?" The kits he referred to were passed out by the national committee to all the delegates, and they contained the usual stuff—aspirin, shampoo, and the like.

"Some smart-ass—excuse me, ma'am, I mean, Kate—snuck rubbers into a batch of them, and the Connecticut delegation is ready to spit, they're so mad."

She laughed. "Now *that's* funny," she said.

He grinned, gave her a nod goodbye, and turned to work his way back through the crowd and out the door. Kate glanced at her watch and felt a catch in her throat. Half an hour to go. A tiny trickle of sweat began moving slowly down her left temple. Was it the balky air-conditioning, trying to cope with a steamy New Orleans night? Not entirely, she had to admit. Gingerly she began picking at a plate of food thrust by an aide into her lap.

Suddenly Abby broke through the crush of people, gave her mother a grin, and collapsed into the seat next to her. The barbecued chicken leg Kate had been balancing on the plate bounced into the air and then down onto the skirt of her yellow silk suit.

"Oh, wow!" Abby's astonished stage whisper was low and piercing, cutting under the babble of excited voices filling the sweaty air. "Mother, why are you eating barbecued chicken right *now*, for Christ's sake?"

"I didn't expect you to knock it off my lap," Kate said crossly as she picked the chicken off her skirt. "And watch your language."

Abby started to retort, then stopped. She pressed her mother's arm in warning. "Look," she whispered, nodding in the direction of Claire Lorenzo, her father's deputy campaign manager. Claire, her face perfectly composed, was staring right at them.

"You're in trouble, Mom." Abby bit her lip. Smaller and more delicately boned than Kate, she had the same darting intelligence in her gray eyes and the same slender hands, hands that frequently mimicked her mother's quick-moving gestures. "I think the Dragon Lady's on her way over."

"The better to measure the size of the stain, I'll bet," whispered Kate, suddenly frustrated. This perfect night, Luke ready to give his acceptance speech, the world opening up, and that damn Claire was about to declare her, Kate, the crisis of the moment.

"Wow, she really *is* coming," Abby whispered.

Kate glanced quickly toward Luke, who was standing in a crowded corner of the room. She felt a thrill of pride. What a good-looking man he was! He was tall, with an athlete's body and a strong, mobile face she never tired of watching. Right now he was enjoying an animated discussion, pulling people toward him by his very presence. The combination of tinkling glasses mixed with the laughter around him sounded like thin ice crackling in a pond. Luke crinkled his face in concentration as he listened to the people who moved into

17

his orbit, his attention making each one feel special. He turned—sensing she was watching?—and offered a comic bow with a grateful gleam in his eye.

We've done it, she thought proudly. It's been scary and risky, but we've done it.

The sound of Claire's voice cut rudely through her ruminations.

"Kate, what a lousy break."

Claire was leaning close, speaking conspiratorially, her perfume subtle and yet enveloping. "I'll shoot whoever gave you that damn cardboard plate," she said with a small smile. Her throaty voice, deepened to a rasp from thousands of cigarettes, commanded attention even when deliberately modulated. At full throttle it could freeze the most hardened political pros. She was also indisputably striking, with copper-red hair and a long, narrow nose boldly carved from pale skin.

Gently she began pulling Kate by the arm, up and away from the sofa. "We'll try some club soda, but we'd better check out your wardrobe," she said, guiding Kate through the crowd toward the bedroom, with Abby following close behind. "What about the blue linen?"

"I'm not crazy about it," Kate objected.

"The background in the hall is red and white. That blue would stand out perfectly. And it would make the linen people very happy."

Kate shook her head with a quick, almost imperceptible motion. "I want to wear something tonight I really like," she said. "And I've done enough for the industry."

Claire sighed. "Okay," she said. "We'll find something."

Luke followed the pair with his eyes as they moved away, then looked inquiringly toward Marty. A stocky man in a wrinkled gray suit, Marty had a stillness of figure that made him a fixed point of reference in a room filled with ebullient, moving people. He was drinking a Coke, positioned on a direct line of sight with the television set, watching. Always watching. Luke's master campaign craftsman was not an attractive man in the best of circumstances, but tonight his chunky body had taken a direct hit from the heat. Damp, acrid yellow arcs had appeared under his arms, causing even the most sycophantic aides to edge away slightly. As Luke watched,

Marty's heavy brows drew together in a deep furrow; he signaled Luke with an imperceptible shake of his head.

Claire would handle this one.

Luke nodded and turned his attention back to the crowd.

Inside the bedroom, the door safely closed, Kate hoisted a bottle of club soda sitting on the bedside table and poured it liberally down the front of her stained skirt. Then she grabbed a towel and began rubbing, but the barbecue sauce just spread in a widening circle through the fabric.

Claire took the towel from her hand. "That's the worst thing you can do," she said. "Can't you see? It's hopeless."

Claire opened the closet and thrust darting fingernails into the hastily hung jumble of clothing. Kate looked down, saw a pair of Luke's jockey shorts lying next to the bed, and kicked them underneath the heavy quilted bedspread before Claire could notice. But Claire was focused on the closet, pulling out the bright blue linen suit and holding it up, her eyes questioning.

"It's the wrong shade for me," Kate objected.

"Kate, it's perfect for television," Claire said in the smooth tone one would use to soothe an irritable child. "I told you, you'll be standing in front of a red-and-white background on that podium, and you'll look great."

Kate stared at the suit with distaste. "No, thanks," she said.

Claire tossed the garment onto the bed with more force than necessary. "You do know you have to be out on that stage in ten minutes," she said lightly.

"Mother, please, choose something," interjected Abby, who was standing nervous guard by the door.

Kate gave up finally on the yellow suit, unzipping what had been up until a few minutes ago the prettiest, most expensive outfit she had ever owned, letting it drop to the carpet.

Someone outside the room pounded heavily on the door. "Everybody about ready in there? The senator is waiting."

Kate tried to swallow a lump wedged in her throat. She knew "the senator" would be charging through that door to collect his family in about thirty seconds if she didn't get her clothes on and get moving. This was the most important night of her life, and here she was in her slip in a lousy hotel room with her husband's jockey shorts under the bed and nothing decent to wear.

Claire ripped the plastic cover off a limegreen shirtwaist dress and held it up doubtfully. This is getting ridiculous, Kate told herself. I'm not getting into a power struggle with Claire over a dumb dress.

"This will do fine," she said, reaching for the shirtwaist.

Claire glanced at Abby, locking her into forced partnership with her eyes. Abby leaned back against the wall, appearing a little overwhelmed, and took a deep breath.

"Don't be stubborn, Mother," she said imploringly. "Wear the blue one, we've gotta get out of here." Kate started to object, but Abby hurried on. "Mom, I wouldn't wear a dress with short sleeves," she said. "The green's pretty, but it's not really your color anyhow. I didn't want to tell you that." Abby was talking now in a rush, oblivious to the flush rising in her mother's cheeks. "Ever thought about going to one of these color advisers, you know, getting your colors done?" she said brightly. "Want to do it together?" Her voice began to trail uncertainly as she met Kate's eyes. "Maybe after we get to the White House."

Wordlessly Kate picked up the blue linen from the bed, yanked the zipper down, and pulled the suit skirt over her head as a second pounding came on the door. Why, she asked herself, was she so furious at the sight of Claire's calm smile?

Luke was pacing impatiently as his wife and daughter emerged.

"Hey—" he said in mild reproof, then cupped Kate's chin, lifting it gently. Kate turned her face upward and felt the soft brush of her husband's lips. All exasperation melted away; nothing would spoil tonight.

Next to Luke, half in shadow, stood Marty. He reached out and plucked Luke's coat sleeve.

"Wait, I want a second with my wife," Luke said, pushing Marty's hand away. He pulled Kate back inside the room and shut the door, ignoring the mass consternation of his aides.

"Honey," Kate said, laughing, "we've got to—"

"Twenty seconds of quiet." He held both her hands in his, closed his eyes, and leaned back against the door. Kate leaned her head against his chest, listening to his rapidly beating heart, grateful for a moment of shared peace. Then he opened his eyes and smiled like a kid. "Come on, let's go claim our prize," he said. And in an instant, they were back in the corridor.

Marty stepped forward, taking no chances this time on losing Luke's attention. His hand shot out, forcing Luke to stop and listen.

"Remember, this isn't a rally," he said quietly. "These people want to cheer and the whole world is watching. Milk those applause lines."

"Give them yourself, Luke," Kate murmured. "That's what matters."

Luke nodded and squeezed her hand, and Kate pretended not to notice Marty's irritated glance as they all stepped into a waiting elevator. She felt suddenly giddy. She took deep breaths as they descended. By the time they had made their way across the ramp leading to the convention hall, she was having a hard time swallowing.

And then they were entering the hall.

Oh, God. Soaring space as far as she could see, a vastness that left her feeling incredibly tiny, a hugeness filled with deafening, exhilarating noise.

She looked up. There, high above the vast hall, were the network anchors suspended in glittering glass booths. She tried to imagine their thoughts; pretended she could script what they were this second telling the nation, ached to hear them say it:

"Here he comes, ladies and gentlemen, Luke Goodspeed, seven months ago just another senator from Illinois, now the nominee of his party, only the third Catholic in history to come this far in presidential politics. Soon you will be hearing him give the most important speech of his life, for tomorrow Luke Goodspeed will take on Republican nominee John Enright in a race for the greatest prize of all, the presidency—" Kate almost laughed out loud with excitement. Luke's national identity was about to take shape. Hundreds of satellite and microwave trucks were lined up outside to beam his speech back to local and independent TV stations all over the country. There, in tiny rooms without windows, producers would log the tape, marking the best soundbites, moving Luke Goodspeed into the forefront of the most important race in the world. Incredible.

Patricia O'Brien

Luke caught her gaze and leaned close. "Bet they're hoping I wind it up fast," he yelled over the noise. "There've gotta be some good parties later in the French Quarter. Red beans and rice, gumbo, Ramos gin fizzes—"

"Sounds good," Kate yelled back. "Shall we skip this and go?"

Together they inched through the crowd, the kids ahead of them, grabbing a hand here, a hand there, waving, smiling, as the band played and people cheered. Luke smiled directly at a paunchy delegate from Iowa, sending the man into a happy cheer. "We're going all the way, Luke!" yelled a woman from New York.

"Let's go, Luke! Let's go, Luke!" The chant was becoming a roar. A woman from Montana jumped on a chair, waving a Goodspeed for President poster, and then three people under the South Dakota banner started an impromptu cancan amidst the pushing, shoving crowd. Oh, God, the balloons! Kate laughed in total joy. Magnificently sized, helium-filled, exploding with color, they floated high in the air from delegation to delegation, from California to Connecticut, from Wisconsin to Hawaii to Illinois, sailing over Minnesota. Even rooted to the floor, mired in the tangle of the crowd, Kate felt she was floating with them. Suddenly she spotted a familiar face bobbing in the milling crowd of reporters; it disappeared, then—yes! There it was again! It was her old friend, Peter Bradford, chief political correspondent for the *Chicago Tribune*, moving through the crowd with them, just outside the protective phalanx of Secret Service agents.

"Hey, Peter, how are you doing?" she yelled impulsively. Peter, a tall man with deep-set eyes and a look of total assuredness, waved back in mock salute. There was a gleam of pleasure in his eye, but he was too much the professional to yell back. The days when he and Kate had covered Congress together as green young reporters were long ago and far away.

Kate put her foot on the first wooden step of the podium and scanned the mass of upturned faces before her. Give me just one second, she thought, just one second to savor it all so I can tuck it away and enjoy it later. Luke grabbed her hand and started to climb the stairs, pulling her gently. All she could think about as she started up the steps was how long it had taken to get there. Twenty years of sitting through speeches at union halls, eating corn dogs at county

22

fairs, courting supporters, waiting out election nights, being the loyal cheerleader, the loving wife, the trusted partner, and never, never flagging. Tonight was the payoff.

"We've made it," she whispered to Luke.

"Don't tempt fate," he whispered back. He kissed her on the top of the head, then threw his arm up in an exuberant wave. From deep inside the crowd, like the growl of a truly splendid roar of thunder, came the words they were hungry to hear.

"We want Luke! We want Luke! We want Luke!"

Abby reached the top step first. Already she was waving to the crowd, her small body on point, graceful as a ballet dancer. Her chin was tilted upward, eyes triumphant, skin polished and clean. Two paces behind came Nat. Maybe it was because he was squinting behind newly strengthened glasses, but suddenly he tripped on the top step, barely catching himself from a perilous sprawl. Kate winced. Nat was at an awkward age.

The band. Kate had been concentrating so much on the cheers, she only now heard the band tearing through the Notre Dame fight song. People were clapping and swaying and singing. "Our song!" Luke yelled with a wink to Kate over the noise.

She grinned back, remembering the fourth quarter of a long-ago Notre Dame–Southern Cal football game when they had first met. It felt like a hundred years ago.

He swung his arm around her. "Aren't you glad we got here together?" he whispered in her ear.

"Yes!" she yelled happily. She looked eagerly again for Peter's face, but it was lost in the crowd. All those years ago her old pal had worried that if she married Luke Goodspeed she would become some kind of wind-up doll—and now look. What did he think tonight?

Members of the Goodspeed family were moving to their special box in back of the podium now, trying not to blink against the scorching lights of the networks. Already in their seats were the two other women in the family—Kate's sister, the "much married" Joan Sullivan Mancini Levitt Duncan, as *Time* magazine called her, and Luke's mother, Louise, slim and tidy in a mauve wool suit, her white hair carefully arranged into sculpted, old-fashioned waves. Joan winked broadly at her sister, which made Kate nervous. You never knew what would strike Joan as funny, but that was the way things went with her. Nobody told her what to do. Three divorces, which had scandalized all their Catholic relatives, especially Luke's mother. Each one had left Joan with a considerable pile of money, which she spent freely—and generously, Kate thought with a rush of warmth, thinking of her sister's contributions to Luke's campaigns. Very generously.

Louise, looking shell-shocked, reached for the hand of a black-garbed priest sitting next to her. Louise was almost a stereotype. In her late seventies, a tiny woman permanently shattered by early widowhood, she was like a box of fine, fragile china. Kate blew her a kiss, hoping she wasn't going to act too vague today.

Kate's eyes rested briefly on the rather soft, round, jovial face of Father Joe Delancey, watching him pat Louise's hand. Father Joe, as the family called him—Luke's cousin and boyhood friend. A good guy. It was Kate's private opinion that Joe played a little too much to the crowd, but what a boon he had been for Luke on the campaign plane with his jokes and memories! Even Marty relaxed and laughed at them on occasion. After all, Father Joe was more than official Best Friend; he was also Luke's unofficial liaison to the Catholic vote. And Marty was never off duty.

Kate's eyes shifted then to Burt Wheeler, Luke's running mate, and his wife, Sally. They stood close together, nice people, both still slightly pop-eyed at finding themselves on the ticket, smiling for all they were worth. Kate felt sudden sympathy. Two days ago, the hardworking, rotund Wheeler was just the longtime governor of New Mexico, and the grandmotherly Sally was busy baking pies for a state Democratic picnic. Now here they are, she thought, linked to us for one of the world's great roller-coaster rides. She started to move toward them for a ritual hug and kiss, but a voice boomed over the loudspeaker, stopping her short.

"Ladies and gentlemen!" The hall grew silent. Ben Ritchie, the governor of Florida, was introducing Luke with a string of lavish rhetorical flourishes. Ritchie had stalled for weeks before finally dropping out of the primaries to help Luke, even when it was clear his own candidacy for the nomination was going nowhere. He was obviously eager to make up for it now.

Then the introduction was over, and the roars that greeted Luke subsided as he stepped to the podium. He faced the crowd, looking past the TelePrompTer into the reaches of the vast hall, the cameras zooming in for a close-up that could not quite catch the true brilliance of eyes that could burn holes through a television anchorman. He ran a hand over his chin, checking automatically for any emerging stubble, and began his speech. Kate crossed her fingers for luck.

"This is our moment, my friends," he began. "Our moment to savor a turning point in the quality of leadership in this country." He gripped the podium, eyes steady, linking himself to the crowd of upturned hopeful faces with an instant, invisible bond. The sound of his voice reverberated through the arched dome above his head, echoing back, down to the undulating sea of red-and-white signs below him. Tiny bursts of light from thousands of flashbulbs filled the hall as people clicked their cameras to record the moment.

Kate closed her eyes briefly, following every word of the memorized speech. This speech was his signal to the country, his justification for his presence in this hall, his credentials for knocking at the door of the White House. His voice rang out, full and firm, as he spoke of the need to shape an America that could reconcile opposing needs and stand united for the future with—as its cornerstone—the strongest and most stable economy in history. Then, and only then, could the country save forests *and* jobs; clean the air *and* keep industry vital; rejuvenate an aging nation, caring for both the elderly *and* the young.

"People are going bankrupt trying to give their parents both dignity and medical care while our government looks the other way," Luke declared. "How long, America? How long?"

Cheers, applause.

"Our lakes are polluted and our air is not fit to breathe," Luke said, pounding his fist on the lectern. "We cannot promise our children a drinkable glass of water. How long, America? How long?"

The roar of support shook even the glass network booths.

Then Kate found herself holding her breath. Luke had reached the place in his speech where he was supposed to reaffirm the party's pro-choice position on abortion, but he moved smoothly on, omitting the section. Her eyes flew not to Luke, but to Marty's barely visible figure at the side of the podium. Luke's campaign manager stared back, his expression flat, and Kate glanced away uneasily.

And then, almost stunningly fast, it was over. The crowd was cheering. Luke raised his arms high, his eyes lit with a light Kate had never seen, and reached for his wife and children.

The Goodspeeds stood together for a magic instant, almost fused in glory. They were not much more than four small specks of color in the hall, but on television screens across the land they were now a potential First Family, as gorgeous as any the nation had ever seen. It was the moment when all things were possible. The moment experienced by only an elite group of political families, some of whom had kept the glory and gone on to the White House— the Kennedys, the Johnsons, the Nixons, the Carters, the Reagans, the Bushes—and some who had not, some who had fallen into the particular oblivion, if not shame, that America reserves for losing presidential candidates. But nothing could spoil tonight. Luke's eyes were glistening as he made his way with his wife and children back from the podium and into the corridor that would lead them away from the arena and back to the hotel, a man lifted out of himself for this moment by the greatest political anointment possible.

The chants echoed and bounced from the walls as they hurried toward the hotel. "We want Luke! We want Luke!" Kate could still hear them as they entered the lobby. The room was jammed. The Secret Service, baggy men in clothes cut a size too large in order to accommodate guns and shoulder holsters, pushed back at the crowd to clear a way through to the elevator being held for Luke.

"Senator, what about those lines you dropped from your speech?" yelled a reporter from the *New York Post*, waving a bootlegged copy of an early draft. "You were going to make a statement on abortion. What were you going to say?"

"Later, you guys," Marty growled from his position at Luke's elbow.

The *Post* reporter was persistent, expertly dodging the hand of an agent. He pushed himself as close as he could to Luke. "Was it because of what happened to that girl in Nebraska?" he yelled again.

Luke stopped, frowned. This was a celebrated case in the news now for weeks. The reporters closed in.

"What happened?" he asked.

"She died, Senator. Just before your speech."

Marty grabbed Luke's arm, but Luke shrugged him off. Kate winced. Poor child. Only fourteen years old, refused an abortion because her parents, devout Catholics, wouldn't give the necessary permission required under the new state law. The American Civil Liberties Union had gone to court to get a waiver—and had lost.

"How did she die?" Luke asked.

"Tried to do it herself. Hemorrhaged."

Luke looked shocked. "That's horrible," he said. "What a terrible waste of a young life."

"Does that mean you're *for* abortion, Senator—or against it?"

Marty began elbowing the reporter away.

"I'm not for women dying like that, if that's what you mean," snapped Luke. He looked suddenly exhausted.

"What are you saying? Are you for abortion on demand? Which is your position, Senator? What about—?"

An agent with beefy hands gave a mighty shove and the *Post* reporter disappeared into a tangle of bodies and camera equipment. "Let's go!" yelled Marty, and the tight human centipede that was the Goodspeed entourage moved on.

At the elevator, Kate saw Marty groping in his suit pocket, probably for a cigarette. The twitch under his right eye was going again, the price paid for twenty-hour days. But nothing stopped Marty, not even a doctor's warning that if he kept smoking he would be dead in five years. He shifted from one foot to the other, obviously and frantically searching his pocket. He stopped. His fingers had closed over what he wanted to find, and his face muscles relaxed in relief. He caught Kate looking at him and gave her a lopsided, shamefaced grin.

"Marty—"

Kate heard Steve Feldon's voice, pierced with anxiety, and felt herself stiffen. Tall, graying, slightly hunched over in a too-new Lands' End poplin jacket, Steve was advancing toward them, smiling nervously. It was Steve—back when he and Luke were both young lawyers in the Cook County state's attorney's office—who first urged Luke to take a run for the congressional seat, and it was Steve who became Luke's indispensable aide after he was elected to the Senate. We wouldn't be here, Kate thought for the hundredth time, this wouldn't be happening, if it weren't for Steve.

But that cut no ice with Marty. "He's too small time; he doesn't

27

see the national picture quickly enough," Marty had repeatedly told Luke. "You can't afford this guy anymore."

"I owe him," Luke would reply. But everybody could see it wasn't working, and aides were whispering that sooner or later Luke would be forced to admit it. It was like killing someone slowly, Kate thought, and it was hard anymore to look Steve straight in the eye.

"I tried to get the news about the girl to you," Steve was saying to Marty, speaking quickly. "But Luke was already—"

Marty whirled, all business, looking at Steve as though he were a piece of spoiled meat. "First rule of politics, Steve," he snapped, cutting him off. "Never leave your candidate vulnerable."

"The crowds were—"

"Forget it," Marty said quickly. He turned his back, guided Luke and Kate into the elevator and stepped in, leaving Steve with a stunned expression on his face as the elevator doors closed.

It was 2:00 A.M. Marty was the last to leave the hotel suite, and Kate locked the door behind him with relief. Briefly she put her forehead against the cool marble of the doorframe. She felt the aching muscles of her face begin to relax. As she lifted her head, she saw Luke staring at her.

"You looked nice, Kate," he said quietly. "I like you in blue. It's still my favorite color."

Was there a small smile hovering at the side of his lips? If she asked, he would deny it. Instead, Kate pulled off her jacket and headed for the bedroom, pausing to brush her husband's cheek with a kiss.

Below them the city's lights looked subdued. Inside, the smell of stale cigarette smoke hung heavy over the living room of the sprawling suite. Luke's hand caressed her shoulder, then moved down to the small of her back, gently pushing her to the bedroom ahead of him.

Kate stretched out on the rumpled spread, watching Luke pull off his tie and shirt with brisk, rapid motions. She felt an urge to slow him down, but he was too wound up. It didn't matter; she liked watching.

Luke stepped out of his shorts and caught his naked reflection in the mirror and frowned. Concentrating, he pulled in his stomach, then let it out.

"Don't worry," Kate said, smiling. "You'll get rid of that working out in the White House gym." She didn't know if there even was one, but it was exciting to think about. Anything about the White House was exciting. Luke, in the Oval Office! They had been married for twenty years and here he was, a man whose picture would be on the front of every major newspaper in the country tomorrow, and she was so proud. The best thing was that only she, Kate, could enjoy watching that slightly protruding stomach darkened with soft and delicious hair. She reached out to touch, to establish her claim.

Luke smiled, a bit abashed at being caught, then stretched his long body out next to her on the bed. His hands cupped behind his head, he stared at the ceiling. "We're only a step away," he said.

"A big step," Kate whispered.

"But only one." He fell silent.

"What are you thinking about, honey?"

"About what all this means," he said slowly. "My God, Kate. Us. The White House."

"It's wonderful." She saw Luke, in her mind's eye, climbing the House podium to present his State of the Union address while she smiled and clapped, wearing a red dress, naturally, watching him proudly from the House gallery. . . .

"The president decides to send troops in case of war," he said, cutting into her reverie. "That's part of the job. I keep asking myself, how does it feel to send young men away maybe to die?"

Kate burrowed close, suddenly focused on the implications. "You won't know," she said quietly, "until and unless you have to do it."

"People forget how powerful the president really is," he said. "If you're going to run for president, you better be damn sure you know what you're doing."

"You do, I know that."

She could feel, rather than see, his smile, as he turned his head and kissed her cheek. "Thanks, kid," he said. "But why me? I've got heroes who really shaped this country. What makes me think I can walk in their shoes better than anyone else? Funny, not many reporters ask it that way; maybe they should."

"What would you say?"

Luke let out a sigh, actually more a gentle whistle of air through his nose. "That's the problem, it sounds corny."

Yes, it did, but Kate liked to hear it. When it came to his heroes, Luke didn't see only the words and the faded photographs. He saw real people, flesh and blood still, even though long in their graves, people who still had lessons to teach to anyone who would listen. At night sometimes he would whisper to her about what the country was and what it could be, and she would close her eyes and feel the strength of his will, pushing. Always pushing.

"At heart you're an idealist," she had said once.

"No, Kate," he had corrected. "I'm a realist with ideals. It's different."

She nudged him now, gently. "Tell me anyway."

"A president should stand for something," Luke said finally. "Like Roosevelt. Or Kennedy. Or, damn it, Ronald Reagan. My father made his share of compromises, and I used to hate it when he'd say, Someday, Luke, you'll understand. And what that meant was, You won't fight for what you believe in all the time, just like me." Luke stirred restlessly. "I know how tough it was for him to build a business and survive, but that makes me sad and angry. I want government to work better, and I think I can make that happen without compromising what I believe in."

She started to reply, but he kept on talking.

"Setting a course, knowing whom to trust—" Briefly he was silent. Then, "It's all politics right now, and I'm not forgetting that for a minute. This campaign, it's a carnival, a kind of goofy carnival; sometimes it's downright embarrassing, isn't it?"

She smiled, thinking of Luke taking part in an Indian rain dance, wearing a miner's helmet for a union convention, and eating frozen yogurt at a Santa Monica shopping mall. Yes, a carnival, who could deny it?

"But if I win, the game's over," Luke said soberly. "Everything changes."

Kate felt suddenly apprehensive. "For us?" she asked.

Instead of answering, Luke turned toward her, then, with a slow, deliberate motion, he unzipped the rumpled blue linen skirt, pulled it down with her panty hose to Kate's feet and let both fall to the floor. His tongue began tracing lazy circles on her belly.

"Not for us," she said, answering her own question. His tongue

30

was moving lower. Unbidden, Kate's hips began to undulate in familiar, sweet motions.

Luke lifted his head and slowly began moving up her body. "I've got an idea," he said.

"What?"

She felt him swell and harden between her legs, and his voice drifted into her ear, a lazy, teasing, sensual murmur.

"How would you like to be fucked by the next president of the United States?"

2

Kate opened her eyes and reached into the tumble of sheets for Luke's body, but he wasn't there. She squinted into the dawn light and saw him sitting on the side of the bed, already dressed in running shorts, tugging on a pair of thick white sweat socks.

"So early?" she mumbled. What incredible energy. He had always been that way, it was one of the things she loved most about him— but running at 5:00 A.M. after a night like last night? She burrowed deeper under the covers.

"You mean you're not coming?" Luke said, a twinkle in his eye. "You're going to pass on this solitary communing with nature?"

"Solitary, my foot."

Luke laughed happily. "I can't wait to see how many reporters keep up with me this morning." He stood and stretched his bare muscular legs, pulled a T-shirt over his head, and blew Kate a kiss. "I'll be back by six," he said. "Catch some more sleep, you'll need it."

Outside, Luke surveyed with mock gravity the sleepy-eyed group of reporters and campaign aides waiting for him. "Tommy," he said, pointing to the moccasin-clad feet of a pudgy reporter from the *San Jose Mercury News*, "those shoes are going to give you trouble."

"Too early to hit the stores, Senator," Tommy replied amiably, pulling a notebook from the elastic band of his sweat suit. "What's your strategy for the South? You gonna take on Enright on offshore drilling in Texas?"

The morning press conference had begun. The small cluster of men and women—led by Luke—began jogging slowly away from the hotel while a panel truck with a pool camera mounted on top and a sound boom swinging perilously close to their noses inched alongside. Only a few gawking early-morning observers were present to watch this awkward mélange of mechanical and human activity jerking like a balky mule down the street. Tonight the rest of the country would see on their television screens the lean, dark-haired candidate of the Democratic party laughing and joking and waving to the camera. But right now the view was limited to the cumbersome choreography of a political moment.

"What's going to be the main thrust of your environmental policy, Senator?" yelled the *Eugene Register-Guard.* "If you're elected, what do you do first?"

"Develop a global environmental plan, one with real teeth," Luke said promptly, speeding up slightly. "Keeping the air and the seas clean takes a world plan now. We don't need another ozone layer disaster."

"Are you gonna try and take Texas?" panted a lagging, persistent Tommy. "Is Enright vulnerable?"

"I'll give it my best shot; I'm not writing off any state," Luke tossed back over his shoulder. "Get yourself those shoes, Tommy."

"Is it true you've promised Governor Ritchie a Cabinet post," puffed NBC, still keeping pace, "for dropping out at the right time?"

Luke frowned. "Nope," he said, glancing coldly at the reporter. "No jobs for favors. You know I don't operate that way."

"Yeah, Senator, but Marty Apple does. Any comment?"

"I call the shots. No promises to anybody."

Luke was breathing harder, reaching full speed, as Peter Bradford loped close to his side, deftly dodging the swinging sound boom above his head.

"Morning, Senator," Peter said cheerfully.

Luke's mood improved instantly. "Morning, Peter," he said. "Ask me something different, okay?"

The two men were already pulling ahead of the rest of the crowd.

"Sure," Peter said affably. "Read that new book on the impact of Hispanics on American culture?"

"Silverman? The Harvard study?"

"That's the one."

"Great stuff." Luke's eyes turned lively with the subject. "Changes your whole idea of how Hispanics are going to vote in the next twenty-five years. Called the guy last week. Want him in my group."

"Your brain trust?"

Luke grinned. "If that's what you want to call it," he said.

"Been meeting with those people for a long time, haven't you?"

Luke nodded soberly. "Four years," he said. "Wouldn't be running for this job without that background." His breath was coming now in short, rhythmic bursts. "No time to learn anything during a campaign."

"Oh, you saying you've learned it all?"

Luke's eyes were twinkling. "You do like tweaking me, don't you?"

Peter grinned this time. "How's Kate?" he asked.

"Ecstatic," Luke said. "Raring to go. Full of energy. Appalled at the idea of my running at sunrise. And right now, sound asleep."

The two men ran together comfortably in silence, covering six city blocks with ease. But a crowd was gathering on the sidewalk, and people were pointing and shouting as more of them recognized Luke.

Luke, with a regretful grimace, glanced up at the sky. "Sun's climbing," he said, then tossed his head in the direction of Peter's colleagues straggling behind, and chuckled. "Better tell those guys to get in shape," he said. "They'll be doing a lot of this in the next four years." With that, he made a sharp right turn and began running back to the hotel, pulling his chunky, loosely connected entourage with him—and leaving the sound truck stuck halfway on the sidewalk with nowhere to turn.

Kate bolted upright, rubbing her eyes, as Luke strode out of the bathroom and over to the dresser to knot his red-for-television tie. His hair, wet from a quick shower, was curling slightly at the ends, something Kate knew he hated. Impatiently he flattened it to his head and peered into the mirror, his face almost boyish in its concentration.

"You're off for the 'Today Show,' right?" He looked so ebullient, so on top of the world, it made her shiver with pleasure.

"Yep," he said, glancing at his watch. "What's your schedule look like?"

Kate knew he would hear her answer and promptly forget; no matter. She jumped out of bed and began collecting her clothes. Luke's aides could peek into a folder at any given moment, if necessary, to tell him where she might be. There was a comfort in that.

"I'm with you to O'Hare this morning," she said as she pulled on a pair of panty hose. "Tomorrow I'm dedicating that new wing of the Evanston Hospital; Abby's going with me. After that, Los Angeles, then Texas, and I'll get to see *you*—" she pointed at him playfully— "on Friday. But I'm due downstairs at the victory breakfast in half an hour. I almost overslept, can you believe it?"

"You're not a morning person, babe, and you never will be."

"Can a morning person find happiness with a night person?"

"He's trying, but stay tuned." Luke grinned and dropped the morning edition of the special convention Hotline, the daily summary of campaign news, gossip, and reaction, next to her on the hotel bed. He hesitated. "You won't like it," he warned, yanking his suit jacket off a hotel coat hanger. "Ernie Stark hit us on abortion. Says I'm a hypocrite and a bad Catholic. Isn't that terrific? I lose the anti-Catholics for being Catholic and the Catholics for not being Catholic enough. I'm going to have to say something."

"He would have hit you on something, anyway," Kate said. "He always does." She quickly scanned the excerpts from the column of the *New York Daily News*'s hugely popular right-wing columnist. It was Stark's usual smarmy stuff.

"Now that he's the Democratic nominee," the excerpt read, "Luke Goodspeed is still trying to play the abortion issue both ways. He publicly claims he supports the law and his party's pro-choice platform—but everybody knows he's privately opposed to abortion. A little hypocritical, wouldn't you say? What you've got, all you poor Democrats out there, is just one more muddled candidate who doesn't know what he believes. This half-baked pol waffles on his Catholic convictions *and* his party's platform. Same old stuff. Watch for a long, embarrassing road to November for the Democratic party."

Kate dropped the paper on the floor and went back to dressing. "He's a stupid jerk," she said. But Luke was not focusing on her.

"They counted on surprising me with the news about that poor

35

girl's death," he said, squinting critically into the mirror at the meager knot on his tie. "You know, I need longer ties."

"I'll order some," Kate said. "Marty should have alerted you."

"No, that was Steve's job; he's the quick-response guy." Luke frowned. "I hate to say it, I don't want to believe it, but he's not up to speed anymore."

Kate sensed Luke was waiting for agreement, but she wasn't ready to change focus. "That girl shouldn't have died; it's outrageous," she said. "All because she was Catholic."

Luke was painstakingly redoing his tie, still focused on the mirror. "What would you say if I told you I checked this morning, and she's a Buddhist?"

"I'd say you were doing your best to defuse me," she retorted with a small smile.

"And you'd be right on the button." He surveyed his handiwork and frowned. "Maybe this tie shrank at the cleaners."

"Maybe your neck is getting thicker," she said, relenting for the moment. "Those cheeseburgers and corn dogs—"

"They don't go to my neck, unfortunately," he said, patting his barely visible paunch. "Better you take on the Church than my ego."

"It's frustrating." Kate hooked a pink lace bra in front with a quick snap, twisted it to her back, then leaned forward, lowering her breasts into the cups. "You know how I feel. Every time I see these women having babies they can't feed or take care of, it drives me nuts." She took a deep breath. "They're told they'll go to hell if they use contraception, and they'll go to hell if they have an abortion, and when they have their babies, they're on their own. It's wrong, it really is."

Luke was watching her machinations with the bra with real interest. "You're amazing," he said. "I've never known anyone who could get dressed so quickly with so little flesh showing."

Kate hesitated. Luke wanted her to back off, but she couldn't. Not yet, anyhow. "How can those bishops be against birth control *and* abortion?" she demanded. "Maybe they mean well, but how can they ignore these women? God help any woman who expects any real help from them when she's pregnant."

"Honey, don't preach."

Now he was warning her.

"I'm not asking you to feel the way I do or say any of this," she began again, "but I will never understand—"

"You will never understand why I don't get as mad as you." Luke paused, which he always did when about to make an extra effort to speak reasonably. "Come on, Kate, you know I'm pro-choice. No conflict, okay? That doesn't mean I have to like abortion, does it? I'm not going to start agonizing, and I'm not going to let the press make me into a Cuomo clone."

"Of course not, I don't want you to do anything of the sort," Kate objected. "But the press knows, and it's the kind of contradiction they love to pick apart."

Luke nodded, more in dismissal of the issue than in agreement. "It's old stuff," he said. "I'm keeping my private feelings out of it. Those Houston ministers never tried to nail Jack Kennedy on *his* personal views about abortion or birth control, so I see no reason why anyone should focus on mine."

"Everybody's going to try pushing you to the wall," Kate said. "The cardinal, Planned Parenthood—"

Luke gently pinched her cheek. "There are a lot of people who understand, maybe better than you think. They may not agree with me, but they realize what a real conundrum it is."

"There are plenty who don't."

"I think I can handle it."

"Hope I can," Kate said with a sigh.

"Sure you can." His tone was gently coaxing. "Just keep smiling whenever you hear somebody denounce me as a hypocrite."

"Or laugh when somebody calls you a baby killer, right?" Kate didn't intend to let a sharp note creep into her voice, but there it was.

Luke touched the tip of her chin, tilting her face upward. "Ever thought of pursuing a fascinating and rewarding career in politics, dear?" he said lightly.

Kate's eyes softened. "I've got one," she said.

"All I'm going to do is restate my basic position; it'll make Marty happy," Luke said soberly. "I think I'll slip it into the Texas speech."

"The less you have to say, the less you'll be pushed by either side, that's what I think."

Luke reached up and ruffled her hair in a characteristic gesture. "Maybe I'll go shoot a spotted owl," he said. "Give the press something important to write about, okay?" He kissed her right temple. "Anyway, remember, we have Father Joe as our secret weapon."

She was being placated; enough was enough.

Patricia O'Brien

"Honey?" she said with resignation.

"Yes?"

"Just don't use 'conundrum' in a speech."

It was a beautiful morning. Later, the sultry New Orleans air would hang like liquid lead over the city, making breathing difficult. The trees would droop and the asphalt pavement would soften under the relentless rays of the summer sun. Later, people seeking relief would straggle gratefully into the cool shelter of the hotel lobby, their eyes glazed from the heat.

But not now. The crowds pouring into the ballroom for the Democratic victory breakfast looked crisp and invigorated, the women bright in crisp cottons, the men all fresh and morning-showered. This was their moment to savor the glories of having finally chosen and focused on one candidate. Today, they had the attention of the country. Their candidate had dominated morning television and the morning papers. The problems, the fights, those would come quickly enough. Today, they held the sun in their hands.

Kate surveyed the crowd from where she waited by the slightly opened door of the holding room behind the stage. She had once hated these breakfasts. There had been times when facing one more plateful of greasy eggs at one more tiny coffee shop in Iowa had seemed an unbearable chore—but not today. People were pouring in, sitting ten to a table in this huge hall. Waiters were rushing to put up more chairs and tables, adding to the rising din as they dragged the chairs around the room. And the sound of hundreds of silver spoons tinkling against china like tiny bells filled the room with an absolutely heavenly music.

Behind her, Kate heard Abby's voice anxiously protesting. "But you said last night—"

"I know, sweetie." It was Claire, responding in a low and hurried voice. "But there's no time. We can't fit you in."

"But—"

"Next time. I promise."

Kate turned around, already calculating how to respond, in time to see Claire give Abby a pat and hurry off. Abby's pretty face was downcast. But when she saw her mother looking at her, she flushed and raised her chin high.

38

"It's not important," she said in response to Kate's inquiring look. "I thought I was getting a chance to speak for a couple of minutes at the breakfast. Claire okayed it last night, but I guess it isn't working out."

Kate blinked. This breakfast was so carefully timed, her own remarks would be wrapped up in five minutes. Had Claire promised Abby a bit of the spotlight in return for pushing the stupid blue suit?

"It would have been tight, honey," Kate said carefully. "We've got to be out of here by nine fifteen."

The deepening flush on Abby's face confirmed her suspicions. Really, Claire was such an operator. Kate saw the crumpled paper Abby was trying to hide in her fist and tried to bolster her spirits.

"Save your notes, honey," she said gently. "You'll be doing more talking than you've dreamed of in the next couple of months."

Abby looked flustered and uncomforted. "Yeah, maybe," she said, before turning away.

Kate took a step to follow her, but was stopped by an unexpected voice.

"Kate, have you got a minute?"

It was Steve. "I've got to get out there pretty quick," she said, feeling a twinge of alarm. "Everything all right?"

"Not particularly," he said. His voice changed from awkwardly casual to intense. "I did my damnedest last night to get to Luke. I'd never let anything blindside him if I could help it, you know that, Kate."

Kate did know that, but her knowledge was only making this harder. "These things happen," she said.

"I'm on the outside looking in these days," he said quietly. "Any suggestions?"

The words hung between them, a Maginot Line between past and present. Kate was struck with how many memories she had of Steve and Luke together—always together, plotting strategy, spinning plans for the future, laughing, sharing jokes—good times. Would it have fallen apart anyway, even if Marty hadn't come onto the scene? Each small problem had fed into another, and the end result was Steve had become less sure of himself, less valuable to Luke as an adviser. Something had wavered between the two men. And she saw little hope of change at this late date. How could she tell Steve that Marty wanted him ousted entirely? It was Marty's job, she thought irritably. Why didn't he tell Steve the truth?

"Luke cares about you, Steve, you know that," she said. "I care about you. We've had some good times—"

Steve straightened his shoulders, and for a second looked like the confident political aide of past years. "None of that matters anymore," he said. "I'm being shut out, and everybody knows it. I can't make a dent in Marty."

The rawness of the appeal stopped the waiting flow of comforting words from Kate. She reached for his hand.

"I'll try to help," she said. She wanted to say more, knew she should say more, but getting those simple, straightforward words out of her mouth was all she could do right now.

An aide rushed up out of breath, her face red. "Mrs. Goodspeed, we need you," she said. "Right away." Kate nodded to Steve, then moved quickly with the aide through the door and into the crowded room, blinking against the dazzling mélange of reflecting crystal and television lights. Below the stage level, the waiting crowd burst into cheerful applause. Kate smiled and waved, then scanned the line of head-table guests with a practiced eye. There was expectation in their faces—not the unquestioning expectation of people who already feel headed for the winner's circle; rather, the calculated stillness of bettors waiting to see how their horse will perform. The fat cats. The heavies. Whatever you called them, this lineup mattered.

"Hello, how are you? I'm so glad you're with us today." To each person—the blond actress who specialized in dirty jokes, the skinny rock star in gold lamé, the portly manufacturer of pharmaceuticals, the governor of Louisiana, New Orleans' leading black activist—to all of them, a murmured greeting, a press of the hand, a direct welcome. Always, the lubricant of appreciation. A drop here, a drop there—it was important, and Kate was good at it.

Kate settled into her seat at the center of the table and turned her attention to the man sitting at her right. For a moment, she couldn't recall his name. He was the builder responsible for massive developments in Los Angeles, Chicago, and Philadelphia, and Marty had courted him assiduously. His grandiose sprawling complexes of hotels and apartment buildings had somehow managed to survive the real estate disasters of the early nineties. Sam Olson, that's who he was. He had channeled liberal doses of money during the primaries to Luke, and was now almost a one-man bank for the Democratic party.

Kate studied the face. It was deceptively soft, with full lips. The baby fat, she observed, stopped at the neck. Lean muscle took over from there.

"Hello, Mrs. Goodspeed," he said, mouth smiling, eyes observing her hesitation. He took a deep swallow of orange juice. "Good coverage this morning," he said. "The best."

"Yes, Sam, isn't it wonderful?" Kate's response was practiced and easy. She eyed two pots of what looked like good coffee, both within arm's reach. The eggs might even be edible.

"Fabulous," he said genially. "Now Luke's gotta get moving. He should start boosting that guy from Liberia—you know, what's-his-name. The poet. Blacks will love it."

Kate poured herself a cup of what looked like a hearty French roast and began sipping slowly before replying. She had almost forgotten, in the excitement of the last few days.

"David Palmer," she said. Luke, as chairman of a Senate subcommittee on immigration, was studying efforts to win for Palmer permanent entry into the country. "It's been a bit sensitive," she said.

"Yeah, and if he doesn't get in, blacks will go batshit, excuse my language, ma'am."

"He's highly revered, we know that," Kate said, annoyed by the phony deference.

Olson chuckled. "Writes good poetry, but made the mistake of getting himself mixed up with one of those terrorist groups, right?"

She thought about what she knew of the case. Palmer was an Americo-Liberian, a poet, one of the descendents of the freed American slaves who had founded Liberia in the mid-nineteenth century. He was famous worldwide now as the "poet of liberation," and had become a true hero to American blacks. Kate was impressed with the dignity and power of his poetry. So was Luke. Unfortunately, Palmer was also still the titular leader of the National Freedom Federation, a group of tribal rebels credited with continuing the chaos of the 1989 civil war, thwarting U.S. efforts to rebuild the country's wrecked economy. He claimed he had broken all ties and was anxious to "rejoin his own people" in the United States. Clearly the government was in no hurry to let him in. In U.S. eyes, the Federation was still officially a terrorist organization, and Palmer was branded.

"We're looking into it," she said.

"Tell Luke to move fast."

"I don't make policy, Sam," she said quickly.

"Not everybody agrees," Olson said, his expression shrewd. "From what I hear, Marty should be a little jealous."

She cast a cool glance. "Sorry," she said. "You're mistaken."

Olson stretched backward, pretending halfheartedly to cover a yawn. "Oops," he said. He reached for a saltshaker and began liberally salting the plate of scrambled eggs before him. "You gotta forgive me, it sure was a late night. I shouldn't be talking so seriously this morning." He smiled lazily. "You looked fantastic last night, by the way."

Kate stabbed at her eggs.

"Thank you," she said pleasantly enough. "I'm told blue's my color."

"Why don't you ride with me to the airport?"

Kate smiled at Claire, gratified to see the startled look she got in response to her impulsive invitation. The Goodspeed party was piling into the polished black cars of the motorcade waiting in front of the hotel, while the New Orleans police and Secret Service agents, looking like waxen statues, held back the crowds. Speed was important. It was already nine o'clock.

"Of course," Claire replied after an instant's hesitation. "I'll join you, but give me a second—I have to make sure Marty has the tape recorder for Luke's interview."

Claire hurried to the first car to catch Marty before he left with Luke and a man from the *New Orleans Times-Picayune*. Kate climbed into a waiting Dodge and she saw a bobbing ponytail over the back of the driver's seat. Good, that kid with the nice eyes was driving—the one who drove a little too fast, but was so anxious to please.

"You know, I like your hair, Bobby," she said.

The back of Bobby's neck turned pink. "Yeah?"

"Yeah."

She saw his eyes crinkle in a grin through the rearview mirror.

"Are you in school?" she asked.

"I start at Yale in January, maybe," Bobby responded.

"Why so late, and why maybe?" she asked.

"I'm hoping for a shot at working full time on Senator Good-speed's campaign," he said eagerly. "I think the senator's going to make a great president."

Kate was touched by his naked fervor. Kids like Bobby were the life's blood of a campaign.

"Well, maybe you'll get your chance," she said. "What are you going to major in at Yale?"

This time Bobby turned his head partway and she saw a sheepish grin. "Driver ed, Mrs. Goodspeed," he said.

She laughed. So he had caught the expression on her face yesterday when he took those curves too fast coming into town. Good, that meant he would drive slower today. Then she peered through the window, watching Claire and Marty whispering together by the car up ahead. The two of them, she thought, always looked like they were plotting something.

She glanced back at the steps of the hotel in time to see her sister stroll out in the company of two female reporters, talking animatedly as the women scribbled in their notebooks. It wasn't so much their obvious interest in what Joan was saying that caught Kate's attention—it was the sleepy, mischievous look on Joan's face. She was probably giving out embarrassing anecdotes again. My sister, Kate thought with resignation—the female Billy Carter.

"Hurry, Joanie," she called, trying to keep reproof out of her voice.

"I've got two new best friends," Joan said with a silvery laugh as she approached, "and I've been telling them some deep, dark secrets. Remember when we went skinny-dipping in Mrs. Kopec's pool and the police hauled us down to the police station? What a bunch of scared, naked kids we were!" She continued walking, still talking animatedly to her delighted hovering companions.

Claire caught the last remark just as she reached the car. "Your sister might pose a bit of a problem," she said, settling into her seat.

"She's fine," Kate said quickly.

"She doesn't care what she says. Doesn't that bother you?"

Not that you'll ever hear, Kate thought. "No," she said. "I'm not bothered at all."

Claire shrugged. "Hear the overnight polls? Luke's up by eight points. Three-point margin of error. Great speech."

Kate was cheered but decided to move straight to the point. This

Patricia O'Brien

was going to be a short ride and Claire wasn't going to be in charge. "Abby felt pretty bad this morning," she said without preamble. "Disappointed. Was there actually some possibility she was going to be able to speak at the breakfast?"

"Oh, it could have worked out if we had had a little more time. But you know how these things go." So smooth and easy.

"I certainly do." Kate kept her voice casual. "But it might have been kinder not to raise her hopes."

Claire didn't reply. Instead she pulled out a cigarette and lit it, inhaled deeply, looked at Kate, and smiled. "You don't mind, do you? It's been a hell of a morning."

Kate shrugged, refusing to be forced into giving permission. "I quit finally," she said, "but it took years."

"For the sake of the children, I suppose?"

"For all of us."

There was a short silence, broken only by the urgent, high-pitched scream of the police sirens guiding the snaking caravan of cars through thinning morning rush-hour traffic. Bobby was driving like a man transporting an armed bomb.

"Do you like kids?" It was an aimless question, even rude. Kate started to soften it, but Claire interrupted.

"Almost had one of my own," she said matter-of-factly. "I was pregnant a few years ago but had a miscarriage. At six months."

Kate caught her breath. My God, at six months? "Oh, Claire," she said. "I'm sorry."

"It was just as well, my marriage was breaking up." Claire looked out the window.

Kate tried to think of something to say. Had she actually thought Claire had no life beyond politics? Here she was, a woman with a resumé other women would kill for, but she hadn't been spared. She had suffered a loss any woman could understand, and Kate suddenly felt an empathy she had never expected to feel.

"That must have made it doubly terrible," she said quietly.

Claire looked straight ahead at some point above Bobby's sun visor. "I kept busy," she said. "That's when Marty and I decided to get together as a political team. We both knew we could produce winners. Driver, will you get closer to the car ahead, please?"

"Okay, ma'am," Bobby replied, hitting the gas.

"I'm really sorry," Kate said.

44

Claire looked at her with an unreadable expression. "For what? This poky driver?" she asked.

"Because it's got to be hard to lose a baby," Kate foundered, wondering why she felt embarrassed.

"You don't understand," Claire said calmly, grinding her cigarette into the car ashtray and then promptly pulling forth another one. "Having a baby would have been a disaster. I probably would have had an abortion if I had had enough time, but I was too busy."

For just an instant, catching a fleeting expression in Claire's eyes, Kate saw something. But then it was gone, and she decided she didn't want to know anyway.

"What did you think of Annie Marshall's piece?"

Kate blinked. A fax of the Annie Marshall piece, as a matter of fact, lay folded right now inside her handbag. Kate wasn't totally sure exactly *how* she felt about it. The headline was a bit breathless: "Kate Goodspeed, the All-American Wife—What Secret Ambitions Rest in Her All-American Soul?" Annie had constructed her piece as artfully as a Japanese flower arrangement, using last night's interview plus others collected in her notebook along the way. A few weeks back, Kate had told her she used to love dancing with the kids in the living room when they were little, joking that it was a way of "easing her itchy feet." Annie had pounced on this as a metaphor for exploring Kate's private ambitions: What about those "itchy feet?" Did she think a woman should run for president? "Absolutely." Would you run? "I am running, in a sense," Kate had replied with a laugh. "As my husband's partner."

Big mistake, Kate thought wryly. The unwritten subtext of Annie's piece seemed to be that Kate might become some kind of power freak in the White House. Kate sighed. Not trapped, not crucified, so she was potentially a power freak. She was supposed to be either a victim or straining to run the country. Annie had really reached on this one.

"She's every bit as ambitious as her husband," declared one anonymous source quoted in the story. "But she'll never admit it. Do we want a First Lady who offers her husband advice on, say, the Balkan war? Makes you wonder where the real Kate Goodspeed is hiding out."

Not in Annie Marshall's story, that was for sure. "It was okay," Kate said with a shrug. "The usual stuff."

"The 'favorite heroine' question?"

"Yes?"

"You should have mentioned Eleanor Roosevelt."

Kate stirred impatiently. "Everybody mentions Eleanor Roosevelt," she said. "There's nothing wrong with Jo March."

"Come on, Kate. *Little Women* is a kids' book."

"She meant a lot to me."

"Next thing we know they'll be asking if you eat russets."

"Who's your favorite heroine, Claire?"

Claire smiled. "Nobody. I prefer men."

"Not even Eleanor Roosevelt?"

"I don't have to admire her."

"You mean, you're not a political wife."

Claire shrugged and changed the subject again.

"By the way—" she said, leaning back, delicately fingering her cigarette—"don't get trapped into charity work for Steve Feldon."

"What are you talking about?"

Claire looked directly into Kate's eyes through the growing haze of smoke in the car. "He wants you to save his ass, doesn't he?"

"He's been with Luke a long time, Claire," Kate said. "We owe him."

Claire sighed. "He's not quick enough, Kate. It isn't enough to be a nice guy. He doesn't have the backbone to take a hint and bow out gracefully."

"He's feeling humiliated. There isn't a reporter in town who doesn't know Steve isn't on the inside anymore."

"He's got to face reality, and, frankly, trying to enlist you is a bit repulsive."

"I don't consider it repulsive," Kate said.

"Of course not," Claire said quickly. "You're too kindhearted. But he'd be a drag on the campaign, and I hope you aren't going to try and make Luke feel sorry for him. It'd be a mistake."

Another silence.

"I'm not a Girl Scout anymore," Kate said pleasantly. "We do need to do something for him, however. That's all there is to it."

"If he'll face facts, we'll let him stay on in the Senate office for now. Maybe something else later."

The promise was mushy, and Kate resolved to talk to Luke at the first opportunity. "I can tell you one thing that would help," she said.

"Give him a front seat with Luke on the ride home today, and make sure the press sees them getting on the plane together."

"That's easy enough," Claire said with a quick shrug. She glanced out the window, hand poised on the door handle. "Good, we're here."

The sirens suddenly stopped as the motorcade approached the chain-link fence where Luke's campaign plane was parked. Luke jumped out of the lead car before it came to a full stop, his body exuding energy and self-confidence. Already, he seemed different. He was the center around which everything and everyone else moved, and Kate saw this as she had rarely seen it—from outside that center—and it gave her a twinge of unfamiliar anxiety. Claire was already out the door; gone without a word. Why did she suddenly feel like an observer and not a participant?

Ahead, the 727 with the steel blue markings of a cut-rate charter company stood alone on the tarmac, its dents and general overall tiredness masked by the soft polish of the morning sun. Even the Democratic candidate for president was going to have to wait for a better charter—there were no planes to spare. "The joys," Marty had said to Luke, "of deregulation." Clustered on the ground near the tail were stacks of weathered tote bags and carry-ons, already undergoing examination by two guard dogs held on a tight leash by a Secret Service agent. Aides were shouting now, glancing at their watches, herding reporters and photographers into a barely held together line preparing to board through the rear of the plane. The media people were a mixed lot. The men were either jovial, rumpled types or thin and tense with stubbled chins. The women stood out in their bright silks and knits, but they had their own rumpled look, and they wore it more self-consciously. All of them, men and women, carried pouchy black bags that encased the flip-top computers on which they banged out their stories, day and night. Bringing up the rear were loudly wisecracking camera and sound crews, a few women in their midst, arm muscles bulging as they hoisted their heavy equipment. The jokes shouted back and forth had more vigor this morning. A new phase of the campaign had begun.

Kate saw Abby and Nat walking quickly past her car and toward the aircraft. Something was wrong; she could tell by the hunch of Nat's shoulders. Then she heard Abby's voice, thin and tense. "You

47

❖ ❖

can't put one foot in front of the other without stumbling," the girl was scolding. "I saw you almost take that header yesterday. Daddy would've been furious if he had seen it." Overhearing, a reporter waiting to board stared at the pair with interest and pulled out his notebook. Kate spied Peter Bradford. Wordlessly she caught his eye as she climbed from the car. Peter nodded, then clapped a hand etched with sinewy lines on the other reporter's shoulder, made some joking comment, and steered him away from Abby and Nat and toward the plane.

Kate smiled after him as he strode away. How strange to think that once, long ago, this man with the long legs and strong, lean chin of a cowboy had been her closest buddy, as fresh and young and ambitious as she. Twenty years was a long time, but she and Peter still shared a bond.

Amidst the milling aides and supporters at the front of the plane, Marty was taking a fast head count. Claire pushed her way through to his side and whispered into his ear, then glided over to Steve at the fringe of the crowd. Kate saw Steve's face brighten, and it saddened her. Things were pretty bad when it took so little to ease his fragile ego.

Now Steve was approaching her.

"Thanks, pal," he said, with a touch of his old spirit. "With a little luck, Luke and I can work this out." He headed to the plane with a swing in his gait.

Outside the fence, a long black car was pulling up. One look, and a waiting aide yelled for Marty. And there he was, emerging from the limo, Kate's breakfast companion—Sam Olson, looking well fed and sure of his welcome.

"We didn't expect this," mumbled an aide, obeying an urgent signal from Marty. "Jesus. We haven't got a seat left on the plane."

Kate watched Marty's enthusiastic welcome, saw him bringing Olson directly to Luke's side. All she wanted to do now was get on the plane and not see what happened next.

Jerry Spanos, Kate's new press secretary, a fresh-faced graduate from the University of Illinois, ran up, stopping her progress. "CBS wants pictures of you running," he said, out of breath. "Will you do it? It'd be great for the youth image. Boost your ratings."

"Jerry, I told you, Luke's the runner in this family, not me."

Jerry sniffed and dug into his pocket for a tissue. He looked distressed. "Nobody has to know that," he said. "I'm just talking photo op."

"Sorry," Kate said, "I don't like to run."

"She doesn't want anybody to see her in shorts," Joan added, coming up behind them.

Jerry excused himself quickly as Kate turned an exasperated glare on her sister.

"Remember that awful picture the *Post* ran of you playing tennis?" Joan said cheerfully. "If anybody exposed *my* thighs like that, I'd enter a convent."

"It was the camera angle," Kate retorted. "My legs aren't *that* bad; anyhow, Luke thinks they're pretty good."

"Better wipe that cross look off your face or it'll freeze on," Joan said. "A reminder, compliments of our dear departed mother."

Reluctantly Kate grinned. "Mother never knew plastic surgery could fix almost anything," she said.

"Well, she knew about cranky kids," said Joan. "And that, I'm afraid, is one thing you've got waiting for you back home."

"I know." Kate sighed. "I don't know what's gotten into Abby."

Together, in agreement for once, the two sisters boarded the plane. Kate settled into her seat, rehearsing a scolding lecture she planned to give Abby when they got home. Only then did she glance out the window at the people still on the ground.

What she saw she would long remember.

There was Steve, his back to the plane, picking up his bag and walking, head high and shoulders stiff, toward the parked cars behind the airport fence. She should have guessed he would be the one Marty would bump. She had guessed it; she just hadn't wanted to admit it.

Suddenly Steve turned his head and stared at the plane. Kate could have sworn he was looking straight at her. Flustered, she pulled back from the window.

49

3

The mood on the plane was unusually quiet, Kate thought—which, in her present unsettled mood, was just fine. Everybody—the candidate, campaign workers, reporters, and even the usually rowdy camera crews—seemed agreed on the need to decompress. She could hear reporters in back of her listlessly tapping stories into their computers, too weary to concern themselves with the front of the plane. No one bothered lobbying for an interview with Luke, and some aides had stretched back gratefully in their seats to catch up on precious sleep. Not Marty, of course. He and Luke were talking to each other across the aisle, and Kate found herself half listening as she stared out at the passing clouds.

"We've got to sharpen the health stuff," Marty said, tapping a copy of Luke's speech clutched in his hand. "We need a better anecdote, you didn't get enough applause with the one we've got."

"Then put in the Brooklyn woman who went blind when her doctor wouldn't accept Medicaid," Luke said. "It's more to the point, anyway."

"Done." Marty scribbled fast, then looked up. "Enright's pushing hard on his foreign policy credentials; we need a brain trust session before you talk to the Council on Foreign Relations."

"Line up Gottlieb, Simmons and—" Luke paused—"that's two from Harvard. Get me Johnson, okay? Princeton. A good balance." He smiled with satisfaction. "I like hearing those guys; I never stop learning from them. They make Enright look like a kid out of kindergarten."

Kate knew Luke had little respect for the Republican party's nominee for the presidency. White-haired, blessed with the bone lines of a true patrician, John Enright had been plucked by Samuel Gilmartin from a nondescript Senate career four years ago and forced through as majority leader. Now, with Gilmartin coasting out of his two terms as President of the United States with high approval ratings, the Republicans were betting on Enright's presidential demeanor to keep them in the White House. Nervously.

"That guy looks like a president and sounds like a president," Marty chuckled. "But the front-porch light is out. He's stone dumb."

"Gilmartin's a smart man," Luke said thoughtfully. "I can't figure out why he insisted on pushing Enright on the party."

Marty shrugged. "Hubris. What else? His mistake, our opportunity."

The plane was descending into Chicago. Luke stretched, yawned, and glanced at his campaign manager. "By the way," he said evenly. "No deals, Marty."

Marty's eyebrows shot up. "What are you talking about?"

"You heard me," Luke said. "No deals with Ritchie or anybody else. And I mean it."

There was a short uncomfortable silence. "You're the boss," Marty said, slapping his copy of Luke's speech back into his briefcase.

The old plane landed with a series of grinding bumps that awoke even the soundest sleepers. Noisily the camera crews hoisted their equipment, preparing for action. But when the doors opened, the Goodspeed entourage was faced with an empty tarmac baking under a pitiless sun. A lone figure stepped forward, hands clawing anxiously at his tie.

"Sorry," he began quickly, looking at Marty. "We've got a little problem. A mix-up in signals, but no disaster." He took a deep breath. "The welcoming reception is over at the United terminal."

"For Christ's sake." Marty's contempt for bad planning was legendary, and the aide dancing on one foot before him grasped for absolution.

"We didn't do it at this end," he said. "It wasn't our fault. Scheduling screwed it—"

"I don't care who screwed it up, it's screwed," Marty said irritably.

"What's going on?" Luke broke in.

Patricia O'Brien

"Wrong terminal," Marty said with disgust. "And we're running late."

Behind him, pouring forth from the rear of the plane, dozens of reporters and photographers milled uncertainly, looking around for the expected reception.

"Senator, there's a huge crowd waiting over there," protested the aide, appealing desperately to Luke. "We just can't—"

"Of course we can't," Luke said instantly. "This is home territory, let's get over there."

"All the locals and network affiliates there?" Marty demanded. "Everybody?"

"Yes, *sir*," the aide said.

"We're going to have a pissed-off mayor," Marty objected. Then, giving up, he whirled on the aide. "What do you intend to do about that?"

"Phone her right away, Senator," the aide said promptly. "Tell her you'll be a little late. And I'll get the traveling press over to United. Fast."

"She'll still be pissed off," Marty said as the aide took off in a dead run.

"I'm the nominee now," Luke said with a grin and a light in his eye. "She'll live with it."

An airport executive suddenly materialized at the gate, a pompous Pied Piper who proceeded to lead the Goodspeed party through the labyrinth of twisting corridors to the United terminal. Kate found herself almost running to keep up, at one point straining to keep Luke in sight. A couple of TV crews and several reporters from the plane had squeezed through the gate and followed Luke in full disaster-alert style—booms thrust forward, cameras running, producers trotting alongside. They did not like this deviation from the expected. It was not in their job descriptions—ever since November 22, 1963—to let Luke disappear from sight for even a minute.

The trek quickly took on a carnival atmosphere. Travelers in the broad white-tiled corridors flattened themselves against the walls, astonished, then excited, as the jumble of people and equipment rushed past. Yes, what do you know, they whispered to each other, that's him all right, oh, yeah, that's the Democrat running for president, you know, the senator, Senator Goodspeed, that's him!

Luke was enjoying himself, and Kate was fascinated by what she

52

saw. He seemed larger. The muscles of his body were pushing out against the confines of his good navy summer suit, or was that just in her mind? How could she be seeing him differently, she who routinely brushed the dandruff off that very same suit as he left the house each morning? Luke's shoulders were swinging, lithe and easy, visibly clearing a respectful space around him. On he went, past gates and coffee shops and rows of metal newspaper-vending machines. Gazing out from those machines, from every one of them, was Luke's likeness, arms thrust upward in a victory salute, triumphant. There he was on the front pages of the *Chicago Sun-Times*, the *Chicago Tribune*, *The New York Times*, the *Los Angeles Times*, and every other newspaper available at O'Hare that chose to mark the political news of the day. Kate delightedly counted the boxes, storing the images she saw of Luke in her mind. This was a universe away from a Senate campaign. She fumbled in her pocket for some coins and stopped at one of the boxes. She shoved the coins in the slot and pulled out a paper, not caring if a photographer caught her in the act. For just an instant she stood still and drank in a full-color, three-column picture of Luke in his moment of triumph, resisting an absurd desire to hug the paper close.

"Mrs. Goodspeed, come on! You'll get left behind!" An alarmed aide was tugging at her sleeve, and Kate hurried on. The crowd ahead was growing, the travelers from San Jose and Des Moines and Detroit and Long Island were craning their heads and they were clapping. He's the candidate, Luke Goodspeed, that's him!

And then they were there, moving through one more chanting, undulating affirmation of Luke's new existence. The reception under the glass-vaulted ceilings of the United terminal was chaotic, cheerfully so, with red-and-white "Let's go, Luke!" banners waving and the all-important cameras recording the scene. Luke didn't have to say much, just to wave and promise through a scratchy microphone a shiny Democratic-led future for the country. Nobody wanted more than that. They just wanted to see him. And then Marty was tucking his hand unobtrusively under Luke's elbow, invisibly guiding him through the crowds like a jockey expertly working the reins.

"See you later, Luke!" Kate yelled as loud as she could as the Goodspeed entourage split into two parts. Luke turned, eyes momentarily searching. He saw her and waved. "See you later, honey!" he yelled back.

53

"Friday!" she shouted. "I'll see you Friday!" It seemed important to remind him.

The drive up to Evanston the next day was peaceful. Kate, Abby sitting next to her, stared out the window of the staff car. She loved to watch the changing moods of Lake Michigan from the Outer Drive on any day, but a warm late-summer afternoon was special. Bathers in bright suits were sprinkled across the white gleaming beaches like grains of colored sugar. Sailboats, bouncing white and free, moved with the water across the horizon, reminding her of the first time she and Luke had ventured out on the lake in a rented Sunfish with a bright yellow sail. So many years ago. Luke had tried to pretend he was a reasonably accomplished sailor. But when the wind shifted, his awkward efforts to tack almost had dumped them into the chilly lake waters. He had tried to right the boat, but the sail kept flapping uselessly in the wind, and he finally gave up, turning to Kate with the expression of a frustrated little boy. "I don't know what the hell I'm doing!" he yelled, exasperated.

Kate was fond of starting her speeches with the story, telling it and retelling it for appreciative audiences, all of whom would laugh and clap when she would hesitate at the end for just a second and then say: "It was, I can assure you, the last time I ever heard my husband say *that*." Maybe it made Luke look a little arrogant, she thought, but it always got the desired response. Marty had even used it in one of the early campaign brochures.

Abby sat quietly next to her mother, gazing at the water and listening to Jerry Spanos explain what would happen at the hospital dedication. It was the usual briefing, and she wasn't giving it full attention. "I wish we could all be lying on that beach right now," she suddenly said.

"You're too famous," Jerry said cheerfully. "Can you imagine what would happen if you went out there? People would go bananas." He sniffed urgently.

Abby pulled a couple of tissues from her purse and thrust them forward. "Doesn't your hay fever ever stop?" she asked.

"Sorry, drives me crazy; you too, huh?" It was a nervous apology. Jerry was young and anxious to please. He blew his nose hard, then sneezed twice for good measure.

"Have we got time for Abby to say something today?" Kate asked.

"Sure," he said, glancing down at the schedule in his lap. "If you shave a couple of minutes off your remarks. It would be kind of nice, actually." He looked at Abby and tried to crack a joke, winking at her in the rearview mirror to show he wasn't serious. "It's a new pediatric wing, maybe you could be our token kid."

"I'm no kid."

Kate saw a flush spread across the back of Jerry's neck. Irritated, she cast Abby a warning glance. Why was she acting so touchy?

"Okay," Abby said, with a clear effort. "I'd like that."

An almost dreamy calmness settled over the backseat of the car, a calmness that lasted until the low, cream-colored buildings that constituted Evanston Hospital came into sight.

"I hear something," Abby said.

"Slow down," Jerry ordered the driver.

Then Kate heard it, too. A rhythmic chanting—a familiar sound.

Jerry was already dialing the site people on the cellular phone to get a fill-in. This was supposed to be an easy hit, a great feel-good stop.

"AIDS or abortion?" asked Kate briskly.

"Abortion," Jerry replied, forcing a matter-of-fact businesslike tone into his voice. "Not big—about twenty people. Just noisy."

The small caravan slowed in preparation for entering the hospital driveway, and Kate pulled Abby back against the seat. "Sit out of camera view," she said to her daughter as the crowd moved forward, spotting their car. "This looks worse than it is."

"Goodspeed's a baby killer!" yelled a woman in a flowered blouse as she tried to get past the Secret Service agents suddenly enveloping Kate's car. Another woman held up a startled-looking toddler in a pair of Oshkosh overalls. "Baby killer!" she yelled. A man in a green shirt holding a bullhorn was weaving through the small crowd, orchestrating the chant. "No baby killers in the White House! No baby killers in the White House!"

A stock demonstration, just a little noisier than most. Kate patted Abby's hand and was surprised to feel a tightly clenched fist. She quickly looked at her daughter's face.

"They always sound alike," Abby whispered. "I hate it."

"They're just trying to put pressure on your father," Kate whispered back. "Don't let it get to you."

"Don't let it get to me? Mother, sometimes—" Abby stopped herself with an obvious effort. "Daddy should be taking these people on," she said.

"That would make more problems," Kate said, more sharply than she had intended. "You know how he feels."

"He's wimping out," Abby said crossly. She folded her arms across firm, small breasts and stared out the window.

"Okay, we're here," Jerry announced with relief as the driver inched his way toward the entrance, past the barrier holding back the demonstrators. "Let's go, ladies."

Kate couldn't stop folding and refolding her program as she waited on the auditorium stage through a long and effusive introduction. Her hands just wouldn't stay still. Why was she so twitchy? Abby had calmed down, if her smiling face was any guide. She had sailed right in and started working the crowd beautifully. Abby knew how to talk to people and ask them questions that made them receptive and eager to listen to what she had to say about her father. She was a great family resource. Kate reminded herself to tell Abby how good she was when they were back in the car. That would help. Still, she couldn't stop folding and refolding the program in her lap.

The applause came, and Kate began her remarks, taking time to recount the accomplishments of the hospital and to laud the contributors and administrators for caring enough about the needs of children to carry through on building the new wing.

"What have we got," she finished finally, "if we don't have our children? We need them healthy and whole, and it is our responsibility to keep them that way." She paused and stepped back, waiting for applause. But in that split second before the audience could react, a hoarse male voice echoed through the auditorium.

"Fight for the unborn!" the man yelled. Kate could see through the lights only a quick flurry of movement and sound and a flash of a man in a green shirt being pushed and shoved toward the rear door. The two television camera crews in the room rushed after him.

"Thank you so much, Mrs. Goodspeed." The hospital's chief administrator was on his feet, his voice booming forth to cover the interruption, inviting the crowd to applaud. "Now," he said, "we are fortunate indeed to be able to hear from a young woman who has

56

herself a strong interest in health care for children—Abby Goodspeed."

Kate turned from the podium and saw with a sinking heart her
daughter's angry face.

"How could you, Abby? How could you?"

The car door had slammed, and Jerry was slumped in the front
seat, pretending not to hear the exasperation in Kate's voice.

"All I did was tell them what I believe," Abby said sullenly.

"All you did was raise the possibility that someone will throw your
remarks at your father on the road and ask him if he agrees with you,
that's all."

"What's wrong with telling them I think abortion is a choice only
a pregnant woman has a right to make?"

"You didn't balance it."

"I don't want to balance it. What's to balance? He ought to come
out strong against those pro-life wackos."

"Abby, it's not that simple, and you know it. You're just indulging
yourself at your father's expense."

"Maybe he'll give me respect for my opinions, Mother. Which is
something, by the way, that would be nice to get from you."

Kate's patience had truly frayed.

"Respect! What are you saying? I'm supposed to respect you for
being reckless on an issue your father has laid out as carefully as he
can? What's going on with you?"

The driver was pulling up to the Outer Drive apartment building
where the Goodspeeds kept a two-bedroom apartment as their official
Illinois residence. Jerry turned around, trying not to look directly at
either woman. "Abby, we're home," he said. "Kate, we've got to get
moving for the airport right away. We're running late."

Abby pushed open the door, her body exuding fury. "Don't you
get it, Mother?" she said. She looked directly at Kate, her eyes
defiant and rimmed with red—but nothing could hide their desperate scorn. "Don't you get it?"

She slammed the door and ran into the building.

Jerry said nothing, his eyes determinedly focused frontward. The
driver looked as though he wished he were very far away. Neither
man made a move.

Kate stared after her daughter. She paused for a long second as bubbles of sweat formed around Jerry's collar. Then she made her decision.

"Take my luggage out of the back, Jerry," she said. "I'm staying here tonight."

Where was Abby? Kate squinted into the gloom of the front hall of the apartment. She could smell the dust wafting out of the laboring old air-conditioner in the living room, but she couldn't see any movement. She put down her suitcase, blinking to adjust to the absence of light. Abby was sitting on the old white sofa, her back erect and tautly molded, staring through the window at the lake waters below.

"This place sure gets stuffy," Kate said, looking around. "I don't think that old air-conditioner is going to last through the summer."

"We won't know, will we?" responded Abby, not moving from her position.

Kate moved farther into the room. "No, I guess we won't," she said. She sat down at the other end of the sofa. "Can I fix you something to eat?" she asked. "A tuna sandwich, maybe?"

"My mother actually opening a can in the kitchen?" A slight smile hovered on Abby's lips. "That's like Daddy trying to drive himself home without getting lost. Do you remember how to use a can opener?"

Kate smiled back, but the familiar gibe was delivered with too cranky an edge. Abby was not acting normally at all. Why did she seem to be spoiling for a fight? What was wrong?

"Okay, what *can* I do for you?" she asked.

Abby was silent for a long moment. "I don't think you can help me," she said finally.

"I know things have been frantic lately, but you've been through this stuff before, sweetie," Kate said, trying to cast as wide and general a net as possible. "We'll have more pressure, more exposure on this campaign, but—"

Abby wasn't listening in the way she usually did; instead she twisted her head around to look at her mother. "Why aren't you on your way to California?" she interrupted.

"I figured maybe you were upset about something and needed my help. Maybe a shoulder to cry on."

"I need more than that."

"Well, honey, if you don't tell me what's going on, I can't help."

"Don't you know? Haven't you figured it out yet?"

Kate paused. Of course, she wanted to know, but suddenly a memory flashed; once again she was the little girl who had accidentally stuck a questing finger into a light socket. She was feeling the same nasty tingle, and she felt a conflicted need simultaneously to probe deeper and pull away.

"I don't intend to play guessing games with you," she said, rising to leave the room. "I think I'll go tackle the tuna. Do you want—"

"Mother. I'm pregnant."

"—mayonnaise?"

Kate stood stupidly as Abby's words hung in the heavy air, changing everything. Through the window, the noise of passing traffic and laughing voices had blended into a fuzzy, comfortable summer sound that suddenly seemed bizarre and out of place.

"What?" she managed.

"Pregnant, Mother, pregnant." Abby's voice was shaking, and she pronounced the syllables slowly, as if saying them for the first time. "I don't know what else to say, don't you understand?"

"Oh, my poor kid," whispered Kate, aghast.

"It happens, you know." Abby's bravado suddenly evaporated and she started to cry.

Kate groped through her shock for the right words; something to put a floor under the news. "Are you sure?" she asked weakly.

"Yes, yes, I'm sure. Please, Mother, stop looking like I hit you!" Abby was hiding her face in her hands, twisting her body away.

Kate quickly moved forward, grabbing her daughter close, desperate to stop the room from spinning for both of them. She felt sick to her stomach. "Oh, baby, I'm here," she said.

Abby burrowed in, allowing her mother's arms to close around her. "Do you know how hard that was to say?" she sobbed, her voice muffled. "Do you? Do you?"

"Abby, Abby," Kate whispered. She was shocked to feel the violent trembling of her daughter's body. This couldn't be true. Abby was too young. My God, she thought, am I blind? How did I miss this?

"What's going to happen to me?" Abby asked, gulping hard.

"Don't worry," Kate said quickly. "I'll take care of you." For just an instant, she flashed to one of her favorite assumptions about Abby's future: a standard corny scene, played out on some well-manicured Ivy League campus. Abby in her college graduation cap and gown. Abby, laughing, holding up her diploma, looking pretty and smart and hopeful. Her fantasy had always assumed an Abby who would make her and Luke look like perfect parents, not an Abby pregnant and desperately afraid. Kate felt a sudden sick stab of shame.

"I'm scared; I'm so scared."

Kate pushed damp hair from the girl's brow and kissed her. "Don't be afraid, honey," she said. "You aren't facing this alone anymore." The thoughts, the guilts, were roaring through her head. She hadn't paid enough attention to her daughter's emerging sexuality. She had seen it, watched as Abby tried lipsticks and eyeshadow and flirted with boys and all the other normal teenage things. But she was always so busy, Luke always so busy—the thoughts were tumbling over each other now. Had Abby used birth control? What about AIDS? Why had she just assumed her daughter would grow up and pull no surprises?

"Let's take this slow," she said. "Have you seen a doctor?"

Abby shook her head violently. "Who?" she asked, despairingly. "Good old Doctor Lafferty, who still offers me lollipops? Who could I go see who wouldn't recognize me?"

"How do you know for sure then?" Kate asked with a note of hope.

Abby cast a look at her mother that was not child to mother, but woman to woman. "Mother, I know," she said quietly, her large eyes wet with tears. "I used one of those home pregnancy kits after I missed my period. And I feel it, I just do. I mean—" Instinctively her hands flew to her stomach, cradling its invisible contents. "I've got to be six weeks along already."

Kate hugged Abby even tighter at the thought of how long she had carried this secret alone. "Who did it?" she asked gently.

Abby tried to push away, but it was a halfhearted gesture. "Don't ask me, please don't," she said. "I feel like such a jerk, I don't know why I let it happen, I—God, I was so stupid."

Kate relaxed her embrace and instead cupped her daughter's small face in her hands, tilting it upward, wishing she could wipe away the humiliation she saw. She debated swiftly how far she should push. Had she been used by someone wanting access to her father—an aide? One of those eternal hangers-on? She knew she was dealing first with the least relevant question, but it was too hard to cut immediately to the heart of the matter. A reporter, maybe? That rock star strutting around in his gold lamé jacket? Kate felt the stirring of anger. It would be nice to have a name, an identity—someone to blame.

"Abby," she began, "he shares responsibility—"

"I never want to see him again, he's gone, anyway." Abby took a deep breath. "I know you're right, but it doesn't make any difference now, don't you see? And it's nobody you know."

The simple declaration gave Kate a piercing sense of separation. How much did she know, when it came down to it, about Abby's life? How much did she simply assume she knew?

"I don't know what to do, Mother," Abby whispered. "I'm so sorry."

"We'll figure it out together, I won't let anything hurt you." Kate felt her confidence returning. This promise was one on which she would deliver.

Abby began to sob. "I can't have a baby," she said. "I have to have an abortion."

Kate opened her mouth to answer, but Abby interrupted with a rush of conviction. "What else is there to do?" she said.

Kate paused. Here they were, now, at the heart.

"I don't know," she said. "Let me think." The dictates of a shaky faith resonated warnings through her soul. An abortion? Oh, God. But Kate could almost feel herself separating inside. The Church didn't prepare a mother for this. She didn't have the answers she needed; the instant certitude to handle this mix of sadness and fear and pain. Instead, here she was, churning with the ferocity of an immediate need to protect Abby—at any cost. Abby, a mother? At fifteen? Unthinkable.

Abby reacted to the turmoil in her mother's face with a plea. "You've always made things work," she said quietly. "For me, for Nat, for Daddy. I need you now. I've made a terrible mess of things, and I don't have anyone else I can turn to."

"You don't have to persuade me, honey," Kate said. "I'm just trying to figure out what's best—and how to do it."

Abby was shaking. "I should have been prepared, but I didn't

61

expect—" She stopped, and then went on. "I'm trying to be grown-up about this." Her voice sounded raspy, like a dull saw. "It's hard. There's a lot at stake with Daddy's campaign, and I know what's going to happen. I'm going to either bring everything crashing down or be something you've got to hide in a closet."

"Abby, no." Kate's heart lurched with pity. How had her child taken on such a terrible weight of responsibility?

"This will ruin Daddy, won't it?" Abby said, undeterred. "People will find out, and then they won't vote for him, will they?"

Kate had to respond quickly and carefully—and force conviction into her response. "No, it won't ruin him," she said. "It will not affect the election. Put that out of your mind."

But it wasn't enough.

"He'll hate me," Abby whispered, her eyes wide and suffering, her certitude chilling. "He thinks abortion is awful, I know he does, no matter what he says."

"He would never, never hate you," Kate said with a catch in her throat. "He loves you very much, don't you know that? You're just distraught."

"He'd be shocked, and you can't say different."

Kate took a breath to say something that would refute this challenge, but she couldn't put together what that 'something' was quickly enough.

Abby's eyes recognized the hesitation.

"I know how to be careful about everything," she said immediately, lifting her chin and looking straight at her mother. "I know how to think about how things look. I remember Daddy telling me, Never do anything you wouldn't want to see tomorrow on the front page of *The New York Times*. We know all about that, Nat and me." Then she folded her hands in her lap and sat back, momentarily serene, as if ready for the camera's eye. The pose was smooth and disconcertingly automatic, and Kate felt an instant of panic. What kid should be worried about things like this?

"Don't, honey," she said. "This isn't about how things look. This is much more important than that."

"I've wanted you and Daddy to be proud of me ever since I can remember," Abby went on. "I was even proud because I never had pimples, not for a single Christmas card, not like Nat."

"Honey—"

"I got the Clearasil and made him sit on the toilet so I could smear it on his face when they got bad," Abby said matter-of-factly. "So you wouldn't know." She looked full at her mother. "I can't hide. I'm trapped and Daddy's going to pay because I let him down."

"No way." Kate took a deep breath. Did she mean this? What would Luke say? She found herself focusing for the first time on the larger implications. This must be kept secret; Abby must be protected. What if a reporter found out? Kate felt suddenly chilled. She reached out and stroked Abby's hair. She couldn't wait. She had to make the decision. Now.

"If it has to be an abortion, then that's what it will be," she said quietly. "Don't worry."

"We can't tell Daddy," Abby whispered. "I could never face him again. I just couldn't handle it."

Kate's heart missed a beat. Keep something this important from Luke? Nothing was left to chance in a Goodspeed campaign; nothing. Have a strategy for everything; that was Luke's basic law of survival. Anything could torpedo you. But she felt a trapdoor opening in her soul; then a long, dark tumble downward. She felt sick to her stomach again. There was more at stake here than Luke—or his campaign.

"All right," she said slowly. "We won't tell him."

The shrill wail of the telephone cut through the air. Kate reached for the phone, and Marty's voice came crackling over the wire, a knife-sharp sound that spilled from the receiver into the room.

"Why aren't you on your way?"

It was so typically Marty. No preliminaries, just demands.

"Abby isn't feeling well," Kate said, slipping immediately into a matter-of-fact professional voice. "I couldn't leave her here alone, and I figured Luke's mother would be enough of a draw for the Hollywood Women's Political Caucus."

"That's debatable."

"Abby's sick, Marty."

An irritable sign whistled through the telephone. "How old is she, Kate?"

She would take none of Marty's bullying tonight. "You know perfectly well how old she is," Kate responded coolly. "So don't try to put me on the defensive."

The line buzzed with static.

Patricia O'Brien

"Well, let's hope she gets better quickly, because we need you in San Francisco tomorrow night," Marty said, ignoring her tone. "Without fail. By the way, your old pal with the Roman collar is trying to screw us."

"What are you talking about?"

"Watch the news."

The connection clicked off. Furious, Kate slammed the phone down.

"He's kind of a strange man, isn't he, Mother?" Abby said from the sofa. "What's he like? I get this feeling he knows everything. I'm a little afraid of him."

"He's hard to read," Kate replied. "I don't think he trusts anybody he can't control. Luke says he lives in an almost empty apartment. Just a bed and a dresser in it, that's all."

"I've never seen any family pictures in his office."

"He's been married twice, has a couple of kids, but he's almost like an empty slate. Luke says he lives for politics, nothing else."

"He doesn't like it when Daddy asks your opinion; I've seen the way he looks at you when he does."

Kate shrugged. "That's his problem," she said.

Abby managed a hollow giggle. "His hair is too black."

"Nobody dares mention *that*."

"I think Daddy could win the White House without him."

"Unfortunately your father doesn't think so."

"I guess the question now is whether he can win the White House with *me*." Abby looked suddenly frightened again, frightened enough for Kate to lean forward and kiss her, then pinch her cheek.

"An old trick," she said gently. "It'll bring back your color."

"I'll bet you learned that from the nuns." A spark of Abby's bouncy warmth was creeping back into her voice.

"Sure I did." Kate laughed. "They'd rather we broke a few blood vessels than wear rouge."

"What would they have done? I mean, if you'd got pregnant?"

Kate was silent for a long time. She sighed. "I don't know," she said finally. She thought for a moment, trying to figure out how to say what she wanted to say next. Then she reached tentatively for her daughter. "Honey—was this something that—just happened?" she said. "Or was it someone you care about?"

64

Abby turned away. "Please, Mother," she said, a warning in her voice.

"It's hard not to ask."

"It was a guy I met, a summer intern." Abby's voice was very shaky. "But I don't want to talk about it. I was just a dope, okay?"

Kate accepted the second rebuff, saying nothing.

"Mother—"

"Yes?"

Abby's face was losing cohesion, blurring with exhaustion. "I can't remember talking with you like this before," she said.

Kate pulled her daughter into her arms again, encountering no resistance. She cradled her head, damp with sweat, and kissed her hair. "I guess I've forgotten how tough it is to be a teenager," she whispered.

Abby's voice, coming from somewhere in her bosom, was too muffled to hear. No matter. Kate held her daughter's crumpling form in one final squeeze and was engulfed once again with the ferocity of caring. Right at this moment, she felt possessed of all the strength needed to do whatever needed to be done.

"Go in now and get some sleep," she said quietly. "I'll take care of everything."

Alone, Kate stared around the room, thinking about what an oddly empty, unlived-in place it really was. The little touches rang false, she decided. The ashtrays on end tables in a house where no one smoked, for one. Or the ceramic bowls stuffed with artificial flowers, scooped up in one fast trip through Crate and Barrel two hours before an "at home" photo session when Luke first declared his candidacy for the presidency. Most of the time, Luke was the only one who camped out here on fence-mending or fund-raising trips. Except for the magnificent lake spread below, there was nothing that anchored the Goodspeeds to this small piece of high-rise turf.

I have things I must sort through, Kate thought, and it isn't going to be easy. She had to figure out a way to help Abby without hurting Luke. It was that stark—there was no denying it. Would he really be hurt? Or would it just hurt his chances for winning the election? She sighed. There was no way of separating the two, not in the lives they were leading now, maybe never. The loss of any semblance of privacy in their lives had never hit home quite this strongly before. She tried to focus her thoughts on Luke. She could see him on the podium in New Orleans, hand raised high; she could conjure up the jut of his chin as he rammed home a point in the last debate; but for the life of her, she couldn't see him sitting next to her here, right now, in the midst of the ashtrays and fake flowers, talking about the desperate plight of their eldest child.

"Luke, listen," she fantasized saying. "Our daughter is a little campaign machine, and that's wonderful for the campaign, but she turned human on us and got herself pregnant." Could she ever say anything like that? No more than she could announce it at a fund-raising breakfast, so she might as well stop thinking about what the shock value of such an announcement would be. She felt suddenly both uncomfortable and vaguely disloyal. She was fantasizing a way of getting Luke's undiverted attention, and that wasn't playing within the rules.

But she had a trick for this kind of unwelcome meditation, and she used it now—she opened a door to her mind where she stored her secret pride. Luke needed her. On every front. When he was thinking about the environment, she was the one who got him to focus on the ozone layer, and she was the one who told him that people were afraid to drink tap water anymore. And when . . .

Stop giving a speech for yourself, she thought impatiently. What were *you* concentrating on when your little girl was slathering Clearasil on her brother to make him politically acceptable? Kate swallowed hard, forcing down her guilt. Her strength came from being sure and very, very steady, and this was not the time to question the past.

Luke, she radioed silently, this one I'm going to handle without you, as I have handled most other family things over the years. Nat's broken arm, for example. Or Abby's first piano recital. Geometry homework, missing hamsters—abortions—they all fall in my territory.

Kate stood abruptly and began pacing the room, stopping to sweep up the closest offending ashtrays and dump them into a drawer. She didn't have to help people like Marty and Claire kill themselves just because it was the polite thing to do. Let them bring their own ashtrays. She caught a glimpse of herself in the mantelplace mirror and noted in the bright late-afternoon light that the skin around her eyes was pierced with a tiny network of unfamiliar wrinkles, the kind that couldn't be covered easily with cream, and just how good a mother was she, anyway?

Kate stared into her own eyes and delivered the challenge. I am an organizer, she thought, a very good organizer, and I have organized Luke's life and my own and my children's lives, and I have done it efficiently enough to keep us all functioning at top form. I have tiptoed around the house before dawn countless times packing for trips to Brussels and Moline and Uganda and child-abuse centers on the South Side of Chicago, and I have never left the house without leaving full instructions with Mrs. Leonard and the kids to cover every contingency. I have never forgotten a birthday or a dental appointment, but somehow I left something out. I forgot to notice my daughter growing up, and I forgot to help her figure out how to do it.

"Mom?"

Kate heard a small noise and looked up to see her son standing in the doorway. In the background, from the small TV in his room, she could hear the sounds of Nat's passion, the ever-present baseball game.

"Nat—" It was hard to keep the surprise out of her voice. "I thought you were at the library."

"I didn't want to go, Harry said he had to go with me."

"Why did that matter?"

"Those wires in his ears. The kids laugh."

Nat wasn't looking directly at her. He was looking at the floor, then out the window. Anywhere but directly at his mother. His eyes looked shocked, and his hand involuntarily went up to tug at his thick, almost curly hair, and then Kate knew.

"You heard."

Nat was desperately seeking a new place to look.

"Yeah." Then he looked straight at his mother, his eyes frightened. "Is she going to be all right?" he asked.

Kate took a deep breath, trying to hold down a flash of unexpected panic. "Yes, honey, she'll be all right."

"What happens when you have an abortion?"

67

It hurt to see the fear in his eyes. "They—stop the pregnancy," she said.

"Could Abby die?"

Kate shook her head. "Not if it's done properly by a good doctor," she said. "And it will be."

"How come she doesn't want Dad to know?"

"Oh, Nat." Kate sighed. "I wish you hadn't listened."

"I couldn't help it."

Of course he couldn't. Why was she turning this into some kind of scolding? "I know," she said. "I just wish you didn't have to worry about this now, too."

"Will Dad have to drop out of the race?"

"No, no." She shook her head vigorously this time. "He'll be fine. But you must promise me you will say nothing. It's very important."

Kate felt a rush of sympathy at the sight of the boy's confused expression. "Come here, son," she said gently. He moved forward and she cradled his face in her hands. She was telling him the rules had changed, and that's all there was to it, and, for once, his father's interests did not come first. "It's Abby's life," she said. "And we have to respect that."

"Yeah, but Dad's running for president."

"That's not everything." The words came out flat and uncompromising, and Kate realized how deeply she meant them. It wasn't everything. There was something else closing in, and she'd be damned if she'd let it engulf her family.

"We always do what's right for Dad."

"That's true," she said with care, picking her way through an unfamiliar minefield. "But this time we first have to do what's right for Abby."

Nat was looking at her directly again. "How do you know what that is?" he asked cautiously.

Kate kept her voice as firm as possible. "I just do, that's all," she said. Nat's face was filled with unformed, unasked questions, but he said nothing, just scratched his head.

"I gotta go study," he mumbled. Reluctantly, Kate withdrew her hand as he turned and fled the room.

Kate picked up the phone almost immediately and dialed the Executive House hotel, too worn out to even ask herself why. Something visceral, maybe. She wasn't even sure there would be an answer, maybe the person she most wanted to talk to right now had already returned home to Washington.

The call was put through immediately, and Kate felt a sense of immense relief as she heard the receiver click off the hook. When she spoke, her voice was not too steady.

"Joan?" she said in a low voice. "Joanie, is that you?"

4

Kate waited in the living room at first, slumped into a chair, watching through the window as the shadows stretched and deepened outside. But it was not in her nature to stay inactive for long. I'll clean out the hall closet, she decided. That'll keep me busy until Joan gets here. She opened the closet door and was greeted with a multitude of smells: the acrid remains of old mothballs, the musty scent of ancient wool, a touch of cinnamon—cinnamon? Kate sniffed experimentally, then dug into the pocket of an old sweater of Abby's. Yes, there they were, a few of the cinnamon drops Abby used to love as a child, hoarded away in her pocket, covered with lint—amazing that they still smelled like anything at all. Kate had a sudden memory of Abby's chubby fingers stuffed into the pockets of this very sweater, remembering the time she tripped on the icy sidewalk, coming up with a bruised nose because she didn't want to let go of her cinnamon drops.

Abby was pregnant.

Kate pulled back from the closet and walked over to the old record player on the far wall. If she was lucky, Luke's Edith Piaf albums would still be here. She smiled. When all her other friends had been listening to Joni Mitchell, Luke had preferred vintage Piaf. He never had followed the crowd. It didn't take long to thumb through the meager collection of faded albums, and she soon found the one she wanted. The record almost slipped through the torn bottom of the jacket, but Kate caught it before it escaped to the floor. It was the first one Luke had played for her in the dusty little apartment on Capitol

Hill he occupied during his first House term. "Seduction by Edith Piaf?" she had teased that first evening, hoping she sounded as sophisticated and self-confident as she yearned to be. It had seemed so important to make him see she was smart and funny and not at all impressed to have his attention once again—that this South Bend "townie" had made her own way to Washington, and *this* time, he would have to court *her*. Kate smiled at the memory. It, too, made a good story for campaign appearances, and nobody had to know how nervous she had felt when she gravitated for the second time into the electrical field of the charming, life-loving Luke Goodspeed. Nobody had to know how much she had wanted to marry him, convinced that this man, of all the men she knew, was the one most likely to make important things happen. She had known one thing, and known it clearly: life with Luke would always, always be interesting.

She placed the record carefully on the turntable, suddenly hungry for the plaintive beauty of the French singer's voice. Piaf's haunting, jaunty rendition of "Milord" flowed through the room, cutting the somber stillness. Kate closed her eyes and leaned against the wall. This was better; she could tackle the closet again. There was therapy as well as a sense of accomplishment in pulling outgrown and worn clothes from their hangers and tossing them into a heap in the hall; she would get somebody to haul them out of here, maybe the Salvation Army. How should she handle this? What should she do? Was she wise enough to save her daughter from harm? There had been so few problems with Abby—with Nat, too, for that matter. They were caring kids, well disciplined, enthusiastic, always supportive. Kate pulled an old pair of Nat's sneakers from the darkest recesses of the closet, his soccer shoes, the shoes he wore to all the games she and Luke had missed. . . .

"We meant well," she found herself saying out loud. The words sounded forlorn in the empty room. On the turntable, Piaf was sorrowing about lost love, and Kate felt a deepening sense of melancholy as she listened. All right, we meant well, but so what? People say that, and then they go ahead and do damage anyway. I've tried to be a good mother, Kate declared silently before the tribunal hastily convened in her brain. I've made mistakes, but I've tried.

She remembered reading somewhere that people who said they "meant well" were people who didn't hear, and they didn't hear until they were ready to listen. Okay. She sat back on her haunches, and brushed old dust from the hem of her skirt, trying to shake her mood. I'm ready to listen, she thought, but I'm not sure what I hear.

The phone rang sharply. Kate froze, choosing not to pick it up, even when the answering machine began to record Luke's rushed and puzzled voice. An image of her husband hearing this news about his adored little girl was forming in her brain, and it was daunting. There was a special relationship between father and daughter; they could share jokes, talk for hours about politics—do so many things together that were comfortable and relaxed, sharing much more than Luke did with his shy, nonpolitical son. But for all that closeness, there were things that could not be shared. Not in the public life this family led. We practice on each other, she thought uncomfortably. We practice perfecting our public selves and we help each other get better and better at it. Is something getting swallowed up? Kate felt a twinge, thinking of the unfair burden now on Nat. He knew something he shouldn't know; nothing was more dangerous in politics. What about here? Within his own family?

Luke's voice stopped; the machine clicked off. No, there was no need to feel guilty about staying in the shadows, protected from his electronic presence. Later, she would call him. Not now. Not until she could talk to Joan and figure out what came next.

Two thousand miles away, Luke stood staring out the window of his hotel room, listening to Kate's calm, businesslike greeting on the answering machine. He tapped his fingers impatiently on the cold wood of the table.

"No answer, huh?" Marty's voice had a definite edge.

"Something's up," Luke said. "Kate can be pretty impulsive, but she sticks to her schedules. She doesn't blow off commitments for nothing."

"Yeah, well, maybe your kid's feeling better."

Luke pulled at the collar of his wilted shirt, holding onto the phone for an instant after leaving his message, as if half expecting Kate to pick up anyway.

"We've gotta get going." Marty was leaning against the door, anxious to get Luke moving. He glanced at his watch and put one hand on the doorknob.

Luke automatically glanced at his own watch. "Maybe she went out for some aspirin or something, and Abby's asleep."

"Yeah. They're okay. Come on, let's go."

Luke hesitated for a fraction of a second only. "Okay," he said, slamming down the phone. "Too bad. She'll be tickled to hear about the White House summons."

"That came off the wall," Marty said. "What does Gilmartin want? Your hide?"

Luke laughed. "Probably. He can't be too happy about George Will calling Enright the 'albatross of the Republican party.' But this is a top-secret special briefing for the two of us, very private; no press."

"I juggled some stuff, and we're okay," Marty said. "It'll be a fast trip in and out of there."

Luke smiled jauntily. "This time," he said.

Back in Chicago, Kate reached for the remote control and flicked on the old television set. Somehow she had never got around to getting the jumpy picture fixed, but at least it still worked.

A flashy collage of images leaped onto the screen: a new commercial for Enright. Kate studied it, curious about the thrust of the first Republican post-convention message. There was John, looking like a courtly banker thinking deep thoughts, reaching out to shake hands with an elderly man in a nursing home and then talking to teenagers in a vocational workshop, while a professional narrator extolled his commitment to "helping Americans improve the quality of life." The man had lived so long in Sam Gilmartin's shadow, he hadn't an original thought in his head. Kate reminded herself not to scoff too much. It would be a big mistake, she knew that, and Enright looked pretty good playing his role. As she watched, she caught a fleeting glimpse of Eleanor Enright, John's wife. Now there was one smart woman, absolutely determined to get her husband into the White House. Luke underrated her appeal. How had Enright ever attracted a wife like Eleanor?

The ad cut to a close-up of Enright lifting a joyous baby high in the air. His arms protecting the child, a sudden burst of light on the baby's face—then freeze-frame. "Yes, John Enright cares about life," the voice-over said. "All life. And you can depend on it."

73

Kate felt suddenly nervous. Only a few hours ago, she would have flagged the ad as evidence that if Luke thought he would be let off the hook on abortion, he was wrong. But now it took on ominous new importance. She considered a quick trip to the kitchen for a glass of wine, but decided to wait for Joan. Where was she? Mother always said Joan would be late for her own funeral; it drove scheduling wild when they tried to slot her campaign appearances. Strange to be thinking of Mother right now. Kate had gotten used to referring to her for the bio writers in one breath as "Margaret Sullivan from County Kerry," not as "Mother." What would she say and do now if she were alive? Kate stared ahead for a moment, seeing nothing. She couldn't visualize the scene; she could not conceive of looking to Margaret Sullivan for help. But still, if she were here . . . Stop it, she told herself. It did no good to build these private little fantasies; if she were truly tough, she would have given them up long ago.

She forced her attention back to Enright's ad. An election was always some kind of Chinese puzzle; you never knew what worked until after it was over. Luke's chances were good, wonderfully good, but he couldn't afford to lose the votes of pro-choice working women. There were a lot of secretaries, paralegals, waitresses, and Wall Street lawyers out there who were fed up with politicians trying to play the abortion issue from the middle of the fence. Luke couldn't risk losing them. Not now. She stirred, restless, wishing again that Joan would hurry up. She hit the zapper; there was the ad again. Fed up with Enright's sanctimonious face, she kept zapping, looking for the evening news.

On NBC, Tom Brokaw was beginning his report.

"Demonstrators filled the street outside the White House today," he announced as pictures of a milling crowd on Pennsylvania Avenue filled the screen, "protesting the administration's failure to act quickly on granting permanent U.S. residence to Liberian poet David Palmer." Kate saw fleeting glimpses of several familiar faces and found herself focusing on the imposing figure of Maurice Norton. A Detroit mailman's son, Norton had risen from a Teamsters local to become the first black to head the AFL-CIO. He was one of the most respected black leaders in the country—and a strong supporter of Luke. We must get onto this, she thought, vaguely alarmed. It was clear from the report that the Republicans would cave in on Palmer sooner or later, and Olson was right; Luke should get credit for leading the way. A picture of Palmer flashed on the screen, a picture of a man with a brooding, powerfully cut face. It's strange, Kate thought, looking into the almost majestic clefts of that face: he looks like a black Abraham Lincoln. No wonder he attracted people to him. It was almost eerie.

The next piece jolted her reverie. "A surprise defection tonight in the Goodspeed campaign," Brokaw began, speaking rapidly, "which could mean a brewing attack from the Catholic Church on the nation's third Catholic presidential nominee."

Kate stared. A picture of an uncomfortable-looking Father Joe flashed on the screen.

"Father Joseph Delancey, a cousin and close friend of Senator Luke Goodspeed, today backed off from a full endorsement of his cousin's candidacy in a hastily called press conference at the chancery, reportedly after being called on the carpet by Cardinal Leo Kovach," Brokaw said. "Delancey denied he was being muzzled by his superiors, telling reporters he had simply 'rethought' his 'unconditional' support after the Democratic Convention and felt a need—as he put it—'to set the record straight early in the game.' "

A shot of Father Joe again. "I cannot in good conscience fully support Senator Goodspeed unless he clarifies his position on abortion," he said in a flat voice. Kate could see sweat on his face as he read from a prepared statement before a cluster of mikes.

"If he takes a solid pro-choice position, are you with him or against him, Father?" asked a reporter.

"Obviously, I remain committed to the Catholic Church's position on this matter," Delancey said stiffly.

"You'd dump your own cousin, Father?"

It was that damn *New York Post* again.

"I would stay committed to the Church," Joe repeated.

"You wouldn't campaign for him then, right? Would you vote for him?"

A chancery aide pushed in front of Joe. "Save your questions for the politicians, please," he said. "That's all, gentlemen and ladies."

Brokaw launched into a quick reprise of the botched abortion case in Nebraska, noting that Luke's comments deploring the young girl's death the night of his nomination had apparently angered Church authorities, who—according to sources—feared it was a prelude to his abandonment of all religious reservations to abortion. "That could have been a costly stumble, possibly shattering the careful centrist position on the issue that worked for Goodspeed through the primaries," Brokaw said. "If the Catholic Church actively fights Luke Goodspeed on this issue, the heat will be on. Right now, the defection of his most loyal clerical ally has got to come at least as an unexpected—" here Brokaw paused for emphasis—"and an *unpleasant* surprise."

The camera cut to Marty, who looked more irritated than surprised. "We defend Father Delancey's right to say anything he wants to say," Marty said smoothly. "If there's any truth to the rumors of coercion, then all we can say is, we're sorry for him and point out the Church is stepping into the wrong arena here. Senator Goodspeed is a good Catholic who has consistently defended a woman's right to decide whether or not to have an abortion within the law. He supports the rule of law—and I'm sure Cardinal Kovach does, too."

Here we go, Kate thought. The first flap of the campaign, that's all it is. But still, she felt jolted. There would be a lot of interest now in whatever Luke decided to say in his Texas speech. Why had Joe done it? His announcement stirred the embers, no doubt about it, besides bumping any video of Luke's tour today of Pittsburgh's nuclear-waste disposal site. The papers would probably put Father Joe on their front pages tomorrow, figuring they had a much sexier story than another take on the hazards of nuclear waste.

Kate sighed. Be honest, she told herself. Am I surprised? No, more sorry than surprised, really. Luke would be jolted, too, but he held an essentially more realistic view of the limits of loyalty than she did. Joe was a good guy, dazzled, if truth be told, by his proximity to the now glamorous presence of Luke, but an easy figure for the cardinal to undercut. He wasn't willing or able to take on Rome. To be fair, it couldn't be easy being a modern priest. The ones who got discouraged left the Church. The ones who stayed seemed stuck in a kind of spiritual time warp. Kate felt a twinge of sadness. She was angry; Luke was right. She was angry for many reasons in part because she felt cheated by the Church. But she had to put all that aside. The most important thing right now was to help Abby.

Luke would be hurt by Joe's defection, but he would move on, fast. "He has to do what he has to do," he would say. And he would refuse to take the betrayal personally. It was a great trait, this hard-headedness of Luke's. Kate stared at the heap of discarded clothes in the hall. "Too bad I don't have it," she said aloud.

The phone rang again, and this time Kate heard Nat pick it up. Please don't be Luke, she pleaded.

"Mom, it's Grandma."

Kate picked up the phone and braced for the flutter of Louise Goodspeed's persistently startled, birdlike voice.

"I'm so upset," Louise wailed. "He can't *mean* it, can he? How can Father Joe be such a *traitor?*"

"He isn't in charge of those decisions, Louise."

"My own brother's son! How could he do this? He and Luke were inseparable when they were kids. I don't know how many times I fed that boy dinner, filling him with steak and potatoes and blueberry pie. He never left a bite on his plate. And gratitude! What about gratitude? I bought him his first good shirt for graduation so he would look decent for a change, and does he remember *that*? What will my friends say?"

All this was delivered in a plaintive, high-pitched lament, and Kate simply waited. It did no good to focus on the almost snobbish piety that Louise shared with the circle of frail widows who were her closest friends. Louise Curran Goodspeed was the daughter of a gruff Chicago meat packer whose proudest achievement was paying off the mortgage on his modest South Side home before his heart gave out. A good man, Luke had told her. A man a daughter could well have been proud of. But Louise had refashioned for herself a vaguely shrouded lace-curtain heritage, an image made possible only because a hardworking Protestant named John Goodspeed had married her and made lots of money before he died. On more than one occasion Kate had been tempted to ask Luke how he had survived his mother's pretensions, but she knew if she did ask, he would just laugh and shrug. He did not like to talk about his mother. He preferred to keep her at a distance and advised Kate to do the same. This, of course, was easier said than done, and, in truth, Kate had grown fond of Louise over the years, even though the older woman continued to suck in attention, sometimes demanding it fretfully. Kate gave herself frequent lectures on the need for patience, but right now she was amused.

"Luke won't lose the election," she said. "All he'll lose is Catholic soft money."

"What's that?"

"Money given to the state parties, not directly to the campaign. Louise, you know what it is."

Louise was calming down, mulling over more familiar wounds. "You're very cynical sometimes, dear," she said. "I know you don't mean it."

"No, I don't mean it."

"Where is Luke? I want to talk to him. What do I do if anyone calls me about this?"

"Luke's in a plane somewhere over Montana," Kate said. "And do not talk to any reporters at all. Just let your machine screen your calls."

"My friends don't like that."

"They don't have sons running for president."

A pause. "Well, that's certainly true." Louise sighed. "Oh, dear," she said.

"Don't worry, Louise," Kate said more gently. "We're in the home stretch, and things are going to be rougher."

"Well, Father Joe should stick to religion. That's what *he's* good at. Not politics."

"Thatta girl." Kate smiled, said goodbye, and hung up.

This time she stayed where she was, staring at the wall, until the doorbell rang.

Joan sat quietly as her sister talked. Her eyes, so much a mirror of Kate's own, never left her sister's face as Kate laid out the details. Kate found the exercise of explaining an almost soothing experience; it gave her reassurance that she would soon have even this under control.

"So there it is," she finished finally. "My kid's pregnant, and I don't know what to do. I mean, I do know, but I don't know how to *do* it."

"That's always the tough part," Joan said, a small smile pulling at the corners of her mouth. She stood up, absently smoothing the fold of her beige linen pants with a pale, well-manicured hand. She always had an easy, casual elegance, the kind that never took itself too seriously—a reflection of her temperament, Kate thought, or at least of the image she wanted to project.

"Are you shocked?" she asked, almost shyly.

"No," Joan replied with a glance of surprise. "I feel bad for Abby, but I'm not shocked. Do you expect me to be?"

"No, not really," Kate said quietly. "I guess I'm the only one who thought she was still a little girl."

Joan considered that in silence. "Hey, you're a mother," she said. "You're entitled." She stood up. "I need a drink."

"I keep asking myself, how did Abby get this—" Kate struggled for the right word, but it wouldn't come—"this *old?*"

"It happens," Joan said. "Any wine in the refrigerator?"

Kate nodded. "Get me a glass, too," she said.

"I thought you were the one who hated the stuff," Joan said. But she rested her hand gently on her sister's shoulder as she walked past. She disappeared into the kitchen, then re-emerged triumphantly holding a jug of Folonari Soave in one hand and two jelly glasses in the other. "We're in luck," she said. "There's enough to see us through the entire planning process."

"She's been struggling with this alone for a month and a half," Kate said. "That's what knocks me out. Totally alone and scared."

"It's a tough thing to go through." Joan put a glass down in front of Kate and poured the pale gold wine. "It's odd, I guess," she continued. "I don't think of anybody in your family being alone, ever; at least that's my impression. You're always surrounded by people." She gave a short, abrupt laugh. "Lord, it would drive me crazy. You can't even have a ripped hem without the whole world noticing."

It was Kate's turn to pause. "That's what's been so tough for my kid," she said finally. "She's had to endure all this within a crowd, and that's the loneliest feeling of all."

Joan surveyed her sister thoughtfully. "You're not allowed to trip up," she said.

"Or deal straight." Kate took a deep swallow of her wine, not wasting time on a sip, trying to hide her surprise at her own words. "Even with Luke." She paused again. "Abby needs help, and I can't tell Luke or anybody else," she said. "If she isn't protected, she could be destroyed. I'd take a ripped hem any time." She glanced at her sister, feeling a shiver of apprehension. She needed to reach Joan, to

cut through the barrier that separated their lives. Did she understand? Please, Kate thought, I really want you to understand.

Joan returned her gaze steadily. "Don't worry," she said. Two
simple words. Tears began squeezing from the corners of Kate's eyes.

"There's a doctor in Lansing I know who can come here, no
questions asked," Joan said, her voice gentle.

"How do we do this without anybody finding out? Is it even
possible?"

"We'll figure out every damn detail and carry it off like a jewelry
heist, and then we'll pray for good luck."

"I'm worried. Really worried."

"That's because you're scared." Joan leaned back into her chair,
listening for sounds. "Is she here?" she said.

"Yes," Kate said. "She's upstairs, asleep."

"Having an abortion isn't the easiest thing in the world," Joan
said. "She's got to be sure it's what she wants."

Kate firmly shook her head. "My God, she's fifteen," she said. "I
want to pretend it's okay to think about her having a baby, but it isn't,
Joanie. It really isn't."

"Yep, I know," Joan said. "What's she saying?"

"She wants the abortion."

"Good."

"There's simply no other choice," Kate said slowly.

"If Luke could only hear you now," Joan said with a grin, then,
hastily, at sight of Kate's stricken look, "I'm sorry, I'm just trying to
loosen us both up a bit. I agree with you totally, you know that. If
you'd said anything else, I would've thought you were nuts."

Kate was beginning to feel the floor under her that she needed, the
support it would take to carry this off. She always felt better when she
was developing a plan, and one was emerging.

"I've got to be assured that he's good—"

"It's a she."

"—that she's good. And that she's got the right equipment to make
it safe."

"She does."

"How do you know?"

Joan sighed. "I know, Kate."

Kate stopped, searching Joan's eyes. Silently, forgetting for the moment her own troubles, she touched her sister's hand. Joan's fingers trembled slightly. But then she straightened, moving her hand away; the moment passed. "It has to be done privately," she said in a businesslike tone.

"Can't it be done in a hospital?"

"Think a minute. There's too much risk of being found out."

"Then where?"

"A clinic. A very good clinic—at night. I know where we have to go."

Kate shuddered.

"She'll be all right." Joan was comforting now.

Kate nodded, not fully convinced. "I've got to be with her."

"You run the risk of being recognized," Joan warned.

"I know," Kate said, feeling a dull ache beginning at the nape of her neck. "But I've got to do it anyway."

Joan sighed. "Not to push this point too far, Kate, but if you're recognized, then Luke takes the dive."

"Abby has to have the abortion."

"Look, I agree. Would Luke?"

Kate straightened and slowly sipped from her glass of wine. "I think he'd be paralyzed."

"Paralyzed?"

Kate was groping. "Caught, I mean," she said. It was hard to explain this to her sister.

"Well, you know your husband, I don't."

"That's not the only consideration." Kate paused, wondering why she felt this so strongly. "Abby would go over the edge if he knew."

Joan put up no further argument. "I'll stay with her in Washington until you get back from—where are you going?"

"I head for California, then Houston. I'll see Luke there on Friday, and then home."

"Okay. When you get back I'll have everything arranged."

"Thanks." Kate reached out and again lightly touched her sister's hand, wanting to hug her, but again Joan pulled away. Joan was not a hugger. "I'll program in a bout of flu as soon as everything is set. And Joan—Nat knows. He overheard us, but he won't say anything."

"Nat? He's such a straight arrow." Joan frowned, showing a flicker of alarm. "How can you be sure?"

81

Kate wasn't up to an analysis of Nat's trustworthiness tonight. "He'll obey me, he knows it's important," she said, hoping she was right.

"Good luck." There was a strong note of skepticism in Joan's response.

"I'll need it, right?" In sudden frustration, Kate gestured toward the thick black trip book resting under her purse on the table by the door. "Look at the size of that thing," she said. "I don't have a single unprogrammed day in my life for the next three months, and this is something Luke and I have dreamed about for twenty years. I'm squeezed, Joan. I can't let him down, not now. But I can't let Abby down either, and I'm muzzling my poor son."

"Stop making yourself feel guilty."

"Got any magic formula?"

Joan shook her head as she drained her glass and reached for the bottle to refill it.

"No, wish I did," she said gently, flashing a rueful smile. "I shouldn't say this, because it won't make you feel good, but I wouldn't be in your shoes for anything."

"Thanks a lot." But Kate smiled back. She felt better anyway.

The next morning, Luke straightened his tie as he walked swiftly through the north entrance foyer of the West Wing of the White House with two silent aides. They moved through the lobby and past a discreet receptionist who nodded them on down a narrow hall. One sharp turn to the left and they were standing at the entrance to the Oval Office.

"Welcome, Luke!" The voice, jovial and commanding, cut through the quietness. Luke strode into the room, catching a glimpse of Enright out of the corner of his eye, but mostly focusing on the imposing presence of President Gilmartin. A bit gaunt around the neck these days, Luke noted, but ruddy from golf and with as strong a grip as ever. He tried not to wince as they shook hands. Gilmartin's eight years in this job had aged him, no question about that, but he still bristled with presence and energy.

"Really appreciate you coming, Luke," Gilmartin said. "One of you two guys will be taking this place over, so I figure it's time for us to have a small chat. Nothing earthshaking. Just preliminary."

Luke's eyes traveled to the presidential seal hanging in back of the president's desk as Gilmartin guided him to a wing-back chair by the fireplace. A hell of a lot of history had taken place in this room. It must be damn tough to give up.

As if on signal, two more men emerged from the doorway: the head of the CIA and Gilmartin's thin-lipped secretary of state. They began what Luke saw at once was a cursory review of major foreign issues: a droning report on the latest Brazilian food riots, familiar statistics on Polish labor unrest and a run-through of intelligence on the most recent Middle East terrorist bombings—most of which had been already reported in *The New York Times*. Enright sat quietly, apparently engrossed, but Gilmartin was fiddling with a pencil. He wasn't paying attention.

Finally Luke interrupted. "Mr. President, most of this we already know," he said. "Is there something special you want to tell me?"

Gilmartin's eyes glinted in appreciation of Luke's bluntness. "Yeah," he said. "The Israeli elections. Trouble for us."

"What do you mean?"

"You think we've had hard-liners in there? This new right-wing party has an unbelievably strong base. They're going to win, and win big."

"That's not exactly classified information, Mr. President," Luke said. "All the polls have predicted that for weeks."

The secretary of state drew his lips tight, disapproval evident. "Our intelligence tells us they want to junk the peace agreement and expel Arabs from Israel and the occupied territories," he said.

Luke kept his eyes on Gilmartin. "I haven't heard anyone in a serious position of power go to *that* extreme," he said levelly.

Gilmartin's eyes flickered, but no one responded. Luke decided it was time to short-circuit the game.

"What do you want from me?" he asked.

Gilmartin leaned forward, pounding a fist into his palm. "I want to say to them, if they start down that road, they've got their last fucking dollar from the USA. They hear that from me, first thing they'll do is go to you and try to whipsaw you. They'll try to play us off against each other. I want to be able to say to them, I'm speaking for you, John—" he nodded at Enright—"and for you, Luke—" another nod in Luke's direction—"and that I'm telling them, whoever is the next president, that policy stands."

"I'm with you, Mr. President," Enright promptly said.

Enright's voice rolled with its usual mellifluousness, but Luke caught a spark of fire in the man's eyes. He made a quick mental note to think about that later.

"Let me see if I understand you, Mr. President," he said, taking his time answering. "You want my support now. If I'm elected, I would then have no leeway in dealing with Israel. Is that right?"

"It's for the good of the country, Senator Goodspeed," the secretary of state broke in. "There's no point in drawing this line if they think they can get a better deal from the next administration."

"Can I see your intelligence information?"

"We can't do that."

"Well, then, you can't expect my cooperation," Luke said dryly. "Things have a way of changing in the Middle East—quite fast." So here it was, a test to see if he could be intimidated by the power of the president. He sighed. Would guys like Gilmartin never learn?

The CIA director looked indignant. "We're talking about a major threat to peace, Senator," he said. "It's critical."

"Maybe it is, but I don't know that yet," Luke said. "And I won't know what should be done about it until I'm president. I'm making no promises to anybody."

Gilmartin's eyes narrowed. "You're looking at this in a partisan way," he said.

Luke smiled. "No disrespect, Mr. President," he said. "But we're a partisan country. I'm not going to tie my hands before I sit where you're sitting."

He heard the other four men in the room sharply draw in their breath. Gilmartin, Luke knew, could throw some pretty impressive fits when he got crossed. All he did now was stare hard at Luke, but Luke could see a glint of the man's famed ruthlessness in his eyes. When he spoke, his voice was calm.

"I'm gonna work real hard to get you defeated, Luke."

"I'm not surprised," Luke replied. "I'd do the same, Mr. President, in your shoes."

A look passed between the two men. It was a look of wary, grudging, mutual respect.

"Well, if you won't help me on foreign policy, I want you to hear something really serious," Gilmartin said. "Hope you brought some aspirin."

He turned to his secretary of state.

"Jack," he said, "call in the Treasury people." He laughed when he caught Luke's inquiring look. "You think the savings-and-loan failures were bad?" he said. "Hang on to your hat, Senator. Wait until you see what's happening with the insurance industry *this* time."

The next few days crawled by for Kate in a blur of speeches and appearances at hospitals, day-care centers, and schools. Normally this was what she enjoyed most—talking to students, urging support of pilot programs for inner-city schools, highlighting the work of especially gifted teachers—but now she felt hollow. Unconnected to her own speeches. Distracted. After careful consideration, she had pulled Abby off the road for the rest of the week. I could keep her with me, Kate first thought, but that would draw more attention. She couldn't make a mistake. She had to think of every detail—very carefully.

Friday finally arrived. Kate sat at the window of the car driving her up to Houston's Four Seasons Hotel and glumly watched the Secret Service going through their usual bustle of clearing a path for her to enter. Luke's speech was tomorrow, and she did not yet know what he planned to say about abortion. People were waving and calling to her and she tried to respond, but it all felt sterile and automatic, more automatic than she'd ever remembered. Her focus had blurred.

"Mrs. Goodspeed, the senator and his staff are waiting for you in the dining room," the concierge whispered as she came through the door. It was just as well, even if she did feel worn out. In a way, it was a relief to face Luke first in front of a group. She walked into the polished, well-groomed interiors off the lobby and glanced around.

There was Luke, comfortably collapsed into a plush-upholstered chair, surrounded by several aides. He looked as though he was chatting amiably with one of the diners at the next table, and she was delighted to feel her spirits rise.

"Kate!"

Marty spotted her first and called out her name; Luke twisted quickly around and grinned a welcome. Kate reached the table, leaned over to kiss her husband, and heard a familiar chuckle to her right.

"She caught you, Luke," the voice said. It was Sam Olson, grinning wide in a full-sized smirk.

Luke looked momentarily annoyed, then reluctantly he laughed.

"What's the joke?" Kate asked, glancing down at a piece of crumpled paper in Luke's hand.

Luke pulled her close into the seat next to him and shrugged. "Nothing new. I've just had an encounter with one of those women who fall all over themselves when they meet a politician. We've seen a million of them, honey."

Kate reached for the piece of paper and spread it out on the tablecloth, noting the silence that had fallen over the table. The handwriting was bold and large, and the message was direct: "You're fantastic." A hastily scribbled phone number followed. Kate quickly laughed, mostly for Olson's benefit, and glanced at the woman over Luke's shoulder. She did indeed know the type—so much so that she tended to make her observations almost clinically. This one had the usual heavy lashes and long legs, arching up from her chair with the usual invitational body language. I give her an eight, Kate thought automatically. A little less mascara, and she could be a ten.

Women always gravitated to Luke. To get excited about it was to waste energy and lose face, and Kate knew better than that.

"They do keep trying, don't they?" she said lightly, then glanced at Marty. "Is the speech ready for tomorrow night?" she asked.

"We're still working on it," Marty replied. "We'll wrap it up after you've gone upstairs."

"That's not necessary," Kate said calmly. "I think you should all come up to the room instead. I've got some thoughts on a few things."

Then she took the piece of paper in her hand and held it over a candle. There were a few nervous coughs as it burst into a gust of flame that surely was visible at the next table.

Luke and Kate's spacious suite was the best the hotel had to offer— invitingly elegant, with soothing beige carpeting and restful peach walls and lots of deeply polished mahogany furniture. Kate looked around admiringly as she and Luke walked in with a cluster of aides right behind them. You took what you could get when you were on the road, and what you got frequently included things like broken heating units and peeling black-and-orange wallpaper, so this was especially nice. It was, she thought with some wistfulness, a place where a man and a woman could curl up under crisp sheets and close out the world. If they lived reasonably normal lives, that is.

"Here's our best effort," Marty said, tossing a single piece of paper on the coffee table in front of Luke. "It's good, it's plain, and it's needed. So much for Father Jello."

Luke smiled slightly. "He's stuck," he said. "Not much he can do about it."

The room grew still as Luke read. Only the sound of Olson digging into a stale bag of potato chips, a noisy, irritating intrusion, broke the silence. What, Kate wondered, was he doing in a private strategy meeting, even if he was bringing in millions to state party organizations?

Luke threw the paper back on the coffee table. "No," he said briskly. "It's got a phony grandstanding tone. Looks like a slap at Joe."

"You can't underreact," Marty said. "Otherwise your cousin's defection makes you look like a wimp."

Luke's eyes turned stubborn. "This reads like a declaration of war on the anti-abortion people, and nobody's going to believe it's anything more than pure politics."

"You're overstating it," Marty said reasonably. "All we've done is make sure there's a little justice in it."

"You bet," Olson interjected, crunching the remains of the potato chip bag in his fist. "Can't risk alienating all the liberals."

Luke looked directly at Kate, ignoring Olson. "My partner here and I don't agree there's a problem," he said. "Pro-choice is pro-choice." Kate returned his gaze, a sense of weariness pulling and engulfing. Maybe she couldn't tell Luke about Abby, but she could do something to protect him if the roof ever came tumbling in.

"Do it, Luke," she said as firmly as possible. "You need the strongest statement possible on the record."

Luke was staring at her. "Mind running that one by me again?" he said.

This time Kate gazed unwillingly into her husband's eyes, wishing she hadn't spoken so flatly, aware suddenly of silence, aware that the others in the room were shrinking back from them. "I just think a little more emotion is a good idea," she said in as reasonable a voice as she could muster. Instantly she regretted her words. Luke looked startled, but mostly he looked hurt.

"Pardon me if I'm surprised," he said.

Olson, oblivious to the tension, leaned forward.

"Can we settle this?" he asked impatiently. "We've got other things to talk about." He stopped. Marty had raised a warning hand.

"I think you ought to read the statement first," Luke said to his wife. Kate picked up the paper and read it, then put it back on the table.

"It's not so bad," she said, a lump forming in her throat.

Luke turned and faced Marty, directing his response to him instead of to his wife. "Well, I don't agree," he said. "I'm not delivering this."

"You're right, Luke." Claire's throaty voice emerged from where she sat in the shadow at the corner of the room, booming forth at its husky, full-volume best.

"You agree?" asked Marty, surprised. He shifted his watchful gaze from Kate and Luke to Claire. "Why?"

"Because Luke will be more convincing if he believes what he says," Claire responded dryly. "Anyone who knows him knows that."

Kate pressed her lips together. She decided to let it pass.

"Okay," Marty said briskly. "Couple of other things. Gilmartin's going after nonvoters with a vengeance this time, and we'd better court them harder than he does."

"Who are they?" asked Kate.

Marty shrugged. "People who've stopped thinking Washington can do anything to solve their problems. The ones who care more about property taxes than income tax and more about their own school district than the Guatemalan elections. We'll keep doing focus groups to fine-tune this, but that's the type. Middle class. Self-absorbed. Midwest, West—hell, everywhere. Claire, keep tracking this, okay?"

She nodded.

"I think Enright's itching to prove he can win this one," Luke broke in suddenly, "without Gilmartin propping him up."

"He hasn't the brains," scoffed an aide.

"Maybe not," said Luke, his voice reflective. "But make no plans without asking yourselves what happens if he tries."

There was a brief moment of silence.

"We need a better antitax message for the South," Marty said. "They're dying down there with this latest recession, and mad as hell because there aren't enough jobs. Wheeler's going to spend extra time there."

"How's he doing?"

Marty grinned. "Working hard, and still thanking the Lord he's on the ticket."

"How's this for the South?" ventured an aide. "Put the cash in *your* pocket, not Washington's." People stared at him. "Hey," he said hastily, "I'm just brainstorming."

Luke had his mind on something else. "I want the focus on the central themes of this campaign," he said. "The things that make us different."

How's this?" Another aide cleared his throat. "We cannot stand still. We are members of a world community, and we must go forward. Always forward."

Ridiculous, Kate thought. You could get away with that in 1960, not now; but nobody was asking her opinion, so she stayed quiet.

"Spongy," Luke said promptly. "Reagan had it right. 'Are you better off than you were four years ago?' Now *there's* a theme."

"Yeah, you're right, but let's deal with that later." Marty was in a hurry. "Let's talk about Palmer."

"About time," Olson said.

Kate glanced at him. No longer was he slouching back in laconic fashion. His eyes narrowed and his body was thrust forward. He wants to be a policy maker, she thought. He figures his money gives him that right.

"Why is the White House holding up the visa?" Olson asked.

"They're just playing to the racists," Claire said impatiently. "They can't last under the kind of pressure they're getting now."

"It's more complicated," Marty said. "I think they're planning to make Enright the hero on this one, probably next week. He's speaking to the NAACP convention an hour before you, Luke. That's when he's going to embrace Palmer, you can bet on it, and we're nuts if we don't beat him to it."

Slowly Luke nodded. "The subcommittee staff checked him out," he said. "Everything looks okay. There are a couple of things—" He stopped.

"Like what?" Olson interrupted.

"What appear to be some crank calls."

"Crank calls?" Olson said irritably. "You're worried about crank calls? Look, you've gotta move."

Kate stiffened. Who did Olson think he was, anyway? She leaned forward. "It doesn't have to be right away," she said quickly. "Luke needs a day or two."

Luke nodded slowly, watching his wife. Marty shot a wary glance at Kate, then at Luke. If Marty only knew the things I really care about, Kate thought; the things really on my mind.

"Okay, let's update Enright," Marty said, moving on. "He's showing some strength on his own. Strong with professionals and managers, which is no big surprise; but he's picking up speed with retirees. You gotta hand it to the guy, he has a way of talking about corporate profits that makes even retired postmen and secretaries feel he's the only one who can keep the economy from going over the brink."

"Smoke and mirrors," scoffed Olson.

"Luke's right," Claire cut in. "Don't underestimate Enright."

"The guy's too flat," objected an aide. "He hasn't got Gilmartin's warmth."

Kate suddenly wanted them all out of there. As if he sensed her mood, Marty stood, signaling the end of the meeting. The others stood also, Olson wisecracking again. Kate smoothed the creases from her skirt, watching Luke; watching Olson. With a start, she saw Marty watching her.

He leaned forward and spoke in a heavy, conspiratorial whisper. "Hey, kid," he said, "we were right." It took her a few seconds to realize he was talking about the abortion statement. He was claiming her as his ally. Kate's stomach began churning again as the group trooped from the room, Marty's remark only deepening her growing sense of having betrayed Luke.

The door had barely closed when Luke turned to her, eyes flashing anger. "So when did you have your brain transplant?" he said roughly. "Or are you one of those ladies downstairs dressed up to look like my wife?"

"Luke—" This was too tough, she told herself. But in her heart she knew she had broken one of their cardinal rules.

"I don't understand," he said. She tried again to answer, but Luke, still hot, was not finished. "Since when is it okay to undercut me in public?"

"You're overreacting, Luke. I changed my mind—"

"Without telling me first? Privately?"

"When?" she asked unhappily. "When was I supposed to do that?"

His face was softening. His anger rarely lasted very long.

"I'm sorry," he said. "It's been a tough day, I don't mean to jump all over you." He coughed. "My voice is giving out again. That speech coach is still trying to get me to speak from the diaphragm, but I can't seem to do it."

"Maybe we're both too stressed out," she said. It was a dive for an easy explanation, but they both wanted it. "It's been a tough week."

"You surprised me, that's all, and I don't like surprises," he said, looking at her curiously. "What about Palmer? I'm ready to get behind the guy, why'd you tell Olson I needed a few more days? I couldn't come right out and contradict you; the rest of them would think we were at each other's throats."

Kate reached out and grabbed his hand, bringing it to her cheek. "I know," she said softly. "I'll try to explain. It's just that we don't have much time to talk anything out privately anymore."

Luke caressed her cheek absentmindedly and didn't press. She knew the signs when he wearied of a topic. "How's Abby?" he asked abruptly.

The sudden sound of her daughter's name hit like a splash of cold water. "What?"

"Abby." He gave her a mildly exasperated look. "You know? Our daughter? Is she still sick?"

"Oh, no, she's fine." It sounded on her own lips like a lame lie, and she felt deeply uncomfortable. "It isn't flu that I'm worried about," she ventured.

"Pressure, right? The kids are under a lot of pressure," Luke said, but his attention was shifting again. He was agreeing too quickly, cutting Kate off. He began moving around the room, picking up glasses, lining them up carefully on a hotel serving tray. "They'll be dealing with a lot more publicity and exposure from here on than they've ever had before, and that's the way it is."

Kate started to walk around after him, feeling a little like an anxious terrier.

"It's tough, though, being a teenage girl," she said, wondering if there was any way past the barrier she had promised to honor.

"This was a pretty big week," Luke said suddenly.

"What?"

He shot her a hurt glance. "You seem so distracted, Kate," he said.

"I'm sorry." What could she say? That he seemed more distracted than she?

"Gilmartin called me in for a backgrounder," he said. "What an operator he is."

"*That's* interesting," she said, trying to give her full attention. "What did he want?"

"He wanted to see how far he could push me on foreign policy, for one," Luke said quietly. "But he got into serious stuff, things I should know about. I appreciated it." He pushed back his shoulders, as if easing an aching muscle. "The insurance industry is in trouble," he said.

Kate looked at him, her attention engaged. "Again?" she said.

Luke nodded.

"This time the biggest pension funds in the country may go down the drain." He sighed, stretching. "That's just one thing." He shot her a questioning smile. "Want to hear more about the nation's infrastructure? Israel? Neo-Nazism?"

Kate smiled back, a bit uncertainly. Family problems seemed almost puny when Luke told her things like this.

It was as if he had read her mind. "It's awesome, Kate," he said. "The—complexity."

She waited expectantly. This had been Luke's first glimpse into the mechanics of the job he wanted badly, and she wanted to hear more.

"And—" she prompted.

"I can't talk about it, honey," Luke said. "You understand. The entire goddamn *world* funnels through that office. You know what happens if you're president? You raise an eyebrow, and the machinery responds. Instantly." He wasn't looking at her anymore; he simply stood by the window, shadowed from the light, angular, removed, very still.

Intellectually she understood. But right now, most of all she understood that she wasn't within that stillness with him. He was removing himself from her, warning her that another barrier was going up, would have to go up, and suddenly she urgently wanted his full attention.

"Sure, I understand," she said. Then the words were scrambling out, tumbling over each other. "I don't want anything to hurt you, Luke, I don't want anything to happen that could be used to attack you later." Don't say too much, she told herself, just raise a warning flag, that's all. "Listen—"

Luke reached out and lightly touched her shoulder. "Relax," he said. The single word offered strength more than comfort. "We'll do fine, Kate; we always do."

As Luke encircled her with his arm, pulling her close, Kate had to acknowledge what she already knew, what years of living with Luke had prepared her for, and it was both a relief—in the current situation—and something else. Luke loved Abby, loved Nat, loved her. That part was okay. But he didn't want to know anything too complicated about them—especially now. She shouldn't complain; he listened to her often enough when she offered advice. But was that really enough? Kate felt a touch of resentment stirring, which only increased her feeling of guilt. Firmly she pushed it away. This line of thinking was totally useless.

"Hey, babe," he said gently, "now explain Palmer."

She cleared her throat.

"Olson thinks he's more than a money man, he thinks he's your adviser," she said. "And I think he's getting entirely too pushy."

"He's always obnoxious."

"I know. But it gets my back up."

"So you decided I should do more checking and the healthy response was to stall."

Kate smiled. They were back on track.

"Right."

Luke chuckled. "My wife," he said. "What would I do without her instincts? Some of them, anyway."

Luke's speech went without incident. Texas's Democrats leaned back in their chairs, well-fed and expectant, loosening the vests of their seldom-worn tuxedos to accommodate chicken Kiev and raspberry mousse, and gave him a rousing reception. Afterward there were questions about Father Joe, a few hostile digs from those reporters wanting more, but there was also something about the response that had a muted quality, and Kate, relieved, found herself wondering why she had doubted Luke's steady approach. Local re-

porters were most interested in knowing if Luke supported a contro-
versial water project, an important but boring topic that soon had the
traveling press yawning. Nothing was more boring to them than local
issues, and for once, Kate was grateful to feel bored herself. The
spotlight, she reminded herself, always shifted eventually. She must
keep her perspective and stay as steady as Luke. Her own peace of
mind and Abby's safety depended on that.

Luke's campaign plane sitting in the fog at the Houston airport
Sunday morning looked ready for a junkyard. All campaign planes
do, Kate reminded herself. But she wasn't prepared for the particularly pungent smell of the chemicals from the toilets as her car drew
up under the open rear door beneath the tail. The wind was blowing
just right. The toilets probably hadn't even been cleaned, which was
disgusting.

"Okay, you guys, stand still so I can get a count!" Marty was doing
a fast check of a ragged line of reporters preparing to board.

"What's the matter, Apple?" yelled a sleepy-looking cameraman.
"Afraid you'll leave somebody important behind?"

"I don't want any hitchhikers," Marty retorted, handing the roster
to an aide. In truth, abandoning a heavyweight columnist or network
star was a sure guarantee of an immediate "campaign in disarray"
story, and Marty was not one to risk any negative development he
could avoid. He was as disheveled as usual, but in a good mood—
even to waving hello to Kate as she climbed the front stairs of the
plane. She forced herself to wave back.

Inside, Kate gazed down the center aisle, past the first-class section
where Luke's entourage was settling in, to the belly of the plane and
the dozens of shouting, joking reporters. Platters of sticky buns and
cardboard containers of orange juice filled one full row of seats, and
two stewardesses passing out the sticky buns were flashing relaxed,
we're-all-in-this-together smiles. Kate felt a twinge of envy. The
reporters really had a community going back there. They had been
living with one another in this airborne cocoon for months, with no
brain-grinding worries about mistakes that could ruin a campaign or
change people's lives. All they had to do was pull out their portable
computers and write their stories, phone them in, and they were
done. The computers made such a funny sound when they banged

away on them—it was the sound of popcorn popping all through the plane, every day. Kate smiled. It wasn't that easy; she knew better. If she hadn't married Luke, she could have been one of those women in the back of the plane. What sort of life would that have been?

She saw Peter as he came aboard, watched him as he claimed his seat from a bewildered local TV reporter, gently explaining the rules of the road: the regulars owned those seats. Yes, for the whole damn campaign. Sorry. The neophyte, learning quickly that possession counted for nothing when you were new, moved quickly to an unclaimed seat. Peter settled in and glanced up, catching Kate's eyes. He grinned, his own eyes dark and merry. "Welcome to my turf," he said, and nodded to the seat next to him. "Got time to talk? Hurry, or we'll lose this."

Why not? Kate glanced back to the front of the plane. Luke was engrossed in conversation with Claire, Marty was sitting next to Sam Olson, and the others were already working on the draft of Luke's next speech. It was bending the rules a bit; she wasn't scheduled for an interview with Peter on this flight, but would it be so terrible to grab a few minutes with an old friend? If Peter made a few squiggles in his notebook, they could pretend it was an interview; he'd like that, Peter always enjoyed a joke. She made her decision.

"Good idea," she said as she plunked herself down and buckled up. Her eyes took on a faint twinkle. "Hmmmm," she said, inhaling deeply. "You're still using that wonderful cheap after-shave lotion. This is my lucky day."

Peter chuckled, leaning forward to pull a dog-eared notebook from his hip pocket for prominent display in his lap. "Hey, lady, I'm just a working reporter," he said. "Don't get overcome."

"I'll try to control myself," she said. It was like the old days, and it made her feel absurdly young. What a time they had had, the two of them, covering the Hill. It was Peter who had advised her, when she was new and scared, to keep a pair of sneakers in the bottom drawer of her desk. "For beating me to the guy we both want a quote from on deadline," he had explained, glancing down at her proudly bought new red Italian pumps with the two-inch heels. "Wear those when we go out to dinner." In the old days, Peter could always make her laugh. He had taught her some of the tricks of covering Congress: knowing where the hidden Senate offices were, for example. If you absolutely had to get a quote from a key senator on a key issue, Peter said, you had to learn where to find the guy when he didn't want to be found and embarrass him into cooperating. It was Peter to whom Kate soon began taking her worries and troubles. He had been a good and steady friend; a trustworthy pal. It was a relief to realize she could be chatty with him still, even mildly gossipy, much more open than with the other reporters. With Peter she didn't have to worry about being dissected.

"I'm pretending you're giving me my Sunday lead," Peter said with a smile, tapping his notebook and stretching out his long, lean legs. "Look a little alarmed; it'll make the other guys nervous." His white shirt was open at the neck, the sleeves rolled up, exposing strong arms thick with dark hair. In the aisle, two women hurrying to their seats glanced at him with more than ordinary interest.

"God, Peter, of course I'm alarmed, you're driving these women crazy," Kate joked. "Or are they jealous because you're sitting with me?"

Peter flashed a challenging grin. "Yeah? What do you think?"

She responded with a sunny smile. "I think it's nice being with an old pal, that's what I think. The ladies can wait."

He was looking very comfortable. "Luke did well last night," he said. "The polls look good. Up four points nationally. He's close to a three-point spread in California."

"Isn't it wonderful?" She sighed happily. "I know you can't say it is, because that would violate your journalistic objectivity, but if you'll raise your right eyebrow slightly, I'll know you agree."

Peter turned full toward her and slowly arched his left brow.

"An enigma," she breathed. "I'm sitting next to a journalistic enigma." They laughed together, then Peter switched the subject.

"I hear Marty wanted a stronger pro-choice statement," he said. "But Claire had other ideas."

"That's the way it looks," Kate said with a small smile.

"Tricky stuff. Those two are quite a pair, aren't they?"

"I don't much like either of them, you know that. We're off the record, aren't we?"

Peter glanced down at his notebook. "Of course," he said quietly. "You never have to ask that. If I want something on the record, I'll tell you."

"They're smart, and Luke likes them," Kate said. "I never feel particularly good around either of them."

"That's no surprise, my friend. They're as conniving as they come in this game. Nobody wants to mess with them, and I'm off the record, too."

"I promise never to tell."

"Cross your heart?"

"Cross my heart."

"I can't figure her out," Kate volunteered, yielding to temptation. "I've watched her through the primaries and she's scary, she's so smart. But she seems like a cold fish to me. Off the record."

"Her first husband was a withdrawn kind of guy. A lawyer," Peter said. "He killed himself. Did you know that?"

"No, I didn't." Kate was startled.

"They weren't together very much," Peter said. "She was in Connecticut when it happened, governor's race, I think, and back on the job the next day. Weird. No one saw her shed a tear."

"Why are the profiles on her always so gushy and praising?" Kate knew she was sounding petulant, even cranky. But Peter would understand. "Just curious, that's all."

He didn't laugh. He considered her question thoughtfully. "She's come a long way in a man's game, and she's never shown a shred of weakness," he said finally. "She's also beautiful. And, as clichéd as it sounds, there's something fascinating about the combination."

Kate's lip curled only slightly, but Peter threw up his hands in mock self-defense. "I only report," he said.

"Luke thinks she's fantastic," Kate said.

"I hear a sour note," Peter said.

Kate sighed. Of course Peter would sense her feelings. How could she expect anything different? And why would she want to? He was her friend, he had been with her through layers and layers of life experiences, and he knew her too well for subterfuge. I am comfortable with him, she thought with a flash of realization. I trust him; he cares about me, not just who I am or what I represent. If he weren't a reporter, she could turn to him now and talk this through. I could tell him about Abby, she thought. He would understand. He would understand the whole damn thing. He would know that I'm afraid, and he wouldn't think I'm weak or foolish or vain. Briefly she closed her eyes, then opened them again, thinking not about Peter, but about her own express-train life. Where was she going anyway?

"First Lady." Try the title on for size one more time. She waited

Patricia O'Brien

for the usual flush of excitement, but what came first was a small quiver of unease. How much did that delightful title really have to do with her most private sense of who she was and what she wanted to be? I've not thought this through, she told herself with some surprise. She found herself working to suppress an unfolding ribbon of un-bidden thought, but there it was anyway, tumbling free through her head. If Luke won and actually took on this incredible, enormous job, he would be living one life, and she and the children would be living another. She had always known it would be different from now, of course. But how would they live? Would Luke always be focused on an agenda larger than hers or the children's? I want to feel he'll still belong to me, she told herself. Whatever that means. Perhaps that's selfish. Lordy, did he belong to her now? She would have to adjust to new rhythms, to new concerns, and nothing in ordinary life would ever be able to compete for his attention with things like riots in Miami or plunging stock prices. That's the way it would have to be. And if I'm worried about that, I shouldn't be here, she told herself. Stop this, she ordered, but her mind raced on. What about the kids? Would the whole family ever watch old movies together anymore? What a silly thought. Still, for just an instant, it was there.

She risked a glance at Peter, forcing a smile. There was no point in thinking like this, for heaven's sake. There was no going back, and she wouldn't want to anyway. She just had too much on her mind right now.

An almost apologetic female voice suddenly boomed from the intercom. "Ladies and gentlemen, will you please sit down and fasten your seat belts? FAA regulations say you have to, remember? We're taking off."

Groans rose from the crowd, and many people, clearly reluctant to comply, took their seats.

"The FAA should keep a spy on board," muttered Peter. They leaned back as the plane rumbled down the runway, creaking and sighing. Both fell quiet as the engines began to pick up momentum. The concrete beneath them was spinning past faster and faster, and finally, the engines roaring with their usual confidence-breaking dry cackle, the old plane lifted from the ground and began its climb.

She turned to him again, still smiling. "Remember the day we met," she said, "when we were covering the first meeting of the new

Senate and waiting outside the Senate chamber, and they all came pouring out, and I didn't know who any of them were?"

"Oh, God, do I remember." Peter chuckled. "You were standing there with your notebook, scribbling down quotes and it was clear you didn't have a clue who was speaking."

"And you stood by my elbow, whispering name after name," Kate said, almost tenderly. "You saved my life."

Peter smiled. "You had real balls, Kate. Remember the time you got past the guard and nailed that Arizona senator for an interview just before he got censured? An exclusive, as I recall. The rest of us were running around shouting how unfair it was to keep the press out. I could have wrung your neck."

"I'm more of a risk taker than you are," she said.

Peter took a second to study her face. "That's for sure," he said.

"You're more the detached observer," she said. "Smart, fast, and safe behind his notebook."

"You're saying I'm stodgy?" Peter looked comically aggrieved.

"Well—" Kate drew the word out as long as possible. Then she twisted in her seat to face him directly. "Here's my challenge, if you choose to take it," she teased. "What's the most daring thing you ever did?"

The plane suddenly jerked, as if racked by an explosive cough. Kate looked out the window, registering every detail. She felt herself straining forward, urging the plane upward. But it wasn't climbing fast enough; it was trying too hard, laboring too much. She glanced at Peter and froze when she saw him gripping the armrests.

"We've got too goddamn many cameras on board," he said.

Get up, get up, Kate said fiercely under her breath, and then, before she could find her voice, she felt a jolt and a shuddering sigh from the aircraft. They were about one thousand feet in the air. Fearfully she glanced again out the window.

The outside right engine had disappeared in a violent spewing forth of bits of steel and a twenty-foot column of flame. Kate forced herself to absorb information as shouts of alarm arose around her, trying not to succumb to the temptation to scramble like a caged rat. Her eyes began to smart. Smoke was filling the plane.

"Here." Peter took a half-filled carton of milk and poured it over his handkerchief and handed it to Kate. His face was set and very white.

Patricia O'Brien

"I want to go up with Luke," Kate whispered. She tried to un-
buckle her belt, but her fingers wouldn't work properly. She saw a
Secret Service agent seated ahead lunge forward into the crash position, crouching, head between his legs. The camera crews in back
of her were grabbing their equipment and scrambling over to the
right side of the plane to film the fire, causing the plane to list
dangerously to the right.

"Get back, you're unbalancing the fucking plane!"

Who said that? Was it Peter yelling at the camera crews? Someone
else yelled that the flames were only a handful of inches from the fuel
lines. It was obvious from their strength that the automatic fire
extinguishers weren't working, and the plane was still sinking.

"Kate—" Peter was trying to say something.

And then Kate was sure they were going down.

Abby, she thought in anguish, Oh, baby, what will you do now?
And who will take care of Nat?

Peter reached for her hand and squeezed tightly. For a long moment, there was no other comfort possible. Kate simply closed her
eyes and waited.

"They got it!"

Cries of relief filled the cabin as the emergency fire extinguisher
finally activated and the flames sputtered out. The voice of the pilot
came over the intercom. "We've had an engine-casing blow, folks,"
he said. "The fire is out. Get back in your seats, that's important. I
repeat, get back in your seats and we'll stay stabilized. We're heading
back to the airport."

The thin veil of smoke was clearing, and the camera crews, suddenly realizing they were part of the problem, obeyed quickly, scrambling back with their equipment. The plane was wobbling slightly,
but the sound of the three remaining engines was strong and steady.
Slowly the plane banked and turned. The smoke in the cabin, sucked
in through the ventilating system, was almost gone now, and Kate
allowed herself to breathe again, but her heart was pounding un-
mercifully. She realized she was still tightly gripping Peter's hand. Or
was he gripping hers? He leaned toward her, reaching for her other
hand.

"We'll make it," he said quietly. "Has something happened to
Abby?"

100

Had she spoken Abby's name aloud? Kate looked at Peter and felt suddenly troubled. The words were from Peter, her friend, but she had the uneasy feeling the eyes belonged to Peter, the reporter.

"Nothing important," she whispered, pulling her hands away.

A sudden bustle of activity near the front of the plane drew the attention of both of them, and Kate looked up to see Luke striding down the aisle in her direction. His face was pale as he fired off instructions to a pair of aides directly in back of him, interrupting himself to answer the questions called out from nervous reporters as he passed.

"Andy, I want the contract with this company canceled immediately," he ordered. "They complain, they've got a lawsuit, got that?"

"Yes, Senator."

"Joe, line us up another plane as soon as we land and we're out of here."

"Senator!" It was the *Cleveland Plain Dealer* reporter. "Is this pilot gonna get us down okay?"

"The fire's out, we'll get down with no problem."

"You guarantee that?"

"I guarantee it." Luke grinned and winked.

Nervous laughter; a few notebooks appeared, but the reporters made no attempt to leave their seats and surround the candidate as was their wont.

"Give us a quote on safety, Senator," yelled a voice from the back of the plane.

Luke raised his chin; Kate felt proud of his steadiness. "I'm telling you all right now, this campaign will never fly a crate like this again," he answered in a voice that carried through the plane. "I'm making safety a number one priority, and you can count on it."

"Costs money, Senator."

"We'll spend whatever it takes. I'm not putting you guys in this kind of jeopardy again." He was now two seats away from Kate, and suddenly he was gazing directly at her with a look of such open tenderness, it took Kate's breath away. "Nor my wife," he added. He reached out his hand. "Come on, honey," he said gently. "I need you up front."

Kate rose from her seat, her legs still trembling, thinking of nothing but getting close to Luke. Together they made their way back up

101

the aisle, she smiling brightly, trying not to show how intently she was concentrating on the sound of the engines.

"It's okay," Luke said as they sat down together in the relative privacy of their seats in front of the press section. He leaned toward her; she felt the touch of his lips on the back of her neck. His arm encircled her shoulders, squeezing her tight.

One of the engines missed.

"Luke—" Kate felt an instant of terror.

"I'm here," he said. She felt his heart pounding with hers.

She glanced out the window. They were coming in low now, on a final approach to the airport. Everything felt steady. The cabin was very quiet.

"You went back there just to get me, didn't you?"

"Of course." His voice was calm. "You think I'm going through this landing without you beside me?"

"I love you."

"I love you too."

"Look." She pointed a shaky finger at another Secret Service agent across from them. He, too, was in a pre-crash crouch.

Luke tried a feeble joke. "A cautious guy," he said.

"Our wills, Luke," she said. "Are they up-to-date?"

"I'll check it out, I promise." He was being responsible, as always. "Just not right this minute."

She tried to laugh. Her nerves began to steady. Was it the comfort of knowing that at least if the plane went down she and Luke would die together? No, it was more than that. They weren't going to crash; she knew they weren't. This was not the end of their lives, something inside told her that, and she felt reassured. They were together, they loved each other, the world was opening up, not closing. It wasn't going to happen this way. Should she say a prayer anyway? It wouldn't hurt.

Outside, the tops of the trees were visible and the engines were roaring smoothly.

"We'll be all right," she said, lifting her face to her husband's and kissing him tenderly on his right cheek.

"You bet," he whispered. "Nothing's going to get us."

The wheels touched the runway. Kate saw for a brief second the waiting fire trucks and the white foam spread thinly across the tarmac. The plane bounced hard, once. Luke lifted her hand to his mouth and kissed it gently. His lips were trembling. Then they were on all wheels, rock-solid against the ground, brakes working, slowing steadily.

Like rolling thunder, a burst of happy applause exploded from the back of the plane.

5

"Abby?"

"Dad? You're all right! Nat! Mrs. Leonard! They're safe!" Abby's delighted screech prompted a grinning Luke to hold the phone receiver up so Kate too could hear their daughter's voice.

"Think they've been watching CNN?" he asked.

"Probably glued to it." Kate laughed. She pressed close next to Luke, the two of them holding the phone now, oblivious to the glances and smiles from campaign staffers and reporters clustered behind them in the Houston terminal waiting room.

"Dad? Mom?" It was Nat, his voice reverting to the higher octave of a year before. "You're okay? You're sure?"

"Yes, son," Luke said. "We're sure. And we're coming home."

"We'll have dinner, all of us, nobody else," Nat said excitedly. "Mrs. Leonard said she's getting champagne, is that okay? Can I have some?"

Laughing, Kate pulled the receiver closer. "Of course it's okay," she said. "And yes, you can. Tonight, we all will. It's perfect." The children asked rapid-fire questions and Luke and Kate, taking turns, answered, their voices filled with jokes and reassurance. I'm grateful we're alive, Kate thought. I'm grateful we have these kids and we're going home to them.

Finally Luke hung up the phone and turned to Kate with a quizzical look. "Mrs. Leonard," he said. "Does she know anything about champagne?"

Kate cocked her head and pretended to consider seriously the

104

question about their housekeeper. "Probably as much as she does about cooking a roast," she said.

Luke groaned. "That means she covers it with water and bakes it in a slow oven for four hours."

Three hours later the campaign was airborne again, with considerable nervous joking as the new aircraft took off. Kate, going to the front of the plane this time, sat next to Luke and held his hand tightly on takeoff. This was where she belonged, not chatting up reporters, even Peter. Luke gave her hand an understanding squeeze and turned to his briefing book, staying absorbed until the plane started its winding descent over the Potomac River to National Airport.

They were home. Hallelujah!

The blast of furnace-like air that greeted them on disembarking felt too much like Houston, but Kate was so glad to be back she seemed to bounce off the plane, impervious to the withering heat. Soon their car was gliding smoothly past the Fourteenth Street Bridge, along the George Washington Parkway, finally turning onto Memorial Bridge to cross the Potomac. Kate loved this view. Ahead was the Lincoln Memorial, its lines spare and white in the summer sun; to its right, rising clean and pure into the sky, the Washington Monument. There was so much history here. Even now, crossing the bridge with the river sparkling below them, she imagined hearing again the cadenced, somber sounds and seeing the caisson of the Kennedy funeral march. She would never forget the sight she saw on television as a child of the riderless horse on this bridge, boots turned backward in the stirrups, escorting the body of the young president to his grave in Arlington Cemetery. Kate shivered and reached again for Luke's hand.

Traffic was light after they wound their way through the crush of what Luke liked to call the Sunday Monument Crowd, and reached the comfortable winding streets of Cleveland Park sooner than they had expected. Only people who had lived in Washington a long time really understood what made Cleveland Park different. It was a neighborhood, a real neighborhood. Down the hill, on Connecticut Avenue, there was a shop where you could get a vacuum cleaner repaired. Next to it, an antique lamp shop. Across the street, a local Irish bar. And a movie theater. Thank heaven, houses were allowed to grow old in Cleveland Park, Kate thought. Peeling paint did not mean social failure. And if a child left a tricycle out and somebody tripped over it in the dark, it was somehow all right. In Georgetown, that kind of thing was frowned on. In Georgetown, tricycles did not fit either the lifestyle or the demands of the scenery. Picturesque cobblestones were tough on tricycles.

The car eased to the curb, and Kate gazed fondly at the weathered, slightly sagging porch that wrapped around the front of their house. It was such a solid, sturdy pile. It looked like a place where kids grew up and left for college and came back to visit after they married and where parents made love and paid their mortgage and grew old together. Luke liked to call her a hopeless romantic when it came to this house, and she couldn't argue that. She particularly liked to fantasize about the old-fashioned slatted porch swing, which Luke had wanted to junk last year. Kate had stayed firm. No way. Maybe the swing didn't say anything crucial about the Goodspeed family, but it said things about fantasies and illusions, about history and personal heritage, about youth and growing old. She could see a child playing on that swing, and that same child later, much later, a frail old woman in a shawl, rocking and knitting on a summer day. Had she seen that one on an AT&T commercial? Probably. But still she could see the old woman; maybe it was herself, that was an interesting thought, and maybe the toddler she could see coming out the door was her first grandchild. It could happen that way. It really could. She thought of Abby and her spirits spiraled downward. She looked closely at the swing as she stepped onto the curb. I'm going to get it repainted, she decided. I want the rust off those hinges.

It was Luke who spotted the cluster of reporters on the sidewalk first.

"What's going on?" he said as one of Marty's aides rushed forward and leaned his head in through the car window.

"This is a perfect at-home session, Senator," the aide said, speaking fast. "Marty says we need it; it's a natural, we've got the nets and the *Times* and the *Post* here, they really want shots of you and your family celebrating your safe return, it's perfect, and they promise to stay in the background."

Luke stared at the aide in disbelief. Kate held her breath.

"No," he said.

"Just until you start eating? Or maybe you could sit there and pretend to eat?"

"No. Tell Marty he picked the wrong night; this dinner's private."

"But—"

Luke was no longer paying attention. He glanced at his watch as he unfolded his legs and bounded out of the car, instantly wired for movement. His energy as he headed up the path was impressive, and Kate found herself hurrying to keep up. The screen door exploded outward, and Nat and Abby were on the steps, exuberantly reaching for both of them.

"Daddy—" Abby threw her arms around her father, her voice catching. "You're home, you're really home."

Luke gathered her close, but not before Kate saw all the lines of his face ease at the sight of his eldest child. "We're fine," he said, stroking her hair, studying her face. "You look so pretty, honey," he said with startled awareness. "There's a bloom to you—"

"Mom's new face cream," Abby said, quickly wiggling away.

"I wish I had been with you," Nat said in a thin voice, stepping close to his father.

"Hey," Luke said, playfully punching his son's shoulder. "I'm glad you weren't."

Kate was shaken anew with a sense of relief and gratitude, but suddenly she was acutely aware of the faint clicking of cameras behind them.

"Let's get inside," she said, hustling her family toward the door. She didn't want to wait long enough for the kids to sense they were, once again, the subject of a media opportunity. She didn't want to stay the extra fraction of a second where she might find herself wondering if Abby's kiss or Nat's hug or Luke's laughter was slightly overexuberant. And she didn't want to find herself turning finally to offer a perfunctory wave in the direction of the cameras. No, not now. Not today.

Waiting inside, with a joyous look on her ruddy, polished face, was the comfortable figure of Mrs. Leonard, the stout, efficient woman who had been coping with the lives of the Goodspeeds for fifteen years. Kate sniffed the air. Mrs. Leonard had been cooking again. She smiled, trying not to catch Luke's eye. Perhaps it was the apple pie that tasted like seasoned wet cardboard. Or the scones that, if dropped, could dent the kitchen floor. Anything, as long as it wasn't the pumpkin bread—she couldn't take that thick, pasty concoction today. Somewhere, back fourteen or so years ago, the decision had been made not to hurt Mrs. Leonard's feelings by telling her the truth about her cooking. I wish, Kate thought ruefully, I could get another crack at that decision.

"You're in for a real treat," murmured a voice.

Kate blinked. Joan was standing, arms crossed, in the gathering shadows in the front hall. Kate's hands went instantly clammy. The question in her eyes as she looked at her sister could not be hidden.

"Everything's taken care of," Joan said in quiet response. "It's going to be fine." She touched her sister's shoulder in a glancing caress. "I can't stand all this happy togetherness," she said with a grin. "You guys can play Ozzie and Harriet; I'm heading home now, see you tomorrow."

"Thank you," Kate said, out of earshot of the others. Impulsively, she grabbed Joan and gave her a fervent hug. "Whether you like it or not," she said. "You're lucky I don't get old Sammy here to give you a big wet kiss." She nodded at the old family labrador leaning against her legs, his sightless eyes trying to figure out what was causing all the excitement.

Joan made an elaborate face, but she didn't pull away. "My God, you've gone insane," she said. "I'm getting out of here."

Kate laughed and waved goodbye, but for the second time today, she had trouble controlling a wobbling in her knees.

Luke was sniffing the air, too. He turned to Mrs. Leonard, fully energized. "Mrs. Leonard, I can smell that pumpkin bread of yours, is it out of the oven yet?" He glanced at Kate, risking a quick, sly wink.

But Mrs. Leonard was not ready for compliments, she was still counting heads for dinner. "Where's Nat?" she said. Her question instantly sent Kate back to the front door looking for her son; this was no time for a press ambush. She needn't have worried. He was on the porch, looking oddly forlorn, talking with a Secret Service agent standing below him on the lawn. Squinting, Kate saw it was Harry Hillman. The man and the boy were together a lot now, and Kate liked the care she sensed Harry felt for Nat. But why was Nat looking so upset? She moved closer to the open screen door to hear them better.

"It's not fair," Nat said truculently.

Kate only then realized Harry was holding Nat's Christmas present from last year—a ten-speed bike. She sighed. Were they going to have to go through this again? Why was Nat so stubborn? Why

108

couldn't he understand he couldn't ride that bike now, and why wouldn't he stop trying to sneak away from the agents assigned to watch him?

"I know it isn't," Harry was saying quietly. "But I can't help it, if you ride, we have to. And that's not the way we can best do our jobs."

"But I've always ridden my bike to school! What's so different now?"

"Come on, Nat," Harry said. "You know what's different."

Kate stood there unseen, wondering if she should say anything. The Secret Service detail guarding the family had told her Nat would probably not be able to ride his bike to school anymore because it was too difficult to keep track of him—like any eleven-year-old, he loved to dart across streets, tear down hills—but getting him to face the necessary constraints was tough.

Nat's jaw was trembling as he gazed defiantly at Harry. "You're a bully," he said. "You're treating me like a baby, and it's dumb."

"No, son," Harry replied heavily. "I'm just a farm boy doing my job. I've told you about the farm."

"Milking dumb cows," Nat sniffed.

"Yeah, and driving tractors. Say—" Harry looked as if he had just had a sudden idea— "when all this is over, want to try driving a tractor?"

Nat, who had scrambled down the steps and was now holding fast to the handlebars of his bike, tugging it away, stopped and looked at Harry. "You mean ride on one?" he said suspiciously.

"No," Harry replied, stepping back from the bike, shoving his hands into his pockets. "I mean drive it."

"I'm not old enough to drive."

"You work on a farm, you learn to drive a tractor. You don't take it out on the highway, you know."

Nat thought about it. "You're bribing me," he said.

"You got it."

Reluctantly Nat grinned.

Harry grinned back, then nodded toward the bike. "Now can I trust you to stash that in the garage for the duration?" he asked.

Nat's face was turned away from Kate now, but she saw him nod, and she saw the look of quiet satisfaction on Harry's face. She wondered if he had kids of his own. All she knew, really, was this tough, highly trained agent whose life was consumed by the discipline of the Service was the man whose job it was to take a bullet for this boy or her or Luke.

"Harry?" Nat was wheeling the bike away when he stopped and turned.

"Yeah, kid?"

"You ever learn to ride a bike on that farm?"

"Nope."

Nat looked triumphant. "I thought so," he said.

Kate smiled, and moved away from the door.

Dinner took place in the dining room on a table set, at Mrs. Leonard's insistence, with Kate's best china and her wedding crystal.

"This is a celebration, Mrs. Goodspeed," she declared. "The best one. Better than the one coming in November."

Looking around at her family gathered at the table, Kate could not deny that. In fact, there was something almost giddy about the evening, something loose and wonderful. By dessert, the four of them were laughing, swapping stories, interrupting each other.

"Dad, remember the time we were playing hide-and-seek and I was hiding from you in the basement and you stood at the top of the stairs and said the game was over, and if I didn't come up immediately, you weren't going to send me to college?" Nat demanded excitedly.

Luke roared. "Do I remember?" he said. "I sure do, and I remember you yelled back up that you didn't care, you wanted to play baseball anyhow."

"Yeah," Nat said in delight. "Maybe I still will."

"Okay, when you're in the World Series, I'll throw out the first ball."

"What about me?" demanded Kate. "Why does the president always get to do it?"

"Because girls can't throw," Nat said.

Abby giggled. "Don't say that to Mom," she said. "You know what she'll do. She'll start practicing in the backyard so she can show Daddy up."

"Watch this pitching arm, kids." Luke grabbed one of Mrs. Leonard's dinner rolls in his right hand and leaned back, winding up for an elaborate pitch.

"Luke—" Kate started to protest.

Luke let go with the roll. It shot in a straight line across the room, hitting the kitchen door with a sharp clunk and dropping to the floor. Instantly the door flew open.

"What all are you doing in here?" asked an astonished Mrs. Leonard.

"Nothing," Kate said hastily. "Really, it's nothing, Luke's just practicing for the World Series, that's all."

Gingerly, Mrs. Leonard fingered the spot where the roll had hit the door. "Whatever you threw, it was heavy enough to chip the paint," she announced.

This was enough to send both Nat and Luke, choking with laughter, almost under the table. Mrs. Leonard shook her head, perplexed, and withdrew. But she was back a moment later, triumphantly holding up a bottle of champagne.

"Hey," Luke said, impressed. "That's *good* stuff."

"Well, of course, Senator," she said with a touch of indignation. "I told them I wanted only the best."

Carefully she withdrew the cork, lined up four crystal goblets, and handed the bottle to Luke.

"Won't you have some with us?" he asked.

"No, sir, thank you. I hate the stuff."

Luke poured a small amount of the golden bubbly liquid into each glass and passed them around the table. He lifted his glass.

"To us," he said.

"To us," Kate breathed.

"To us," Abby and Nat echoed.

It was a moment Kate wanted to box and put away. She felt enveloped in the kind of sanity and warmth only Luke and the kids could provide.

"We live with this campaign every minute of the day," Luke said in sudden rumination as he looked around the table. "We never get away from it." He took a sip of wine. "But we have tonight," he said quietly. "Tonight is ours."

Abby lifted her glass, her hand trembling slightly. "I wish tonight could last forever," she said.

111

"Senator—" The door swung open, and Mrs. Leonard's head appeared. "I hate to bother you, but you've got a phone call."

Impatiently Luke shook his head. "Tell whoever it is to call tomorrow," he said.

"It's Miss Lorenzo, Senator. She said it was important. Something about a schedule change."

Luke hesitated. Kate felt Abby's eyes on her, watching. I'm not going to make any fuss, she told herself, that's silly.

"Go ahead, honey," she said. "We'll wait."

"Yeah, you never know." With a squeeze of Kate's hand, Luke got up and left the room.

Kate tried to keep the glow on the moment, but Luke's absence left a slight pall. "What do you think of your first champagne?" she asked her son.

"You really want to know?" Nat said earnestly.

She smiled. "Sure I do."

Nat made a face and stared at his glass with puzzled disappointment. "It's really awful."

Kate laughed. "Don't feel bad," she said. "I don't like the stuff much myself."

Normality was so fleeting.

The next night, a few hours after Luke left for a speech in New York, Kate and Abby slipped into the backseat of a nondescript rented Chevrolet and, with Joan at the wheel, eased off into the darkness.

There was no sound in the car, just a permeating bone-cold tension. Abby sat curled into a small ball in the backseat, her face pressed against the window, as Joan pulled into an empty parking lot and flicked off the ignition. Joan pulled out a half-empty package of Oreo cookies and offered one to Abby, who shook her head negatively.

"How can you *eat*?" she said.

Joan bit into a cookie, ignoring her niece, eying the night-shrouded medical building in front of them. It was totally dark. "We wait for the doctor to turn on the light," she said. "Then we go."

Five minutes passed. Then ten. Kate felt she was back on yesterday's plane, struggling again with the fear of impending disaster. But this time she must succeed in pretending to be calm. For Abby's sake.

Kate tried to put an arm around her daughter, but Abby seemed to be somewhere else and gently pulled away. "I'm all right, Mother," she said by way of explanation. "I just don't want to be touched right now."

Kate turned to the window again, straining to see something that would signal what they were to do next.

"I'm surprised at how easily we got past the border patrol," Joan said as she absently tapped the steering wheel with a broken fingernail painted cherry red. "I thought those Secret Service guys ruled your lives. Do you get to go to the bathroom alone?" Incessantly her finger tapped.

Abby giggled, a high-pitched sound laced with tension. "They're more embarrassed than we are," she said.

"I told them we wanted private time," Kate said. "The night crew is young; they try to please. Stop making that noise, Joan. I can't stand it. When are they going to turn on that light?"

"Any minute," Joan said. She glanced back at Abby. "Keep that scarf tied on tight," she warned. She looked with a touch of amusement at Kate. "You don't shine in a babushka, dearie," she said.

Kate smiled slightly, fingering the edges of the ridiculous fringed cotton scarf tied beneath her chin. Shining was the last thing on her mind. Her heart was thumping too fast. She tried her old game of I'm-not-here, the one she used when she was eleven years old and getting her teeth filled at the dentist's. I'm not *really* here, she thought, I'm sitting somewhere else, somewhere safe, watching this on television and Abby's with me and we're laughing about how dumb that woman who looks like me looks in a babushka. . . . She sighed. It wasn't working. She, Kate, *was* here, in an empty Bethesda medical center parking lot, and, yes, it was the middle of the night. She shivered involuntarily.

Could they pull this off?

"Finally." Joan's whisper was relieved, but also triumphant.

Yes. Finally. The light was on.

Blazing. Too obvious. Good, someone was pulling down the shade, muting the effect, making it less of a beacon.

"Let's go," Joan said.

Abby began to whimper. A disturbing sound. A child's sound.

"Don't," whispered Kate. "We have to be quiet."

"I can't believe I'm in this spot," Abby sobbed.

"Sweetie—"

Abby was sobbing louder. The sound was carrying, cutting through the still night air of the empty parking lot.

"Hey, no problem," Joan said calmly. "You don't have to go through with it." She stretched as far as she could in the front seat, cradling her head in her hands, the light from the medical office window sparking off a ring of dull, twisted gold on one of her long fingers. "Go ahead, have the baby," she continued. "So what if we'll be reading about Luke Goodspeed's bastard grandchild in Ernie Stark's column? Who wanted the White House, anyway?"

"Joan!" Kate protested.

"Make up your mind," Joan said, this time with absolute, deadly calm.

Kate couldn't stand it; she touched Abby's face. "Honey, you do not have to go through with this if you don't want to," she said, just as calmly as her sister. "You say the word, and we are out of here. There are other solutions, I mean it." Joan was not going to get away with her bullying.

Abby paused, then put her hand on the door handle and pushed hard. "I'm okay now," she said, her voice shaky. "I want it, Mother. You're tough, Aunt Joan."

"I do what I have to do," Joan said cheerfully before slipping out of the driver's seat. "Now stick close to me and say absolutely nothing until we're inside that building. Do you hear me? Absolutely nothing."

The trio moved quickly across the parking lot toward a side entrance, the sound from their low-heeled shoes muffled on the pavement. Joan pulled out a key to insert in the door.

Kate heard a slight rustling behind them.

"Hurry," she said, her eyes darting back and forth from the door to the bushes. What was she hearing? A bird; maybe a dog. That was it, a stray dog roaming, trampling the leaves underfoot, pushing forward. . . .

Then, unbelieving, she saw the shape of a slender woman with pale skin in a white dress emerge from the shadows. Her dress was gauzy, floating around slender legs, and she moved toward them

114

with a bouncy step. She had the determined, perky smile of—of what? Of a high school cheerleader.

"I know why you're here," she said in a strong, confiding voice, looking straight at Abby. "And I'll bet this isn't what you want to do."

Kate stared in momentary confusion. The woman was young, maybe early twenties, very pretty, almost vulnerable-looking, with eyes big and bright under heavily penciled, impossibly arched eyebrows. Who was she?

"Get out of the way," Joan suddenly yelled. "Don't you come near us."

The woman ignored her. Her tone changed, taking on an urgent, coaxing note as she took another step closer to Abby. "You're so young," she said softly. "You know what they do, how they try to shame you? They bring out big boxes in the daytime and wrap them around girls like you to hide you as they bring you in, to hide your shame, hide your fear—"

Abby stood frozen in place. The woman moved closer, edging between them and the door. "Don't let them do this to you," she implored, never taking her gaze off Abby. Her eyes, almost imperceptibly, were changing. They were becoming even brighter, like candles in flame. "What's your name?" she said. "I know what you're going through, don't let them hurt your baby, I can tell you're scared, listen to me—"

Joan shoved her, trying to clear a path, but the woman was reaching for Abby's hand. "You know what it is, I know you do, it's murder, that's what it is," she said, her voice taking on the crooning cadence of a prayer. "Murder, murder, think about it, for the love of God, you're murdering your baby."

"Oh, God," moaned Abby.

Joan shoved at the woman, forcing her back a step, and wrested the clinic door open. She pushed Abby and Kate through, then followed, pulling the door shut as the woman lunged forward, thrusting her long, slender hands almost into their faces, screaming.

"No, no!" she cried. "Murderers!"

"Get in the elevator," Joan said, holding the door against the sound of fists hammering outside.

Abby began fluttering like a wounded sparrow.

"Go *on*," Joan yelled. "I'll get us out of here. I promise. Now, *go*."

115

Patricia O'Brien

Kate put an arm around Abby and stumbled with her into the elevator, glancing back at her sister. What she saw made her heart hammer ever harder and more painfully against her ribs. Joan's face was contorted, twisted into an expression Kate had never seen before. Maybe it was the light, or the strain, but her face seemed suddenly unnaturally dark, and as the elevator doors closed, Kate realized for the first time what it meant to see a face literally black with rage.

It was over; Kate could barely believe it.

A pale shaft of weak moonlight crept across the Goodspeed kitchen, illuminating the shapes of the two sisters as, hours later, they sat down to share a quiet cup of coffee. It was three in the morning. Upstairs, filled with Valium, her ordeal over, Abby was drifting into sleep.

"How is she?" Joan asked as Kate tiptoed to her chair after a check on her daughter.

"Worn out," Kate said wearily. "Resigned, relieved." She shook her head. "She doesn't want to talk about it. All she said just now is she's glad she did it, that I shouldn't worry. Joan, she's trying to comfort *me*."

"She's a good kid."

"I could hear what was going on." Kate squeezed her eyes shut, holding back stinging tears. "I could hear her, in the examining room, crying."

"It happens," Joan said. Kate heard the exhaustion in her sister's voice, but she couldn't let the memory go. Not yet.

"I felt totally helpless, Joan. I couldn't do anything for her."

Joan reached over and squeezed her hand. "You already had," she said. "And you were there with her, she didn't have to go through it alone. You were right about that."

"It wouldn't have worked without you," Kate said quietly, and was rewarded with a thin smile. It was true—she could never have handled this without Joan's help. She shivered at the memory of how close they had been to detection. "How did you know that woman would be gone when we came out?" she asked.

"I didn't," Joan said. "But I would have torn her hair out if she had

116

stuck around, I guarantee you. I walked out there just before you came down, and she was gone." She gave a short laugh. "Those people don't give a damn about anything except their own fanaticism."

"She seemed so young. Almost frail."

"Don't be fooled, Kate."

"You hate her type, don't you?"

"I don't like anyone telling me what I can and can't do." Joan offered no further explanation. Instead, she looked at her sister with an almost meek expression. "I know I've quit, a thousand times, probably," she said. "But I really need a cigarette. Got one?"

"No," Kate said. "But I've got three ashtrays in the apartment in Chicago. Next time we're there, feel free."

"Good try, dearie." They smiled wanly at each other across the table.

"How do you know she didn't see our faces?"

"It was too dark."

"You can't be sure of that."

"I can't be sure of anything, but I'm positive she didn't get a clear view of our faces. We saw her better than she saw us, because of that white dress. Don't get too spooked, okay? She was just a Right-to-Lifer on a routine patrol of the clinic. They don't usually hang around that late."

"Our luck."

Joan made a quick, clucking semimaternal noise. "The problem's taken care of, and Abby is all right," she said. "I'd say 'our luck' is pretty good, considering."

"I know," Kate said in a low voice. "I hope she's going to stay all right."

"She'll put it behind her very fast," Joan said. "She's young, but she's tough. Where's the sugar?"

"On the shelf above the microwave. Is she?"

"You better believe it," Joan replied, standing to search for the little blue-and-white sugar bowl Kate had brought home last year from Portugal. "We had a few heart-to-heart talks this week." She gave a short, wry laugh. "I must say, it's a new experience to be chief confidante to a kid." She pulled the bowl down, took the lid off, and made a face. "Lumpy," she said.

117

Patricia O'Brien

Kate felt suddenly jealous of the time missed with her daughter. It was not a new feeling, and it didn't help to tell herself she should by now be used to periodic stabs of this sense of loss.

"She thinks you've been terrific," Joan said gently, as if reading her sister's mind. "Mother of the Year. Honestly."

Kate's lips trembled. "She sold more cookies for the Girl Scouts than anyone in the neighborhood," she said. "How did she change so fast?"

"Hey, I don't have to buy them all from her every year anymore. It wasn't too fast for *me!*"

Kate smiled. Joan would not allow her to get maudlin.

"You're still fighting this abortion, I think," Joan said, watching her sister closely.

Kate opened her mouth to protest, then reconsidered. "Maybe I am," she replied. "I don't know why."

"Don't you? I think it's pretty easy to figure out. You're still carrying around a few tons of Catholic guilt."

"I don't think it ever goes away," Kate said.

Joan took a deep breath, but this time her voice didn't come across as tough as she apparently intended. "Well, take my advice and shake it, or it drives you crazy," she said.

Kate looked with interest at her sister's face through the gloom. Had Joan's break with the Church been painful? She didn't know. It was strange, actually. They looked alike, laughed alike, walked with the same quick stride, and wore the same shade of lipstick, but they hadn't shared much in common for years. I've never asked her if she regrets not having children, Kate thought with a touch of surprise. I guess I just assumed she was more interested in traveling the world and meeting interesting people, but there's a lot I should know, and I don't. Maybe I've been slotting her too easily; taking her for granted. But even as she thought these things, she knew why she knew so little. Joan, she reminded herself, was not easy to reach in the best of times.

"It's the campaign, not the Church that I'm worried about," Kate said.

"That's not your focus, Kate. I know it isn't."

"You don't understand," Kate said. "I have to think about the campaign, don't you see? Keeping this from Luke means he could end up looking like a hypocrite."

118

"I know you won't like this, but I think sometimes he does anyway," Joan said. "He wants everything both ways."

Kate spread her arms, palms up. "Don't we all?" she said.

"Sure," Joan replied. She looked at her sister with such comical satisfaction that they both laughed. "What I mean is, Luke has choices," Joan said, turning serious. "On this, you didn't."

Kate shrugged. "I'm not second-guessing myself," she said. "But the fact remains, Luke is more vulnerable now than he was before—and he doesn't know it."

"It can't be helped. Right?"

Kate was silent for a moment. "This was a gut decision," she said. "I'm used to taking time, thinking out all the implications."

"Well—" Joan stretched her legs out under the table and yawned mightily. "When your kid's pregnant, you don't have the luxury. This is the way it should be, and I say you've done it right, but then, I'm the flaky sister nobody totally trusts." She dropped the self-mocking tone. "I know you're worried about what this could do to Luke's campaign," she said, "but I also think you're trying to please Mother, if you don't mind a little half-baked psychoanalysis."

Kate abruptly laughed. "If you only knew how funny that is," she said.

"Try me."

Kate shook her head. "Look," she said, "I gave up trying to please Mother long before she died."

"No, you didn't." Joan pursed her lips and looked down her nose, instantly adopting the lofty vantage point of the therapist. "You just *think* you did," she said. "You thought you were some kind of renegade, skipping Mass and running around being a reporter in Washington, but you were the good one. I know it's a terrible burden to bear, but that's the way it was, my dear. I was the one Mother despaired of. Not to speak of how our pious, dear departed father felt."

A vivid memory rose in Kate's brain of the somber, detached man who had spoken so little and died in his sleep of heart failure at the age of forty-five. A man she and Joan never really knew; something to regret, and maybe, someday, to talk about. But he was not the parent she was wrestling with right now. "You're wrong," she said. "She wanted you. She didn't want to have me."

"Where did you get that idea?"

119

"Oh, come on, Joan." Kate was feeling a touch of impatience. "I was the baby who came a little early, remember? The eight-pounder who debuted at seven and a half months?"

Joan smiled. "Oh, that," she said.

"Yes, that."

The two women sat in silence.

"You know what you need?" Joan suddenly said.

"What?"

"A sugar bowl with a better lid, and a sense of what the hell."

Kate smiled. She felt touched by Joan's bravado. "Okay," she said. "What the hell."

Joan didn't answer right away. She picked up her coffee and stared into the night gloom that filled the corners of the room.

"I think you're very conscientious, a good candidate's wife," she said slowly. "You do the kind of dutiful things you're supposed to do, I guess, like sending out those family Christmas cards every year." Her voice turned lightly teasing. "But has anyone ever told you Nat always looks like his shirt collar is a size too big?"

Kate smiled again. "He hates being short," she said. "I keep telling him he's going to shoot up all at once and be as tall as his father any day now."

"Then again, maybe he won't," Joan said.

Kate sighed. "I'll deal with that if it happens."

"Lordy, to think of what I've been spared."

Kate speculated briefly on whether the joke was over; you never could tell with Joan, who tended to be serious when she was joking, and joking when she was serious. But tonight Kate did not feel quite the same propensity to follow the dips and curves of her sister's moods. Somehow, in the half-lit kitchen, with the children sleeping and the house quiet, she found there were some things she wanted to say.

"I've been fed up at times," she said, half timidly. "Which you probably think is ridiculous."

"Ridiculous?" Joan said, a little startled. "I think it's normal."

This probably wasn't a good idea. Kate had rigid rules about sharing too much of her private life; maybe, she thought suddenly, I'm not too forthcoming, either. "Remember when Luke decided to run for the Senate?" she said cautiously. "That crazy time?"

"Sure."

"That was the toughest," she said. "He was running everywhere constantly. I had a refrigerator full of Lean Cuisines for the kids and me, because we hardly saw him."

"Didn't that hurt Mrs. Leonard's feelings?"

Kate made a face. "We overdosed on her cookies, and she felt better."

"I still think you were born for this life."

Kate smiled, got up, pulled a package of breakfast rolls out of the pantry, and put two into the toaster oven. "Was I?"

"No question about it," Joan replied without hesitation. "You are perfect in the role. If they gave Academy Awards—"

"Enough," Kate said. "This isn't acting, it's politicking."

"Do you ever get lonely?" Joan was suddenly dead serious, and Kate had to take a second or two to adjust.

"Sometimes," she said.

"When?"

Kate wished she had remembered to ask Mrs. Leonard to buy more milk. There wasn't going to be enough for cereal, and she was dying for some, with a banana. Any bananas? Her eyes scanned the top of the refrigerator. No bananas. Her husband was running for president of the most influential, powerful country in the world, and she had no bananas.

"On the road," she said. "In crowds, when I have to shake more than a couple of hundred hands at a time."

"Adulation is tough, but that's not exactly what I meant."

"Okay," Kate said with a stiff smile. "It's been a perfect life."

Joan dipped her head in graceful apology. "Sorry," she said. "I'm not trying to pry."

"Well, I'll tell you," Kate said. This was her sister, and she suddenly wanted no more of their usual prickly sparring. "At one point, I was hoping Luke would quit Congress and join a Chicago law firm. He had two good offers, and we wouldn't have had a financial worry in the world." She sat still for a moment, remembering. "My friends from school had freer lives than mine," she said. "Not as interesting, probably, but freer. I found myself envying them once in a while."

"Funny, I never think of you envying anyone."

"How strange that sounds," Kate said slowly. "You know why? Because I've been jealous of you."

"Why?"

121

"Same thing—your freedom."

"If you only knew," Joan said, an oddly wry note creeping into her voice. "It gets just as lonely when you try to live too many lives at one time." She sipped halfheartedly at her fourth cup of coffee.

"Luke knew I felt shut out and alone a lot," Kate continued. "But he had to do what he needed to do." She hesitated. "I knew he would be a good senator. And I knew we would get back on track as partners."

"Did you tell him you were thinking about a divorce?"

Kate's eyes flew wide open. "I was?" she asked.

"Of course," Joan said airily. "Doesn't everybody?"

"I doubt it," Kate said. "I think you should cut your rates, Doctor Freud. Grade C analysis, I'm afraid."

The two sisters smiled at each other.

"Okay, what about the good things?" Joan said after a pause.

Kate leaned back, enjoying now the chance to ruminate out loud. It was a luxury, one in which she couldn't often indulge. "Remember when Luke and I dated that first summer in South Bend?"

"I sure do. You used to take the telephone into the bathroom and turn on the shower so no one could hear you talking. And I was stuck in the hall, dancing up and down, waiting to get in."

"And then he left for Harvard, and I never heard from him again."

"Until, miracles of miracles, the handsome young congressman spied the beautiful young reporter in the halls of Congress—"

"Right." Kate giggled. "The rest is history."

"Or another Style Section piece."

"I think it was Luke's leaving that convinced me I was going to do something different with my life."

"You certainly got interested fast in government and politics. God, Mother hated it when you brought home *The New York Times*." Joan grinned at the memory. "She said it was the messiest paper she had ever seen."

Kate chuckled. "I was reading everything I could and leaving fingerprints on the walls."

"I thought you'd be the one running for Congress someday," Joan said.

Kate was silent for a moment, thinking. "When Luke and I met that second time," she finally said, "we shared a lot of ideas about what we wanted to do with our lives and how we wanted to change

122

things. How we could do things *our* way. That's part of what our marriage is about." She paused briefly. "Everything about life tastes better; I guess it's like seasoned food. When we go to a hospital or a union hall and I see people watching and listening to him, it's a thrill."

"His speech, your thrill?"

"Don't you see? I'm part of it. When I hear the applause after he talks, and I know we built the ideas together, I feel the applause is for me, too. When we're sitting at breakfast and I read about kids shooting each other every night in Detroit and Chicago and Washington, I can look across the table and say to the man sitting there, 'Let's do something.' A bill. A speech. A plan." She spread her arms wide. "I'm married to a guy I admire and love. On top of that, I feel important and worthwhile. Who could ask for more?"

"How about now? This campaign?"

Kate shrugged. "This one's tougher."

Joan thought about that for a moment, then shook her head. "I can't imagine staying focused on one man for very long under any circumstances," she said with a barely audible sigh. "Lord knows, I've tried."

She was still fingering her coffee cup, but there was a hint of something in her voice that stirred a protective impulse in Kate. She studied her sister. Joan had dressed with her usual casual elegance for the middle-of-the-night trip to the abortion clinic. Unlike Kate, who, chilled, still sat wrapped in an old raincoat with her hair askew, Joan was in full makeup with her hair looking freshly blow-dried and wearing a spotless soft green wool skirt. Intimidatingly perfect. But for one of those rare instants in their lives, Kate thought she saw past the easy perfection. Joan isn't vain, she realized suddenly. She's determined to create an illusion which she totally controls. Kate felt she had been allowed a peek beyond the illusion, but she knew that with one blink, with one wrong word, the moment would be gone.

"Maybe you just got mixed up with the wrong guys," she said.

Joan put down her cup and laughed lightly. "Oh, hell, I had fun," she said. The moment was indeed gone, but Kate wanted to offer something back.

"I know I have to relax a little," she said, "but Luke and I have a lot at stake, and I'm not quite sure how to do it."

Joan gave her sister an amused, openly fond glance. "You'll make

123

◆◆

a great First Lady," she said. "But you've got to promise me something."

"What?"

Outside the sky was fading from black to a gray-blue, and the moon hung low on the horizon. Dawn was approaching, and all the strain and tension of this bizarre night was in Joan's response.

"Just don't start feeling sorry for yourself," she said, "when you get what you want."

6

In New York, an hour later, the same gray-blue sky began turning gold with the first touch of the morning sun. Luke, alone in his hotel room, hastily swallowed a cup of warm coffee delivered moments before by a sleepy-looking waiter. The phone rang.

"Big day today?" said Claire.

Luke looked longingly at the empty coffee cup. "Yeah," he said. "Atlanta, Miami, overnight in Walla Walla, Washington—the damn schedule zigzags like the medical chart of some guy in cardiac arrest, but then, it always does."

Claire laughed appreciatively. "Well, take a look at *The Times*; it'll make you feel better."

Luke stretched to retrieve his copy of *The New York Times*, which rested under the food tray. He glanced at it quickly. There he was, on page one.

"Looks good," he said with a yawn. "Hey, they played Enright below the fold. Lucky me."

"Nothing more than you deserve. Take a look at the editorial page."

Luke flipped to *The Times*'s lead editorial, a horse-race piece examining the first days of the general campaign. Enright was still looking like a captive of the Right, *The Times* declared, and hadn't yet escaped Gilmartin's imposing shadow. Luke Goodspeed, on the other hand, *The Times* went on, was out of the gate and running well.

"Not bad," Luke said, pleased.

"Not bad?" Claire said with a laugh. "It's great! I think this 'champion of tough caring' slogan is catching on."

"Hey, your idea," Luke said warmly.

"It wouldn't work if it wasn't true," Claire said.

"Thanks," Luke said. He glanced at his watch. "Anything I need to know?"

"You're up-to-date on the California water fight?"

"I've got the stuff you faxed yesterday," Luke said.

"Good." Claire's voice was crisply professional. "It's very touchy. Don't let anybody pose you by a Hollywood pool, or they'll be screaming in Berkeley. Oh, by the way—" she allowed herself an almost girlish giggle—"did you see the Doonesbury strips on Enright?"

"Claire," Luke said in mock exasperation, "when do I get time to look at the comics?"

"You don't get any fun," she protested.

"I could use a laugh once in a while," he said. He glanced again at his watch. "Damn, I've gotta move."

"See you soon."

Luke hung up the phone, stretched, tucked the newspaper into his briefcase, and snapped it shut. He decided not to wait for the aides due to meet him in the room in ten minutes. He was early; the hotel was quiet. He would go downstairs and see if he could get a hot cup of coffee.

He walked into the hall, absently pulling the door shut behind him before checking to see if the hallway was empty. The Secret Service agent waiting outside jumped instantly across the narrow corridor to summon an elevator. Luke heard the lock click at the same second he saw a man dart from the shadows toward him. He stiffened, registering impressions fast. The man was about sixty years old, black, with powerful, gnarled hands and hair the color of polished pewter. Not carrying a weapon.

The agent whirled.

"Senator Goodspeed, I must talk to you," the man whispered, calmly enough.

Luke, watching the man's face, held up a restraining hand.

"Check with my press secretary," he said amiably. "He'll be downstairs in a few minutes."

126

"No!" The man's hands were trembling. "It must be you, and it must be now. It's about David Palmer. Please listen."

This was no ordinary supplicant, the voice was too firm. But it was the desperate expression in his clearly intelligent eyes that gave Luke pause. "Okay, I can give you a second," he said. He moved toward the elevator as he spoke, eying the opening door. He put one foot inside.

The man made a sharp, bleating noise and moved quickly to hold the door open with his shoulder even as the agent, hand on his holster now, lunged forward to put himself between the stranger and Luke.

"I mean no harm," the man said hastily in liquid, cadenced English. "My name is Edward Young, and I need to give you information about Palmer, information you must have."

"Move away!" ordered the agent.

"Palmer," Young said, his voice louder. "You know who I mean! Palmer is an evil man, he cannot be allowed to come into this country. Please, you are a man with courage. Please listen."

Luke paused.

"Wait," he said to the agent. He held the door open and studied the man. Young's slight frame was trembling uncontrollably. He had to know he was taking a risk. But there was something fiercely dignified about his lined and weathered face, and he was standing his ground.

"Say that again," Luke said. "And explain. Fast."

"Can you believe it?"

It was Jerry's agitated voice on the phone at 7:00 A.M., waking Kate from a thick, soupy sleep. " 'Sunrise Edition' is pissed because they didn't get an exclusive the day after the convention," he said. "They said they were promised one, and they won't have Luke on again if he does 'Today' live the same day. I can't believe these jerks."

"What do I need to know, Jerry?" Kate was trying hard to wake up.

"Polls," Jerry said, sounding efficient. "Luke is doing good with California women. Up two points. We've got two thirty-second spots rotating now. Good graphics. You're looking good in Florida. They like your wrinkled linen look."

127

"I'm sick of wrinkles; anyhow, it's almost fall. I'm not wearing any more linen."

"Wrinkles work."

"Then find me some cheap wool. Very cheap."

"We've got a pile of interview requests, can we go through them?"

"Sure."

Jerry cleared his throat. "*Modern Maturity*; that's the AARP magazine, huge circulation; they want fifteen to twenty minutes at their headquarters."

"What topic?"

"We choose."

"Okay; tell them ten minutes."

"Hayden Publishing; a briefing for their reporters in Washington. They own twelve papers all over the country; suburban outlets; very strong. Three TV stations, and twelve cable systems. Luke's doing a dinner with them."

"How much time?"

"Thirty minutes. It's worth it, Kate."

"Put it on."

"Norwegian News Agency; twenty-minute phone interview."

"Put them low on the list; and make it five minutes. U.S. interviews come first."

"Right. We're all set on the *USA Today* family profile."

It was all so ordinary, but it felt bizarre.

Kate looked up and saw Abby, pale and silent, standing at her bedroom door. She said goodbye, quickly cradled the phone and sat up, trying to clear the fuzziness from her head. Only two hours of sleep, and no chance for any more, not today. There was too much to do.

"How are you, honey?" she asked.

"Just fine." Abby's voice, unlike her own, was clear and firm. "Mother, I want to get back out campaigning," she said.

"Now?" Kate said, surprised. "It's too soon, Abby. You need to rest for a few days. School starts—"

"I'll stay home for a couple of days, but Mr. Buford—you know, the new principal?—said I could start school late if I wanted to," Abby said. She smiled with a touch of adolescent smugness. "He's a Democrat."

128

"But—"

Abby spoke again, steady as a rock. "I'm an asset, Mother," she said coolly. "Daddy needs me."

Kate's head felt suddenly full of echoes from the past. Maybe this was exactly what Abby needed, but it felt too quick. It made the experience too—what was the right word? Too ordinary, she thought. She couldn't articulate what she was worried about, none of it would make sense. "I'll think about it," she said. "Now I want you to go have a good breakfast. You're looking too pale."

Abby smiled for the first time, a calm, oddly victorious smile. "Mrs. Leonard is burning me some bacon right now," she said. "Want some?"

By the end of the week, Kate was somewhere in Pennsylvania. It was after midnight and she was in a hotel room, thrashing about on a lumpy mattress. The phone rang and she reached for it, pulling it under the covers. Thank God for her nightly connection with Luke.

"How'm I doing?" His voice was scratchy and tired.

"Great, honey."

"What'd the nets use tonight?"

"CBS used the San Jose rally. Good visuals. I liked the sound-bite."

"Which one did they use?"

"Nuclear-waste dumps. Eleven seconds, four over their average."

A low whistle. "Pretty good."

Kate hesitated; surely Luke already knew. "Enright said he supports Palmer getting his visa," she said. "The convention gave him a standing ovation. That just about clinches it."

"Yeah, I know."

"Are you sorry you waited?"

"No," he said quietly. "You were right, I need to check out a few things."

"Keep me posted."

"Absolutely."

"There's a rally scheduled in New York to keep up the pressure for admitting Palmer," Kate said. "It looks like Enright is going to be part of the show. Isn't Gilmartin playing it out this way to make Enright look stronger?"

"Yeah, Marty's roaring about it." She heard a quiet chuckle. "I'm giving him heart palpitations. How am I looking? Tired?"

"A little, to be honest."

"A little more Pancake Number Two under the eyes?"

"And over the beard."

"Don't get worried, honey," he said. "Everything will be okay."

She felt a rush of caring. "We'll make sure of that," she said.

"I love you," he said. His voice was fading.

"Me, too," she said. "Goodnight."

The days began to flow by. Fast. There was no time to think about anything except the campaign. Luke was everywhere—shouting himself hoarse at a rally in California's Central Valley, leading a torchlight parade in Seattle, thanking supporters at a banquet in Manhattan. Kate had learned how to travel in a reasonably civilized manner, and fashion editors were calling her now for tips. When she read her advice in the magazines, her routine sounded wonderfully efficient, but in truth it never worked quite as smoothly as it was supposed to. She kept two complete sets of cosmetics in separate plastic bags: one for home; one for the road. But she was always dipping in one for a particular eyeshadow or lipstick, and then forgetting to return the borrowed item to the proper bag. Still, she was secretly proud of her packing. She rolled everything tightly into sausage shapes, which horrified Joan, and then stuffed them into her favorite carry-on suitcase. "That cannot come out properly," Joan protested as she watched the process one day. Kate assured her that, yes, indeed, most clothes stayed relatively unwrinkled, except for the damn linen. When they didn't, the trick was to turn on the hottest water possible in the hotel shower, hang the clothes on the shower bar, and let them steam. Kate learned to loathe hotels with headless hangers; just to be safe, she always carried a real one of her own— along with a small magnifying mirror. And never, never did she carry the vial of emergency hair color for touch-ups in the same compartment with her clothes.

"Ouch," said Joan, thinking about the potential damage, should she do so.

"I haven't done it," Kate assured her. "But Eleanor Enright did, two years ago. Believe it or not, she's the one who warned me."

"I hear your press people are fighting with your scheduling people," Joan said, changing the subject.

"You're really staying tuned into the gossip, aren't you?" Kate said, amused. "Scheduling decided Luke should bag Evans and Novak, press was horrified, and yelled until the show went back on the schedule, then someone messed up the appointment for the David Frost interview—I was in South Carolina, if you can believe it, when he showed up with his crew at the house, and I hear he was livid—" Kate paused for breath.

"Oh, Lord," Joan moaned. "I don't need to hear any more."

"That's life in a campaign," Kate said with a small smile. "So why won't you get out there and help us shake some hands?"

Joan shook her head firmly. "You know I'm not a campaigner," she said. "I'll stay wholesome for the duration, but I'm not getting out there or you'll have me speaking to the Future Farmers of America. And I'm no good on price supports."

Kate shrugged; this was nothing new. Her thoughts turned to Abby. She was flying everywhere now to campaign for her father, and she spoke not a word to Kate about the abortion. It was as if that night in Bethesda had never happened, which at first alarmed Kate, but slowly the pretense felt justifiable. The event was fading for her, too, and when she did remember it, it was vague and hazy as a long-ago dream—a very bad dream. The world was normal again.

Another night, another town. Another peal of the hotel phone. Kate reached for it groggily.

"How am I doing?"

"Great, honey."

"How are the kids?"

"Nat's getting razzed at school every day now. Some of the kids are calling him 'Son of Luke,' can you believe it? Not mean stuff," Kate hastened to add. "From what he tells me, it's just separating him out from the crowd, and he doesn't want to be separated out from the crowd."

"Hey, fame has its price. He shouldn't let it get to him."

"You know Nat, he hates being the center of attention."

"How's Abby?"

"Working hard, a valiant 'Daughter of Luke.' The press adores her."

"That's my girl," Luke said quietly. She could sense his proud grin, but he said no more, instead shifting the topic. "Enright's been getting a lot of time on the nets."

"He sure has." Kate spoke lightly, not wanting to emphasize a growing worry. Enright was indeed capitalizing on Luke's silence on Palmer, even managing to make himself look like a champion of civil rights, a tough feat to pull off. "Any developments, honey?"

"Not yet," he said. "Soon."

"Is it tomorrow you do the press conference in front of the decaying bridge?"

"The one in Flint?" A rustling of paper. "Yeah. That's tomorrow."

"The nets will use that, wait and see," she said. "That bridge is so horrible, it's spectacular."

"Should I wear a coat and tie or go casual?"

"Coat and tie. You want to be Mr. Serious, the man who can do something about the nation's decaying infrastructure. Horrible word."

"Yeah," Luke agreed amiably. "It puts people to sleep. Thank God you know how to dress me long distance."

Kate burrowed under the covers a little, cradling the phone closer. "I'd like to do a little *un*dressing," she said. "But it doesn't work long distance."

A funny noise rattled through the receiver.

"What's that?" she asked.

"That's me, kissing you through the phone. Very passionately."

Kate giggled and planted a wet smack on the cold plastic. "That's me, kissing you back." She felt like a teenager.

She heard the comforting rumble of Luke's laugh. "What if I grabbed a plane and crawled into bed with you later tonight?"

"I'll keep your side warm, just in case."

"Hell, I'm not even sure what town you're in."

Kate giggled again. "Neither am I."

"Oh, well, it was a good idea, anyway. Saw a CNN film clip of you talking to that Texas child-care coalition. Great job. Throw in the polls every chance you get."

"I do, but that's not always the soundbite."

132

"Keep trying. And, honey?"

"Yes?"

"That pink lipstick was great. Better than red."

"Gotcha."

"Love me?"

"Madly."

"Good night, babe."

Kate lay still after cradling the phone, staring at the ceiling of the barren hotel room. She felt strange, somehow—what was it? Somehow undernourished, that was it. She stirred restlessly, annoyed with herself. She certainly had no complaints of any importance. There was no more of Luke's touchy abrasiveness, thank goodness. They had passed that, fortunately, but nothing the two of them talked about these days dipped much below the surface. She poked hard at the pillow, impatient with her own musings. She was just tired. But the feeling wouldn't go away. Okay, it was hard to find time to dig into any possible problems—maybe she had spoken too lightly about Nat's feelings? She smiled in the dark. The teasing, the sexual play, was fun. But everything had an overlay, a political agenda. It would be nice if things would calm down enough so she could get enough sleep and stop brooding on little things at busy times. Relax, she ordered herself. But that wasn't quite enough to allow her to turn over, scrunch up, and go to sleep.

She squinted hard up at the unfamiliar ceiling. She truly could not remember where she was. She knew it was two in the morning. She knew she would be addressing a breakfast meeting in five hours. But where was she? She turned and reached for the local phone book tucked inside a cheap Formica bedside stand.

What do you know, she thought. I'm in St. Paul, Minnesota. Hello, St. Paul.

Some mornings, even cheating with the telephone book didn't work—not when, after getting only three hours sleep, she was so tired she could barely see her toothbrush. So Kate played a game with herself on the long plane trips, concentrating on figuring out where she had been. It was against the rules to peek at her schedule. Was it Los Angeles, where she had spoken to the Hispanic educators? Or was that Chicago? What about the visit to the day-care center last week? Was that Minnesota or that little town, what's-its-name, on the northern peninsula of Michigan? She'd worn her boots, and there was a sprinkle of snow. Where was that, anyway? No time to figure it out. The plane was landing, somewhere in the Midwest.

The days were disappearing now as fast as butter melting onto a hot griddle. Gone. Days with a frantic, dreamlike quality, a brutal, galloping sequence of farms and towns and cities and events and broken suitcases and lost toothbrushes and clanging hotel pipes and endless, endless press releases, radio spots, television ads. Luke was campaigning nonstop, and they rarely saw each other. Kate was all over the country, everywhere, giving speeches, smiling, shaking hands, mending stockings with clear nail polish, sleeping in her clothes, and staring at the blinking red message light on one hotel phone after another—the message light that never seemed to turn off.

Finally it was late September.

"Hey," Kate whispered through the phone to her husband one night while burrowed under the covers of a bed in a room in a hotel in a town somewhere in Michigan. "We're going to see each other tomorrow! In Los Angeles. Can you believe it?"

He laughed. "Can't wait," he said.

It began as one of those days a campaign manager dreams about. It was better than good. People surged out onto the sidewalks, lining up ten deep to cheer and shout as Luke led a parade up Figueroa, over Wilshire, and then up Hope.

"Christ, look at the crowds!" yelled Marty, as the parade moved toward the Public Library. "Luke, stand up in the car!"

Luke stood and pulled Kate up with him. It felt wobbly, standing in a moving car, but exciting. Office workers leaned out of their windows, shouting and cheering and tossing perforated strips torn from computer paper down on the little caravan of cars. They'd had their orders from Marty's advance team, and they followed them, making sure plenty of paper fell on a laughing candidate standing tall and strong in a bright red car while the West Covina High School band huffed and tootled the stirring Sousa marches still guaranteed to put lumps in the throats of most middle Americans. It was supposed to look great on the evening news, and it would.

"Mother, look!" yelled Abby as she tugged at Kate from her place sitting next to Nat on the back of the open car, pointing at the pudgy conductor of this campaign symphony. Marty was walking along the edge of the crowd, arms swinging, chatting with a steady stream of reporters, and grinning, actually grinning. Caught in the exuberance of the moment, mother and daughter laughed. "Amazing, isn't it?" Kate said. "Miracles happen!"

Once more Abby tugged at her mother. "Mother?" she said, nodding toward Claire, giggling. "She's getting thinner, can you believe it?"

Indeed she was. Walking slowly with the parade, shmoozing with reporters, Claire looked refreshed, not wilted; glowing, not glowering. The somewhat lumpy softness of convention time had given way to a smooth, easy look. Kate, suddenly self-conscious as she balanced her toes on the edge of the seat, fingered the soiled collar of her own green silk shirt.

"Wow, I like her dress," Abby said, still watching Claire. Kate took a good look at Claire's soft scoop-necked wool and noted only one detail. The damn dress was blue.

That night, Luke was restless as a prowling cat. Back and forth he paced in their room behind the graceful facade of the Beverly Wilshire Hotel, his hair wet from the shower, wearing nothing except a short white terry robe that left his muscular hairy legs exposed. Kate watched him, proud, but wondering. He couldn't seem to allow himself to savor the evidence of today's smashing success. He couldn't sit still. It was almost as if the nerves in his body were dancing on top of his skin. Every few minutes he stopped before the television set, zapper in hand, flicking between news shows.

Los Angeles was getting a full dose of today's parade and rally on every television station. Together, Kate and Luke watched the parading images in bemusement: there was Luke, standing tall, brushing shredded computer paper out of his hair, laughing, squinting into the sun. Zap. Luke Goodspeed, arms stretched out, speaking passionately about his plan for affordable health care. Zap. Luke Goodspeed reaching for Kate's hand, raising it high with his. Zap. It was saturation coverage, even for a presidential campaign, and Kate wanted him to enjoy it, but apparently all he could do was watch.

Patricia O'Brien

"What's wrong?" she finally asked.

"Nothing," he said. "My skin's too jumpy."

"Look!" Kate pointed to the set. Surely this would relax him. There was the pale countenance of John Enright standing next to ABC's Lynn Sherr, who was grilling him on the latest poll results for the ABC campaign roundup. Luke allowed himself a smile as he listened to the figures: a five-point gap in Florida, and he was ahead. Enright's lead was dropping in Texas. Kate stole a casual glance at her husband. Good—he seemed to be absorbing the fact that he was now holding the national lead by four points.

"Honey, you're not working right now," she said quietly. "It's okay to relax and enjoy."

"There's too much other stuff going on," he said, almost fretfully. "It's not as good as it looks."

Kate turned her attention back to the television set.

"What's your reaction, Senator Enright?" Sherr asked on the screen.

"This race is far from over, and that's all I'm going to say," Enright said serenely, leaning into the microphone. "You ladies and gentlemen of the media shouldn't forget that."

Enright didn't seem all that worried, and briefly Kate wondered why. He looked like a man with a surprise up his sleeve.

Luke sprang up and continued his restless sojourn around the room. There was no way, Kate thought, simply no way, for him to sit still tonight. She felt troubled.

"What's wrong?" she asked again.

Luke didn't answer at first, walking instead over to a huge oak table by the window that overlooked Wilshire Boulevard. On top of the table was an unopened bottle of champagne resting in a bucket, and next to it a basket of fruit sent up by the hotel management, a lavish arrangement of oranges, pears, apples, apricots, and bananas. Luke picked up an apple and took a deep bite, then resumed his aimless pace.

"Nothing, nothing at all," he said. He stopped, apple poised in midair. He seemed to be hearing something. "Who's cheering?" he asked, a puzzled look on his face.

Kate listened. "I don't hear anything," she said.

"I do," Luke said, walking over to the window to peer at the ground eight stories below. He let out a laugh. "This is ridiculous,"

136

he said. "Those people out there are still applauding me. I can hear them. There must still be a crowd in the streets."

Kate walked over to the window and looked out onto a virtually empty Wilshire Boulevard. On one corner, a man walking a giant black poodle stood waiting for the light to change. She saw no one else.

She turned to peer deeply into her husband's drained and exhausted face.

"Luke, there isn't anyone out there," she said softly. "I think what you're hearing is the air-conditioner. And I think it's time you got some sleep."

Her words had the effect of stripping away the nervous energy that had kept him pacing. He settled heavily onto the sofa next to her.

"We've got a bad poll coming out tomorrow. I'm slipping with blacks, and Enright is picking them up."

"We'll live with it," she said comfortingly.

"Kate, how can you say that?"

The phone rang.

"Hi," Luke said to the voice on the other end. "Yeah, I'm beat. Yeah, I know it's only a dip, but it could mean trouble."

There was a silence, and Kate found herself, with no luck, trying to pick up the voice on the other end of the line.

"Thanks," Luke said. His voice seemed more relaxed. "I know. No, don't worry, it's okay." He flashed a smile at Kate. "She doesn't mind. No, really. I appreciate it. Get a good night's sleep, we start early." He laughed. "Yep, I know. As usual."

"Who was that?"

"Claire. Just checking in."

"She could have waited until morning."

Luke didn't bother answering; he just shrugged.

"What I meant was," Kate said, picking up their interrupted conversation, "Enright can't ride his endorsement of Palmer too far, he hasn't got a record that can stand up."

"I wish it were that simple," Luke said. "I'm getting pressure coming from every direction now." He waved a tired hand. "Those nuts on the far right, for example. They'd do anything to keep Palmer out of the country. They're a bunch of flat-out racists, and if I don't back Palmer, it looks like I'm one of them."

"This man you told me about, the one who grabbed you at the

elevator—what's his name?" Luke had told her very little about the encounter, just enough to make her nervous.

"Young. Edward Young."

"Who is he? What did he want?"

Luke hesitated. "I can't go into too much detail yet," he said. "I don't know enough. He's Liberian. Drives a cab in Manhattan. He told me he's been following my campaign for months. He told me he sat in his cab and listened to my acceptance speech and decided then I was the candidate with the courage to do something." Luke grinned ruefully. "A little guy—but brave. He could've got himself shot when he grabbed me at that elevator. He claims Palmer is a drug dealer who will stop at nothing to get a base in this country."

Kate's heart pumped faster. "Do you believe him?"

Luke sighed. "I wish I could say he's a phony, but I don't think so."

"Honey, that's incredible. What are you going to do?"

"Get plenty more information, and get it fast." Luke frowned, his restless mood returning. "When you get this busy, you get sloppy," he said, half to himself. "I can't afford to get sloppy. I can't afford to overlook a single thing. Then you get somebody who stabs you in the back—" He was rambling, and Kate was having trouble following his train of thought.

"You mean Father Joe?"

Luke's brow furrowed. He nodded. "Plain Joe; forget the collar." An uncharacteristic mocking note crept into his voice. "The guy I taught to swim; the kid who was so skinny he couldn't keep his bathing trunks up."

"Maybe you should talk with him; do something to ease this."

"And play right into the cardinal's hands? No, thanks."

"We don't really know why he pulled out," she said. "They must have yanked him back pretty hard."

"I never thought he'd buckle so easily," Luke said. "I thought he was tough enough to stand up for himself."

"Maybe that's too much to expect of a man in his position," Kate said. "Anyway, it's not his strength you're upset about, it's his loyalty."

"Yeah," he said. "Loyalty, God, you need it in this business. But you can never count on anybody too much."

"You can count on me."

Luke shot his wife an absentminded but affectionate glance. "I know," he said. "You're great."

I'm getting patted on the head, Kate thought. It was enough to make her push her point a little farther.

"We're always here for you," she said. "Nat and Abby and me."

"This is the toughest race I've ever been through," Luke said, as if he hadn't heard her. "I'm not complaining, mind you. That's the way it should be. But the closer we get, the more I want it." He flashed her a tired grin. "You are looking at naked ambition, honey. With every crummy dinner in every crummy hotel, I want it more." He slapped his fist into the cup of his left hand. "You know what's great! Coming into a small town two hours late, rain falling, and finding a city square packed with people. Waiting for me. Just some little place in Ohio or Texas or eastern Oregon—that's the good part." His eyes were too bright, and he was rambling again. "I wonder if I still know how to drive a shift car," he said.

Kate laughed in true astonishment. "You didn't know how to drive one before," she said. "What do you expect, a miracle?"

Luke briefly closed his eyes. He scratched absently at his leg, the folds of the robe falling back from his haunches. "Jesus, I'm tired," he said. He stood and aimlessly paced the room. "This takes every ounce of energy, every damn ounce," he said. "Those people today, they want a winner. All of them out there today, waving and shouting and clapping, accountants and secretaries and restaurant cooks and kids in jeans—they want a winner. They want me to sound like one and look like one, and they're with me as long as I never let my shoulders hunch up or my face sag, and if my feet ache, they don't want to know it."

Kate made a comforting noise and waited.

"I'm not complaining," he said again. "Lord, no. It's the damnedest thing. I felt like General MacArthur standing in that car today." He looked at her sheepishly. "My dad told me about that big ticker-tape parade after Truman fired him. I didn't know a damn thing about the general or his mucking around in policy, but I sure wanted a hero. Heroes rode in parades, and people showered them with shredded paper, and it sounded good to me. I wanted to be a hero."

"Well, you are, now."

139

Patricia O'Brien

Luke sighed. "A hero? Come on, babe. I'm not sure there are any anymore." He took both her hands in his. "You're with me all the way, right?"

Kate blinked in surprise. "Of course," she said.

"No matter what happens?"

"Yes," she said firmly.

"We're partners. We can trust each other."

Kate kept her hands still in his. Very still. She thought of Abby, but what was done was done. "We're only human beings, honey," she said carefully. "We do the best we can."

Luke was not preparing to probe. His eyes shifted elsewhere. "That's right," he said. "We do the best we can."

"We've survived a lot of things," she said. "But if I don't get you to bed pretty soon, I'm not sure you'll make it till tomorrow."

"Will you rub my neck?"

"I'll rub your neck."

Luke scraped at the stubble on his face, looking suddenly like a tired child. He pulled the terry robe closer and moved toward the bedroom.

"Luke."

"Yes?"

Her eyes were concerned; uncertain. "You are absolutely campaigning too hard," she said.

A few weeks later Luke flew back in from the road to vote on a Senate clean water bill.

"Look, I've got to keep my constituents happy," he told Marty, when he objected. "Steve's right, I've got to be there for this vote."

"Who gives a fuck about dead alewives in Lake Michigan?" demanded Marty.

"I do, Marty. Remember? I represent Illinois."

That ended the discussion. This one was Steve's call, whether Marty liked it or not.

Steve was quick to relish the moment, basking in the reflected glory as Luke's Senate colleagues scrambled close to shake the hand of the Democratic party's standard-bearer. From the gallery reserved for the families of senators, Kate watched her husband threading his way through the rows of polished mahogany desks to his seat and felt a swelling of pride. You could smell the excitement, taste it, in this chamber. Those self-assured men down there in their expensive suits clapping Luke on the back and exchanging hearty greetings just might be talking to the next president of the United States, and they couldn't afford to forget that for a minute.

"Mom," Nat hissed, as he peered over the railing, "Senator Lauraux wears a *rug*."

Abby giggled. "Look at some of the others," she whispered to her brother. "He isn't the only one."

Kate put a warning hand on Nat's pointing finger and glanced over at the press gallery. It was full, a good sign. She saw the reporters crowded into the front rows crane their necks over the edge of the balcony, watching Luke's every move. What he did mattered. Everything he did mattered. There was a distinct smell of victory in the air, and it had nothing to do with any environmental bill.

After the vote, Kate joined Luke under the Ohio Clock outside the Senate chamber, where he shared a few more minutes of conversation with his fellow senators, before they headed for the east entrance and their waiting entourage. "I used to think getting into this club was the high point of my life," Luke whispered as they hurried through the corridor, lush with its intricate rust-and-blue mosaic floor. "Now, look. They're envying me." He grinned, obviously enjoying himself. Relishing was the better word.

They reached the top of the stairs.

"Here they come!"

Reporters who had been lazily lounging against trees, joking, deciphering their notes, listening to their tape recorders as they waited, suddenly surged forward like dancers hearing a cue.

"There's Ernie Stark," Steve whispered into Kate's ear.

You could tell by looking at him that Stark didn't like to wait—not for anything or anybody. He stood immobile, bored, gazing up the glistening white stone steps. Like a snake, Kate thought. Ready to strike.

Luke was cheerful as he reached the clamoring reporters, clearly ready to chat, instead of heading directly for his car. Steve, hovering close, looked pleased. He elbowed away some lesser campaign aides and pushed himself close to Luke's side, claiming what used to be his unchallenged turf.

A few local Illinois reporters tried to ask questions about the bill,

141

but the campaign press quickly and impatiently drowned them out.

"How's the campaign going, Senator?"

"Do you think you're going to win?"

Luke swung easily into his usual answers, and the reporters scribbled away in their usual manner as Kate cast a curious glance in Ernie Stark's direction. He wasn't trying to ask anything. He was just standing there, a runty little man with coal-black hair. He was staring. Not at Luke—at her.

Kate felt queasy. She was glad when Steve stepped forward, thrusting his hand in the air with a semblance of his former authority. "That's all, guys," he said crisply, waving the camera crews away. "We've got a campaign going here." Everybody broke for the buses, and Kate moved to a waiting mini-van and took a seat.

Ernie Stark glided like an eel through the crowd toward the mini-van. He reached the open window by which Kate was sitting and grasped the pane. She could see newsprint stains under his fingernails.

"Hi there, Mrs. Goodspeed," he said. "Campaign's goin' great, huh?"

"Yes," Kate said, trying to pull back from the window.

Ernie leaned closer. "Hey, that's great," he said. "Don't get a chance to see much of your husband, do you? That's what happens, I guess."

The mini-van began to move, but Ernie Stark hung on.

"Do you feel lonely, Mrs. Goodspeed?"

"Not at all." Kate was startled. "Why do you ask?"

"Being alone, without your husband and all."

"I'm not alone, he's right there," she said, pointing to the van ahead.

"Yeah, riding in a different car, huh? Gee, I'm sorry."

"Hey—" He was moving faster now, as the van picked up speed. "Hey, Mrs. Goodspeed, how are the kids taking it? How's your daughter?"

What happened next was shocking. Steve, standing near Kate in the van, suddenly leaned past her, an angry glitter in his eyes, and slid the window shut on Stark's fingers, catching them tightly. The van was picking up speed. Ernie Stark tried to pull his hand away, but he could not wriggle free. He let out an angry howl, then broke into a stumbling run.

142

"Steve!"

Kate struggled to push Steve away and release Stark's grimy fingers from the window. The van was picking up even more speed, and she saw the anger in Stark's eyes turn to fright as he tried to run faster. She pushed the window open, releasing his hand, then looked back and saw him stumble to his knees on the concrete. A string of curses hit the air.

"You could've killed him!" she burst out, frightened.

"He's too tough a bastard," Steve said. The words were scornfully dismissive, but his thin frame was trembling with anger. "A scare won't hurt him. Anyway, he had no right to throw that at you."

"What do you mean? What was he talking about?"

But Steve was through talking. Stubbornly he shook his head and got up. "Gotta work on this press release," he said, waving a piece of paper. "I'll write in the back of the van so you can get some rest." And then he was gone.

7

Kate found herself staring at the morning paper a few days later, trying to control her shock. "Well, Ernie Stark finally answered my question," she muttered to herself. Angrily, she pitched the paper into the kitchen wastebasket, startling old Sammy, who gazed at her through puzzled, rheumy eyes.

"You can do anything you want with it," she whispered to the dog. He staggered up to lick her hand and then collapsed again, too old to launch a counterattack, even for Kate. She gazed around the old country-style kitchen that reflected so much the casual disorder of their lives, forcing herself for the moment to concentrate on the simple and mundane. I must scrub the grease off the teakettle, she told herself. Empty the garbage. I must do small chores and think about this.

She heard a noise and looked up. Abby was standing at the doorway, clutching the edges of her faded down robe, the robe Luke liked to joke made her look like a pink Pillsbury doughboy. Her face was deathly pale.

"I already read it, Mother."

"It could be something else. It could have nothing to do with you." It was the only thing Kate could think of to say.

Abby leaned over and pulled the paper out of the wastebasket, stared down at the column, and began to read aloud.

" 'You would have thought Luke Goodspeed, the Democrats' Golden Boy, would be above reproach in most departments,

144

wouldn't you?' " she read, mimicking Stark's arch prose. " 'Well, we understand there's a secret out there. A secret that could undermine his straight-shooter, all-American image. Watch this space.' "

"Honey—"

Abby dropped the paper and looked at her mother with terrified eyes. "What are we going to do?" she said.

Kate took a deep breath, trying very hard not to convey to Abby how worried she was by Ernie Stark's attack. She knew what she had to say, and she knew it wasn't going to be easy.

"We have to warn your father," she said as gently as she could. "Just in case."

"No, please."

"If we don't, he's going to get blindsided. We're leaving him vulnerable, Abby."

Abby leaned back against the door, huge, silent tears swelling from her eyes. "I can't live with that, Mother," she said softly.

"If there's a better way, honey, help me find it."

Abby could say nothing, and Kate felt a great swell of pity. Abby was trapped. She was going to have to not only risk losing her father's respect to save him from public humiliation, she would face public humiliation herself. Of course, it was too much. How could it not be?

"I'll do everything to help you through it," Kate said. "Everything I can do."

"Nothing will make it better."

"Your father will be stunned, we know that," Kate said. She searched for a way to comfort her daughter. "He'll be confused and angry and embarrassed. But he'll support us, he'll stand by you. You know he will."

"Mother, he'll feel I betrayed him. Deep down, he'll feel I hurt him in the worst way possible. Publicly."

Kate hesitated, not sure which tack to take. How would Luke react? Was Abby right? There was no precedent for any of them jeopardizing Luke's public image. In truth, his reaction was an unknown. That gave her the uncomfortable sensation of a situation slipping out of control; worse than that, it made her uneasy about how far she could reach into her husband's psyche before touching a stranger.

145

Nonetheless she kept her voice firm when she finally spoke. "I'll handle this," she said. "I'll make sure your father understands."

"He won't understand." Abby was now pacing agitatedly, wringing her hands as if caught in a corner with no way out. "All he thinks about now is winning this election, everything is geared to that, and it's Marty and that creepy Claire who tell him what to think and what to say—"

"Abby, calm down," Kate said, concerned about the edge of hysteria creeping into her daughter's voice. "That's not true."

"Well, I think it is." Abby shot a defiant look at her mother. "You don't see it because you don't want to see it. You and Dad shake hands together on a platform every two weeks and head off in different directions, but I've been traveling with him a lot, and I know what's going on. He's like a machine, always huddling with one of them on the plane. . . ."

Kate was determined not to feed her hysteria. "Honey, you're losing perspective," she said. "Your dad is running harder and faster for this than for anything in his life—"

"*That's* for sure."

Kate stopped and took a deep breath, reminding herself she was facing a frightened fifteen-year-old, not the polished young woman whose stellar performance in winning votes for her father won praise from everyone. Too much so, probably. It was a mistake to think Abby was more mature than her age; it was another way of pushing adulthood on her too soon. A lot was expected anyway. From the first time she had trotted around in a crunchy starched pinafore handing out leaflets with her daddy, a lot had been expected of her. How many times had she, Kate, wanted her children to act older than they were? Too many times, she told herself. Maybe I've let myself fashion them to fit Luke's press releases. The thought was bizarre. Her hands began to tremble.

"Abby—" she began.

Nat's slight form suddenly appeared in the doorway behind Abby. His face was very red, his glasses round and big on his face. "I can't stand listening to this," he said in a choked voice. "That creep will ruin Dad, and it's all your fault, Abby."

"My fault! What do you know?" Abby protested, whirling on her younger brother. "What do you know about how it feels to go through something like this? You—you're just a twit who doesn't know enough about anything!"

"Stop it!" Kate commanded. The shock of Nat's unusual outburst had thrown her off balance.

But Nat's defiance was already crumbling. He sat down at the kitchen table, kicked hard at the table leg, and grabbed the sports section of the *Washington Post*, turning away from his mother and sister. "The whole thing's shitty," he mumbled, and then, cracking his knuckles, tried to bury himself in the Monday football scores.

Abby was not about to be ignored. "You think you can blame me and then just hide behind the paper," she said, gulping tears and clutching her robe. "Stop that disgusting noise and listen to me. You've never had to make a single grown-up decision, all you ever do is play those stupid Nintendo games and throw dirty clothes around your room and—"

"Abby, stop." Kate tried to be calm, but her heart was caught by the pathetic sight of her daughter standing there, her face not yet free of baby fat, trying to proclaim her adulthood. "Don't, honey."

"Don't, honey," mimicked Nat, from behind the paper. But he had stopped cracking his knuckles and was biting hard on his lower lip.

"You're hiding, just like Daddy," Abby shot out.

"Sure, blame him," Nat shot back.

Kate stood up. "That's enough," she said angrily. "You're not enemies; stop acting that way."

The room fell silent, so silent the sound of the ticking clock in the dining room could be heard. Kate saw in one illuminating moment what she had never seen on the faces of her children, and hoped never to see again. They were ashamed; baffled, frightened, and ashamed. They didn't deserve this.

"Now here is what's going to happen," she said, speaking slowly. "We may have a crisis on our hands. You guys know what's at stake. We have to warn your father, there is no other way around it." She took a deep breath, not having the slightest idea what she should say next. "I'll talk to him this morning," she said finally. "We'll work it out because we always have before."

"This time it's different," Abby whispered.

Kate pulled her resistant daughter close and simultaneously en-

147

❖ ❖

circled Nat's shoulders with her other arm. "We've always done it before," she said firmly. Was she just some kind of coach giving a locker-room pep talk? No, she thought, I've got to deliver for these kids. I've got to deliver for my family.

"We've done it before and we'll do it again," she said. "I promise."

Later, Kate stood by the bedroom window combing her hair and staring past creamy antique lace curtains to the gently sloping lawn outside. It bothered her that she couldn't recall noticing whether the leaves on the big maple in front of the house had turned their usual fiery red this year. That was something she always looked forward to, and now many of them already lay in damp windswept piles across the yard, crunchy and sweet-smelling underfoot.

She dressed carefully, choosing a wool paisley dress of cherry red and gold. It was her comfort dress, the one, she liked to tell Luke, that made her feel snug in the coldest weather. In truth, she needed more than a little comfort now.

She heard the car door slam and saw through the window her driver lounging against the side of the car. Behind him, in the most deliberately anonymous car on the block, the ever-hovering Secret Service agents sat stoically. She was more used to them now, even though Harry was the only one who had become almost part of the family. She peered closer at the car. She could see the other agent she liked, the cute one, Megan Thaler, who helped Abby trim her bangs last week. The agents were easy and pleasant, and they all appreciated a plate of cookies every now and then, even Mrs. Leonard's cookies. It must get terribly boring, Kate thought.

She quickly pulled out her favorite gold earrings. They were heavy clip-ons that always ended up pinching her ears, but it was very important today that she look and feel pulled together—small lobes be damned. She put the earrings on and hurried downstairs.

"Let's go to campaign headquarters," Kate told the driver.

The young woman's freckled face registered confusion. "Aren't you headed for the airport, Mrs. Goodspeed?"

"No, not today. Luke's at headquarters for a meeting, and I have to catch him before he leaves for Oregon." Still the driver hesitated, and she saw she had to reassure her. "Don't worry," she said dryly, "I'm not violating my schedule."

This old wreck of a building is as dilapidated as ever, Kate thought as she hurried up the steps of the old shoe store, now reborn as the official "Goodspeed for President" headquarters. If anything, after months of hard use, it looked worse. But then she saw the huge new posters of Luke in the windows and felt a surge of pride. Not many women got to see their husbands in double life-size photos. Then again, she smiled to herself, thinking of what Joan's reaction would be, how many would want to? She pushed open the shabby front door.

Inside, the high-pitched peal of telephones blended with the sound of shouting aides and chattering phone-bank volunteers, producing a decibel level that made Kate's ears ache. She picked her way carefully past boxes in the corridor stacked with scheduling books and office supplies to Marty's office. Everything was a mess.

"Hey, grab those newspapers!" yelled a volunteer, pointing frantically at a wobbling stack of papers stacked next to the coffee machine. Too late. With a sloppy thud, they fell into a trash can filled with damp mounds of still-steaming coffee grounds. Kate moved on, eying a large message board covered with stacks of pink message slips thumbtacked next to clippings of news stories touting the Goodspeed campaign. Did anyone ever answer all of them? In the press office, four television sets, each tuned to a different network, were lined up on top of a set of cheap pressed-board bookcases. All sets were on, with the sound turned down, their flickering images routinely ignored until the evening news shows began. That was the signal for turning the sound up to full volume.

The door to Marty's office was closed, but she could hear raised voices. She looked questioningly at Jackie Beecham, his secretary, a tiny woman from North Carolina with huge dark pupils and a nervous, pursing mouth.

"They've been in there awhile," Jackie whispered, eyes widening at Kate's unexpected presence.

"Luke knows I'm coming," Kate found herself whispering back. She hesitated, then turned the knob and walked in. If she didn't get

Luke out of there, the meeting could go on forever. She didn't want to stand outside and wait, not when the volunteers on the phone bank were eying her curiously.

Luke was standing by the window, looking oddly mulish, hands plunged into the pockets of his suit. Marty was sitting on the edge of a wobbly scarred conference table, his eyes quiet, expressionless. Clair was picking at her perfect fingernails.

Luke jumped as Kate walked in. "You're early," he said.

"Have you seen Ernie Stark's column?" she asked, without preamble. The haze of smoke that hung heavy over exposed pipes, peeling paint, and grimy windows was suddenly stifling, and Kate had to exert extra control over her voice to speak normally.

"Yes," he said, his eyes widening in surprise.

"I need to talk to you about it," she said. "Alone."

Marty cast her an amused glance. "Don't overreact, Kate. It's just a campaign glitch."

"It's more than that," she managed, taken aback.

"I don't think Kate knows what's going on," Claire interrupted soothingly. "We need to fill her in."

"In a minute," Luke said. "Excuse us, okay?" She felt his arm under hers, guiding her through the door into a small closetlike inner office. The room was so close, she could feel the sweat trickling down between her breasts.

"Honey, that column—" she began.

"Never mind about that," he said. "You were right to stall, Kate. Palmer isn't what he seems to be. For sure."

Kate caught her breath sharply. "Young was right?" she whispered.

"Yes."

"Oh, my God." Shocked, she forgot for the moment her own concerns. "Are you sure?"

"Young says he's bringing us proof," Luke said. His eyes were very bright. "If it's solid, Enright looks like a fool. I'll oppose Palmer and get points for doing it. Couldn't be better."

"Don't forget the people who admire and respect him, honey; they'll be shocked." It wasn't like Luke to focus only on the politics.

He paused and shot her a quick glance. "I haven't forgotten, Kate," he said quietly. "You're with me, no matter what happens?"

"Of course," she said. "You don't have to keep asking that."

150

"I know, but you never can tell." It was an odd response, but before she could question him, he took her again by the hand and propelled her back into the room where the first thing she was aware of was Claire's watchful, immobile face.

"Marty, tell her," Claire demanded.

Marty moved toward the window and then sank into a swivel chair. Kate stood at the doorway as he swiveled slowly back and forth. "We've known for a few days that we've got a little problem," he said, not looking at her directly. "Stark's apparently found out what it is."

Kate briefly counted the beats of her thudding heart.

"It involves our friend from New York," he went on.

"What—?"

"Sam Olson. He picked up the New Orleans hotel bill for the entire staff, and everybody here just figured the bill was late. So it didn't get reported to the Federal Election Commission."

"That's against the law."

"Yes, we know that," Claire broke in, a small, patronizing smile flitting across her face.

"Well, how could you let it happen then?" Kate said sharply. "I can't understand why he's around so much; he thinks he's too important."

"Look, let's face it, we wouldn't have gotten this far without him," Marty said. "We were squeezed for money on this and he thought he was doing us a favor. Paying the bill is no problem, we've just got to keep Stark from riding it into the headlines. Damn Stark! All he wants is a character issue."

So this was it? The dimensions of the problem were shrinking rapidly in Kate's mind. The pain in her chest began to ease. No, it was too easy. Was this all it was? Be careful, she told herself. Be sure.

Marty spoke up again, sounding exasperated. "When Stark plants an item like that, we get a dozen reporters on our necks," he said, waving a stack of pink phone slips. "We're paying the bill today and filing fast, and Olson's falling all over himself with apologies."

Kate had a hard time envisioning Olson apologizing for anything, but she wanted to believe. She wanted very much to believe. "I'm sure he is," she said. "I wouldn't think he would want reporters poking around too much in his affairs."

Luke studied his wife with something akin to—what was it?— relief? "You don't seem very worried," he said.

151

"It sounds like a nonproblem, that's why," she said with almost transparent relief. It would not do to convey the depth of her feelings. Euphoria would be mighty suspect.

Jackie popped her head in the door. "The ad team from New York is here," she said.

Marty turned toward Claire, an eyebrow raised.

"It's a good concept," Claire said. "You'll love the storyboards—bad closing shot, but fixable." She smiled at Kate. "A new thirty-second spot on Enright's environmental record," she said. "The last one cost him three points in California."

Kate edged toward the door. There was just a hint of polite exclusion in Claire's voice, and she sensed it was time to leave.

"You wanted to talk?" Luke suddenly asked.

"Oh—" Kate's hands fluttered for an instant. "It can wait," she said.

"We'd still like to do a little damage control on the filing story," Marty said in a genial tone. "You're old pals with Bradford, aren't you?"

"Peter? Yes."

Marty leaned forward, the table under him creaking in protest. "Maybe you could drop a word to him."

Kate was surprised. "Ask him to sit on a story?" she said. "He'd never do that."

"Not sit on it," Marty said quickly. "Just balance it out a little." He smiled. "Maybe he'd do it for old times' sake."

Lord, Marty had a heavy touch. "That's a little crass," she said. She found herself wishing Luke would say something, but he stayed silent.

"Hey, just a joke. It isn't a big deal, so don't worry about it if you don't want to do it," Marty said. "We'd just like him to know this was an honest oversight." And then, as if the thought had just occurred to him, "Look, we'll give him an exclusive preview of the new ad," he said. "How's that?"

In her present relieved state of mind, Marty's arguments were beginning to sound reasonable. "I'll think about it," she said.

"Only if you want to," Luke said, finally speaking up. There was an edge of apology to his voice.

"No, I'll do it," she said, suddenly deciding. It was a small enough favor if it mattered to Luke.

"He's on the trip to Oregon tonight, isn't he, Marty?" Luke looked questioningly at his campaign manager. Marty nodded. "Better nail him this morning," he said.

Kate caught a current of tension in the room and felt a sense of nagging doubt. But the release of her own tension was so relieving, so delicious, she chose not to think about anything else. Why should she? Abby's secret was still safe. One thing at a time.

The three sat staring at each other after Kate's exit, the tension palpable now that they were alone. Marty spoke first.

"I think she bought it," he said.

"Bought *what?*" Luke demanded.

"Bought our story about what Ernie Stark is up to."

Luke angrily turned his back on the two of them and walked to the window.

Claire shot Marty a fierce, warning glance. He shrugged, then switched the subject.

"You told her about this Palmer thing?"

Luke nodded his head. "Of course."

Marty looked taken aback for a moment, then slipped quickly into gear. "I'm telling you, Luke," he said, "the whole thing sounds crazy. David Palmer, the new patron saint of American blacks, a front for a major drug cartel that funds the National Freedom Federation?" But his eyes were hopeful. "What's the guy's name again?"

"Edward Young," Luke said. "He's been driving a cab in New York for five years, ever since he left Liberia. So far all of what he says checks out." Luke paused. "He's a smart man, Marty; no phony. Well-educated, determined, and scared to death."

"We've got a lot to gain if it's true, if we handle it right." Marty's chunky figure seemed tensed for a fight; he paced, his hands clasped behind his back. His mouth was drawn thin and tight. "But if it isn't true, we could get creamed."

"He says he's got a ton of documentation."

"When does he get here?"

Luke glanced at his watch. "Any minute."

"Has he gone to the immigration people?"

"He says he's tried everybody; nobody will listen to him. I'm his last hope."

153

Claire was watching the two men, appraising them both, but her primary attention was clearly on Luke. "You started to tell us about his daughter before Kate came," she prompted.

Luke nodded. "Young makes no pretenses," he said. "He was deep into this cartel himself until his kid died of an overdose."

Marty let out a short snort, remarkably like the bark of an impatient dog. "So he saw the light."

"Yeah, Marty, if you want to put it that way," Luke said in his most laconic manner. "He saw the light. He got the hell out of Liberia, chose a new name, and went underground as a New York cabbie. Trying to blow the whistle on Palmer could get him killed, that's why he's so scared."

There was a knock on the door. Jackie opened it and fastened her eyes on Marty. "Mr. Young is here," she said.

"Send him in."

Edward Young took two steps into the room and paused. His right hand clenched a worn, rumpled tweed cap; his left held a plastic shopping bag. He stood stolidly, almost anchored to the floor. He cleared his throat and looked at Luke.

"It's a pleasure to see you again, Senator," he said quietly.

Marty squirmed in his chair. "Let's get down to business," he said.

Young stared at him.

"It's okay, Mr. Young," Luke said. "Mr. Apple is my campaign manager, and—" he nodded at Claire—"Miss Lorenzo is my deputy campaign manager. You can trust them."

Young held out the shopping bag. "I've brought what you want," he said.

Marty thrust out his hand, took the bag, and began pulling papers out.

"What's here?" he said.

"Everything I could put together quickly. Affidavits from former couriers. Documents on where the drugs were picked up, where delivered, where the money was sent to be laundered. Bank records, everything."

Luke moved swiftly to Marty's side, picking up the documents, scanning them fast. "Do they link Palmer to the operation?" he asked.

"Not by name," Young said. His hands shook slightly. "It's clear who they're talking about. The people who put those papers together, they know."

Marty snorted impatiently. "That's not good enough," he said. "Can you produce these people?"

Young looked about him, uncertain. "Senator," he said, ignoring Marty and speaking directly to Luke. "We are all afraid. All of this will take time."

"What do you want from us?" Marty challenged.

Young's eyes, burning hot, switched focus. "Fight him," he said. "Don't make this easy for him. Read these papers, you'll see how he's connected. Don't let him be a false hero."

"I'll fight him," Luke said, "if we've got solid proof. But you must understand, I run a great risk here if this material gets shot down."

"We need more." Marty studied the face of the man before him with shrewd eyes. "I think you have more."

Young's gaze stayed steady. "Yes," he said softly. "There is a tape."

"Of what?"

"A meeting with Palmer."

"Well, hell," exploded Marty. "Bring it to us!"

"It will be difficult." There was a long pause. "It is in the hands of a courier. But if you must have it, I'll get it." The tension in his face was so pronounced, even Marty paused.

"We're asking you to put yourself at risk, right?" Luke said slowly.

Young smiled, the skin crinkling into deep folds around his eyes. He spoke then from the experience of a world none of them knew. "Senator," he said quietly, "I'm always at risk." He took the tweed cap and pulled it down low over his gray hair. "I will leave you these papers," he said, nodding at the documents on Marty's desk. "You'll learn a great deal about Mr. Palmer."

And then he was gone.

For a moment, Luke, Marty, and Claire sat in silence. Then Claire spoke. Her hair was pulling loose from a carelessly fastened rubber band, her eyes were rimmed with tiny lines. The total effect was one of unusual softness.

"You believe him, don't you," she said, looking at Luke.

"Yes," he said. "I do."

Marty groaned, clapping a hand to his forehead with such force it

155

left an immediate angry imprint. "We're not getting enough to take a chance," he said. "Why you?"

Luke whirled. "Why *not* me?" he said. "I'm on the damn sub-committee that pushed this whole thing along and made it happen. I'm one of the reasons Palmer is poised to land in this country. Who else, Marty?"

Marty dropped his show of indignation. "Luke" he said quietly, "if you don't get behind the Palmer people, we risk a huge chunk of the black vote."

Luke kept his face impassive, but Marty pressed on. "You know exactly what I mean," he said. "This guy is their hero. He's Bishop Tutu and Nelson Mandela rolled into one, and black leaders see him as the best role model they've got for their kids. You pass on this, you've got at least seven states jeopardized—including Illinois and Michigan. You pass on this, and black leaders will be after your hide—especially Maurice Norton."

Maurice Norton was indeed a man to be reckoned with. As the powerful head of the AFL–CIO, he made no secret of his determination to improve the lot of the most endangered age group in America—young black males. Marty leaned closer, the lower part of his jaw almost perceptibly hardening.

"This is *the* black issue right now," he said slowly. "We're going to get ninety to ninety-five percent of that vote, and we can't risk losing any of it—we need it, Luke. Anything else, we've gotta do some hard thinking." He paused for maximum effect. "You want to be the first Democrat to lose the black vote since Stevenson?"

Luke flung his hands out in exasperation. "For Christ's sake, lay off the politics for a minute, will you?" he said. "If this thing is as bad as it smells, I'm not ducking it. Do you understand what Young is telling us? Palmer will be setting up bank accounts in this country as a front to launder drug money and ship it back to the Federation. Do you see the implications?"

Marty hardly paused, speaking fast and bluntly. "Sure, I see the implications," he said. "But I don't trust this guy. I don't think he has any tape. My job is getting you elected. That's what I'm concentrating on, and that's what I intend to do. Enright's picking up points on this, points we can't afford to lose. Everything else comes second. That doesn't mean we don't look closer at this later, but *not now.*

You can do a helluva lot if you're president. And you can't do shit if you lose."

A silence fell. Marty's anger had splashed over the room like a spray of buckshot.

"I'm not going to throw this election away, I can assure you," Luke said finally. "But I *am* listening to Young. And I'm waiting to see if he comes up with that tape before I back Palmer. That's the way it is, Marty."

"Yeah," Marty replied disgustedly. "That's the way it is."

Luke's eyes flickered; he had not missed the intonation. He glanced at his watch. "I should call Kate," he said, half to himself. "She had something on her mind."

Claire searched his face.

Luke raised an eyebrow, as if asking a silent question.

She reached with one hand for his arm, touching it lightly. "I was just thinking," she said, "what a good soldier Kate is."

Suddenly Jackie's head popped through the door, her large eyes urgent.

"Oh, hell," Marty yelled. "Send in the damn storyboards."

Figuring out how to talk to Peter on short notice was a little awkward. Kate finally decided to call and ask him to drop by campaign headquarters before he left for the airport, but an officious-sounding editor answered the phone and immediately recognized her voice. The man's voice turned instantly to butter. He's putting the news room on full alert, Kate thought dryly. It was ridiculously corny, but maybe she should have tried holding her nose. Yes, he assured her, Peter would be there very soon. He, the editor, would make damn sure, Mrs. Goodspeed. Right away. Kate hung up feeling uneasily like a cheat. Peter was probably going to be hauled off another story while his editor salivated over some possible exclusive that didn't exist. She could only hope Peter would understand.

An hour later, Peter walked into the campaign conference room with his tie askew and a black garment bag slung over his shoulder. His eyes had the look of a man with too many things to do in too little a period of time.

"Hi," he said, eying Kate curiously. "What's up?"

157

"Nothing much," she said, nonplused. "I just wanted to talk about a couple of little things before you leave. I haven't seen you since we were preparing to die together." The feeble joke did nothing to erase the curiosity in Peter's eyes.

"You were worried about Abby," he said bluntly.

"That was nothing," she said. "Family stuff."

"Family stuff's important."

She tried to ease the tone of the exchange. "Speaking of family, how are your kids?" she said.

Peter sighed, the sigh of a man who knows he's temporarily on someone else's timetable. He threw his garment bag over the back of a chair, and sat down. "Fine. In Florida with their mother. I don't see them nearly enough."

"I guess politics is as tough on reporters' lives as it is on politicians' families," she ventured.

Peter looked at her with an expression half amused, half exasperated. "It was a lousy marriage, which you already know," he said. "Kate, no offense. But I'm sure you didn't ask to see me to talk about my ex-wife or my kids. What's up?"

"Did you read Ernie Stark's item this morning?" she said.

"I wondered if that was what this little summons was all about," he said, a hint of wariness in his eye.

"Peter, it wasn't a summons." She didn't like the tone of this at all. "I just wanted to talk to you about it. Not for attribution."

"Understood, Kate. Always." Peter had pulled forth a notebook and pen and was looking at her expectantly.

"One of our contributors got too helpful and inadvertently caused us a problem," she began.

Peter sat still, pen in the air. "Sam Olson," he said.

"Yes, how did you know?"

"Hey, it's predictable."

"Well, he picked up the New Orleans hotel bill and never submitted it to the campaign, so there was no FEC filing. One of those crazy things. The campaign just overlooked it."

"So?"

Kate was flustered. "Well, we're filing as fast as we can, and we're hoping the media won't leap all over the story and make it more than it is."

"Oh," Peter said softly. "Who's this 'we'? Kate, I do believe you are trying to exert a little damage control with your old friend Peter."

Kate flushed. "I suppose I am," she said. "What's so terrible about that?"

Peter began tapping on the conference table with his pen, looking past Kate to the wall beside her. "This isn't exactly new information," he said. "Martha Reilly is writing a piece on it for tomorrow."

Kate was thrown off balance. "Well, then, can you—?" above all, don't ask him to exert any influence to change the story—"can you fill her in on the facts?"

"She knows them."

"Maybe she doesn't appreciate how inadvertent it was on our part," she pressed.

"I told you, she's got all the facts."

"We've got a great new environmental ad," Kate said, now badly flustered. "Want a preview?" She felt herself babbling. "Exclusive, naturally."

Peter cast a cynical look at Kate and shook his head. "I'm feeling manipulated, my friend," he said quietly, closing his notebook and tucking it into his outside suit pocket. "I'm not butting in on another reporter's story."

It was his almost pitying look that threw Kate. This was a stupid situation. How could she have let herself get into it?

"I'm sorry, that's not what I'm trying to do," she said stiffly. "There's so much tension now. We're so close—"

Peter stood up to go, the expression in his eyes unchanged. "Marty knew we were doing this piece," he said. "I guess he didn't tell you that. As far as your overly helpful developer friend is concerned, he hasn't done you any good, but he won't destroy the campaign." Peter paused, looking suddenly thoughtful. "My bet is, Stark's got something else cooking," he said.

Kate stiffened. "What do you mean?"

Peter shrugged, then picked up his garment bag and turned to go.

"I don't know," he said. "But Ernie doesn't give a damn about FEC stories; too boring. He probably thinks he's got some hot story."

Kate froze. She had to make Peter stand still for a moment; she had to find out what he knew. "Do you know anything? I mean, could this be something to do with personal things?" she managed.

159

Peter stopped in mid-motion.

"I mean—" Kate found herself hurrying on before he could speak, desperate to find out if Abby was indeed in jeopardy—"could it be anything about—family members, or anything like that?"

"Not that I know of," Peter said slowly, surveying her face.

"You're sure?"

"I'd probably have had some kind of tip, and I don't."

She knew Peter. He was telling the truth. Her stomach quivered with relief. Abby was safe. It was all right. "I can't imagine—" she began.

Peter was staring uncomfortably at a spot above her head, shifting his garment bag as if it had suddenly become an intolerable burden. "I won't ask why you're asking," he said, "because you obviously don't want to tell me. But I'm going to have to follow up on this. You know that."

She nodded.

"If something's bothering you, stay alert."

"What do you mean?" she parried.

"Look, maybe it *is* the FEC." He drew a deep breath and gazed at her kindly. "But you know politics. Just keep your dukes up, pal."

"Peter—"

"I've gotta go. Let's talk later."

Kate was in a fury when she stomped out of headquarters and headed home. Never again would she let herself in for an embarrassment like this. Marty thought he could manipulate everything and everybody. He didn't care if he compromised her with Peter. And Luke! He hadn't seemed concerned. He had responded distractedly, as if his mind were already on other things. Her anger grew hotter, encompassing her husband. How could he have let her in for this? At least she could breathe easier about Abby. Peter had some of the best sources in the country; he would know if something serious was going on. If Stark wasn't hyping the FEC story, it was some other minor tidbit. That's the way he always worked. Lots of innuendo.

She reached the house to be greeted by a disconcerting sight. Joan was standing on the front porch, looking uncharacteristically disheveled. Her hair was tucked back behind her ears and her face, devoid of its usual carefully applied makeup, looked almost childlike.

"Damn it, Kate," she burst out. "I'm the one in this family who causes problems, remember? I'm the one who's supposed to be flailing all over the place, not you and the kids. What am I doing here? I feel like I'm holding you all together!"

"What's the matter?"

"Nat and Abby are fighting like eight-year-olds, and I can't stand either one of them anymore, so I'll see you tomorrow morning, okay?"

Kate relaxed. Here was a situation she could do something about. "I think I can calm them down," she said. "I've got good news." She felt a tight band lift from her chest. Take one thing at a time, she told herself. Abby is safe; and that's the most important thing. "The best there is," she said.

The next morning, Kate stood beside the kitchen table with the coffeepot in her hand and stared inquiringly at Joan. "Want some?"

"With that lumpy sugar of yours? No, thanks."

Kate shoved a box of Sweet 'N Low across the kitchen table toward her sister and proceeded to pour. "This is better for you anyway," she said.

She sat down and moved her chair slightly, stretching comfortably in the warmth of a beam of morning sun pouring through the window. She was in charge again. Being in charge meant being able to *do* something, and finally she had been able to do something that could wipe the pinched tension from the faces of her children. She had faced them head-on and had told them that the secret that bound them so claustrophobically was safe. Ernie Stark, the sleaze, was not going to expose Abby. Abby could pick up the morning newspaper now without wanting to throw up, and Nat could stop fearing the anticipated jibes of his classmates. They had looked at her with such naked relief yesterday when she told them that she herself had looked away. She never again wanted to see those expressions. Never. Kids shouldn't have to deal with what they were dealing with, she said to Joan as she poured the coffee and passed a cup to her sister. Kids—

"So what *was* Stark hinting at?" Joan broke in. "And that better be decaffeinated." She had regained her aplomb and reapplied her lipstick. She, too, was relaxed.

"It is." Kate got up to reach for the milk before answering the rest of the question. "Sam Olson picked up the New Orleans hotel tab for the campaign, and no one caught the mistake until this week," she said. "ABC's doing a piece."

"That's all? How is that personal?"

"A reflection on Luke's character, I suppose."

"Ernie usually does better than that."

"I know."

"It doesn't quite fit."

Kate slumped deeper into the sturdy oak chair. "Well, that's it, anyway," she said, trying to speak with calm finality. Why was she not mentioning Peter's parting remarks, his warning, if that's what it was? Because it all sounded a touch too melodramatic, that was why.

Joan's attention was moving on to other things. "Your kids—"

"Abby is still a baby," Kate said, her brow furrowing, "and Nat is locked up so tight most of the time, he just exploded over this." She sighed. "I understand Abby better, I think. I don't always know what's going on in Nat's head."

"Well, he's pretty withdrawn, and I hate to give you one more thing to worry about, but there it is," Joan said. "He's a shy kid who thinks his father is the greatest hero of the Western world—for as much good as that does him."

"You've been dumping on Luke too much," Kate said, feeling suddenly defensive.

Joan smiled. "Sorry," she said. "But I don't understand the guy anymore. He's never *here*, even when he's here. He's like the guy who steps off the screen in that Woody Allen movie, what was it called?" She paused. "*The Purple Rose of Cairo*, that was it. Let me ask you, does he put the toilet seat down? If he does, I'll like him better."

Kate couldn't suppress a grin. "Yes. He does."

Joan cocked a quizzical eyebrow. "*All* the time?" she demanded.

"Hey, enough. All right?"

"Okay, I'll get a little serious," Joan said with a sigh. "Does he know Nat felt miserable when he flunked his big history test last week? Does he know the kid hides *Playboy* centerfolds under his mattress? And I wasn't snooping, either. Mrs. Leonard found them."

Kate blinked. She hadn't known Nat flunked his exam—she had forgotten to ask. And the centerfolds were a surprise.

A tiny smile hovered over Joan's lips. "New information?" she said.

Kate reacted defensively, almost by instinct. "All young boys do that sort of thing," she said. "It's no big deal."

But Joan was not pushing; instead she casually glanced down at the morning paper. "Hey," she said with a laugh, picking up the front section. "See this ad for Palmer? I've jumped into politics and didn't even know it."

"What are you talking about?"

"Look."

Kate quickly scanned the full-page ad, an emotional tribute to David Palmer, which exhorted Americans to "Join the Organizations Listed Below" and support Palmer as "An Authentic Hero." The endorsements of at least thirty prominent business and civil rights organizations filled half the page.

"See?" Joan pointed at the name of one of the organizations, the Black Education League. "They provide scholarships for urban black kids. It's Maurice Norton's baby, and my favorite charity." She laughed again. "I support them, probably single-handedly."

"Joan," Kate said, feeling cautious, "this might not be good for Luke."

Joan's eyes widened in surprise. "Why not?" she asked.

"Because he's worried about Palmer," Kate said. "He apparently isn't the hero American blacks want him to be." She hesitated. "I'm sorry. I can't fill you in on the details. Not yet."

Joan's surprise turned quickly to indignation. "I get it," she said. "This ad is supposed to put pressure on Luke to endorse Palmer, right?"

Kate nodded.

"Maurice knows damn well I give a lot of money to the League," Joan said, half to herself. "He's thanked me often enough." She drummed her meticulously burnished nails on the table and frowned. "I'm being used," she said suddenly.

"I don't know if you are, but it looks a bit odd."

Joan snorted. "They figure I'll pressure Luke to come around," she said. "Either that, or people will find out I'm part of that ad campaign and he'll be embarrassed."

Kate couldn't help a smile. "For someone who hates politics, you figure things out pretty fast," she said.

"Sister dear, if you have as much money as I do, you develop a sixth sense about being used."

"What are you going to do?"

"Get Maurice to take the League off that list or withdraw my money," Joan said promptly.

"Don't do anything too quickly," Kate said. "It might make it worse."

"I'll follow your lead," Joan said with an impatient shrug. "But I'm really pissed." She sighed. "I'm probably too involved with your life now anyway. I guess I'm at loose ends these days." She stretched out her small frame and ran restless fingers through her disheveled hair, tousling it further. "I've married an Italian and a Protestant and written two books on interior design and bought and sold four houses and collected more antique armoires than anyone needs in a life-time," she said, half to herself. "I've endowed hospitals, hosted AIDS benefits, and supported several designers, and I'm bored." She looked up at her sister good-naturedly. "I sure don't mean to be dumping on you about the kids, sis."

Kate smiled in spite of herself. "I think you're mellowing out remarkably," she said.

"I've got to go back to living up to my reputation," Joan said. "Maybe I need a new husband. Or another book." Her eyes suddenly sparked. "By the way, I hear Sam Olson is getting a divorce."

"Joan, don't you dare even *think* of it."

"Don't worry, I'm waiting for the perfect man. He's probably not born yet, but I've given him a name."

"And what's that?"

"Sean. Sean Martin, actually. A perfect name."

Kate laughed. "If he hasn't been born yet, can he be a baby first?"

"If he's a *cute* baby."

They were both laughing when the phone rang.

"Kate?"

She didn't want to hear Steve's voice. It was beginning to feel cloying, almost sticky, like burrs attached to her clothing, and Kate had an uncivil urge to push him away.

"Hi, Steve. What can I do for you?" She made her voice brisk, impersonal, rushed.

"I need to talk to you," he said. "Things are getting worse. Marty's out to get me for good."

There it was, that raw desperation again. How long could she hold this man's hand?

"I've done what I can, Steve," she said.

"I know that, I'm not expecting a miracle. Look—I want to explain some things. I don't want to cause you any trouble."

"That's not going to happen."

"Marty's not the guy to get Luke elected," Steve said feelingly. "It isn't enough to be Machiavellian."

"Steve—I really have to go."

"Just a few minutes, Kate. Please."

The burrs were multiplying, sticking everywhere. Kate was torn between old loyalties and a growing dislike for a situation she could do nothing about. He had to get it through his head that she had done all she could.

"Look, I can only spare about twenty minutes."

"The Roma Café, in fifteen minutes—is that okay?"

Kate thought quickly of the old Washington landmark restaurant on Connecticut Avenue with its jungle murals and the fierce tiger and bear standing guard at the door. It was a busy place in the evening but usually deserted in the late afternoon. Her watchdog agents could have coffee in a back booth, and it was better than telling Steve to come to the house. It might be hard to get rid of him then.

"Okay."

Joan studied her sister as she pulled on a coat. "Be careful," she said. "I think that guy's over the edge."

"I feel guilty, I don't know why," Kate said, her eyes troubled. "I've talked to Luke, but he's too busy to pay attention."

"The point is, you can't help him."

"I want to do something," Kate said. "I just wish he wouldn't act so much like a victim. It makes me nervous."

"A little projection, maybe?"

Irritated, Kate pulled the door shut behind her with an extra tug. She hadn't bothered to answer.

Steve looks more haunted than ever, Kate thought as she slipped into one of the Roma's red leather booths. His jowls had sagged alarmingly, robbing his features of a sharpness that used to convey authority. She felt again the stirrings of pity. Maybe he never had had the right stuff for a national campaign.

"Marty's going to fire me," Steve blurted out without preamble, his voice low.

"I haven't heard that," Kate said, startled. She wished instantly that Luke had prepared her.

"They won't tell you, because you'd get Luke to stop it," Steve said.

"Steve. I'm sorry." What else could she say?

"Luke's been brainwashed by Marty, that bastard," Steve said desperately. "Trust me, Kate. I know. Marty wants me dumped now so I'm out of the way before there's a chance for something at the White House."

"You've worked long and hard for us," Kate said quietly. It wasn't fair. Maybe it was smart, maybe it was necessary. But it wasn't fair. "I'll do what I can to help you if you decide to start looking for another job." She said it as gently as she could.

Steve's eyes shifted away. "Are you telling me something, Kate?"

"If it's done, it's done," she said. "It's probably time for you to—to look for other options."

She quickly saw her mistake.

"Look for other options!" Steve said, his voice mocking. "Have you been brainwashed, too?"

Kate felt suddenly defensive. "Steve," she said. "I can't make them want you. Maybe what I'm saying sounds harsh, but I want to help you understand that and move on. You've got to make the next move yourself."

An anger was simmering, an anger she had never seen him display. "Oh, I've tried," he said sharply. "I've tried."

Kate forced herself to pause and study Steve's face. It had the strange, rough look of an unfinished drawing where the details don't quite add up to a whole. The furrows in his forehead had deepened markedly, giving him the appearance of being in constant pain. More than that, he had developed a habit of clenching and unclenching his hands in a despairing, wringing motion, the motion of a man with nowhere to go. She needed to be very tactful.

Then she made a second mistake. "Maybe you've worked too long for Luke," she said in what she hoped was a gentle manner. "Maybe it's not healthy. What I'm saying is, you have to take charge of your own life."

Steve studied her from under half-lowered lids.

"Can you take this plain?" he said quietly. "Marty's destroying me, and Luke is letting it happen. You think about it. I've spent a lot of years paving the way for Luke and shaping him up for this race. Now he's remote, removed—up on his goddamn mountain, and I'm expendable. Luke doesn't need me anymore. And when he doesn't need somebody these days, they go off his screen."

Kate found herself checking out the location of the suddenly comforting presence of the Secret Service. The two agents were idly sipping coffee on the other side of the restaurant, looking incongruously small under the huge stuffed head of a wild-eyed deer. They were not looking directly at her, which was just as well.

"I'm not going to sit here and have you talk about Luke that way," she said. "He's my husband, and he's a fine man. You're over the line, Steve. If you're going to talk like this, I can't help you."

"Well, you just listen to me," he said with escalating intensity, his eyes as unnaturally bright as those of the dead deer on the wall. "You think you're protected? Well, you're not." There was an ominous quality in his words that Kate could not ignore. Steve paused, then, "That's all I'm going to say."

"You're going to explain that statement, and then I'm heading out the door," she said, just as fiercely. "You've no right to do this."

Steve slumped back in the booth, considering. Then he straightened up.

"Read Ernie Stark's column this morning?"

"Yes, and I know what it's all about."

"Do you, now?"

"Yes, I do." She could show no anxiety, no tentativeness.

Steve appeared first to be struggling within himself, and then something won. "Oh, no, you don't," he said. "All I can say to you is, keep an eye on your husband." He started to rise, and she had to stop herself from grabbing at his jacket sleeve.

"You've lost it, Steve," she said.

"I've lost it?" He was standing now, looking down at her with an expression born of months of accumulated fury. "No," he said. "Luke has. All my life he's been Mr. Morality. The man you could

167

count on to be a straight arrow. Decent. Well, not since Marty and Claire took over his life. Especially Claire."

"What are you saying?"

"What I'm saying is, Claire has her claws in Luke, and he isn't fighting it. I saw a few little scenes in New Orleans when they didn't think anyone was looking. He'll be fucking her any day now, if he isn't already. And if you don't believe me, you'll end up the same way I did—trusting this guy and believing in him, and then you'll get shot down, too."

"I don't believe a word you are saying!"

"Your problem, Kate. Not mine."

"Get out of here," she managed to say through clenched teeth.

"Happy to oblige."

For all his anger, there were tears in Steve's eyes as he turned on his heel and strode out of the restaurant.

8

It wasn't possible to put the scene in the Roma aside, no matter how hard she tried. She drove home, shaken by the ferocity of Steve's despair, her feelings alternating between pity and anger, asking herself how he dared try to rip apart and stomp on the person who had done more for him than anybody else in the world. She ground her teeth, her dentist's warning against the habit forgotten, and only slowly, reluctantly faced the fact that she wasn't able to totally block out Steve's words.

Kate pulled up to the curb in front of the house, stepped out, and locked the car. She did not want to dwell on the certitude she had heard in his voice. But that certitude, echoing in her head, drove her to the telephone.

She dialed campaign headquarters, reminding herself to keep her voice light and pleasant. Yes, she told the head of scheduling, she knew she was expected for campaign appearances in Minnesota and Wisconsin, but something had come up, and instead she would be joining Luke in Oregon. No, Marty had not been informed. She could hear the rapid shuffling of paper on the other end of the line, a muffled consultation with an aide.

"Kate, we just can't do that," said the scheduling head in a horrified voice. "You're expected at a fund-raiser for the governor in Minneapolis and—"

"But I *am* going to do it. That's what I'm telling you."

More whispering at the other end, then the scheduler's voice again. "This poses a major problem for us," she said. Her tone had turned crisp.

Well, Kate said, she knew that was true, and it was certainly too bad. But there it was. And would the scheduler do Kate a favor? Inform Marty that he needn't bother calling, because she was leaving on a five o'clock commercial flight. Thank you very much. And goodbye.

Kate hardly needed to acknowledge to herself that the head of scheduling probably now, at this moment, wanted to wring her neck. The words the staff would be bandying about at headquarters were easy enough to guess. Thoughtless. Irresponsible. Probably imperious, too. She stared out the window at the almost bare limbs of the oak tree, knowing one thing, and knowing it fully. She had to see Luke.

Marty made no attempt to stop her. The flight to Portland went smoothly. It was oddly relieving to be on a scheduled flight for a change instead of on a campaign charter, and she found herself puzzling that one out. At first it felt more comfortable because she could observe people who weren't totally focused on her presence. But after the plane took off, when Kate settled back into her seat with her thoughts, a numbing wave of loneliness swept through her. There was no one here she could turn to, no one here who would ever understand. She didn't believe Steve's smarmy charges, not for a minute; this was politics, just smarmy politics. Kate lowered her head to hide her eyes. I want someone to hug me, she thought. I want to be told everything's all right. Carefully she forced herself to sort through the events of the last few days. What was Ernie Stark hinting at? It wasn't the stupid filing flap, she knew that, maybe she had known it right away, even before Peter rejected it so flatly. I'm being conned, she thought. But why? About what? Marty liked secrets for the sake of secrets; it didn't have to be something major for him to play cute games. She had been so focused on keeping Abby safe, she had been missing things. Maybe I'm conning myself, she thought. I can't stand Claire, I'd believe anything about her, and that's the truth. The loneliness was deepening, actually chilling her bones.

"Excuse me, are you using that blanket?" she asked timidly of her seatmate. A large man, about mid-thirties, with carefully trimmed hair, lifted his head from a magazine and turned toward her. "No, go ahead," he said. "Please. It's yours." He peered into her face, and Kate braced for the inevitable moment of recognition. "Are you all right?" he asked, a frown of concern on his face. "Want me to get the stewardess to bring you some coffee?"

"No, thank you, I'm fine." She smiled gratefully as she wrapped herself in the blanket. He was still looking at her, still concerned, and suddenly she realized she didn't want him to go back to his magazine.

"Are you from Oregon?" she asked.

They chatted off and on for the rest of the flight. He was a computer programmer, a Republican, his name was David Roper, and he had three children. No, he had not recognized her, he acknowledged after a while, not at first. Yes, he and his wife loved Oregon. A great life, but they only hoped they'd have enough money to send their children to college when the time came. Kate felt her spirits rise. Was he aware of the modified voucher plan her husband had proposed for improving the public schools? And Luke's college tuition plan for young families? No, he was not. It sounded interesting. By the time the 747 landed at Portland Airport, David Roper was her friend. They exchanged warm handshakes, wishing each other good luck, and Kate had an instant of insanity when she wanted impulsively to ask if she could, please, follow him home for dinner. Just to bask in unconditional approval for a few more hours, that's all. Would his wife have a fire ready in the fireplace? Could she toast her toes, please, and expound a little more on the urgent needs of secondary education?

Wistfully she watched him go. When, she asked herself, will I be able again to do something so relaxing, so quiet, so normal as to visit a real home, and sit in front of a real fire, to do nothing but talk and laugh with real friends? There was no answer for her question, so she turned her attention to a car and two fresh, watchful agents waiting for her just outside the terminal entrance. Kate half expected a baffled Luke brooding in the backseat, which was ridiculous, of course; he had better things to do than sit out at the airport waiting for her. Instead she found an overly polite aide who greeted her with the caution of a diver approaching a shark. The signals were out, obviously. The imperious Kate Goodspeed had decided on a whim to go to Oregon, and cared not a whit that she had wrecked the campaign's schedule. Back in Washington, she knew, aides were scrambling to make up excuses for her canceled trip and probably fending off curious reporters who knew that in a presidential campaign the schedule was law. Unless something better came along, of course. Nobody liked to admit it, but a speech to the Boy Scouts of America was always dumpable for a last-minute invitation from, say, "Nightline."

Kate gazed from the window at the soft rain falling on the Douglas firs, hardly hearing the nervous aide prattle on about a few quick appearances she had lined up for Kate's "unexpected" appearance in Oregon. The onstage part of her brain simply was not engaged at the moment. She was feeling uneasy and revved up for battle, but against what? Luke would think it funny; he would have a joke or two about her impulsive nature, but her behavior wasn't at all professional at the moment. She rubbed her ear; it hurt. I'm catching a cold on top of everything else, she thought. I'd better not kiss Luke directly on the lips; he can't afford to get sick. He would laugh at that, of course. Luke was convinced no germ could ever lay him low, and so far he had been right, scorning all the vitamin C Kate religiously took every day. I'm more fearful than he is, she thought. I want safety. If you really do, said a small interior voice, what are you doing *here?* Precisely, her brain replied.

Nat's diffident, worried face rose next in her brain, and she felt a surge of gratitude to Joan for stepping in to stay while she took this trip, no questions asked. I must focus more closely on Nat, she thought. I must watch and understand more and try to get inside his head. It was different with Abby; she could make a more visceral connection with her daughter. There were things a boy needed that she couldn't wholly give, and even if that wasn't the way it should be in a perfect, nongender-conscious world, that's the way it was. Kate sighed. This was a child who immersed himself in video games, and neither she nor Luke understood the world he entered when he played.

She brooded about Claire. So smart, so competent, and undeniably beautiful—all things that brought her considerable admiration. Was she, Kate, just jealous? Was it that simple? She leaned her cheek against the cool dampness of the window and reminded herself, as she had been doing since she left the Roma Café, that she could not take seriously a man who was obviously sick, a man made vindictive by defeat. Steve was lashing out at anything and anybody, and she mustn't lose sight of that.

Oh, whispered the small voice deep inside, there's nothing new about women being attracted to Luke. You know that. That's a fact of life. Be real. Kate sat very still until a slight wave of nausea passed. Yes, she had seen more than her share of women circling her husband like delicate vultures. It was certainly within the realm of possibility that something might have happened, or almost happened—she chose not to finish the thought. No, it wasn't unthinkable. Lord, after all her years in Washington, she knew better. The older Senate wives, the ones with marbled hairdos and set smiles, used to counsel the younger wives over tea in the Senate Dining Room. Watch for signs of trouble, they would murmur under the chatter of voices, but, my dear, always know when to confront and when to look the other way. Kate would smile and murmur back appreciatively, feeling sorry for these women. The truth was, she knew, they spent their lives looking the other way.

But then again, surely she was acting precipitately. It was the strain of the campaign, the strain of other worries. Luke would not do anything that would jeopardize the trust between them. They knew each other too well; they loved each other too much. Anybody else; not Luke. Even if for some terrible reason he was tempted, wouldn't the fact that he was running for president stop him? Oh, quit being so pragmatic, said the inside voice most capable of dealing lethal blows to her heart. He wouldn't do it to *you*, not ever.

She straightened her back, rubbed her ear again, and tried to focus on the aide. "Could you please get me some ear drops, something for an earache?" she said. "Try the hotel drugstore, okay?" The aide nodded, made a note.

The rain was falling heavily by the time the car reached the Benson Hotel in downtown Portland. Kate moved through the elegant lobby, past the dark polished woods of the graceful staircase, fingering the key to Luke's room provided her by the aide.

"Senator Goodspeed's in Eugene for a speech and won't be back until after eleven o'clock," the aide said upon giving her the key. "We've let him know you're here, so he's expecting you. Can I order dinner for your room?"

173

Kate shook her head, anxious to free herself from his presence. "I'm fine," she said. And now, she thought, punching the elevator button, I wonder how many phone messages will be up there from Marty?

"Kate—what are you doing here?"

She wheeled around, flushing as she recognized the voice. There was Peter, standing almost directly behind her.

"A change of plans," she said, punching again for the elevator.

"That's funny," Peter said lightly. "You're supposed to be in Minnesota. What's up?"

"Don't grill me, please." It felt good to snap out the words instead of contriving an evasive answer. It felt absolutely wonderful for about ten seconds, and then Kate wished she could recall them.

Peter moved swiftly to her side and drew her back from the elevator. "That was not a response from the candidate's wife," he said gently. "That was Kate Sullivan. What's wrong? Can I help?"

"Peter, I'm sorry," she said, pushing his hand away. "I'm just embarrassed."

"Because Marty set you up to manipulate me? Hey, forget it. You didn't know. Why are you here?"

Her earache was getting worse; where was that aide with the ear drops? She didn't dare let herself crumble in front of Peter. She didn't dare burden him with her fears and concerns; it wasn't right. How could she get him to pull away? "Right now," she said stiffly, "I wish you'd just leave me alone."

Peter, looking genuinely concerned, hesitated at the rebuff. The elevator doors were opening, and she moved forward.

"I'm not trying to get a story," he said. "I just want to know what's wrong, and whether I can do anything to help."

The elevator doors were closing, and Kate felt suddenly torn. A few minutes of conversation, a little lightheartedness—maybe she would feel better.

No.

"I'm sorry," she said. "This is private." The metal doors pulled together with a final muted thud and he was gone.

The red light on the telephone was blinking as ominously as the light on an approaching police cruiser. Kate picked up the phone and called the desk.

"Three calls for you, Mrs. Goodspeed, from Marty Apple," the hotel operator said brightly. "He said to call him before you do anything; it was urgent." The operator, impressed with her own message, paused to let its importance sink in.

"Anything else?" Kate asked.

"A call from Claire for the senator," the operator replied. "No—make that two."

"Thank you very much." Kate cradled the phone and decided to wait for Marty's next call.

"Kate! Glad I got you, how are you, kid? Missed Luke, huh?" Marty's voice was hearty, projecting just the right note of concern.

"I have to talk to him," she said.

"Nothing so terrible about that." His voice was still hearty. "Anything wrong?"

He's worried, she thought. That jolted her. "We've been apart too much," she said, keeping her voice conversational.

"Hey, so what's new?"

"Steve came to me—it's private, Marty."

"Spreading rumors. Right?"

"What are you implying?" she said cautiously.

"Snide stuff, I'll bet. Hanky-panky."

His words cheapened her fears, leaving her more uneasy. "Are you talking about something I should know?"

"I'm just telling you, you've been hearing the sneakiest kind of campaign gossip. Am I wrong?"

"This is between Luke and me."

Marty apparently chose not to hear. "Steve's no pillar of truth," he said. "Fact is, he's full of shit."

"Look—"

"Believe me. You're hearing the rantings of a guy who's over the edge. He didn't dump it on you calmly, I'll bet."

"He was furious."

"And lying."

Kate paused to consider. "Luke and I will talk about it," she said. It seemed important to break through Marty's proprietary tone.

"I hope you'll take my advice and go easy on this," Marty said. He

175

was less hearty, more tactful. "We've got other problems, and Luke needs your support right now."

"Because of the FEC filing? That's a red herring, Marty."

"No, not that." Marty's voice became brisk, businesslike. "Enright's capitalizing on Luke's stall on Palmer. Did you see his new ad?"

"Not yet."

"He's getting good handling; Luke's right, he's developing some fire. He really wants the job. Then we've got one of those damn little land mines that pop up every now and then. Luke doesn't know this yet, but the cardinal is using Delancey to take another swipe at him."

"Why?"

"Are you ready?" Marty paused for effect. "Luke's mother stirred them up."

"What?"

"She told a reporter today that her son has every right to say what he thinks and that the Church should get its nose out of politics."

Kate laughed in spite of herself. "Good old Louise," she said.

"It may sound funny, but they're mad," Marty said. "They've got Father Jello—"

"Don't call him that."

"Suit yourself," he said. "Delancey's being hauled out for an anti-abortion rally in downtown Chicago next Saturday, which, naturally, makes it an anti-Goodspeed event. They've got us in a squeeze, you know. You and Luke will be on the podium with Kovach in Chicago that night for the Catholic Interracial Council dinner, so you'd better brace for a chilly reception. You see what I'm saying, don't you?" He paused again.

"Marty, I don't need a primer on how to act when things get politically touchy."

"I'm counting on it." Marty's voice lost its bossy tone, and she found it impossible to ignore the real feeling she heard over the wire. "He's awfully close to the biggest prize of his life—and yours," he said. "Remember that."

The energy was draining from Kate, and she had to get off the phone.

"I know what I have to do," she said. "Goodnight."

Hours went by. Was it one in the morning? Two o'clock? Kate smelled the woodsy scent of Luke's after-shave before opening her eyes, and waited, groggy and confused from sleep. What was supposed to happen now? She couldn't remember.

"Kate, Kate. Marty told me you were here."

Luke's strong hands were bundling her close, pulling her from the chair where she had collapsed in sleep, half carrying her to the bed.

"What time is it?" she managed to ask.

"Eleven-thirty, Oregon time," he said. "Two-thirty in the morning, Washington time. You must be exhausted."

Kate was waking up now. She could feel the ache in her stomach, the tension in her head again. She wanted to sleep, to forget this.

"Do you know why I'm here?" she asked.

"Tell me." He put a hand under her chin and tilted her head upward, holding her gaze. His eyes were grave and dark, burdened with weariness. She felt a sting of concern.

"You don't look well," she said.

"I'm just tired," he said. "The days are going faster and faster, and we've got to be able to turn on a dime now more than ever before." He took his hand away and began to smooth out the hollows beneath his eyes, rubbing so hard the skin pulled downward, flattening out the planes of his face. "We've got a sticky problem coming up with the cardinal again," he continued. "Can you believe my mother? She's so contrite, she's ready to throw herself in front of him for mercy."

"What did you tell her?"

"I told her to stay off the damn phone," Luke replied. His voice was dry. "We've got a debate coming up and a new ad campaign and Enright is going to grab any ammunition he can get. I'm lucky I've got Marty, he keeps a cool head when things get rough. Did I tell you about Enright's new ad?" All this he said rapidly and with increasing vigor as he stood and began to pace.

Kate did not want to be pulled into a discussion of the latest campaign crisis. "Steve came to me with a terrible story," she said, and then simply could not go on.

Luke looked surprised, then noncommittal.

177

"Shoot," he said.

"I've never asked you this before," Kate said quietly. "It's the corniest question in the world, but I have to know the answer." This was even harder than she had expected. "Are you having an affair?"

She couldn't say Claire's name.

Luke stopped dead, his gesticulating hand poised in midair. "Marty was right," he said. "Steve's lost it. I'm firing him."

So Marty had already briefed him. Kate waited, too proud to ask the question again.

"No." Luke's face was calm, his eyes heavy with new fatigue.

"It's not true?"

"It's not true."

What more did she want? She should let go of this right here—not one more word—and then she felt the words coming anyway. Something, she thought irritably, is wrong with the circuitry in my brain.

"He said it was Claire." She hoped he would laugh.

Instead, Luke held her at arm's length, surveying her as if she were a ball of tangled string to be untied. "You're fixated on Claire," he said. He seemed to speak out of genuine puzzlement. "Isn't there enough going on, Kate? Do you have to give me this to worry about?"

"I'm sorry." The words were automatic, deeply ingrained, quick to surface. I was born saying them, Kate thought. Did any woman ever manage to root them out of her psyche? If so, she would like to know the secret.

"Honey, Claire is an asset, not an enemy," Luke said in a milder tone. "How do I convince you of that? I wish you didn't feel so eternally in competition. That's it, isn't it?" He didn't pause for an answer. "She's a solid, sensitive person, and she's helped me—you, too—a lot. I'll tell you something—" He paused.

"I'm listening."

"Remember when she backed me on the abortion statement?"

And when I didn't, Kate finished silently. But she nodded.

"Well," Luke continued, "she told me why later. This may surprise you." He paused. "Claire had a miscarriage. A few years ago."

Kate opened her mouth to say, yes, she did know, but Luke went on.

178

"She feels a terrible sense of loss," he said. This was said so feelingly, an astonished Kate could not interrupt.

"She cried," Luke went on. "Can you believe it? Strong, tough Claire Lorenzo? She said it was the worst loss she ever experienced."

Oh, this was too much. "Worse than her husband's suicide?"

Luke's eyes opened wide. "Jesus, Kate. What sort of nasty crack is that?"

"I just wondered."

"They were about to separate."

"I'm sorry." There was no way out of a second apology.

Luke appeared not to have heard. He sat down on the side of the bed and began stroking Kate's forehead. "There's a lot more to Claire than you give her credit for," he said. "And she's an enormous asset to me. Please remember, we've got a lot at stake here."

Kate closed her eyes and gave herself over to the gentle pressure of her husband's hands. It was time to be soft, not strident, and she stretched out on the bed, her arms encircling. His lovemaking was elaborate, drawn out; maybe a little too elaborate. She knew Luke on the campaign trail. When he was hitting four and five states a day, giving speech after speech, he didn't perform like a fantasy lover at night. Stop complaining, you idiot, she told herself. Still, where in heaven's name did he get the energy?

"Hold me," he whispered afterward, pulling her to the warmth of his side of the bed. She rubbed his back, scratching gently with her fingernails, and he promptly fell asleep. Kate lay still, staring out the hotel window. It was strange to think she shouldn't be here. She had traveled across the country for comfort and certainly had no complaints about what she had found. But here she was, lying next to her husband, feeling like a kid skipping school. And there had been, yes, there had been a sense of unreality about their conversation and their lovemaking. Kate tried to grin to herself in the dark, because what she was thinking should be funny, and it also probably explained all her niggling anxieties—except it felt weird.

"We weren't on the schedule," she whispered.

The air from the open hotel window the next morning smelled fresh and clean, free of haze and fog. Kate inhaled deeply and breathed out, wishing she could package the air and move it to

Washington. Her doubts seemed totally small and silly in the sunlight. Luke moved rapidly around the room, dressing to leave, as they talked quickly in the kind of shorthand they used to cover a lot of ground as fast as possible. Impressions, polls, attitudes, staff problems. Family. She told him Nat had flunked his history exam and felt very bad, and Luke's brow furrowed in concern. He promised to call Nat that night, to bring him on the next campaign swing—could he afford to be out of school for an entire week? If not, a day together next Sunday. Then he looked at his week's schedule and quickly amended his promise. Half a day. A library dedication, damn it. Kate sighed; Luke ruffled her hair and kissed her neck.

"Joan's furious at Norton," Kate said. "Did you see the Palmer ad? She funds the Black Education League."

"Yeah, I know," Luke said. "She told Marty. She should sit tight and do nothing, okay?"

Kate nodded. Luke was clearly reluctant to talk more.

"It's what I suspected earlier," he said. "I'm probably going to be sticking my neck out alone on this one."

"Not alone, Luke." She studied him for a moment; hesitated, then made up her mind. "Luke—" she felt compelled to say this—"don't fire Steve."

"I have to; he's nuts."

"Maybe," Kate said, "but we have to get him medical help—something."

"Don't worry," Luke said. "I'll handle it." He smiled at her. "Glad you're here," he said gently. He pushed back a wisp of hair from her forehead. "Are you sticking with me for a while?" His voice was casual, welcoming. Not a word of chastisement for kicking over her schedule. "If you are, I'm heading for Los Angeles tonight."

The sun from the window now filled the room, and Kate felt acutely embarrassed about the abrupt nature of her impromptu trip. Luke was being gentle, but there was something she had to face. She shouldn't be here; she should never have come. She wasn't doing her job.

"I suppose I could still make that dinner in Minnesota," she said. "Although why a Democratic governor in Minnesota needs help getting reelected, I don't know."

"You feel like it? Are you sure? Marty would fall on his knees and kiss your feet," Luke said, grinning. "Rest here for a while. If you decide to go with me, I'll see you on the plane after the rally this morning. If not, good luck in Minnesota."

When Luke left, Kate took a long shower and made up her mind. Dripping wet, she stepped from the bathtub and picked up the phone. No problem, a cheery voice at Luke's local office said. We'll have you on a plane within an hour, Mrs. Goodspeed.

Kate got out of the hotel without running into Peter again and made the Minnesota dinner in time to nibble at a heavy custard dessert soaked in brandy that kept her up most of the night. The governor was most appreciative of her presence, and Kate, in a fine burst of energy, shook hands with every important Democrat in the room before leaving.

Her conscience was easing. The best kind of absolution, she told herself, comes from hard work.

The next morning, leaning her head back and closing her eyes on a plane back to Washington, she felt more tired than she had ever felt before.

The week went by quickly. Kate was back in the good graces of the scheduling department, and, just to make sure she stayed there, she took on a few extra campaign stops for the end of the week. San Jose. Tucson. A social workers' conference in Philadelphia. The lining in her coat pocket, recently resewn after falling apart under the weight of hotel room keys she kept forgetting to turn back in, ripped again. Back home, Nat retook his history test and passed it on Thursday, a feat he proudly announced when his father called. Luke was properly enthusiastic, although he threw in a little lecture on studying harder next time.

By Friday, the week had changed from a nightmare to a tour de force for Kate. She was back in a world she could handle, and things were clicking. The tempo was picking up in the campaign, reaching that classic point of semi-hysteria that signaled an end in sight. Now the newspapers were printing polls every day—CBS–New York Times one day, ABC–Washington Post the next, NBC–Wall Street Journal the day after that. They all showed the same thing. Luke's margin was narrow and increasing slightly—but no breakthrough. Anything less than a 4 percent lead was within the statistical margin of error, so neither side was celebrating. Maybe running for president

Patricia O'Brien

shouldn't be easy, Kate told herself on the plane back from Philadelphia; maybe you have to suffer. She foraged fretfully in her purse for her inflatable pillow. But she was disappointed, uneasy, at the closeness of the race. She wanted a nice, comfortable coast into Election Day, naturally, and if *that* wasn't the mark of a spoiled baby, she didn't know what was.

"Jerry," she said loudly, over the engines of the small, bucking plane. "Where is my pillow?"

Jerry dived for a black satchel under the seat. "I brought an extra one," he said with good cheer. "I don't know what you do with them, Kate—eat them?"

"My coat pocket's torn again," she mumbled, watching Jerry inflate the limp piece of plastic he pulled from the bag. She needed a nap. She definitely needed a nap. Gratefully she took the rubber pillow and settled back, her eyes closed.

"Jerry," she said, "what would I do without you?"

It was her good deed for the day. Now, sleep.

Friday night, finally home, Kate pulled on a comfortable set of old sweats and sat down to watch herself on MacNeil-Lehrer. Abby curled up tight on the sofa next to her, and together they watched as Kate's face flashed on the screen.

"The pace of the campaign seems to be taking a toll on the candidate's wife," Jim Lehrer said in a quick voice-over. "Mrs. Goodspeed is a veteran campaigner, but these days she's looking a little hollow-eyed and frazzled. Perhaps that's why she made an unscheduled midweek trip to Oregon to see her husband, a needed break for what campaign manager Marty Apple described as—" Lehrer paused, offering an amused smile with the words—"as a little conjugal rest and recreation."

"You did look kind of—um, tired," Abby volunteered when the piece was over.

"Naw," said Nat loyally. "Maybe just a little, that's all."

But it was true, she didn't look good. Kate peered at the television screen and decided she looked every minute of her forty-five years, which shouldn't be quite as upsetting as it was. She liked the fact that the country knew her age, she had told Luke; it made her much less self-conscious out on the stump. She liked it most of the time, but not tonight. She looked worse than frazzled, she thought. She looked dumpy.

182

That's what made Joan's surprise suggestion the next morning sound like such a great idea.

The two sisters sat together with Nat and Abby, eating breakfast, Kate glumly watching another piece of unflattering tape of herself on "Good Morning, America."

Joan watched her, chewing thoughtfully on a stale corn muffin. "Look, you've got a rare day free before going to Chicago for that supper with the cardinal," she said. "So why don't we go shopping? Buy you some clothes? Maybe get some concealer to hide those bags under your eyes?"

This was sudden. Go to a store? Shop in the middle of a campaign? "Do I look that bad?"

Joan ignored her question. "It's better than hanging around in this den of technology," she said.

The fax machine, a no-nonsense steel presence in the middle of the kitchen, suddenly rang and clicked on.

Joan jumped. "How can you stand that thing?" she asked.

Kate walked over to scan the first sheet out of the machine— a statement for her to approve for the Muscular Dystrophy Association's annual fund-raising banquet. "Can't do without it," she said.

Mrs. Leonard bustled in and handed Kate a package. "From the office," she said. "They want to know which shots you want in the new brochure."

"Why do you need another brochure?" Joan asked.

"It's for Texas," Kate said absentmindedly, paging quickly through the shots. "Give them this one," she said, and handed the package back to Mrs. Leonard. She walked over again to the fax machine.

Joan sighed. "Let's get out of here," she said. Her voice took on a playful quality. "Think of the expressions on the faces of the Secret Service when you tell them we're headed for Neiman Marcus. They'll die."

"I think it's a great idea, Mother," Abby said with sudden enthusiasm. "Can I have the Special K?"

Kate passed the box of cereal. Why not? She had a few precious free hours. The day was crisp and beautiful, the sun was shining through the kitchen window, the kids' spirits were up, the polls were holding steady, and it was ridiculous to spend the day worrying about being snubbed by the cardinal.

183

Joan looked up with another thought. "Is Maurice Norton coming to this dinner tonight?"

Kate nodded. "I think so," she said.

A small smile worked its way across Joan's face. "Well, what do you know," she said softly. "Think I'll tag along for the trip."

Kate wasn't really listening; she was savoring the idea of shopping. "I could use some new things, I guess," she said slowly. "I haven't been in a real store in over a year."

It was more than just the fun of seeing a lot of clothes at one time and buying what *she* wanted instead of what a shopper chose and sent over. She wanted to feel pretty again, to notice what she put on when she dressed at 6:00 A.M. in a hotel room. She was tired of plain winter suits with skirts long enough to cover her knees when she sat. And she would never get the stain out of the dress she dumped the orange juice on flying through that awful ice storm over Chicago. Her bras—well, fortunately no photographers ever saw the tired state *they* were in.

Mrs. Leonard, looking harassed, a thin bead of sweat on her upper lip, walked back into the room.

"Mr. Spanos is on the intercom," she said. "He wants to know if you want the manicurist this morning."

"No," Kate said, feeling a little testy. Did Jerry have to respond quite so quickly to Jim Lehrer's report? "I'm going out shopping. I don't want my nails done today."

Joan laughed. "What a crazy life you lead," she said. "You need a new sofa, and instead you've got a manicurist."

"Plus I have to have my roots done twice as often," Kate said, grinning. "I hope my hair survives the campaign."

She had made up her mind. "How do we do this without causing a riot?" she asked.

"Leave it to me," Joan said with casual confidence. "Remember? I'm a born shopper. *I'll* set it up with Neiman Marcus. *You* get to tell the Secret Service."

It *was* a big deal, Kate told herself later as the smiling manager of the store escorted them from the front door of the store on Wisconsin Avenue to the escalator. Red silk ribbons had been hastily strung between the Estée Lauder and Elizabeth Arden cosmetics counters to mark a path, and curious shoppers were watching and murmuring as Kate and Joan entered. Waiting photographers snapped their pictures, setting off little festive pops of light. This was everyday stuff for people like Princess Diana and the Queen of England. But walking between the ribbons, amidst the scents of powders, perfumes, and soft leathers, Kate suddenly felt like a child playing dress-up once again, a pretend queen walking in pretend royal robes, smiling regally at her subjects. Keep your head, it must be the red ribbons, she decided with some amusement. They certainly added a fantasy quality. But wasn't her whole life right now something of a fantasy? This wasn't the real Kate walking through Neiman Marcus. The real Kate came rushing in on Saturday mornings in a pair of jeans and sneakers to check out the sale racks before treating herself to a frozen yogurt downstairs. The real Kate loved looking at Chanel handbags and those gorgeous Hermès scarves, but would never dream of buying any of them. The real Kate was too busy keeping her monthly American Express bill paid up.

"We've set aside some lovely things for you to try," the manager murmured, hurrying them to the lush confines of the designer salon and a private dressing room. The entire salon was roped off with gold cord, and Kate felt suddenly silly. What was she doing here? Why would people fawn so over a candidate's wife? Were Americans that hungry for temporary kings and queens?

"Don't disapprove," Joan whispered, reading her mind. "You're putting glamour in their day."

Joan had done superb advance work. A smiling woman in discreet gray and wearing tiny gold earrings was already unzipping a tissue-soft wool suit in burnished melon. "We have several things waiting," she said. "I know we'll find something you love."

I love this and I haven't even got it on, Kate thought as she eased the skirt over her head. She buttoned the skirt, donned a gray silk blouse and pulled on the jacket, then whirled in a circle for her sister.

Joan grinned. "I'm jealous," she said.

"It probably costs a fortune?"

"No, I told them to choose stuff within a realistic price range."

Kate smiled, determined not to look at the price tag on the suit. Not quite yet. "Your realistic price range or mine?" she asked.

"Yours. I promise. You can look now," said Joan.

Kate peeked at the tag, feeling like a teenager. She grinned.

"We spent two million on last week's ad campaign, and here I am, worrying over a three-hundred-dollar suit," she said. "I'll take it."

"No, you won't. Not until you've tried on a dozen more."

"Remember when we played dress-up with old curtains?" Kate giggled at the sudden memory. "Mother collected them from the neighbors, I'm sure she did; she knew how to keep us busy."

"Yes, but you always played the queen, and I had to be your lady-in-waiting," Joan said.

"I used to be jealous because you always looked better, even if I was the queen," Kate retorted.

"My inborn fashion sense, I guess," Joan said with a smile. "Here I am, dressing you again!"

Kate felt suddenly, wonderfully happy. It was true, she and Joan had used those hours of play to try on identities and weave stories about themselves, fantastic stories, and here they were now, living one of the greatest fantasies of all. Slowly the room filled with a jumble of clothes. A mauve knit dress, perfect for traveling, a sweater embroidered with peacocks—

"Peacocks?" Kate said doubtfully.

"Beautiful, Mrs. Goodspeed," breathed the lady in gray.

"If you don't want it, hand it over," said Joan, with more than a hint of interest.

How delicious it was to be making this kind of decision. "It'll look better on you," Kate said, tossing the sweater to her sister and reaching for an emerald green wool dress.

Then came the lingerie—an armful of lace panties and bras in soft blues and pinks, satin nightshirts in glowing cream, and a wrap-around travel robe in cream-and-beige silk.

Kate put on the robe and stared at herself in the mirror. "I'm feeling so much better," she said. "The underwear is too expensive, but I can't live without this robe." She giggled, turned to Joan, and struck a pose.

"Very pretty. You hardly notice the bags under your eyes."

"Prettier than Claire Lorenzo?"

Joan studied her briefly. "Are you worried about her?" she asked.

Kate thought about it for a moment. "No, but I think about her," she said.

186

"So that's what Steve did to you."

"Nobody did anything to me, Joan. I'm just wary."

It was three o'clock before the last clothes were tried on, chosen or rejected, and cleared from the dressing room. It was amazing, really, how for the space of an hour and a half the campaign had all but disappeared from Kate's mind.

"This is like being back in the real world," she said at one point, and Joan had laughed. "Don't let anyone hear you say that," she said. "Neiman Marcus is not exactly the real world, dearie."

But it was a wonderful place to play. With some regret, Kate watched the lady in gray bundle off the last garments to be wrapped in white tissue paper and boxed for delivery to the house in Cleveland Park.

"Playtime's over," she announced, glancing at her watch. "We've got to get moving."

The trip back downstairs caused even more of a stir. Word had spread through the Mazza Gallerie that Mrs. Goodspeed, Senator Goodspeed's wife, was actually shopping at Neiman Marcus, let's go take a peek, they've got the place roped off, but if we pretend to be headed for the ladies room, we can get right up to the Secret Service agents and maybe we'll see her leave.

"What'd you buy, Mrs. Goodspeed?" yelled a good-natured reporter who had been stuck with staking out the designer department until Kate and Joan emerged. A photographer jumping around like a small toad took pictures as they headed down the escalator. Women shoppers pressed forward, craning and whispering. Kate smiled and waved, already wondering if she should have chosen a less obviously upscale store for her very public shopping trip.

Downstairs, the crowd was even greater. The elegant red ribbons had been torn open and the two agents were grim-faced as they cut a route past a display of silver comb-and-brush sets.

"What happens if you tell them you want to stop and buy a purse?" muttered Joan.

Kate grinned and started to whisper a reply. She stopped in mid-sentence and caught her breath sharply.

"Anything wrong?" Joan asked.

"Look." Kate could hardly speak. "Over there."

"Where?"

"There! That woman—"

Joan stared, but the milling group was just a blur of faces. "I don't see anything."

They had reached the front door and were quickly guided out to the waiting car. Kate sank into the backseat as far back as she could, all color gone from her face.

"What's the matter?" asked Joan.

"It was the woman with those funny penciled eyebrows. I know it was her—"

"What woman? What eyebrows?"

Kate briefly squeezed her eyes shut and opened them again to look steadily at her sister.

"The woman who tried to stop us at the abortion clinic," she said. "She was standing in the crowd."

Joan's expression did not change, but her face seemed to freeze. "She could not possibly have recognized you," she said firmly. She didn't so much say it as mandate it, but it didn't help. Kate was shaking; she had never expected to see those eyebrows again.

Later that afternoon, the campaign plane took off for Chicago. The flight was fifteen minutes late in leaving, burdened by an extra contingent of media anxious to see firsthand how much of an impact the disapproval of a powerful prince of the Church would have on the campaign of Luke Goodspeed. Things were heating up nicely from the perspective of a reporter after a good story. The Chicago rally—with an uncomfortable-looking Father Joe Delancey prominently featured—had been huge. To darken the day's picture a little more, Enright was not that far behind in the latest CBS poll. And Marty was getting nervous about Catholic voters. He was keeping the campaign-tracking polls on this one in his back pocket, but Luke's support among working-class Catholics was clearly moving downward in response to hierarchy criticism. Suburban Catholics were inching toward Luke, which was the good news. But very slowly.

"Goodspeed doesn't have a lock on this election, that's for sure," the *Los Angeles Times* reporter said to the CBS correspondent as she pulled out her computer and began banging out an early story. "I'm kind of glad; things were getting too boring." Suddenly she looked out the window of the plane with an expression of horror on her face.

"Oh, my God," she said, as the plane moved forward down the tarmac in preparation for takeoff. "That's my suitcase sitting out there!"

CBS looked up absently from checking his notes. "I'll lend you a toothbrush," he said. Then he caught sight of her bag and one other huddled forlornly beside it on the tarmac, receding swiftly out of sight. He paled.

"Mine, too!" he yelled, banging futilely on the window.

A ripple of sympathetic laughter moved through the cabin, but there was nothing to be done. Just one more hazard of the road; one more story to tell when the political wars were over. A little spice at this stage was welcome. Who wanted a boring end to all these months of traveling, speechifying, handshaking, parading, waiting? Who wanted any end to it at all?

From the back of the plane came the sound of a harmonica. Someone was playing Willie Nelson's "On the Road Again."

"Hey, our theme song," the *Wall Street Journal* said to the *Charlotte Observer*. "God, I haven't been off the road in two months."

"Yeah?" said the *Observer*. And because he was new at covering politics, he told the truth. Just said it, straight out. "You know," he said sheepishly, "this is more fun than working."

At the front of the plane, Kate found herself glancing frequently at her husband. Luke was tense, his usually mobile face set in solid, almost stern lines.

"It's just a dinner," she felt compelled to whisper.

"I'm having random, murderous thoughts," he whispered back, trying for levity.

"At this point in a campaign, everything seems like a crisis," she said. "The cardinal can't hurt you."

"It's not the cardinal; the cummerbund for my tux is back on the bed."

"Are they getting one in Chicago?"

"So Marty tells me." Luke simply refused to smile.

"Remember when you went to the dinner for the president of Turkey and didn't know it was black tie and changed clothes with the waiter?" Come on, Luke, Kate urged silently. This one always makes both of us laugh.

Luke tried a halfhearted smile, but couldn't sustain it.

"You're not worried about the cummerbund," Kate said. "Admit it."

"Okay, I admit it." Once again, he absentmindedly rubbed the hollows beneath his eyes. "You know better."

"You'll always have somebody after you, Luke."

"I don't need Kovach fucking me over," he said roughly. "I've got more important things to worry about."

Kate patted his hand, but she wondered: When had he started talking like Marty? It was unsettling.

The dinner was a huge affair. Two hundred circular white-clothed tables filled the downtown hotel ballroom, each crowned with a wire stand holding a black-numbered sign. The crowd blended and flowed, a shifting kaleidoscope of men in crisp black and white and women in reds and greens and purples, as couples searched for the tables to which they had been assigned. Kate found herself noting the sloppily sewn beige taffeta swathed across the long, raised head table as she and Luke moved up the steps to take their places. It was an unusually tacky setup anchored with sprawling arrangements of fake flowers that would not show up well on television. But perhaps, she told herself, the council had not expected so much press attention. Her eyes searched for Cardinal Kovach. There he was, quietly regal in his scarlet biretta and robe, looking as calm as Luke looked tense. The cameras were already clicking and whirring. The crowd seemed to surge forward in a single wave of craning necks and rustling voices, all eager for a view of the coming confrontation.

The plan was simple. Luke and Kate would walk directly to the cardinal with smiles on their faces and voice a quick greeting before taking their seats and turning their attention to other guests. Timing was crucial, for if they lingered too long and the cardinal snubbed them, that would be tomorrow's story; if they were too brusque, *that* would be the story. They would aim for a neutralized photo opportunity, a bland and polite picture for the front pages and evening news. Timing was all.

"Here we go," whispered Luke, grasping Kate's hand.

Cardinal Kovach looked up as they approached and began to rise, a benign expression on his full, bespectacled face, his hand moving in a quick motion which Kate's eye did not follow. She was already finding it hard to put out of mind the rigidity of the boundaries he represented.

"Your Eminence," Luke said in his fullest and warmest tones, "what a pleasure to see you. You know my wife, Kate, I'm sure."

The cardinal pulled himself up very straight, his biretta glowing under the television lights. He was a tall man, unexpectedly muscular, with eyes as blue and piercing as Luke's. Kate was struck with the smooth flow of authority that emanated from his presence, and she found herself resisting. He represented so much of what she found detached and dehumanized about the Church, but he also represented a security of habit and belief closer to her than all others. It was a powerful, drawing force.

"I wish I could say the same, Senator," Cardinal Kovach said in a strong, grave voice. "But I must first plead with you to heed the Church. You are a Catholic, and you have much to answer for. Your cousin is praying for your soul. I would be remiss if I did not take this opportunity to remind you of that."

The directness of his public scolding was unexpected. Luke seemed off balance, his expression almost surly, and Kate was suddenly anxious for him. He needed poise for this, not some rough-edged Marty Apple response.

"This isn't the time to discuss our differences, Your Eminence," Luke said, smoothly enough. "Tonight is the time to dwell on what unites us." He began shifting his weight to edge away, but the cardinal stepped forward, closing the gap.

"These are troubled times, Senator," the cardinal said. "We think Father Delancey has the right and duty to speak out against your views, even if he is your cousin and one of your closest friends."

Kate folded her hands in front of her, a simultaneously protective and obedient gesture. This one must be handled by Luke; she would have to smile steadily and do nothing else.

Luke returned gravity for gravity, but she heard the sharpening edge of his voice. "Sorry, Your Eminence, but this is one subject on which we aren't going to agree," he said. "Why don't we sit down and enjoy the evening together?"

The cardinal bowed slightly, stiffly. "We who remain true to the

191

Church will remember you in our prayers," he said. Each word was spoken deliberately and slowly. He switched his gaze to Kate, studying her briefly, speculatively, with shrewd eyes. Kate found herself unable to move, even though Luke was putting pressure on her arm.

"We will pray for you too, Mrs. Goodspeed," the cardinal said. It was like having a spotlight swung into her eyes; the light was refracting, and it hurt.

Kate didn't plan what she said next, the words just came out. Just one single, crazy swipe of the sword.

"Don't waste your time, Your Eminence," she said. She remembered to keep her voice low, but the look of chilly reproof on the cardinal's face was surely being preserved on film by at least some of those infernal cameras below the podium. Instead of curtailing her recklessness, it only spurred Kate on.

"You see—" how absurd to try to explain, but there it was—"I don't really need your prayers, Your Eminence. Well, actually—" she sensed Luke's eyes burning into her back—"I may well *need* them." She took a breath, and allowed herself some of the bluntest words she had spoken publicly in years. "But I don't really *want* them."

9

"Could you have restrained yourself just a little?" Luke whispered as they took their seats. "Didn't you see him pull over the open mike? Or are you trying to make enemies for the hell of it?"

To those only a few feet away, his smile was easy and full. Only Kate could see the anger throbbing in the muscles of her husband's face.

"I saw him move something—" She was now appalled at her own rash action, then hurt by Luke's words. "Why are you so angry?" she whispered back, turning so her thick, dark hair shielded her face from the crowd. "Why didn't you warn me?"

"How could I?" Luke snapped. "Where was your common sense? That mike was almost under your nose. Why did you have to say *anything*?"

Kate's attempt to control broke. "Luke, I'm sorry," she said. "I didn't see the mike, okay?"

But Luke seemed to be urged on by feelings she didn't understand. "Marty's right," he said. "You don't listen to anybody, do you?"

It was too much. "Since when is *he* in charge of defining *me*?" she said.

At that moment, the band struck up the Notre Dame fight song, and alumni sprinkled through the crowd began to cheer and sing. Luke widened his pasted-on grin and waved, slipping an arm around his wife's rigid shoulders.

"Smile," he ordered. "They're singing our song again."

They spoke hardly at all after the dinner, and Kate brooded as much over Luke's tongue-lashing as over her own bad judgment. That hadn't sounded like Luke, not the Luke she knew. But I was wrong, she told herself. I'm worried and twitchy and I wasn't as careful as I should have been. But I can't tell him that because I can't tell him about Abby.

They slept that night like strangers, each carefully keeping to opposite sides of the bed. The next morning, with nothing discussed, Luke prepared to leave the Chicago apartment.

"Claire's coming over to see what kind of damage control we'll need to clean up last night's mess," he said, his hand on the front doorknob. His words were stiff, but his face was the face of a man who hadn't slept very well. "I'll see you Thursday night."

"Why Claire?" Kate wanted to tell him she was sorry, but this she hadn't expected. "And what's Thursday night?"

"Because she's got common sense, that's why. And Thursday night's the night of the mock debate, which you've apparently forgotten."

"Luke. Don't be so harsh." Yes, she had forgotten the mock debate, the dress rehearsal for the last debate of the campaign. The real thing would be next week at the University of Massachusetts in Amherst, and it would be the final major campaign event before the election. But she didn't deserve this.

He hesitated, his hand still grasping the doorknob. They fought rarely, managing most of their disagreements with marital dodges and feints, but it was clear from his face that this was something different. "Look, we talked about loyalty, remember?" he said. "In Los Angeles? And Texas? And before that, you promised you wouldn't embarrass me with any Church bashing. Why, Kate? Aren't we in this together? You seem disconnected; kind of detached."

"Disconnected?" This was totally unfair. "I should never have said what I did, but I've been working nonstop for you, and you know it."

"You don't listen, Kate, you do what you want to do."

"Pardon me," she said with spirit, not liking the fact that she couldn't get a grasp on what was really at stake here. "But you used to call that my independence, and if memory serves, you've had no complaints about it for twenty years."

She was losing his attention, as if he already had something more important to think about. "Nothing matters more than you," she blurted out, distressed. "He was just so sure of himself—I can't explain it. Please don't be angry."

Luke's face softened, but the look in his eyes was still unfathomable. "I'm sorry," he said quietly. "I've got a lot on my mind."

Kate said nothing, fighting frustration. These were Luke's deflecting words, and they were truly powerful—more now than ever before.

He reached out and touched her face briefly. "You'll be civil to Claire? Promise?" He meant it as a light touch, she knew, but it didn't quite come off. He bent and kissed her quickly. "You'll work it out," he said, and he was gone.

Claire wasted no time. She showed up before Kate could finish her first cup of coffee, which left Kate feeling irritated, deprived of the hard, cutting edge of caffeine.

Claire slipped into one of the cane chairs in the kitchen with the ease of someone who had come to chat about nothing in particular. But the ease was mechanical and practiced, leaving Kate with the feeling that she was once again being defined as a problem.

"There was no real need for you to come," Kate said with limited grace. She poured some coffee, congratulating herself on her steady hand. She would be damned if she would show one hint of embarrassment.

Claire did not look directly at Kate. Her hair was pulled back into a severe knot, a style that would be unattractive on many women, but which on Claire served only to accentuate the sculptural perfection of her face. The very difficulty of carrying off such a hairstyle made Kate feel the hopelessness of trying to compete with good bones.

"Great coffee," Claire said, sipping in experimental fashion. "Did you get this from that little shop on Rush Street?"

"No. Somewhere, I can't remember. Maybe somebody gave it to us."

195

Patricia O'Brien

"I'm fully aware you don't want me here, so let's not waste time," Claire said with a small smile. "Let's figure out what to do about the cardinal."

"He set me off," Kate said. "It's hard to explain."

Claire looked blank. "I don't care why," she said. "I only care what we do about it. The *Tribune* got it into their late edition, and we'll see more this evening on the news. Let me run some things by you. A note to Kovach? A statement explaining what you really meant? Show up at Mass today?" Claire looked quickly at her watch. "You could make a Mass."

Kate felt quite calm. "No," she said. "I don't go very often, and the press knows that. So does Cardinal Kovach, which is probably why he wants to pray for me."

"Then let's compose a private note," Claire said patiently. "To keep him from capitalizing on this."

Kate was silent for a moment, thinking. "I don't think he will," she said finally. "He'll just say something like 'Mrs. Goodspeed appears troubled by her husband's defiance of the Church.' Something like that. They don't want me, they want Luke."

"A short note wouldn't hurt then," Claire pressed.

"I don't want to write the cardinal," Kate said firmly. "I have nothing to say to him."

Claire sighed. "You did last night."

"The worst thing I did was get Luke angry," Kate said. "The cardinal doesn't matter."

Claire lowered her eyes briefly at mention of Luke's name, as if to excuse herself from a private dispute. "At this stage, everything matters," she said. "We really can't afford to take chances."

"Let's see first if Kovach demands an apology," Kate said. "He won't, I'm quite sure. I know Catholics better than you do." She suddenly decided to play a bold card. "I understand you and Luke had a little chat," she said. "About your miscarriage."

"So he told you," Claire said, with no hint of surprise. "Actually—" she smiled—"you're the one who started me thinking about my real feelings. I began facing them after our little talk in the car." She caught Kate's skeptical look. "I've got an image to keep up," she said. "I'm not made of stone, you know. I was trying to hide how bad I felt."

196

"You did a good job of that."

"Well—should I have bared my soul?" Claire laughed, but her voice took on a slight edge.

"You had no trouble confiding in Luke," Kate countered.

Claire's one-word reply was quite blunt. "True," she said. Her eyes were thoughtful as she rose to dump her coffee into the sink.

This was not expected. Kate tried to come up quickly with a rejoinder, but Claire spoke again. "It's easy for you," she said, running the coffee cup under a sluggish stream of water. "You don't live out of a suitcase every day of your life; you've got kids, a home. I've learned to appreciate friends when I find them."

For an instant she looked almost fragile. But then she straightened, and the illusion was gone. "Okay, you win," she said in a brisk tone. "No note, no apology. You'll be here tonight, right? I'll track the news and get to you if we have to shift course." Another quick glance at her watch before she gathered her things and headed for the door, crisp and businesslike. "By the way, your sister caused a stir last night, too," she said.

Kate felt a twinge of alarm. "What happened?"

"She spilled a glass of wine down the front of Maurice Norton's tux."

Claire was watching her and Kate decided not to give the expected response. If she knew her sister, it had been a carefully staged accident, but she wasn't about to give Claire the satisfaction of saying so.

"Red or white?" she asked.

"I didn't ask." Claire pursed her lips, still gazing thoughtfully at Kate. "I've got to get back to Washington." She turned to leave. "We'll talk later."

It turned out to be a victory for Kate—of sorts. Cardinal Kovach did not get indignant over her rejection of his offer of prayers. When asked for a statement on the encounter at the dinner, he focused instead on Luke's "misguided arrogance in the face of God's teachings." Several reporters made a point to ask him for a specific response to Kate's acerbic statement, but the cardinal contented himself with a brief, pained answer: "We will of course include her in our prayers anyway," he said.

Kate congratulated herself, since it was clear no one else would. At least right now, the cardinal was more concerned with exhorting the faithful to "turn their backs" on the Democratic candidate for the presidency than with the status of Kate's soul. It would take until the end of the week, when the campaign's tracking polls had something to report, to see whether his strategy was cutting into Luke's support base.

On Tuesday she found herself restlessly waiting for a phone call from Luke. When had he stopped calling every night? That wasn't possible these days, she knew that. But one call, grabbed on the run from somewhere or from the plane—he had that cellular phone—he could do it, of course he could. The fact that he hadn't called meant he was still angry. This was too much time to go by without patching up an argument, especially now.

Kate brooded. She should have come up with something more to explain her outburst. She knew from past experience what the last weeks of a campaign could be like, but the pressures this time were really heavy. Quit kidding yourself, she thought. It isn't just the pace. It's a tension, an apartness between me and Luke.

The phone rang. She grabbed it.

"I couldn't hear what he said, but Luke looked like Mr. Plastic on that podium," Joan said.

"And what did Norton look like when you spilled the wine on him?"

"I accidentally spilled it," Joan corrected her airily. "Big difference."

"Would I doubt your word? What did he say?"

"Sputtered a lot. I offered him a napkin; I was a good girl." She chuckled. "He knew damn well what it was about."

Kate sighed. She didn't feel her old anxieties about policing Joan; Joan could take care of herself.

"Joan, am I changing? Is Luke changing?"

"Ask me in November."

"No, I'm asking you now."

It seemed strange to be turning to her sister for a reality check. Was she leaning on a frail reed?

"You both are," Joan answered quietly. "But don't ask me to explain how. Hey, so am I. You know what I enjoy? I enjoy leaving. So what am I doing these days? Helping Nat with his homework, taking you shopping, eating Mrs. Leonard's pumpkin glop—"

"Don't forget tossing wine at Norton."

198

"*Spilling*," Joan corrected. "Don't worry about *that*. Maurice and I understand each other."

Kate smiled. No, she decided, Joan would not snap. Nor was she a reed weaving and bending in the wind. She could count on that now. It felt rather like having an umbrella tucked away for a rainy day.

How strange.

Kate stood in the back of the church, amazingly, alone. She was somewhere in Bethesda. Precisely twenty minutes had been spent in the Immaculate Heart rectory with the Iranian Family Rescue Foundation. So efficiently had the meeting proceeded, the cars weren't here yet to take her to the next event.

"Would you like to see our church, Mrs. Goodspeed?"

There was unexpected time to kill; what were her hosts going to do with her? The strain was showing on their faces.

"I'll stop in for a second by myself, thank you."

The instant the heavy oak doors closed behind her, Kate knew why she was there. She breathed in deeply, inhaling the vestiges of incense from the morning High Mass. She wandered up the side aisle, past the dark, forbidding confessionals. What terror they had inspired in her as a child! "Forgive me, Father, for I have sinned. . . ." Whispered misdeeds, laid out with anguish before an invisible priest, humbly, breathing deeply before he spoke in an effort to avoid inhaling his bad breath—the memories were solemn, real. She closed her eyes, and just for a moment she could see a lineup of little girls in blue serge uniforms and feel the cold wooden beads of her mother's rosary fuzzed with the lint in the lining of her jacket pocket.

She walked toward the altar, up to the heavy oak altar rail, and stared at the familiar bed of flickering red votive lights. Beneath the layered rows lay a thin bed of white sand dotted with the charred remains of matches. Each light signaled a prayer; a plea for help, a prayer for a dead soul. They had always fascinated her, these anonymous prayers. Kate found herself struggling once again with her deepest conflicts of belief. No one knew who had whispered those prayers, who had reached for a match—except, perhaps, God? And when the match would strike the wick, did only God know why one more ruby-red glass cup had flickered to life? Such a comfort it was for petitioners to realize they could make the sign of the cross,

199

genuflect, and leave the church and that their prayers would still continue to undulate upward: prayers for the sick; petitions for mercy; prayers for good fortune; prayers for the dead. Did they fool themselves?

Kate took a deep breath, her spirit eased by the lights. It didn't matter. She, too, would be a petitioner once again, and offer a prayer.

Trembling with sudden emotion, she knelt on the narrow, wooden riser and reached for one of the slender red-tipped matches, simultaneously pushing a folded dollar bill through the slot for offerings. For the first time since the night at the clinic, she allowed herself to remember again the sound of Abby's crying. She bowed her head. She could hear it; she could remember every sound from behind that closed door. She stared at the rows of small glass cups filled with their tiny flickering flames. They were mesmerizing, comforting. It suddenly seemed wholly appropriate to hold a small private ceremony of loss.

She lit a fat new candle and watched the flame flare high. For a long moment, she saw nothing else.

"Kate?"

The strong male voice, even though modulated, cut harshly through the air of the quiet church. Kate jumped violently and whirled around. Behind her, back a few paces, was Father Joe Delancey.

"What are you doing here?" she said, startled.

Joe smiled uncertainly. "I was about to ask you the same thing." He looked unnaturally pale and slightly less rotund than she remembered.

She recovered first. "This is not exactly a pleasure, Joe," she said, edging away from the votive lights. Calm down, she instructed herself. He can't possibly know why you were kneeling there.

"Wait," he said quietly. "I promise I'll skip the hearty, good-old-Father-Joe number. It sounds too much like an old forties movie, anyway."

"I always thought so," she said. His Roman collar still pushed up the skin of his substantially thick neck, she noted, and the spidery veins dappled across his face were more prominent than ever.

He risked a slow smile. "You really gave it to the cardinal," he said.

"It was stupid of me."

"You wouldn't have done that unless you were under a lot of tension, and I'm the one who put it on you. Kate, I'm sorry. That's all. This isn't the time to tell Luke that, so I'm telling you."

"Have you tried?"

"Father Jello getting past Marty Apple?" Delancey cast her a wry look. "What would you think of his chances?"

"We don't call you that," Kate said quickly.

"No, but Marty does, and he's the boss."

His words were true enough to make Kate fidgety. "Why did you let the cardinal use you?" she asked.

"He invoked the discipline of the priesthood," Delancey said, his voice sober. "I had no choice."

"What about your own conscience, Joe?" she asked. "You know who Luke is and what he stands for, and you know what you did to him. You make it sound as if you're some kind of prisoner."

Delancey walked toward her from the shadows, but only to stand before her, his hands folded in front of him. "You're always at war with the Church, aren't you?" he said. "You have been for as long as I've known you." He didn't say it as a denunciation. He said it sadly.

"I think it controls through fear, and I long ago saw the damage that does," she said. She took a deep breath. "The Church is no friend of mine."

"Spoken like a rejected suitor." He risked a small smile again. "Can you put aside your anger and think about just one thing? The Church is made up of fallible humans who make mistakes, and none of us is immune."

"Joe, that's all very nice, but you betrayed Luke, and he never forgets when that happens." Her own words made her uneasy in a way she hadn't expected. They sounded smug and self-righteous. What about her own betrayal? Was that indeed what it was? "That's too harsh," she amended. "But you did undercut him."

This time his smile was very gentle. "So did you," he said.

Kate dropped her eyes in confusion. For heaven's sake, Joe was not talking about Abby's abortion.

"With the cardinal," he said, watching her closely.

"That's between us," she said.

"You're right," he said. He reached out this time and took one of

201

◆◆

her hands between his; she did not pull away. "I want to be a good priest," he said. He spoke very slowly, as if listening to each word as he said it. "That's the focus of my life, and I can't forget it or I destroy myself. But I'm also not going to be used anymore by Church politicians, I promise you that."

"I'm not questioning your sincerity," she said, her voice troubled. "But doesn't that depend on the cardinal?"

He didn't flinch. "Yes, to a certain extent," he said. "He's a politician; he's got his agenda. But he's a priest, too, and he has to respect my need to honor my family as well as my church. We've talked. He listened. We have an understanding. In other words—" he smiled—"I shut up about Luke and they leave me alone."

Why was she so unendingly skeptical? "What happens if you have to make a moral decision he doesn't agree with?" she challenged. "Is 'shutting up' an option?"

"It hasn't happened that way."

"Yet, Joe."

He nodded calmly. "Yet," he repeated. He looked at her closely. "You've got something bothering you."

Kate turned her face away. "You're a priest, you're supposed to be wise," she said finally. "What happens when you confess to one sin and hold back another?"

"Which one's worse?"

"Neither wins any prizes," she said. Reluctantly she smiled as he reached for her hand and gave it a squeeze.

"Can I help?"

"No." Kate straightened; pulled her coat closer and checked her watch. "I'm not cutting you off," she said. "I don't mean to sound cold. But this is something I truly can't talk about."

"I'm grateful you've listened to me," he said with warmth. "And any time I can return the favor, I'm ready. You can get pretty mad at anybody who steps on you or yours, but you're a generous-hearted human being, Kate Goodspeed."

She smiled. "Thanks, Joe," she said. "But I'll be a very late one if I don't get out of here in thirty seconds."

Delancey stepped back. "What a coincidence, running into you here," he said. There was a funny little twinkle in his eye. "On my turf, yet."

"This was no coincidence, was it?"

He shrugged. "Helps us both to clear the air a little, if possible. There's a lot of life after this campaign."

Kate raised a single eyebrow. "There is?" she said. She reached forward and this time she was the one to touch hands. "Don't worry," she said, and then wasn't sure what she meant. "Take care, Joe."

Quickly she walked down the center aisle to the dark oak doors and pushed them open without looking back.

Kate rolled over in bed, burrowing her head into a wonderfully soft down pillow that would probably set her sneezing in a few minutes, but the comfort was worth it. She squinted at the clock. Damn, it was broken. Home tended to be a lot less efficient than a hotel, but it felt delicious to be in her own bed in her own room in Cleveland Park. She had finished her latest swing through the South in record time, thanks to good advance work. She lay quietly, listening to the familiar, comforting sounds of the kids getting ready for school and a house creaking in the autumn wind. Clanging cereal bowls, a barking dog, a tree limb scratching at the bedroom window . . .

"Nat, you ate all the Special K!"

"I did not, the box was empty!"

Kate got up then and pulled on a robe. It was Mrs. Leonard's day off; Kate would make the special Irish oatmeal for Nat and Abby—an autumn treat. She didn't like to cook, never had, which was probably a major character flaw, but she had resisted connecting nurture with pots and pans and measuring spoons for so long now, even Luke liked to laugh and say there was little hope of ever getting her into the kitchen.

Why didn't he call?

Kate stood at the top of the stairs, tying her robe close against the chilly morning air.

"Hey," she called. "How about some hot oatmeal?"

An hour later, she moved about the kitchen, scrubbing the oatmeal from the pot before it hardened, loving the plainness of the morning. The children were gone; the house was silent. She picked up her favorite old yellow mug, dumped the cold coffee, and placed the mug on the top rack in the dishwasher. Luke thought she should throw the old pottery out, but she was reluctant. There were only a few pieces left of the dishes they'd bought when they were first married. She liked seeing them on the shelf, and she didn't mind drinking from a chipped mug.

Why didn't he call?

She felt a drifting sense of melancholy and began to hurry through the job. Enough, she lectured herself. You've been on the road, juggling kids and problems and loneliness before. Just get on with it. She punched the "On" button, and the noisy sound of rushing water filled the kitchen, almost drowning out the sound of the ringing phone.

"Mrs. Goodspeed?" It was one of the Secret Service agents posted outside. "There's a lady here to see you."

"Who is it?"

"A Mrs. Feldon. Mrs. Lisa Feldon."

Steve's wife. Ex-wife, Kate corrected herself. She hesitated.

"Want me to get rid of her?" the agent asked, noting her hesitation.

"No." It seemed too cowardly. "Please just send her in."

Lisa Feldon. It took some concentration to bring an image into focus. Kate remembered only a mousy little woman with small, nervous hands who had worked with Steve for a while in Luke's office, back during his first term in the Senate. Kate could recall only a few awkward dinner parties. Lisa was the type of person Kate never knew where to seat. Next to the senator just back from a fact-finding trip through Central America? He would fall out of his seat with boredom. Next to the Czechoslovakian economic counselor? Disaster. Next to Luke? He'd be polite, but it was expecting too much. So back and forth the little white place cards would go, first here, then there, and all the while, Kate would wonder why Lisa was so shy. It hadn't come as much of a surprise when she and Steve split. Where was she now? Kate thought she remembered something about her working in a school in Baltimore. Was she a teacher? Or maybe a child-care worker?

The woman who came through the door clutching a purse with worn straps was as drab and gray as Kate remembered. Just paler and older. And still wearing her thin hair in an out-of-date back-combed pouf.

"Lisa," Kate said with practiced warmth, reaching out her hand.

Lisa Feldon nodded a restrained hello, looking into the living room with guarded curiosity, surveying the undeniably old furniture. Two chairs in faded green slipcovers flanked the east window that opened onto the porch. An ancient tweed-covered sofa with thick, soft cushions sat beneath the south window, next to an elaborately molded turn-of-the-century mantel speckled with holes made by tacks which had held family Christmas stockings of the past. The fireplace itself looked bare and too clean, a reminder of how little time the Goodspeeds spent nowadays in the room. The bookshelves, if you looked closely, were covered in a fine layer of dust.

"Everything looks about the same," Lisa Feldon said as if to herself, taking time to scan the room, not even looking at Kate.

"We don't have much time for redecorating projects," Kate said with a small laugh. Things did look a bit shabby, she thought. She had to do something about that creaky old sofa. "You know politics."

A cloud passed over the woman's pale countenance. "I certainly do," she said.

Kate felt suddenly awkward. This was silly—why was she standing here, letting Lisa do an almost clinical appraisal of her own living room? She cleared her throat. "What can I do for you?" she asked.

"I came to talk to you about Steve."

"I don't think I can—"

"He's disintegrating," Lisa said. "Luke's going to knock him out on his ear. He'll have no job. He'll have nothing."

"Steve's having some kind of breakdown, Lisa," Kate said quickly. "Luke will help him, I can promise you that."

The woman looked at Kate with frank disbelief, but her voice was detached. "Steve needs Luke," she said, running nervous fingers across the clasp of her purse. She paused. "I don't know why. I've never known why."

She suddenly looked so lost, Kate took pity on her. "Would you like to sit down?" she suggested. "I'll pour us some coffee."

The woman nodded, and chose one of the green chairs in the morning sun. She held the coffee mug Kate brought her as gingerly as if it were a fragile china cup, her eyes darting around the room.

"The first time I came here, it was kind of a surprise," she said in a suddenly chatty tone. "I think I expected something more glam-

205

orous. You know, antiques and things like that." She said the word "antiques" with the slow savoring of someone who respects the word as part of a foreign language. "I was here the night Luke decided to run for the Senate," she said. "That's when I first met you."

Of course. What a long time ago it was!

"I remember that night. I remember Steve standing over there—" She pointed at the fireplace. "He was happy."

Kate remembered, too. Steve and Luke had been crazy with excitement that night; like a pair of kids.

"Do you have any idea what it was like to work for Luke Goodspeed?" Lisa asked, a peculiar brilliance in her eyes.

"I'm not sure what you mean," Kate said.

"I'll tell you." The woman cradled her coffee mug, staring down into the dark brew. "It meant taking care of him, all the time."

"Oh, now—" If Lisa was going to try and paint Steve as some kind of servant, she might rethink her attempt at cordiality.

"Like a baby." Lisa gave a short, mirthless laugh. "Once, on our anniversary, I went all out making a special dinner. I can't remember what, now, maybe roast beef. And corn on the cob; Steve loves corn on the cob. He was late getting home, as usual, and we were just starting to eat when the phone rang. It was Luke, calling from the plane. Know what he said?"

Kate didn't really want to know, but she sat, silent.

"He said, 'Steve, I'm landing in fifteen minutes. Can you come pick me up?' And you know what Steve did?" A small smile played at the corners of Lisa's mouth.

It was a familiar scenario, there was no denying it. "I probably do," Kate said.

"Sure you do," Lisa said softly. "Steve put down his fork and put on his jacket and went to the airport to pick Luke up. It happened all the time, but that night it really burned me. Do you know what I wish I had had the nerve to say in those days?"

Kate braced herself; she wasn't sure for what.

Lisa leaned forward, the skin around her lips puckered tight. "I wish I had said, 'Tell him to get a cab,' that's all," she said fiercely. " 'Tell him to hail a goddamn cab!' "

Kate bit her lip. She could argue this if she wanted to; she could point out that Luke certainly never had forced Steve to do anything

206

he didn't want to do. Luke needed people around him who knew how to respond fast. For heaven's sake, if Luke ever had been forced to find his own way home from the airport, he probably would have lost his way. It was something of a family joke, really. Luke hardly ever drove himself anywhere, but she couldn't say that to Lisa.

"You're not describing a master-servant relationship," she said quickly. "They were friends."

"He didn't own Steve," Lisa said. "We had a right to a private life."

"Of course you did," Kate said. "But you know how it works in this town." She was beginning to feel she was being used as a sounding board for reasons not at all clear. "What is it you want from me?"

"I don't want anything," the woman said, her voice breaking. "I just want to say some things I've never been able to say."

The two women sat staring at each other in silence. Then Lisa shifted her gaze to the window, ruminating out loud.

"You and I never knew each other very well," she said.

"That's true," Kate replied.

"Frankly, I didn't like you very much. No offense."

Kate uncrossed her legs, ready for flight.

"You were in the same cocoon Luke was in," Lisa went on. "Sort of plastic. Toothpasty. Entitled."

"I'm sorry you feel that," Kate said, her voice deliberately cool. "Look, I have to cut this short—"

"Yes, entitled." Lisa seemed not to have heard her. "It's a description that fits. I'm sorry, but it does."

Kate stood quickly. Lisa followed suit, but in more leisurely fashion.

"Excuse me for talking so plain," Lisa said. "It's rude and terrible and all that. But you haven't heard anything said straight in years. All I'm trying to do is tell you some things that are true, and maybe get you to notice." She paused, searching Kate's eyes. "I don't know, maybe I've wasted my time." She smiled again, a tired smile now. She looked very vulnerable. "Have I?"

Abruptly, Kate sat down again. She wasn't sure why.

Lisa spoke very patiently. "I'm not being polite or kind," she said. "But why, when I think Steve is dying inside, shouldn't you have to face knowing it?" She sat again in the green chair, putting her coffee

207

mug down carefully on the glass coffee table, wiping a smear of lipstick off the lip with her finger, and shot Kate a quick glance. "It's been a year and a half since he left me. I'll bet you didn't realize it was so long."

Kate couldn't remember. Had she ever known precisely when Steve and his wife broke up? Not really. Steve's personal life never had been much of a topic of conversation, hardly ever surfacing during the years he worked with Luke and spent time with Kate and the family. It hadn't seemed strange, then—just natural. But it seemed strange now. What that meant, she couldn't think about until Lisa left and she could clear her head.

"He said I nagged him too much," the woman said. "It's true, I did. Now he's alone, but actually we both are. You know what it is? What I want to say?"

Kate felt another rush of pity. "I'm getting a pretty good idea."

"Good." She captured Kate's eyes with a level gaze. "Men like Steve live for men like Luke, and then they get thrown away when they're not useful anymore. I think it's awful."

"Are you aware of what Steve said to me?" Kate asked. The wounds from Steve's words in the Roma were still raw and, sick or not, his actions had been inexcusable.

"Yes, I am."

"Lisa, I know you care for him still, but it was terrible. We'll get him medical help, but Luke can't be expected to go any further than that."

Lisa laughed, a short burst of raw sound. "Oh, I know," she said. "He didn't mean to hurt you, but that doesn't matter anymore. It's too late. You know who was his new best friend for a while? You'll love it."

Puzzled, Kate waited.

"Ernie Stark."

Kate drew her breath in sharply, so sharply that Lisa stared.

"How do you know that?" Kate said.

"He told me. Boasted, is a better word." Lisa's tone softened. "He's a hurt man, Kate. He had to peel away from the guy. I think he's sorry and he's scared."

"He's made a terrible mistake." It was all Kate could manage.

The light in Lisa's eyes was fading. She stood, picked up her purse and clutched it close. "I'll go now," she said. "I know I should say

I'm sorry I bothered you, but the truth is, I wanted to bother you. I've wanted to say these things for a long time. Goodbye."

She walked toward the door with Kate close behind, turning as she prepared to leave, gazing at Kate closely as if memorizing her face.

"I still don't think I like you," she said. "But I'm not as angry as I was. I guess—" she sighed—"I guess we're both alike in a way. But I'm free now. You're the one who's stuck."

She turned her back and walked out the open door, not waiting for a response, leaving Kate to stare after her.

"Immigration's moving ahead," Luke said angrily, speaking louder into the special secure-line phone to overcome the noise of his landing plane. "My people on the subcommittee say they're sure the government is sitting on something, but they're letting Palmer in anyway."

"Then drop it," Marty said, his voice tinny and chopped with static. "We need a wider lead; Enright's using every edge he has. Did you hear he fired Gilmartin's guy?"

"No."

"He got mad when the press laughed at him for visiting the American flag factory. Can you believe the Republicans tried that phony gambit again?"

Luke chewed hard on a fingernail. "Nothing from Young yet?"

"Nothing. Luke, the guy can't deliver."

"Yeah, but this thing smells. We're picking up too many hints."

"No hard evidence."

"Gilmartin knows Palmer's a dangerous man, I'm convinced of it. But nobody is going to move a finger because of the campaign."

"Get even when you're in the White House."

"I'm not ready to drop this," Luke said quietly.

Marty answered with care. "You've gotta pick your battles, Luke. Don't let them be forced on you."

"No chance," Luke said, and then fell silent.

"I'll leak this to the *Times*," Marty said. "They'll get it out in the open. Just send Young to them; let them do the dirty work."

"I already suggested that, but Young doesn't trust reporters."

The static on the line crackled as the plane descended faster, hitting the tarmac at Washington's National Airport with a rude

Patricia O'Brien

bounce. Windows rattled, coffee cups tipped, and jeers of protest erupted from the press section in back of the drawn curtain. Compliance with safety regulations had become casual; one of several reporters standing in the aisle when the wheels hit the ground took a tumble.

"I want Palmer stopped," Luke said, ignoring the noise. "I'm going to Dale Lasati."

"The head of Immigration and Naturalization?" Marty said. "If you do, you might as well walk out on Pennsylvania Avenue and tell the world."

"That's exactly the point," Luke said. "I want Lasati to take this right to the White House. He can stop Palmer."

"Yeah, and then Gilmartin patches it up for you with blacks, right?" Marty's voice cut through the static with heavy sarcasm. "You think you don't get fingered as the hit man?"

"Marty, you're great at your job," Luke said. "You run the campaign. I'll handle this. I'm getting mad as hell, and I'm not going to be a party to letting this guy in the country."

"You get your hands on that tape, and I agree," Marty said. "If you don't, get him after the campaign."

"I'm going to try to reach Young."

"We need to talk; I'll meet you at the house."

Luke shook his head in the negative. "After the mock debate tonight."

"You won't do anything between now and then?"

"Breathe easy. But I'm not changing my mind."

Kate lifted her head at the sound of a knob turning and let out a deep sigh of relief. Luke was home, finally.

"Okay." She nodded to a bored camera crew sprawled on chairs in the kitchen. The crew snapped to attention when they saw Luke and moved for the dining room, equipment clanking.

"He's here. Mrs. Leonard, is the table set?" Mrs. Leonard nodded, and Kate turned to greet her husband as he stepped into the kitchen. I hope he remembered we're shooting this campaign video, she thought, and then, as she caught the weary look in Luke's eyes, she realized, with a sinking heart, he had not.

"What's going on?"

210

She attempted a bright smile. "The Goodspeed family at dinner," she said. "Remember? Our next commercial?"

Luke threw his briefcase onto a chair and sighed irritably. "I was hoping to catch a little rest," he said.

Why, Kate thought resentfully, do I feel apologetic for something his campaign set up? "It won't take long," she said.

Joan appeared suddenly at the door, glancing swiftly from her sister to Luke. "I've got a gift for you, Luke," she interrupted, a smile playing at the corners of her lips. "Looks like you need one. Here." She walked over to the kitchen counter and picked up a small package and offered it to him.

Luke hesitated, then took the package. "What is it?" he asked.

"It is definitely not a bomb," she said. "Open it up and see."

Luke ripped off the tape and opened the box. Inside was a sequined psychedelic shirt in hot orange and purple.

Joan laughed. "Luke, you should see your face," she said.

Luke was smiling finally. "Okay," he said. "What's the message?"

"An alternative shirt for an alternative lifestyle, maybe," Joan offered, a twinkle in her eye. "Or just something simple to wear to your inaugural."

"In other words," he said, clearly pretending to furrow his brow and think deeply, "loosen up?"

"Something like that," Joan said, her gaze steady.

"Gotcha." Only then did Luke turn and look full at his wife. "Sorry to be so cranky," he said, pulling the shirt out of the box and holding it up for fit. His voice was suddenly lighter. "What do you think? Will it work with a tux? Or are the colors not right?"

Kate laughed with relief, impulsively moving forward and giving him a hug.

"I'm sorry I didn't call," he whispered into her ear.

"I'm sorry for the whole thing, for everything," she said. It didn't matter, she would apologize for anything, she was so relieved at the break in tension. Standing on pride was a mistake.

"You were right," he said.

"About what?"

"The cardinal," he said. He tugged playfully at a strand of her hair. "You psyched him out perfectly. See? I'm admitting I was wrong. Surprised?" He smiled expectantly.

Discreetly Joan slipped away to help Mrs. Leonard, who was lay-

211

ing out platters of pumpkin bread on the dining-room table. Luke and Kate stood alone. She reached upward gratefully and touched his face. "No, I'm really happy," she said. "I hate fighting with you, Luke, it makes me sick to my stomach."

"Ouch." He winced, and his hand flew to a scratch on his cheek.

"Oh," she said, alarmed, looking at her hand. A jagged, broken prong was jutting out of the setting of the turquoise ring he had given her for their tenth wedding anniversary. "I'm sorry," she said, flustered. "I've got to get this fixed, but I keep forgetting. Luke, there's a lot to talk about. I had a visitor today. . . ."

He was stealing a glance at the red-and-white kitchen clock above the door. "Can we talk later?" he said. "Time's running short."

Kate's words rushed forth. "Steve's ex-wife, remember her?" she said rapidly. "She's a strange woman. Honey, we need to talk."

"Okay, okay," Luke mumbled, rubbing his cheek and moving toward the door. "Everybody wants to talk."

"I'm not everybody."

Luke caught the edge in her voice and quickly changed the subject. "This should be good tonight," he said. "I'll wipe the floor with Lyons. Too bad it isn't Enright himself. Remember the last debate? This one will be even better."

"Bob Lyons? He's playing Enright?" Luke was already halfway out of the room. She wanted him to stand still for just a few minutes more, something he clearly didn't intend to do.

"He sure isn't playing me," Luke said with a grin. "Let's go choke down some pumpkin bread for the cameras. Those lights will melt the wallpaper off if we don't hurry."

Kate automatically moved to follow him, stepping carefully over the maze of wires and cables that stripped the room and the people in it of anything approaching normalcy. My God, it's nothing more than a stage set, she thought. Everything in our lives is public now; nothing is spontaneous or done simply for fun. She felt a stab of nostalgia. Luke wouldn't be pitching dinner rolls to the kids again in this room for a long time.

The auditorium buzzed with voices as reporters roamed the aisles, collecting as many morsels and tidbits of information as possible from staff aides and supporters before the debate began.

"Jerry!" yelled one woman reporter in a baggy gabardine jacket, running up to Jerry Spanos as he prepared to duck behind a stage curtain in the rented hall. "Listen, I need stuff, come on, some color, anything! Okay?"

Jerry paused. "Okay," he agreed, "but I'm not the best guy to talk with—"

"Look, I'll take anybody I can get," the woman interrupted cheerfully. "I've got an early deadline."

"Shoot."

"Any special camera angles?"

"Don't know."

"Same makeup? He looked pale last time."

"They're brightening it up."

"What color is his suit? Same one he'll wear next week?"

"It's gray; I don't know if he's gonna wear it for the real debate."

"What shade?"

Jerry blinked.

"Dark gray?" she said, impatient. "Medium? Light?"

"Medium, I think."

"Is it true your media consultants decided that?"

"What do you mean?"

"I hear Marty's strategy is to make Enright look as ancient as possible, and they think a gray suit gives Goodspeed a more youthful look than a blue one. Right or wrong?"

Jerry shrugged his shoulders. "Hey," he said, "I work for Kate, I don't know. She likes blue."

The woman rolled her eyes. "Jerry, you're no help at all, damn it." She spotted Marty across the room. "Hey!" she yelled, following a crowd flocking in that direction, and she was gone.

The seats in the hall were filling rapidly with several dozen carefully selected guests—people chosen to give upbeat reports to the press about Luke's prowess after the mock debate was over. Marty, standing now in a cluster of reporters, was carefully pointing out that Enright was by far the more accomplished debater, and Luke was working hard to compensate.

"Come on," said *Time* magazine, a little gnome of a man, and a long-time veteran of the campaign wars. "You're just trying to lower our expectations."

"Casey, how can you say something like that?"

213

The other reporters laughed and scribbled away. It was all part of the game, but Casey persisted. "Is he up-to-date on the Brazil food riots? What about the oil spill threatening the beach at Cannes?"

Marty held aloft a thick, impressive book bound in black. "Here's the issues book," he said solemnly. "Take a look at how thick it is, guys. Believe me, Luke Goodspeed knows the issues. He's ready for anything."

"Color of tie?"

"Orange."

"What happened to yellow?"

"Passé."

"What about red?"

"*Very* passé."

The crowd had a boosterish, festive air, Kate thought, as she followed the Secret Service agents working a way through for her and Nat. She was glad Bob Lyons was playing Enright. Lyons was a tough, hard-driving lawyer who wouldn't drop out of character in the role at the wrong moment. He would make Luke work hard—after all, he'd done this before.

They reached their seats, and she studied the stage. The podiums were exact replicas of the real ones for next week, the size and placement of which had been decided in lengthy negotiations between the two campaigns. Enright was short, Luke was tall, so Enright would be allowed to stand on a riser to compensate. She couldn't help a smile. Somebody surely would sneak a photographer in back to get a shot of Enright on that riser. Marty probably had it all arranged.

Nat, here with his mother under orders, looked uncomfortable and bored in his chair, slumping down each time someone stopped by to shake Kate's hand.

"Sit up, Nat," she whispered, annoyed, and at the same time rather liking the fact that he was wiggling like a normal kid. It eased a worry.

Someone slid into the seat next to her and leaned close. Before turning, she knew who it was.

"Kate." Peter touched her hand, and she looked into his eyes. They were troubled. "I can't stay," he said rapidly. "They're clearing press out right now. But I've got to say something."

Kate felt very conscious of Nat listening on her right. Peter seemed too absorbed to even notice her son's presence.

"What is it—?" she began.

He cut her off. "I owe you," he said. "You've got trouble coming."

For one still moment, she thought Peter was going to lean closer and hug her in front of everybody, but he stayed where he was.

"I'm sorry, kid," he whispered. He straightened, started to move away.

"No—" Kate jumped to her feet, grabbed the lapel of his suit, then, flushing, let go. "Wait."

Peter's voice held a warning she could not read. "Kate, I can't." He moved swiftly down the aisle, working his way to the exit. Kate started to follow him, then stopped. People were looking at her curiously. Damn, she couldn't leave now. She couldn't go charging down the aisle after Peter like some brainless idiot; it would look terrible. Outwardly calm, she turned around and walked slowly back to her seat.

"What was that all about?" Nat asked, his fingers clenched to the arms of his chair, as she sat down again next to him. "What did Peter want?"

Kate kept her tone soothing. "I don't know," she said, patting her son's hand. "Nothing, I'm sure. You know Peter—he's just being dramatic. Chasing some story, I guess."

Nat nodded, but she saw his knuckles whiten as he continued to clench the chair. She closed her eyes, swallowing apprehension. Peter wouldn't try to scare her, he wasn't like that. Something was up. What was it? The blood in her temples began to pound, but she forced herself to smooth her brow, act serene, and focus on the stage. The mock debate was about to begin.

Marty was walking to the center of the stage, calling out to the electricians to focus the spots. His manner was carefree and breezy as he put up a hand and quieted the small crowd.

"We're ready to start, folks," he said. "The playacting tonight is serious, so please try to respond as if you're watching the real thing. The best way is to forget this here is our friend Bob Lyons—" Lyons was stepping up to one of the podiums—"and imagine you are watching Shorty—whoops, I mean John Enright." A titter spread through the group, and something approaching a twinkle appeared in Marty's eye.

"He's so phony," Nat mumbled.

Kate didn't answer. She had to relax. She concentrated on how well the normally cheery fifty-year-old Lyons had created the illusion of being Enright. He stooped slightly and became a dignified decade older; he squinted, and it was eerily clear he needed bifocals. Absentmindedly he began tapping the tiny mike on his lapel with his index finger. The mannerism was perfect. And he even had Enright's thick, elegantly white hair.

Luke was stepping up to the other podium, looking serious. Kate forced herself to focus on the stage. This was the most important dress rehearsal of his campaign, and Luke couldn't be better stoked with information and one-liners to cover every conceivable situation. If there were gaps, if there were problems, tonight was the night to find them and solve them. She searched her husband's face eagerly, looking for something, noting something in its contours she hadn't expected. He didn't just look leaner and sharper, he *was* leaner and sharper.

"Hey, Dad," Nat said softly, "give 'em hell."

It quickly became apparent that Lyons was not planning on giving Luke an easy ride. The session rapidly grew tough, with Lyons boring into Luke, searching for every conceivable weak spot. He found a few. At one point, Luke slammed his fist on the podium and shot out a denunciation. His cheeks were flushed. He was into the game.

Suddenly Bob grinned. "Gotcha, Luke," he said.

A ripple of relieved laughter moved through the crowd. "Let's work on that," Marty called out from the first row, his voice genial. Luke made a joke; the mock debate moved on.

It was then that Kate heard a murmur of movement behind her. She glanced around. One of Luke's aides, shaking his head, was handing a folded newspaper to another aide seated next to him. He glanced at the paper, frowned, and turned to see who to pass it to next. Curious, Nat reached for it, his hand pulling it away even as the first aide tried fruitlessly to ward him off.

Kate's attention went back to the stage. Luke was denouncing the Republican plan to once again cap the Social Security cost of living adjustment.

"Senator, your party has spent decades making proposals that would cost the country too much money," Bob shot out. "I see a defensive man in front of me who represents the past."

216

Luke leaned forward, smiling, almost as if his reaction hadn't been planned. "The only defensiveness in this election, Senator, comes from the party that's forgotten about the elderly in this country," he said. "They're my parents and your parents, and they're not talking favors. They're talking rights. And the Democrats are the ones hearing them."

A surrogate questioner on the panel of "reporters" faced Luke.

"Senator, there are rumors circulating about your private life that are raising questions in the last days of this election," the questioner, a campaign aide from the Chicago office, asked. "Do you see yourself as a solid family man?"

Luke looked taken aback. At that moment, Kate felt something drop in her lap. She glanced down and saw the folded newspaper, then looked at Nat. His face was drawn and white. Kate picked up the paper and saw it was an obscure alternative publication from Los Angeles that frequently ran dubious stories, claiming they were too "hot" for the mainstream press. She was focused on Nat's clear distress, which was why she sensed rather than heard the shrillness in Luke's response.

"What the hell is that question supposed to mean?" Luke shot back from the stage.

"Senator, people are asking," protested the aide, his playacting facade slightly askew. "Maybe nobody will touch it, but—"

Marty stood up and strode closer to the stage. "Let's put that one aside right now," he said. "We'll work on it later."

But Bob Lyons, the lenses on his reading glasses glinting in the light from the overhead spots, was too deep into his role to pull out now. "Issues of character are part of the issues of governing," he thundered. "You can't dodge a question like this, Senator."

Luke flashed him a quick, irritated look. "Knock it off, Bob," he said.

Kate didn't see the expression on Luke's face, nor did she hear the embarrassed titter that swept the audience. She was too absorbed in reading the front-page story spread across in her lap.

"You can be sure nobody in the so-called 'respectable' press will touch this one," the story began. "Not this close to the election. But there is reliable information that Luke Goodspeed, the first Catholic candidate to win his party's nomination for president since John F. Kennedy, is carrying on an affair with a high-placed campaign aide."

There was much more, but Kate was too stunned to read it all. Or was she? She had to think about that, but not now. Later. She became suddenly conscious that people were craning their necks to look at her, whispering quietly.

"Mom, what's this all about?"

"It's a sleazy rag," she said, straightening her spine. "Don't take it seriously." She looked quickly at her son and saw nothing but confusion. She turned her face away; this was no time to communicate worry. "And don't change your expression," she said. "People are watching us."

The mock debate was over, and Luke was searching for her; she could see him moving toward her through the crowd.

"Luke—" She edged back into an alcove of the auditorium, and then he was bending close.

"What's the matter?" he said.

Silently she handed him the newspaper and watched his face stiffen. "My God, what garbage," he said, throwing the newspaper aside. "This is *National Enquirer* stuff." His scorn was dismissive and total.

"Luke—"

"Honey, I've got to go; the plane's waiting," he said. His tone was patient, but hurried. "We'll talk about this and anything else on your mind, but later, okay? Don't let this stuff upset you. How'd I do?" He kissed her lightly, quickly, not waiting for an answer. Troubled, Kate kissed him back. And then he was gone, caught up in the rush of aides and reporters.

But something had changed. She felt it in her stomach.

The next morning, Kate awoke from a light sleep, sat up in bed, and swung her feet onto the carpeted floor, searching through the gloom for her slippers. She had slept uneasily, and her head was still filled with the sounds of her dreams—harsh, unrelenting sounds. She had awakened several times with the sense of falling through space with nothing and no one to stop her fall. Now there was a lump of apprehension in her throat that she tried to swallow down, but it wouldn't budge.

She eased her toes into the furry confines of pink mules and allowed herself another moment to sit on the edge of the bed. The alarm would not go off for another half hour. The light was cutting through the darkness more rapidly, and she could now faintly see the outline of her campaign schedule on the bedside table. Kate stared at the two sheets of computer paper stapled together and remembered what was first on her schedule: a live appearance on "Sunrise Edition," the nation's number one morning talk show—a special hour-long interview with the wives of the Democratic and Republican presidential nominees. That meant she was about to share a couch this morning with Eleanor Enright and chat about what it meant to be a candidate's wife.

Eleanor: the woman who had rolled more bandages for the Red Cross, kissed more children, addressed more Christmas cards, treated more constituents to gracious tours of the Capitol than anybody. One of the smartest, most political wives in town. Kate felt pressure collecting in her head. In truth, this wasn't the day she wanted to face Eleanor.

That's what's changed, she thought suddenly. That rag from Los Angeles has me on the defensive, and I resent it. Was she awake enough yet to know if that was the truth? Yes, she told herself, that's the truth. And the lump in her throat was not going away.

❖ ❖

10

Kate saw Jerry Spanos cast a nervous sidelong glance at her as they walked together through the glass doors of the television studio. She smiled encouragingly. She suspected Jerry hadn't been particularly happy at first with the lower status of working for her and not Luke. He had seen himself as something of a nursemaid, she was sure of it, but now they were almost buddies. And buddies in this business were hard to come by.

"Don't worry," she said. Jerry opened his mouth to speak just as a bright-faced woman in a gray tweed jacket swooped down on them from the other side of the reception area. "Mrs. Goodspeed, it's terrific to see you," the woman interrupted in a voice from the diaphragm, flowing with energy. "We're delighted to have both you and Mrs. Enright. To think you could both take time from your busy schedules and do this for us is really terrific. How are you? How's your family? A killer schedule, right?" Together, escorted by the voluble young greeter, Kate and Jerry walked down the narrow corridor leading to the makeup room.

A middle-aged woman with orange-tinted hair and a prim demeanor stood to greet them as they entered. "Ah, Mrs. Goodspeed, too much campaigning," she said gravely, studying the face of her subject. She quickly softened her greeting with a smile as Kate settled into a pink leather chair and faced a wall of mirrors. "Do what you can," Kate said calmly. Her eyes closed as she felt the first cold stroke of the makeup sponge on her left cheek, thinking, I'm not going to let Jerry get me worried.

"Mrs. Goodspeed. Hey, this is a real pleasure." Jack Braden, the executive producer of the show, had entered the room and was grinning widely into the mirror. His dark gray sports coat was casually impeccable, his manner professionally genial. Was he checking out the bags under her eyes? Kate wished the makeup woman would work faster.

"Is there water for Mrs. Goodspeed?" Jerry said, his voice a touch officious.

"Of course." Braden didn't even glance at him.

"I want to check the seating," Jerry persisted. "Mrs. Goodspeed needs a straight-back chair."

"We'll get whatever chair you want," Braden said, still not looking at Jerry. Instead he spoke to the makeup woman, meanwhile staring at Kate in the mirror.

"Put some more of that stuff under her eyes," he said.

The set was a mock living room. Walking onto the sound stage, past the dark hulking presence of the cameras and the hidden folding chairs where guests usually sat waiting their turn, Kate found herself searching for Eleanor Enright. Eleanor and she were friends, of a sort. After all these years as Senate wives, they shared an unspoken understanding. Was she counting on that today?

A pale beige sofa sat dead center on the raised set. In back, invisible glowing spots simulated the morning sun peeping through a fake window. Seated on the sofa was the show's popular middle-aged yet cheerleader-fresh host, his winsome blond partner, and Eleanor. They all smiled brightly at Kate.

"Hello, Kate," Eleanor said.

Tennis tan, wired with energy, her gray hair silvered and tamed, Eleanor Enright sat poised and confident in a skirt exactly the right length, her clothes discreetly good, as usual, and very low key. The family money never showed. Back in Kate's first days as a Senate wife, Eleanor had been fabled for her helpfulness. She advised on where the best schools were, what grocery stores delivered, where you could get a good haircut, and where you could find a plumber who would come on weekends—all the things new Senate wives needed to know. But nothing—not money, not friendship—ever interfered with Eleanor's job of moving her colorless, careful husband to the top. She had awesome discipline.

221

"How are the children?" Eleanor said. "Growing fast, I'll bet."
"They certainly are," Kate responded with an equally bright smile.
"In school?"
"Yes."
"Not watching this morning, are they?"
A shadow of something passed over Eleanor's eyes and then it was
gone, and Kate wondered if she had seen anything at all.

Behind the nonreflecting glass of the control room a stocky technician chomped on a large wad of gum as the senior producer, a
young woman with crisply cut blond hair, paced nervously. Her
name was Charlotte Vronsky, and she was new and ambitious, one
of the bright young women of television who had reaped the payoff
for hard work and good luck. But it meant never resting for a minute.
Work was everything; it had to be, especially with a tough boss like
Jack Braden.

She flashed a smile toward the only visitor in the booth, a tall man
standing quietly in the rear. He held a notebook in his hands, a
signature symbol that justified his presence, but he wasn't writing.
Instead, Peter Bradford's eyes were fixed on the monitor. He looked
almost as tense as Kate Goodspeed, but he broke his concentration
for a moment to smile back at Charlotte, and she was grateful.
Getting him inside the control booth for the show was bending the
rules a bit, but Peter was known as a nice guy who could be charm-
ingly persuasive. She did not admit this to herself directly, but in
Charlotte's busy brain there was a secret thought: maybe, just maybe,
he might be grateful enough later to want to share a drink or dinner.
Things got pretty lonely sometimes in the condo.

The host, Dick Trenton, a beaming man in a bright plaid tie, was
rubbing his hands. "I'm happy you both agreed to do this, I really,
really am," he said. "It means a lot to the country to know just *how*
you live in this *relentless* spotlight, and how you *cope* and—" he
spread his arms in a happy gesture—"and everything else." His eyes
went blank for an instant. Charlotte's voice was in his earpiece.
"Twenty seconds, Dick," she said. The stage manager standing
next to one of the cameras bellowed an echo: "Twenty seconds."
"Now, down to business," he said briskly. "You've both met Jana
Jewell, my new partner, right?" The blonde tossed her hair and

smiled. Eleanor and Kate dutifully smiled back. "Jana's with us fresh from Los Angeles," Dick went on, "and the four of us are going to have a good time this morning." He peered past the lights to a small enclosure filled with expectant, smiling, upturned faces. "We've got our studio audience ready and *raring* to go," he said.

Charlotte's voice cut in, low. "Five seconds, Dick."

"Five seconds!" echoed the stage manager. "Four, three, two . . ." and with a wave of his hand, Dick swiveled to Camera One, his arms wide and embracing.

"Hel-lo, *America!*" he crowed.

Kate sneaked a glance at the studio clock. Ten minutes past the hour. It was terrible to get bored early in a show, dangerous, in fact; but lordy, this team was predictable. She and Eleanor were playing an easy game of Ping-Pong with their questions: What sort of First Lady would you be? Would you redecorate the White House? Would you attend cabinet meetings? How much influence should a First Lady have over her husband? What's too much? The usual. Kate settled back, sensing herself working comfortably with Eleanor to strike just the right balance.

"Mrs. Enright, what attributes should a First Lady have?" asked Jana brightly.

"Well—certainly, stamina," Eleanor replied with a light laugh.

"What about character traits? What flaws should the public look out for?"

"Hmmm." Eleanor was pursing her lips thoughtfully. "That's harder," she said. "Lying, obviously, is unacceptable. Also—well, rudeness."

"Can you give us an example?"

"Oh, my." Eleanor let out a sigh. "I do think religious leaders should be respected," she said. "Some issues are very volatile of course—but, as wives of the men who want to lead this country, I think we are obligated to treat these people with unfailing courtesy."

Jolted, Kate looked at Eleanor and then forced a mask over her face. She was suddenly on the defensive. Be careful, she warned herself, say something positive about Cardinal Kovach, then get off the subject—

But the anticipated question didn't come. Instead, Jana pressed forward with Eleanor. "You said something else," she said. "Lying. Tell us more."

"Well, when one tries to keep secrets—" Eleanor paused. She looked only at Jana, avoiding Kate's eyes. "It isn't a healthy situation."

Kate tried to interrupt, but Jana's interest in Eleanor was avid.

"What kind of secrets?" she asked. "Perhaps rumors—of a candidate's extramarital adventures?"

"I certainly think rumors must be addressed," Eleanor said firmly.

"Mrs. Goodspeed—" Jana was leaning forward, looking less winsome, her voice lubricated with concern. "Tough times, huh? How does it feel to be hearing all this stupid gossip about your husband?"

The studio audience sat very still.

"Je-*sus*, look at that," the technician in the control room chortled, shoving his gum to the side of his jaw and pointing at Kate's stunned face. "She looks like someone hit her."

"You're reading into it what you want," Charlotte said quickly.

"Honey, I'm reading what I *see*."

"Take Camera Three," Charlotte ordered. "I want a four-shot here."

"No."

Charlotte whirled around. Jack Braden, arms folded, had stepped into the control room and was standing behind her, staring at Kate's face on the Camera Two monitor. Peter, who hadn't moved, was staring, too.

"Stay on Two," Braden said. "And take it a little tighter. This is good."

"All campaigns endure rumors," Kate was saying, trying desperately to keep the shakiness she felt out of her voice. "There's no truth to this one, and nobody's going to believe it. I've got better things to do than pay attention to malicious attacks."

She hoped she had hit the right note of forcefulness, but the studio audience was unnaturally quiet. She glanced coldly at Eleanor. There was pity in Eleanor's eyes, a remote pity, the pity reserved for the death of an endangered species, perhaps the snaildarter or the spotted owl. The decent, gracious Eleanor would feel real pity. This apparition before her did not.

In the control room, Charlotte reasserted herself. "Go to commercial," she barked into Dick's ear.

"Hold it," Braden shot back. "Let this play out a few more seconds." But Dick had already reacted to Charlotte's order. "Stay with us," he said brightly to the camera, "we'll be right back." The red light on the camera blinked off.

"Eleanor—" Kate leaned forward, taking advantage of the reprieve to face her adversary—"how can you do this? It's me, Kate—remember?"

"I don't know what you mean," Eleanor said quietly.

"You certainly do," Kate said, her hand firmly over her microphone. The two women stared at each other, and Kate had to swallow a torrent of words. She had no choice. Once again they were on the air.

In the control room, Charlotte hissed into her headset, "You got him?"

"Sure do," came the reply. "He's already patched into the board and ready to go."

Charlotte turned to the technician. "Let's take Enright, now," she commanded.

"This'll surprise them," he said as he pressed the right flashing button connecting the audio board to the set.

"Now, some questions from our television audience," Dick announced. "Just a few—" he gestured toward the camera—"so that some of you out there will also have a chance to talk with the woman who will be First Lady."

"Hello, Mrs. Enright!"

The male voice boomed over the intercom, through the studio and out onto the nation's airwaves. Eleanor blinked, then executed a perfect double take. "John," she said with delight, "is that you?"

Kate felt a cramp twisting her stomach. Eleanor was doing a great job of feigning surprise as she plunged into a brief, chatty, carefully scripted exchange with her husband, while Dick and Jana fairly wiggled in their chairs with excitement.

"Gotta go now, honey," Enright said. "Time to get back to work." He chuckled. "Time to win an election."

"America's listening, John," Eleanor said liltingly. "Hope everybody forgives me for being shameless about plugging my husband, but you're the man for me and you're the man for the job. Right, everybody?" The studio audience laughed and clapped. A couple of people cheered.

225

Kate's disdain for this hokey little exchange was almost immediately engulfed by a totally humiliating realization. Watching Eleanor, she was looking at what she herself was supposed to be. She was like the talking doll Abby had as a little girl, the one with the string in the back that you pulled when you wanted it to say bright, happy things. But wasn't she just doing her job? Kate felt queasy. I do this kind of thing for Luke, she thought. It's as natural an act as breathing, and there's no reason it should be any different for Eleanor.

"She's got class," said the technician, nodding admiringly toward Eleanor's image on the monitor.

"Matter of opinion," Charlotte snapped. "Keep that camera *off* Kate when we come back." Her mouth tightened, and she waited to be overruled. But from behind, only silence. Jack Braden had vanished, off to sell the nightly news on using footage of Kate's stricken face.

"Peter?" Charlotte said, turning around. His face was shadowed. She took a step toward him. "Hey, got time for a cup of coffee when we're done?"

"Sorry," he said gently, moving out of the shadows. "I have to get back to the office. Thanks anyway." He quickly squeezed her arm, and turned to go.

Charlotte watched him leave. She had done all the right things, and he was not angry with her, but she also knew she would never sip wine with Peter Bradford. She saw an expression on his face she didn't understand. She shook her head with a burst of furious impatience at the world, at men, at television. Then she picked up her notes for the next day's show. She would study them at home tonight and remember to be a little obsequious with Jack tomorrow.

It was over. Done. Kate and Eleanor stiffly shook hands.

"Wasn't this a great show?" Dick said to the studio audience. "Wasn't it *great*?" The audience clapped and clapped. Jerry was there, his face grim, thrusting his hand forward to help Kate down from the set and to move her quickly out of the studio and into her waiting car. Peter stepped quickly through the crowd and touched Kate's hand. "Not easy," he whispered. "You did fine."

226

Startled, she scanned his eyes anxiously. "Are you writing about it?"

"No."

"Thank you."

She began moving automatically, smiling brightly, waving good-bye. She almost made it to the door.

"Mrs. Goodspeed? Kate?"

Kate stopped dead in her tracks. That voice. She turned slowly, knowing what she would see.

A kind-faced woman with short white hair, probably early sixties, dressed in a pair of pants and a floral sweater, stepped forward from the crowd, offering her hand. Her expression was hopeful but tentative.

"I wanted to see you again," she said, almost shyly. "Remember me? Constitutional History? You were my best student. I hope you don't mind."

Woodenly Kate thrust forward her hand and forced a smile.

"Not at all," she lied.

In a Midwest airport hotel room, a tired place with wafer-thin walls covered in mustard yellow foil wallpaper, Luke stared at the television screen, then flicked off the set. His face was drawn, his eyes shot through with tiny, crackling lines of fatigue.

"Not so good," Marty said, from a corner of the room.

"Kate looked like someone shot her between the eyes," Luke said slowly. "I never want that to happen again."

"We can fix it up; I've got a plan."

Luke did not respond; his face grew even more somber; his eyes more distant.

Nervously, Marty cleared his throat. "Thinking about Young?"

"Yeah."

"When did his wife call you?"

Luke briefly closed his eyes, then opened them again.

"About four this morning," he said.

"So the guy's dead." Marty said the words matter-of-factly, with no emotion.

"Yeah."

"You believe her?"

227

"I know pain and fear when I hear it in someone's voice, Marty. Edward Young's dead."

"What happened?"

"She heard a car drive up shortly after midnight, then somebody rang the doorbell. She opened the door, and there he was, on the doorstep." Luke paused, rubbed a hand through his hair. "Shot once in the back of the head. That cap of his was stuffed in his mouth."

"Jesus."

"He died trying to get us that tape."

"You don't know that."

"Hell, I can't prove it. But I'll bet he risked his life for that tape, and he lost. Now his wife and the others are too frightened to help us."

There was a short silence. "It's too bad," Marty said finally. "But there's nothing we can do about it."

"Don't wash your hands of this too fast," Luke said quietly. "I'm convinced. I'm opposing Palmer. Lasati's doing nothing; none of Gilmartin's people plan to do a damn thing. Eventually, there'll be an investigation, and I know where I stand. Right now."

Marty sighed. "So what?" he said. "Nothing's going to stop Palmer. His mug is everywhere—posters, magazines, church foyers, TV—you name it."

"Look, I may not *be* president yet," Luke said, his voice low, but with a hard edge. "But I'm going to goddamn *act* like one."

"We've got enough damage control ahead of us, Luke." This time, Marty's voice was heavy.

Luke ignored him. "I want the statement released through my Senate office," he said. "I dictated it two hours ago."

"Do us both a favor. Stall for a few more days." Marty paused, giving each word deliberate weight. "You know why."

Luke sat still, saying nothing. He picked up a dry piece of toast off a room-service tray and chewed it slowly. "I'm not waiting until after the election, if that's what you're thinking," he finally said.

Marty picked up from the bed a piece of paper covered with Luke's handwritten scrawl and read it carefully before answering. "All right," he said. "But we've got to do some groundwork first with blacks." He waited, letting his words sink in. "Next Sunday, okay?" he said. "The day after the debate. No later."

Luke considered this, frowning. "Okay," he said, with an abrupt nod.

The phone pealed, sharp and loud. Luke reached across the bed and picked it up to Steve's voice. Instantly his body stiffened.

"Luke."

"What the hell do *you* want?"

"I'm reading your statement opposing Palmer, and it's right on the money. Everybody else is too scared to do anything. I just wanted to tell you that."

Luke stared into the receiver. "After the way you trashed me with Kate, you just get on the phone to tell me you like a statement?" he said, his voice vibrating with anger. "What exactly do you want? Absolution?"

The silence was short but total. "No elaborate agenda," Steve finally said, speaking carefully. "I'm sitting here in the Senate office and I'm still working for you, as far as I know. All I wanted to tell you was I'm impressed. It's the old Luke. I owe you that."

"You've made a mistake, Steve. You are no longer working for me."

This time his words were greeted with total silence.

"I would have dumped you the day you talked to Kate," Luke said. "But I've been holding off to find the right time. I've just decided this is the right time."

"I gave you your excuse, right? But I had to hear you say it before I could really believe it," Steve said flatly. "And now I have."

"Yeah, you're hearing it. You're fired."

"Maybe I owe you something, just one last thing, and then I'm out the door, okay?" Steve paused, taking a deep breath. "You're on some damn detour, Luke, and it'll catch up with you."

"You threatening me, Steve?"

"No. I've done a lot of things, but I haven't done that."

"You better start packing your things."

"One question," Steve asked.

"Yeah?"

"Do you think I was trying to destroy you? You think about it for a second. You think about everything we've done together. Do you think that? No, wait a minute. Do you *believe* that?"

"All I go on," Luke snapped, "is what you did to me last."

A sudden sharp snort of laughter from Steve. "You make it easy for yourself, don't you."

"I keep my focus, if that's what you mean."

"Maybe we both could have done a better job of that."

"Steve, you slandered me. To my wife. That's unforgivable."

"That was a big mistake, and I'm deeply sorry. But nobody's been more loyal to you in your life."

"Sorry, buddy, it doesn't look that way from where I sit. We're done."

"I hear you. Goodbye, Luke, what the hell, huh?" Again, the sharp, strained laughter. "That's politics."

The connection clicked off.

Luke slammed the phone back into its cradle with such force that the bedside table shook. He stared at it for a moment and then turned to Marty. "I want him cleaned out of there before the end of the day," he said.

Then he stood and strode to the bathroom to shave.

The New York Times printed an especially small paper Saturday, which meant a smaller news hole than usual. Kate's denial of the Los Angeles tabloid's story ran inside, with no picture. But the Associated Press version out on the wires to hundreds of papers played it big. Her denial—coming as it did on a national television show seen by hundreds of thousands of people—legitimized the story. Reporters everywhere scrambled to follow up. The *Washington Post* played it on the first page, describing in detail Kate's stricken demeanor. A fuzzy still from the TV show, full face, ran above the fold. In it, Kate looked as if someone had slapped her, hard. The *Post* story included a paragraph quoting a member of the studio audience as describing Eleanor Enright's "grace and even demeanor" during the "awkward" questions about "the increasingly detailed rumors."

In his cluttered office, Marty Apple sat alone, drumming his fingers, the papers in a jumble around him. His brow was furrowed.

"Marty, I got her. She's on the phone."

He nodded to his secretary and picked up the receiver.

"The footage on CBS was the worst," he said without preamble.

"You should have briefed me on what might happen, Marty," Kate said calmly. "That's your job. Damage control." Her voice was clear and firm.

"You didn't have to fall apart, Kate," he said. "I can't pull a window shade over you with every little crisis."

"Correct me if I'm wrong, but I don't think this is a little crisis."

His silence gave her the answer she expected. Marty cleared his throat. "I've got a plan, and I need your cooperation," he said.

"What is it?"

"I want you in Chicago Monday morning."

"Why?"

"For a joint press conference with Luke."

There was a long silence.

"You want me to be the dutiful wife, right?"

"Kate, your husband is being smeared," he answered. His voice was slow, elaborately patient. "You're under too much strain, kid," he said.

Kate sighed. "Spare me, Marty."

"I've got to say it plain, okay? You looked like you were falling apart, and that gives more credence to these damn rumors. We have to have this press conference now, and you being there is crucial."

"Are you actually saying this is my fault?"

"We pull together on this one, that's what I'm saying. Okay?"

"I don't know."

Again, a short silence.

"Don't stall," Marty said, his voice quieting. "There isn't time."

Kate smiled grimly. "There never is," she said. "Clear your schedule, Marty. It's time you and I had a little talk."

Marty was a man who prided himself on knowing when to make a tactical concession, and he responded quickly. "I'll be right over," he said.

"No."

It was the first flat-out no from Kate, and Marty, taken aback, didn't respond right away.

"Make it an hour from now. I'm busy," she said.

"It's more convenient right now."

"No, it isn't. I'm going over Nat's math homework."

The line clicked softly, and it gave Kate satisfaction to know Marty was holding a dead phone.

Kate stared down at the page of scrawled math problems Nat had left beside the phone. She allowed herself a faint smile. Her son's homework was completely indecipherable, but it provided an excuse for putting the meeting with Marty on her terms instead of his. There was a novelty in that.

She listened. The house was unusually silent. Mrs. Leonard was enjoying a rare day off, and she had unplugged the fax machine. Nothing the campaign could send over for her attention seemed urgent today. A few old friends had called—awkwardly, warily trying to say the right thing. "Are you okay?" they said. "I'm okay," she replied. "The press is *awful*," they said. "Any rumor in a storm," she replied. They didn't ask if the rumor was true. They didn't ask how Luke was taking the news. They treated it like a death, which, in a sense, it was. Kate stared at the phone, thinking of Luke's mother. Poor Louise. Should she call her? What would she say? Would it just put pressure on her loyalty to her son? Maybe it was better to wait, to see if Louise herself chose to call.

When the phone rang again, it was Joan. "I'm here," she said simply.

"I know," Kate replied. She wanted to say more; she wanted to express her thanks. But that was all she dared say. Joan was angry at Luke, she could hear it in her voice, and it was wiser not to tap into it. She needed Joan's support, not her anger. It might strike too dangerous a spark in herself.

She fixed herself a tuna sandwich, spreading low-fat mayonnaise over two thin slices of wheat bread. At the last minute, she remembered to cut up a little celery. Maybe today she would eat that dark chocolate bar tucked back in the freezer. What would the world do without chocolate? She worked methodically, rinsing out the tuna can, carefully tucking the tin lid inside the can before depositing it in the garbage. She folded her sandwich inside a paper towel. She was too restless to eat it sitting down.

In the dining room, the fruitwood grandfather clock Louise had given her son and new daughter-in-law as a wedding present chimed the hour. Kate walked slowly down the hall, munching wheat bread and tuna, listening to the soft clicking of her heels on the weathered oak floor. She glanced at the clock, remembering Abby as a six-year-old explaining to her little brother how it worked. "This is the heart," Abby had instructed importantly, pointing to the pendulum, "and the things in back are the muscles, and then it's got a nice voice to tell us what time it is, and that's why it's a good clock."

"What's a bad clock?" Nat had asked.

Abby never hesitated. "The one that wakes up Mommy and Daddy to go fly away on an airplane," she said.

Kate had tiptoed away, storing the story, softening it and weaving it in with other anecdotes of their busy lives, forgetting it eventually, and now as she stared into the dining room, she could almost see her small children again. Would she see this scene the same way, would it be so stunningly freeze-framed, if it had been stored inside a video camera instead of only her memory? Would it make her as wistful? Would it preserve reality better or simply distort it more? Once, coming back with Luke from a Senate trip to Europe, Kate had sat across the aisle from a woman who spent the entire flight watching vacation film on her portable camcorder. Periodically she would pass her husband the camcorder and he would watch a while and then pass it back—all in silence. They were validating reality, Kate decided. Their vacation wasn't real until they could watch it on tape. It was such a curious detachment from experience. Was she living the same way?

Kate slowly climbed the center stairs, fingering the graceful old Victorian balustrade. The carpet beneath her feet was worn but still sturdy. At the top of the stairs she stood at the door to Nat's bedroom. She opened it gingerly, feeling like an intruder. Chaos. Clothes everywhere. Bright-colored posters of rock stars covered the walls. She didn't recognize any of them. In the corner, angled awkwardly against a chest overflowing with T-shirts and white gym socks, was Nat's old guitar. Did he still play it?

She stepped into the room. On a table beside the bed was Nat's computer. The gray, blank screen told her nothing, but it was the core of her son's imaginative world. What was in the thing? On the south wall, a bulletin board crammed with notes and pictures provided an easier peek into her son's soul. She peered at the jumble, touching nothing: here was a notice of a school swim meet; there a picture of Luke ripped from the *Washington Post*. In the center of the board, a *Time* magazine convention cover featuring the victorious, smiling Democratic candidate. Beneath it, two "Goodspeed for President" campaign buttons. Under the *Post* photograph Kate spotted the birthday card she had sent Nat last year from New Hampshire—bought by an aide and signed by her in a hasty scrawl. She didn't remember mailing it.

She stepped out of the room and down the hall again. It was like

233

collecting faded snapshots as she walked. Old laughter, children chasing each other, the dog scratching the bedroom door—she stared into the room she shared with Luke. With its soft lavenders and blues, the room verged on being too feminine. But Kate saw it as a refuge from chaos, a place where she could read alone or lie with Luke between the cool softness of pale cotton sheets. The mood was sensual. Luke had never complained, although he did joke about Kate's weakness for lacy bedpillows. Was she imagining it, or could she smell Luke's favorite soap? She sniffed again, carefully, closing her eyes. No, she couldn't remember smelling it for a long time. Did Luke use it anymore? It must be the scented paper lining the closet shelves.

Downstairs, the screen door creaked open. Marty was knocking heavily on the door.

"Coffee?"

Marty stood stiffly in the front hall, looking awkwardly out of place. He grunted once in response to Kate's query. Taking that as yes, she turned and walked into the kitchen, leaving him standing alone. She slowly filled the kettle and flicked on the gas, then took down two coffee mugs from the cupboard. Poised for a moment, hesitating, she put them back and pulled two china teacups and saucers out instead. She gazed with a modicum of satisfaction at a fragile handle never intended for a man's fingers.

She heard his step and turned. He had followed her into the kitchen and was staring at the teacups as if he could read her mind.

"If it's all the same to you, I'd rather have a mug."

Kate nodded. Marty was already pacing purposefully.

"I don't have much time," he said. "We're running out of options."

Kate measured out rounded teaspoons of instant coffee, lifted the steaming kettle, and poured, her hand steady. Marty kept pacing. I'm going to break through to this man if it kills me, she thought.

Marty pulled a cigarette from the pack in his pocket and began to light it.

"Please don't smoke," Kate said.

Marty's expression was almost comical. He froze for an instant,

234

then blew out the match and replaced the cigarette in his pocket without comment.

"Okay, you're telling me I'm on your turf, Kate," he said, sitting heavily in a chair. "Let's go on with it; I'm in no mood for games."

Kate whirled on him. "Marty, what is this tough-guy stuff?" she said. "Do you realize how insulting you are?"

"Hey, I'm not insulting you," he said. He seemed taken aback by her direct attack. "I've made a special trip here for you—okay?"

Kate handed him his coffee in a mug and watched his thick fingers grope for leverage with the handle. "I want to know what's really going on," she said. "I want you to face me and tell me straight, and I don't want to be patronized."

Marty nodded and pulled his chair close to the kitchen table. "If I've been rough on you, I'm sorry," he said. "But I'm focused on the job at hand. We've got plenty of problems, you know that. My feeling is, you personalize things too much—you get too emotional, okay? When you do, you risk screwing up the campaign."

Still standing, she noted how gray he had become. It made him seem suddenly almost vulnerable.

"How are your kids, Marty?"

He shifted in his chair. "Fine, no problems."

"Do you ever see them?"

"Hey, spare me, this isn't the point of anything."

"Where are they?"

He spread his hands, visibly annoyed. "Here, there, anywhere—this isn't relevant, you know. Got a spoon?"

Kate handed him a spoon, sat down with her coffee, and watched him dig out two large mounds of sugar from the sugar bowl and dump them into his mug, leaving a thin trail of spilled crystals on the table.

"I don't think of you as someone with a home," she said as he licked his thumb, pressed it onto the spilled sugar and licked it again.

"I should be the one feeling insulted, now."

"No, I mean it," she persisted. "I can't see you with a home, and I get this strange feeling—I don't know what you believe in."

She saw something flicker in his eyes. Marty swallowed half his cup of coffee in a gulp and brushed an impatient hand across his chin. "I believe in the person I work for," he said. "Maybe you don't think so, but it's true. You think about the people I've worked for; they all believe in the same things you do and Luke does; they're the ones that oughta be running the country—is that so bad?"

He was switching gears again, almost imperceptibly. "If we're being blunt with each other, I want to say something," he said. "You think I'm nothing but a con man. I know you do." There was a question in his usually unreadable eyes; he actually paused to see if she would protest. Kate said nothing, and he went on. "Well, if that's what you think, you're wrong," he said. "You want to know about my kids, right? A little human-interest material, right?"

"Marty, I'm not a reporter."

"Well, you used to be." It was said with such force, Kate was taken aback.

"Okay, I'll tell you. They're twelve and thirteen now; two boys. Real jocks, I'm told; live with their mother. Missouri. The youngest plays soccer, captain of the team. . . ." Marty could have been reciting the alphabet. He stopped abruptly, casting her a look that seemed almost sly. "Satisfied?"

"Do you see much of them?"

"With my life?" He laughed. "Are you kidding?" He put out his arms, palms up, in an imploring gesture. "If I'm a con man, aren't we all? You? Luke?"

"Are you conning me now?"

Marty sighed. "Look, we're trying to win an election," he said. "And you don't get medals in this business for doing your job right."

"That's the kind of thing I can't stand," she said, shaking her head in irritation. "You talk in tough-guy clichés and you don't say anything." She leaned forward, almost imploringly. "Marty, talk to me about something. Talk to me about the difference between a truth and a lie."

The room was very still.

Another shift of gears. "I know how to do my job," he said. "That's my brand of honesty. Doing it right."

Kate wanted to grab him by his arms and shake him, but she felt suddenly more frightened than angry. This man trying to shape Luke had no shape of his own, nothing she could connect with or understand. He was like a slithering fish. What ridiculous impulse had given her the idea she could break through to him in any way? If she

236

had entertained any thoughts of getting him to understand she was struggling with a sense of things slipping and sliding, that she needed some sense from him of what was going on, they were gone now. He lived in another world. All she could hope for was that Luke had not completely moved to that world with him.

"Let me at least get straight what it is you want from me. No—" Kate quickly amended— "what it is you want me to *be*."

Marty watched her warily.

"Okay. You want me to be unquestioning, unchallenging, totally focused on the campaign—have I got it right so far?"

"So far."

"I should always do exactly what you tell me to do."

"Yep."

"Wear what you want me to wear."

"Yep."

"Say what you want me to say."

"You got it."

Kate felt an impulse to laugh but she quelled it. Marty was totally serious. "Don't you understand I'm never going to be that kind of wife?" she said. Instantly she corrected herself. "That kind of person?"

Her choice of words hovered in the air, sounding strange. But there was no denying the truth anymore. Something was happening inside her. There was a wall, an absolutely impenetrable wall between her and this man, maybe between her and Luke and everybody else in the campaign as well, because something was happening and she was now, finally, beginning to understand what it was. She was not just a piece of the campaign machinery anymore, not just "Senator Goodspeed's lovely wife," not merely a smiling source of strength to be marketed to America's voters. She was herself. An individual. I'm making my own decisions now, she thought. I have to.

"Why not?"

"Because it's not possible," she said.

Marty leaned forward, talking rapidly. "You think I'm kidding around? I'm not. Am I old-fashioned about this? You bet. You married this guy, Kate."

"Yes, I married him, not you. I reject your claim of ownership."

237

Marty shook his head impatiently, his anger barely under control. "A campaign is a war," he said. "It has battles, and battles need strategy, and everything you do or the kids do or I do or Luke does has *got* to be geared to winning the goddamn war. Why is that so hard to understand?"

"You may be out to win a war," Kate retorted, "but you're not going to do it by leaving my body on the battlefield. This campaign isn't the whole world."

"Yes, it is."

She pulled back, weary. There was no use arguing the point. Yes, it was the whole world. For Marty. For Luke. For Claire. But not for her; not anymore. "Let me tell you something about the world, Marty," she said. "It has kids in it. My kids. It has people in it who care about each other and respect each other and are married because they want to be." She bit her lip. She might be getting into an area of wishful thinking, but she couldn't think about that now. "Nat and Abby are an important part of my world. I'm not around for you to manipulate, nor are they. And I have a husband, not just a candidate, in my bed at night."

Marty leaned forward, muscles tensed. He was really trying to convince her, his focus was authentic and unmistakable. "You keep all that by doing what we need you to do," he said. "I need you, Kate. Luke needs you. The balance could tip if we're not careful. Our focus groups show Enright's looking stronger, more his own man. His education ideas are getting serious press attention, and now we've got this damn rumor hanging over us. You know what's going to happen Monday? We're going to start sliding. Our tracking polls are already showing it. We're going to get the shit kicked out of us unless you and Luke can get the press to pull off. I want to keep Luke on the campaign trail tomorrow, looking normal—I'll keep the press away. I don't want him back here. You love your husband, right? Show it. Show it with every movement, every muscle. Be noble, loyal. Line up the kids, I want them there, too. Put your chins up in the air, hang together, convince those jackals you're toughing out the rumors. We'll get the worst of them later. When we win. Now, I'm going to ask." He leaned back, and locked his eyes with hers. His voice went very soft. "I'm going to beg. Are you going to be at this press conference or not?"

238

There it was. She knew what her answer had to be. There was no way out of this; she had known that all along. Even as she felt herself separating from the reality Marty was describing, there was the call of loyalty. She couldn't let Luke down. This wasn't the time or place to rewrite the rules.

"Tell me why I'm there, Marty," she said. "And lay it out straight."

"To back Luke up, plain and simple. We'll prepare you, don't worry. You won't get any more surprises."

"Is my husband sleeping with Claire?"

Marty shook his head. "No," he said. His gaze stayed steady.

Kate chose to make him wait a moment longer. "I'm never going to be a robot again," she said.

"Hey, whatever you want."

Kate stared at Marty for a long moment, not trusting anything she saw in his face. But it was done, she knew that.

"All right," she said.

He broke into a wide, crooked grin. "Good girl," he said.

"For Luke. Not for you."

The grin was spreading over his face, giving him an almost eerie look of jolliness, like a world-weary Santa Claus. "Shit," he said. "I don't care."

Nat, hugging close the folds of an old and baggy tweed sweater, sat hunched forward on the top step of the back porch next to his mother. Both of them squinted against Sunday's harsh sun.

"I don't want to go, Mom," he said.

"You don't have to decide right away."

"Aren't we supposed to fly there tonight?"

"There's a bad storm front moving into Chicago," Kate said. "And I've got a speech this afternoon. So Marty's chartering a plane for us tomorrow morning. We leave at six."

Nat scratched his head, saying nothing. His freckled face was very pale.

"Nat," Kate said gently. "I won't force you."

Nat shot his mother a startled, grateful look. "I'm mad at him," he volunteered hesitantly. "He told me he'd call tonight, and I know he's gonna try and talk me into going. That's why I'm mad."

"I know you are." She didn't want to probe any deeper.

"Aren't you?"

There was a wind building, a wind just a touch too cold for sitting in the shade on the porch steps. Kate shivered. At least it will wake me up, she thought. At least I'm not sitting inside reading the follow-up stories in the Sunday papers. How much should she say to Nat? Was it a mistake to be too honest?

"I'm feeling pretty bad," she said. "And I'm worried."

Nat shook his head, started to speak, then stared hard at his shoes. He said nothing.

"He needs me, Nat," she said simply.

Nat scratched at his head with an agitated motion and started to say something just as the phone rang. He looked at his mother in instant alarm.

"Shall I get it?" she asked.

The expression in the boy's eyes faded, replaced by resignation. "Naw," he said.

He disappeared inside the house, and Kate burrowed her face into her lap to protect it against any more abuse from the wind. Long moments passed. She waited. When Nat reappeared, he didn't sit down, choosing instead to stand by the screen door, absently poking his finger through a small rusting hole in the mesh.

"Dad made his pitch," he said.

"What did you tell him?"

"I said okay."

"Is it okay?"

"He said he needed me. Real bad."

"Is he still on the line?"

The hole was getting bigger. Nat pushed hard at the edges, peeling them back. "He said to tell you thanks for taking the time to come. He said he'd talk to you later tonight."

Kate considered that in silence. "What else did he say?"

"Abby's already with him. He said she wants you to bring her new green dress with the white collar if it's back from the cleaner's." Nat minced the words, making them small and sharp.

"Don't be so hard on her, Nat," Kate said softly. "She's having a tough time."

Nat was shoving viciously at the ragged hole now, intent on pushing two fingers through it. "Then how come," he said, his voice as shredded as the edges of the split wire, "I'm asking, Mom, how come then, she's getting *dressed up* for this?"

That night Kate sat alone on the edge of her bed in her room. Her speech at the American Association for Higher Education's convention had gone well, even though she had walked through it in a daze. She should try to sleep; tomorrow would be tough. She knew Nat was still awake in his room, maybe staring at a Nintendo game; she could see a faint ribbon of light coming from under his door. Everything was ready. Marty had faxed several sheets of possible questions she might get at the press conference—with the answers he "suggested" she give. "Nothing to worry about," he had scrawled across the top of the first page. "Just memorize these; don't deviate." Kate stared at the pages scattered across the bedspread. Nothing to worry about.

The phone rang.

"Kate?" Luke's voice was low and hurried. "Hey, honey. You all ready?"

"Luke, I feel strange," Kate said, her voice breaking. "I don't know why we're doing this."

"The rumors are killing us," he said firmly. "We have to defuse them. I'm sorry; it's tough on you."

"Luke—"

"Honey, I don't have time to talk; I've got a speech in ten minutes."

A well of frustration and anxiety was about to spill out from her insides. "I don't care," she said. "We *have* to talk."

"Not now, Kate. Look, get some sleep. We'll talk tomorrow."

"Luke, I have to know the truth. Are you—?"

"I can't talk now, babe, okay?"

"But—"

The line went suddenly dead.

Unbelieving, she hugged the receiver closer to her ear. Luke had hung up, actually hung up, while she was trying to talk to him. She replaced the phone, stood, and began walking with uncertain steps toward the bathroom. She stopped. She was staring into the full-length mirror on the door. For a long moment she searched the reflected image of her face. She would not think about this, she decided—not now.

241

Slowly she began to remove her clothes. First, the beautiful melon-colored wool jacket; Joan was right, it really was a great color. Then, fingers shaking, she tried to unfasten the tiny pearl buttons of the new gray silk blouse, another of her Neiman Marcus choices. She definitely would push all of this away, she definitely would not think about it. The first grease stain on the blouse would be a disaster, but Joan was right about that, too; if you could do it, buying good-quality clothes made a major difference. I cannot allow this to engulf me, she thought. She removed the blouse carefully and laid it on a nearby chair, then turned back to the mirror. Her eyes narrowed critically. Her breasts were still full and reasonably high. Not those of a twenty-year-old, but not bad. She unhooked her bra, a serviceable one; not particularly sexy. How many times had she unhooked it under the caressing gaze of her husband, the man she could trust above all other people? When was the last time he had paid her body any real attention? I don't care what those lace bras from Neiman Marcus cost, she thought. I'm ordering them. Half a dozen of them, damn it. They had made love, oh, yes. Or was it just sex, just release, just the elimination of tension? Was that all he needed her for now? Her panty hose came off next—a great new color, gray-green, perfect with the melon-colored suit. It was nice to be so color-coordinated. Had he really been there for her, his soul, his heart, as well as his body, or had she fooled herself? She slipped off her panties; they were trimmed with a rather meager bit of lace. Also a little too much on the serviceable side. Did he care anymore?

Finally she was staring into the mirror at her naked body. Was she just a fool, one more woman tricking herself into believing she was loved when she wasn't? The pain was piercing. I need just a few minutes more to get used to it, she told herself. That's what I need. She traced the image of her body with her eyes inch by inch, sparing herself nothing. Her stomach was reasonably flat, her hips nicely molded, if a bit generous. Her legs had never been as long and lithe as those of a ballet dancer, for heaven's sake, but they were holding up well. Luke used to tell her they were beautiful—when had he said it last? Could she remember? The inspection continued. No veins; not many, anyhow. Where had she gone wrong? What mistakes had she made? How could she have kept this from happening? She stared and stared until the image in the mirror began to blur.

"No, damn it," she whispered. "I didn't do anything wrong. He did." Her body was trembling. She straightened, thrusting her breasts forward, pushing her shoulders back. She would not allow herself to feel like a reject. She would fight. Claire was younger, yes; her breasts were probably firmer, her stomach without a ripple. So what? There were much more important things than youth and beauty, weren't there? She watched her chin go up, saw her image grow clearer as the tears in her eyes dried. Then her full voice, not a whisper, hit the quiet air like crackling shot.

"All right," she challenged her image defiantly. "What's she got that I haven't got?"

Peter walked through the *Tribune* bureau, tucked into an office complex on K Street, the thick beige carpet muffling the sound of his footsteps. He looked around. Only a skeleton crew this afternoon: a bored-looking weekend editor and two reporters crouched like small animals before humming computer terminals. The reporters' plyboard cubicles clustered on each side of the long, narrow room were painted alternately pale beige or gold, giving the bureau the look of a high-class hair salon. At the far end, facing out toward the front door, was the glass-enclosed office of the bureau chief, Burt Barrows. A big, beefy man, he sat idle now behind the glass, watching Peter approach.

Peter felt rather than saw the two reporters glance sideways at him as he continued on down the narrow aisle. They weren't dumb. They knew Barrows wouldn't be in here on a Sunday if something wasn't up.

Peter opened the office door and approached, establishing and maintaining steady eye contact. Barrows, the furrows across his forehead making him appear much older than his fifty years, sat back in his chair, making no pretense of feigning interrupted work. He was fond of Peter. He considered him the best reporter in the bureau, and this wasn't going to be easy.

"I hear you were in the control room," he said.

"My day off, Burt. One a year or so isn't asking too much, is it?" Peter spoke easily, calmly.

"You saw Goodspeed's wife fall apart."

"She didn't fall apart."

Barrows shrugged. "Okay, she didn't fall apart, and you didn't write a story. How come?"

"It wasn't a story in my opinion."

Barrows shoved a pile of newspapers on his desk in Peter's direction. "A lot of people disagreed with you."

Peter didn't bother to glance down. "Yeah," he said. "I know they did."

"What am I going to do with you, huh?" Barrows was exasperated. "You've been friends with Kate for years, and that's helped us plenty—I'm not denying it. But you've got a job to do, Peter. You were right *there*, for Christ's sake. You can't protect her. You're a *reporter*."

"I'm not trying to. The wires had it covered."

"You would've had access to her. That would've given us a big edge."

Peter smacked his right fist into his left palm with such abruptness that Barrows jumped. "I'm no voyeur," he said angrily. "There's enough of that in this business already."

Barrows looked searchingly at his top reporter. "Maybe you're getting a little too close to this story," he said quietly.

"Friendship's okay when it pays off with an exclusive interview, right? But it's supposed to go out the window when we start competing with the supermarket tabloids." Peter leaned forward, staring at Barrows. "Aren't you asking to have it both ways?"

"No, Peter. *You* are."

Peter looked away. "I don't know the answer," he said, half to himself. "Reporters shouldn't have friends who aren't reporters, that's the only way, but that doesn't work either. So we're hypocrites."

Barrows opened a drawer and pulled out a half-empty box of cigars. "Want one?" he offered.

Peter shook his head.

Barrows lit one of the cigars and puffed slowly, with obvious pleasure. "My wife won't let me have these in the house," he said. "God, they're good."

"They're taking up a petition in the newsroom to pressure you to stop."

"Shit, I know. Why don't they just stay out of my glass box?" Barrows said, encompassing his office with a wave of his hand as a curl of acrid smoke rose to the ceiling. "Then I could kill myself in privacy." He tapped loose a thick, wobbling ash. "Peter," he said slowly, "I'm pulling you off the Chicago press conference."

Peter instantly stood, stretching his long legs as if they had grown very stiff. "You can't do that, this is my story," he said.

"I'm assigning Annie Marshall."

"That's a mistake."

"She's a good reporter, whatever you think of her style."

"She doesn't know politics."

"She knows people."

"We're out to nail Goodspeed one way or another, right?"

"This is a presidential campaign, and it looks like the front-runner is *shtupping* his deputy campaign manager," Barrows replied levelly. "We're just days from the election and the story is about to explode. You don't see that? Look—take a couple of days off. You're a helluva good reporter and you deserve a rest."

Peter's face was calm but pale. "No way," he repeated, standing his ground.

"I mean it, Peter," Barrows said. "Miami. Two days. Sun, sand and stuff. What if I said I was paying?"

Peter laughed in spite of himself. "You wouldn't do that in a million years."

Barrows grinned briefly. "True." He leaned forward. "You don't want another reporter on your turf and you don't want to cover the story," he said. "So what do you want? My job?"

"I'm covering the story. The campaign's the story," Peter said with measured precision.

Barrows's natural frown lines reappeared. "You tell me you've no appetite for this circus tomorrow, yet—" He paused in mid-sentence. Abruptly he pushed himself away from his desk, his decision made. "Okay. Go ahead and go. If anything major develops, write it. Annie can write the 'I'm innocent and my loving family supports me' piece. But get us something good, Peter. Find a way to get out front on this."

Peter smiled faintly. "If this were a movie, you'd be telling me my ass is on the line."

"Your ass *is* on the line." Barrows sighed. "So's mine, if I can't break myself of these damn things." He picked up the cigar, gazed at it thoughtfully, and puffed before speaking again. "If this really were a movie, I'd be handing you a plane ticket to Miami," he said.

"You don't believe in vacations, Burt. You've always said they rot the mind."

"You could go visit your kids or something."

Peter spoke quietly. "I'm okay," he said. "Don't worry."

Again, a noisy sigh from behind the desk. "I have my little square inch of principle, and I'm standing on it." He looked thoughtfully at the ceiling. "Can't remember who said that; Ben Bradlee, I think. Go catch your plane."

11

This, Kate thought, scanning the lobby of the Palmer House, is truly a carnival. She felt Nat's hand turn slippery and sweaty in hers, but she held it tight as campaign aides shoved forward to break a path.

"Outta the way! Outta the way!"

Microphones thrust forward; camera booms swung close. "Mrs. Goodspeed, is this going to ruin your husband's chances to be president?"

"Mrs. Goodspeed, how do you *feel?*"

"Nat, have you talked to your father?"

The voices were shrill and tense, and the faces that shoved in close twitched with exhaustion.

"She won't say anything," mumbled the *Houston Chronicle* to the *St. Louis Post-Dispatch.* "Why do we bother? It's a total waste of time." He shook his head in disgust, then pushed deep into the crowd, shouting, his notebook ready.

Kate wanted to cover her ears. God, everything was in the same decibel range.

"No interviews," yelled one stocky aide with burly, flailing arms. "Move back, you guys, the questions get answered in an hour!"

The crowd only pressed closer.

"Mrs. Goodspeed, what do you feel—?"

Mercifully, the elevator doors opened. Kate and Nat were pushed in by the aides; the reporters pushed out. The doors swept closed, barely missing the hand of one reporter. Suddenly, silence.

"Jesus," said the aide with the burly arms, wiping his brow and punching the button labeled "Penthouse." He shook his head. "Those crazy assholes." He looked quickly at Kate. "Sorry, Mrs. Goodspeed."

She made no reply. Nat gently pulled his hand free and she saw him flex his fingers. She hadn't realized how tightly she had been holding on.

The doors opened on a wide hallway busy with aides rushing back and forth. Kate could hear the sound of a wire ticker.

Marty was waiting. No Luke.

"Hi there," he said. The tail of his shirt, carelessly shoved in, was sticking out of his trousers like a forgotten restaurant napkin. He faced Kate, his face wreathed in a fixed smile. There were tiny beads of sweat on his upper lip.

"Where's Luke?" she demanded.

"He'll be back in fifteen minutes," Marty said, glancing swiftly at his watch. "He's calling Olson. Old Sam's mad as hell about the Palmer release."

"What Palmer release?"

Marty looked at her, then looked away. "Luke hasn't had time to tell you yet, I guess," he said casually. "He's opposing Palmer's entry into the country. He'll announce it the day after the debate. Sam's so mad he's pulling out his support; too bad, he's been a good catalyst for soft money, but we're doing all right on that front. Norton's raising hell, too, but that's no surprise."

Kate started to say something, then stopped. Luke had excluded her from his decision, and that realization only deepened her feeling of isolation.

"Excuse me, ma'am." A waiter in a white coat, pushing a room-service cart ladened with half-eaten breakfast rolls and lettuce curling brown at the edges, was waiting to pass. She stepped aside.

Marty's hand shot out, stopping the cart. "Can we get you something, Kate?" he asked quickly. His tone turned as solicitous as a servant's. "Fruit? Sandwich? Room service's got some great coffee. It's even hot."

Kate looked at the cart's contents, her stomach turning, and shook her head. "Where's my daughter?" she said, holding out a plastic bag. "I have her dress."

Marty took the bag and signaled to a young man standing among a cluster of hovering aides. Eyes eager, the boy sprang forward instantly. Marty handed him the dress with quick instructions. "Second room on the left, and hurry. The kid's been frantic for this."

"Yes, sir."

"I'll go," Kate said, moving forward.

"Wait," Marty said. "We've only got a couple of minutes; we'd better get organized. Fast."

Kate sensed Nat shifting restlessly at her side, and actually felt his desire to flee. We might as well get it over with, she thought with a sick feeling of anger. "Then do it," she said. "Fast."

9:45 A.M. They were in the elevator, plunging down, reaching the lobby, aides pressed close against Kate and the children. She could hardly breathe. Only as they stepped into the hallway did she see her husband emerging from a door hidden behind a curtain, moving forward quickly to join his family. Kate was shocked to see the hollow look in his eyes as he gazed at her, a look stripped of all the rough toughness of recent weeks. She moved forward and touched his arm, alarmed.

"Bad day," he said with an attempt at a grin that wouldn't stay in place. "Let's go, kid."

There wasn't time for a single extra word.

The Palmer House ballroom was jammed. Reporters filled every chair and latecomers were squeezing together along the wall as camera crews fought for setup space, yelling at each other and anybody in their way, creating general chaos as Goodspeed campaign aides tried vainly to keep a path open to the podium.

"This is not a polite business," a reporter from the *Minneapolis Star-Tribune* remarked to Peter.

"Yeah."

"Hear about the polls?"

"What?"

"Taking a dip, my friend." The reporter grinned. "We're going to see a dive if Goodspeed doesn't do something to save his ass. I'll bet Marty Apple is sharpening his resumé."

Suddenly there was a commotion at the back of the room.

"What's happening?" Annie Marshall had darting, lively eyes that saw and routinely stored the kind of detail that made her feature

249

stories such biting little classics. But she was short, and she was having trouble seeing anything. She tapped impatiently on Peter's shoulder. "Come on, Peter, tell me, I can't see a thing, is she doing the noble wife number? Any makeup on?"

Peter glanced at her with shaded eyes. "They're on their way," he said shortly.

"Let me in front, okay, so I can see? Come on, Peter, you're too tall!" Annie, irritated, was straining to push past a camera crew that had materialized suddenly in front of her.

Peter stepped back, but not before he managed to exchange one quick glance with Kate. She tried to smile in recognition when she saw his face searching for her through the crowd. But her teeth were too dry for her lips to move easily, and she could not. His eyes were kind, too kind, the kindness reserved for humiliated friends. But he was her friend, maybe the only one in this room. She shivered.

Annie, ever the recorder, followed Kate's gaze directly to Peter's face. "What's the matter?" she said, her eyes alert with interest. "You look like you're going to throw up."

Peter made no attempt to answer.

"Let them *through!*"

The Goodspeed family reached the podium platform at the back of the room, but not before Kate digested the sight of Abby's stunned, almost shell-shocked face above the white collar of her favorite green dress. Kate felt a surge of sadness. Abby was understanding now what this was all about, looking wildly around, realizing she was for the first time on the receiving end of a hunt filled with blood lust; you could smell it. Her daughter would not today be doing what she had expected to do. She would not today be acting out the fantasy of rushing forward to defend her father. Kate felt helpless. She had tried to prepare Abby for the reality, but it had been impossible. Luke moved to the podium, a bizarre wedding-cake structure topped with a scrambled array of microphones and tape recorders. Kate, Abby, and Nat stood behind him in a protective arc as he raised his hand for quiet.

"I have a statement to read, and then I'll take your questions," he said. The statement was brief, and he read it calmly, standing erect, his voice firm. His face was very pale.

Kate concentrated on keeping her face composed, casting about for a suitable object to focus on as she positioned herself under the blinding lights. She settled finally on the back of Luke's neck, or rather, the fuzzy edges of the slightly fraying collar of his white shirt. Interesting how the escaping threads turned to powder, wafting a millimeter or two away from home to settle on the back of his navy blue suit—or were those little white flecks actually dandruff? She watched the skin of his neck scraping the edges of the collar as he moved his head, each time flaking off another puff of airy, disintegrating fabric. Perspiration was collecting in the roughened edges, turning them faintly yellow; you couldn't see it all that well yet unless you looked very closely, but it would be quite pronounced on the inside seam.

Lordy, she thought suddenly, I'm diagnosing a case of what the ads used to call "ring around the collar." She had a sudden, crazy desire to laugh.

Her concentration shifted to Luke's words, but it was an effort. She heard him call the rumors of an affair "the workings of petty minds" and listened as he called on "the responsible members of the media" to put their coverage of the campaign "back on the high ground." It was becoming a blur.

Then came the reporters' questions, cautiously asked. It was clear Luke was not going to present them with anything approaching a clean confession, and finally someone fired off a question about Palmer. Abruptly, the mood of the room shifted. The questions came faster, Luke's voice became stronger; this was firmer ground for both sides. What about the anger building in the black community, Senator? What about the Congressional Black Caucus's vow to schedule Palmer poetry readings every night on the steps of the nation's capitol until Election Day? Is this pressure to get you moving on an endorsement?

And then just one question, boomed out by *The New York Times*.

"Senator Goodspeed, have you—look, this isn't easy to ask—but, are you or are you not sleeping with someone other than your wife?"

The room was very silent, except for the soft whirring of the cameras.

"I refuse to dignify these charges by responding to them," Luke replied somberly. "I want this campaign to be fought on the issues, and, by God, I believe that's what the American public wants, too."

His demeanor was perfect.

A strong, determined female voice cut through from the crowd. "Mrs. Goodspeed!"

Luke turned partly around, meeting his wife's eyes with an oddly vacant yet pleading smile.

"Yes," she said, composed, trying to forget Luke's expression.

"Do you think your husband is answering the question?"

"My husband says he is, and I believe him."

She could see the face of the reporter now; it was Annie Marshall.

"Do you believe he's faithful?"

There was no oxygen in the room; she felt she was strangling. "My husband will always have my complete and full support," she said.

"But you didn't answer my question!"

Other reporters were ducking their heads, looking embarrassed.

"Yes, I know he is," Kate replied.

A shifting sigh moved through the room. People were leaning back in their chairs, looking at each other, stirring uneasily. A line was being approached, and editors would be passing judgment on how their reporters performed at the edge of that line. Editors wanted more, editors always wanted more, more of everything except criticism of themselves. Right now they were in their offices watching the stoic faces of Luke and Kate and the children on their television monitors or screens and they were thinking of advertisers and public disapproval and, yes, a very risky line was being approached.

"Mrs. Goodspeed—"

"Oh, come on, isn't that enough?" Luke said, in a rasping voice. "My wife already answered your questions."

Abruptly, the crew from Chicago's CBS station turned off its cameras and shut off its lights. A few reporters halfheartedly leaned forward again as if to press further, to ignore the signal, but a necessary tension was easing away.

"Why are they stopping?" Annie muttered to Peter. "He hasn't answered anything. Can he get away with this?"

Marty stepped to the podium. "We're wrapping this up, guys," he said, his manner muted and easy. "Senator Goodspeed has a campaign to get back to."

A second television crew started breaking down its equipment, and more lights blinked off. Luke began to move away from the podium, to work his way through the crowd, pulling Kate close to him and holding her hand. Abby and Nat followed their parents.

"Okay, guys, let 'em through."

No one shoved forward this time; it was almost as if the Goodspeed family had suddenly become irrelevant. Television correspondents were doing hasty stand-up reports in front of their cameras and print reporters were closing their notebooks. One local television reporter let out an audible snort. "They're like dolls," he said, his voice cutting across the room as Luke and Kate and the kids passed by. "Yeah, dolls. Barbie and Ken hit the big time."

"Cool it," someone said with a forced laugh.

Kate heard, and felt a blush spreading forward from the back of her neck. It was a blush caused by shame and fueled by anger, and it burned like the sun.

With aides flanking them like armor, the Goodspeeds moved through the holding room and toward the back elevator. Luke attempted to take Abby's hand, but she shook him violently away. Then Marty moved in, separating Luke from the others, but only after whispering in Kate's ear, "Terrific job, kid. You were great."

Kate barely heard the words. Instead, she found herself staring directly at Claire Lorenzo.

Claire looked different. Her skin was as smooth and clear as ever, but her face seemed pieced together into an uncertain montage. Suddenly she turned and caught Kate watching her; she raised her chin with a touch of her usual cool competence and began to turn away.

Kate moved forward swiftly, suddenly blinded with pain.

"Who do you think you are?" she whispered. "What are you trying to do?"

Claire's pale face revealed no emotion. "Don't waste your anger," she parried in her best low-register staccato.

"You're exactly like Marty."

"If you mean, do we both want to see Luke elected president, you're right. You want to torpedo that?"

"I don't crave a win as much as you do."

"I don't believe it." Claire smiled her habitual, one-sided smile. "You've been in this game a long time, and you're no amateur."

"Don't talk to me about games," Kate heard herself say, her voice

253

dangerously out of control. "And do me a favor, please. Keep your hands off my husband."

"Don't, you're diminishing both of us." Claire's voice was flat, but not without feeling. "If you want to see me as the cold-blooded ambitious homewrecker, I can't stop you. But I've got two things to say, and I hope you're listening."

The arc of space around them was widening. Someone had whispered urgently into Marty's ear, nodding to the two women, and Kate saw him suddenly whip around and move in their direction.

"Number one," Claire said. "Blame me if it makes you feel better, but it takes two for something to happen, not one. And second, be careful. Keep in mind what we both want."

"How do you know what I want?"

"Oh, I know." Claire smiled briefly. "Keep your head."

Kate was quivering with anger. "You should have followed your own advice," she said.

Claire frowned this time. "Look," she said, "you *owe* him this one."

"You don't get it, Claire, you really don't. This isn't a trade-off."

"The White House? That isn't enough?"

Kate stared into Claire's eyes and saw again a flash of what she had seen before: a fragility that belied the toughness. The woman's mouth was actually trembling. Was it an act? Maybe she was all bravado, not strength. But it didn't make any difference. No difference at all.

"No," she said. "It's not enough." And knew, finally, that she meant it.

"Then you're not as smart as I thought you were," Claire said calmly as Marty's hand fell heavily on her shoulder and began moving her away.

They were upstairs in their room. Away from the mad press scene, away from the nervous aides. Finally, Kate faced Luke. She held herself taut, staring straight at him. She waited.

"Okay," Luke said quietly. "Let's talk."

For one split second Kate thought wildly of declining the invitation. She raised her chin high. "It's true, isn't it?" she said, her voice unsteady.

For a moment she imagined he was swaying. He gripped her by

the shoulders as if to hold both of them safely in place, but there was no place to be safe in; it was as if they stood together on a kind of a high, narrow diving board, a board dipping and bending now under their weight.

She pushed herself off and plunged into the void. "You are sleeping with her," she whispered.

"I was." Luke took a deep breath. "Yes."

"Oh, God." The words hit like an electric charge, and for a moment she felt perilously dizzy. Her heart raced; sweat broke out on her forehead. She hadn't expected to feel such shock. Hearing Luke finally say the words made it irrevocably true. Her strength evaporated, flowed from her body, and she began to tremble violently. "How could you do this to me?" she blurted.

"Kate, I'm sorry. So damn sorry."

"Why?" she demanded, her voice cracking. "For God's sake, why?"

"I can't answer," he said in a low voice. "I can't explain."

Something was building, heaving upward inside her body, pounding against skin and bone, demanding to be heard. "You bastard," she said, her voice choked and trembling now. "How dare you say that! How dare you think you can get off that easy!" Her hands tightened; she felt her nails digging deep into her palms. The heaving, the pounding, were getting louder. This was rage, total, encompassing rage, and it was building. How could he stand here in front of her and say something so stupid? Who did he think she was? How much was she supposed to swallow?

"I know it isn't enough; Kate, I'm sorry."

"Then answer my question!" she screamed, the torrent breaking forth and flooding out. "Give me something I can understand, something that doesn't leave me humiliated, that doesn't leave your family humiliated!" With one fist, she pounded her own chest. "Remember me?" she screamed again. "Remember? I'm Kate, your wife! How in the name of God could you hurt me like this?"

Luke started to speak, but she suddenly raised her hand and delivered a stinging slap flat across his cheek. She would wipe that resigned expression off his face, she would, by God, deliver some pain of her own. She raised her hand again and froze. The jagged setting of her turquoise ring had actually broken the skin; she could see tiny pinpricks of blood through the stubble of his beard.

255

What was happening to her? How could she do this?

Luke grabbed her hands, pulled them down tight to his sides, holding her close even as she struggled to wrest free. "Kate, stop it," he demanded.

She couldn't. She threw her head back, looked full into his face and spat.

Luke dropped her hands and turned away, rubbing at the spittle with the sleeve of his jacket. "Christ, what's happening to us?" he cried.

Spent, Kate sank into a chair. "You tell me," she whispered. "You tell me."

Luke fell into a chair directly across the room from his wife. "I've cheapened us both," he said in a heavy voice. "I've ruined us."

"Maybe yourself, but not me," Kate shot back, her voice breaking. "I won't let you do it, Luke. I'm not going to let you do it."

Luke yanked at his tie, pulling it loose until it hung from his neck like a hangman's knot. "I don't love her, I never did," he said, fighting for control of his voice. "I'm trying to answer your question, but God, I don't know how to do it. I'm having trouble answering it for myself. It's ego, Kate. That's what it is." There was sweat on his brow. "It's my own damn fault."

No, she wouldn't let him off that easily. "Try," she said, breathing deeply now, making each word come out strong and clear. "I want to hear something from you that's true."

Luke stared past her, still working on his voice. "Look, you won't believe me, you'll think I'm just looking for excuses," he said. "But for months now, I've seen myself everywhere, newsstands, television, magazines—God, you know what it's like. Everywhere, okay?" He shook his head, his face desolate. "It's an experience unlike any other, and I got caught up in it."

She was not hearing this. She could not be hearing this. Her chest was aching, her eyes stinging. "You're telling me you slept with Claire because you couldn't handle your own celebrity?" she said. "I don't believe it."

"I'm telling you I began believing too much in it when some people told me I was special."

"Like Claire. Right?"

"Yeah." He looked straight at her. "That's right."

"You are a bastard," she said softly. "You are a vain, pompous bastard."

Luke turned his head, as if to ward off another blow. "Call me anything you want," he said. "I deserve it."

So here, finally, was the reasoning. She, Kate, had not given him enough. She, Kate, had been inadequate to his needs. How slick; how perfect. She was not buying it. "I've been telling you you're special for twenty years, damn it," she whispered. "Why wasn't that enough?"

"It got lonely," he said, looking very weary. "It sounds self-pitying; maybe it is; maybe you'll think so."

She stared at him, remembering their nightly phone conversations from all the strange motels, the silly long-distance kissing games. . . .

"Lonely? With me on the phone to you every night, at least when you chose to call?"

Luke shook his head. "You can't understand, I don't expect you to," he said. "I'm trying, okay?" His eyes had a caged look; he wanted a way out. "Maybe I'm only going to make it worse. How do I say this? Claire was inside the tiniest of circles with me; she understood what was happening every minute of the day, she was part of it, and she was the only one I could talk to." He searched Kate's face hopefully. "This is terrible to hit you with, but she became an important part of my life."

Kate winced. How many blows could she take?

"What about Marty?" she challenged. "Why didn't you sleep with Marty, if all you wanted was a campaign soul mate?"

He glanced up at her, baffled. "Why do you want me to hurt you?" he asked.

"You can't make it worse," she said, her voice choking.

"Okay, you want me to say she's beautiful. And sexy. She is."

The rage inside her was lurching through tissue and bone again. "And what about me?" she said. "Your wife?" She spat out the word, it was her credential. Her puny, laughable credential.

"You are more beautiful. And more sexy." Luke breathed deeply, fighting for time. "And I've been a total fool."

"No, more than a fool, Luke," she said, shaking her head. "More, much more. How could you parade me out there this morning, knowing I'd be forced to lie?"

257

"You haven't known the full truth until right now." His chin set stubbornly. "I saved you that."

She stared at him, unbelieving. "You didn't save me anything," she said, stunned. "You trapped me into a humiliating and degrading lie."

Luke put a hand to his forehead. "Kate, I'm sorry," he said. "I've hurt you terribly—please understand I know that now. Please."

Did she believe him? She searched his face, hungrily trying to find the familiar. Oh, there was regret. She could see that; it was etched across his forehead like a raw wound. But did he regret what he had done? Or did he regret being caught? Kate searched angrily; she couldn't be sure. She didn't know, she simply couldn't trust her feelings anymore.

"I was an arrogant prick, Kate. Have you ever heard me say that before?"

"It's about time," she lashed back.

He managed a thin smile. "Fair enough," he said.

There was an agenda, she had to go through the entire thing. "How could you lie to me in Oregon?" she whispered. "You held me, we made love—"

"Kate—" Luke briefly closed his eyes. "I didn't know myself, then."

Again, Kate searched his face, this time with a colder anger; she could feel now the gnawing pain of uncertainty. Maybe he was telling the truth. And then again, maybe he wasn't. Her heart was pounding so hard now, she could barely breathe. She would probably never know.

"You've forced us through this absurd, shoddy press conference just to perpetuate a lie," she said. "All three of us standing there, your loyal backup musicians, singing the same tune—"

"Kate, I had no choice!" Luke said, his voice stronger.

"Luke, I'm thinking about our whole lives," she said shakily. "I've been playing a role for you for years and years. I got so good at it, I didn't even realize I was doing it. It's been eating me up, bit by bit, to the point where I've almost lost the chance to know who I am. I don't want that. I don't want to be so lost. That's what I've been. Lost. And I think you've been lost too. Luke, I'm scared. I'm scared that you can say there's no choice. A week ago, you probably felt you

258

had no choice but to keep lying to me because I might wreck your campaign if I found out about Claire. Maybe I would have, right? And that would have been the worst thing possible, right? I don't think you want to examine too closely what I'm telling you, because it might turn out you'd be better off telling the truth, and the truth's too risky." She looked at Luke and saw he was shaken. His eyes were sunk deep into their sockets. Again she saw—could it really be true?—a spark of fear. Or was it pain? Could it be pain?

"You've got a right to be angry," he said. "You have every right to be. I don't expect you to forgive me right away, but I have to hope you will. In time. I've got to believe that."

It was fear. Yes, it was. "Nice speech, dear," she said, her voice breaking. "Who wrote it?"

Luke jerked back involuntarily. "What did Claire say to you down there?"

"She said you had to win, that I owed you."

He considered this silently. "I was wrong to get involved with her," he said, picking his way through the words as carefully as a soldier through a minefield. "But she's totally committed to winning this race—she does care."

"That's supposed to make me feel better?" Kate said, astonished. "Don't you understand, you're her ticket to power? Don't you feel the slightest bit used? I hope you do, oh, God, I hope you do, because that's the way I feel. That's what's been done to me!"

Luke threw up his hands in a despairing gesture. "Look, okay," he said. "Maybe I was her ticket to power, whatever that means, but I'm not now!"

"Look at her!" she cried. "She's still hanging on, I can see that. What a scummy game you and Marty play!"

Luke's head rose, eyes desperate. "What do you want from me?" he burst out. "I was a fool, a total fool to do this, not because it was dumb politically, but because I love you, okay? Do you believe that? Will you believe that? What are you saying? You want me to *keep* seeing her?" His eyes were almost wild now with bafflement. "Is that it? What is this, some kind of perverse sisterhood?"

"You've lied to me, you've betrayed me!" She wanted to scream the words at the top of her lungs, but if she did, she might not be able to stop. Who was this man? Was this Luke, the man she had loved

259

from the time he was a young congressman, the man who had hugged her tight when her mother died, the man who taught her the right way to row a boat on a summer day out on the C & O Canal, the man she had curled up next to in bed night after night, week after week, year after year, for half her life now?

"Kate," he said, his voice growing alarmed as he sensed the depth of her despair. "I can't believe this is happening either; Kate, I wouldn't hurt you for the world."

"Oh, God, that's funny."

"Honey, keep your head."

"That's what Claire said." The lurching, pounding rage was slouching down into a damp puddle in her heart, leaving her without its anesthetizing strength. In its place was a bitter, permeating pain. So that was what it all came down to—a joke; a joke on her. She covered her face with both hands.

"Please go away," she said simply. "Leave me alone. Go talk to your kids. Do something to help them. I can't bear the sight of you, not right now."

A moment passed. Kate did not look up. Then she heard Luke reach for the door. She felt a puff of air from the hotel corridor as the door closed behind him.

Down the hall, in a much smaller room, Marty closed another door behind him, waiting for the quiet click before turning fully forward to face the woman sitting on the side of the bed.

"You had to talk to her," he said, speaking very slowly. "You had to screw it up."

"It just happened." Claire sat very straight, meeting his gaze. The slight bump in the middle of her nose gave her a faintly pugilistic air.

"No, it didn't." Marty's voice was flat. "You fell for Luke, that's what happened. I could see it coming months ago, but I didn't think you'd get so goddamn careless. We both knew Stark was sniffing around. You threw everything away."

"Don't be so dramatic, Marty." Claire reached for a cigarette from a mangled pack on the nightstand. "I'm not going to sit here and defend myself. I'm as good at this business as you are, and this is a blip on the screen. We'll still win."

"Maybe Luke can. Maybe I can." He stared at her. "But not you, Claire. You've lost. You have fucking lost."

Claire barely moved and her lips parted only slightly. "Isn't it amazing?" she said. "I'm not shaking in my boots. The terrible Marty Apple is telling me I'm finished, and I'm not scared at all. And we both know why, don't we? Send me packing, Marty, and *Luke* is finished. Everyone will assume he's guilty, and you damn well know it."

They stared at each other. Then Marty backed off. "You're no good to me now," he said, less roughly.

There was the barest of hesitations, then Claire inhaled deeply, blowing the smoke out in a slow, deliberate swirl. "You don't mean that," she said calmly, with a hint of amusement. "We do all right, you and I."

Marty stared longingly at the cigarette. "Don't be so sure," he said. "You've blotted your copybook, Claire. You won't be quite so much the shining star from here on in."

"Let me count the clichés," she said, rolling her eyes. "We can use them in a speech." She picked up the pack from the side table and pulled it slightly open, revealing two remaining cigarettes, then smiled at Marty. "Let's be real," she said.

Marty's body appeared to sag; his face was tense and watchful.

"Anything we do together, if we keep our nerve, we can do right and end up looking good," Claire said. "That's the way it works as long as memories stay short—and they do." She laughed. "They always do. Want one?" Deftly she tossed the pack. Marty stooped, caught it before it hit the floor.

"Sorry," she said.

"You've got to stay in the background," Marty said, as if nothing had happened. The sharp, scraping sound of a match against a matchbook, then a flash of flame. Marty lit the cigarette, inhaled deeply. "I don't want to see you around for a while."

Claire laughed. "Just stay available, right? Until you need me, right? You're keeping someone around who blotted her copybook?"

Marty said nothing.

"I can wait you out any day," she said softly.

"Your copybook is looking cleaner every minute."

Claire looked at her boss in amusement. "Love your flexibility, Marty," she said.

"I like survival," he said.

261

She lifted a water glass from the bedside table and held it aloft in a mock toast. "To survival," she said. Marty did not see the slight tremor in her hand.

Kate was staring out the window a few moments later when she felt again a puff of air from the doorway. She turned. Abby and Nat, guarded looks in their eyes, were walking toward her. Abby was clutching her brother's hand. The two of them stood together, self-protectively, as if behind some invisible shield. The sight of them broke Kate's heart.

"Come here," she said, opening her arms wide. Silently, swiftly, they moved into her embrace. There was a wetness on Nat's cheek, a tremble in Abby's arms, and the abandon with which they hugged her sent shivering reverberations straight down her spine.

"Are you all right?" she asked.

Nat nodded silently and turned his head to hide his eyes, but he didn't pull away. "Yeah, I guess so," he mumbled.

Tremulously, Abby looked up at her mother. "What do I say to him?" she asked.

"What are you feeling?"

"I know it's true, and I want him to admit it," Abby said. Her voice was shaking. "I hate Claire!"

"Is that what you want to say?"

Abby lowered her eyes and shrugged her shoulders helplessly. "I don't know. Mother, what will happen? Will people laugh at us?"

"I can't answer that, honey," Kate said gently. "But they can't hurt us if we don't let them."

"Daddy's letting them," Nat broke in, kicking at the door.

Kate felt very tired. "The most important thing," she said, "is to hang on to your own sense of yourself." She didn't know if Nat understood; the words were inadequate. Nor was the charade yet fully played out. In an hour, the Goodspeed family was scheduled to climb back on the campaign plane and fly home to Washington. It had been planned as a calm and dignified end to a major public relations coup. Kate smiled bitterly; what a joke. She was trapped in a role. So were the kids. All she could deal with at this moment, in her current state of numbness, was figuring how to play those roles out. I have to protect Nat and Abby, she thought. The publicity is going to be awful. But she wasn't quite sure how, which made the monumental job of going on from here in this campaign that much worse. Not to speak of her marriage.

"Mom, do I have to go to school tomorrow?" asked Nat.

This decision was easy. "No," she said. "You don't. And we will unplug the television set as soon as we get home. Got that?"

They nodded.

"Mom—" It was Nat, again, his eyes squinting up, not looking directly at her.

"Yes?"

"You okay?"

Kate felt a wave of helplessness. What could she say to her children after what they'd witnessed downstairs? Their father had toppled from his pedestal. What did they need from her?

"Mom's strong," Abby said, and her voice was trembling.

That's what they needed. Real or not, right or not, they needed right now from her the same kind of assurance they had needed for years.

"Don't worry," Kate answered, feeling as if she spoke from deep within a cave. "You're right. I am strong."

At that very moment, in New York, Ernie Stark, at his desk in his office at the *New York Daily News*, flicked off the TV set, sat back in his chair, and stretched lazily. Watching the Goodspeed press conference would have been irritating a few hours ago, but not now. This was so much better. A grin familiar to some of his victims was widening slowly across his face. His black hair glistened under the morning sun streaming through the office window.

Stark was happy. Certainly not because he had just watched Luke Goodspeed successfully stalling on a scandal that should torpedo his campaign. Normally, that would have ruined Stark's digestion for the entire day—at least until he could check the tracking polls. But now it didn't matter. He glanced contentedly at the document sitting before him on his desk. His grin grew even wider as his gaze searched the street below. He was watching the progress down the street of a morning visitor who had simply shown up at his door—a very indignant woman. A little self-righteous, perhaps, but what a delicious story! Stark sighed, the relishing sigh of a deeply contented man.

263

◆◆

This was much better than firing off a column on Goodspeed's tawdry affair—too many people were writing about that now. It had lost its freshness. Yes, this was much better.

He reached for the telephone and dialed the number for the Palmer House in Chicago.

"Hello? Mrs. Goodspeed's room, please," he said in his twanging, nasal voice. "Will you please tell her it's Ernie Stark?" A silence. "She's busy?" He chuckled. "Well, tell her it's urgent she call me right back. Yes, that's it. Stark. From New York."

It was the middle of the afternoon in Washington, a few hours after the Chicago press conference. Lisa Feldon sat numbly in a chair in the waiting room at George Washington University Hospital's emergency entrance. Her face was parchment pale. Across from her sat a white-haired old man in a thin gray raincoat, talking softly to himself. A woman across the room with hair bundled into a blue Lurex hairnet eyed her curiously. Next to her, two teenagers sat in a trancelike state as music thundered into their heads through earphones.

Lisa ignored them all. She huddled down, hands shoved into the pockets of her down coat. She sat as close to the door as she could, staring at two brown splotches on the cool green tile leading to the hidden emergency room beyond a pair of steel doors. Suddenly the doors swung open and a thirtyish woman in a white coat emerged, her eyes swiftly scanning the room.

"Mrs. Feldon?"

Lisa stood slowly.

"We won't know for a while," the doctor said gently. "He got here late."

"He didn't call me soon enough," Lisa said in a shaky, uncertain voice.

"They're pumping his stomach," the doctor said, drawing back from Lisa's emotion. "I can't tell you anything more right now." She turned and vanished through the doors.

Lisa sat down again and looked over to see the lady in the blue Lurex hairnet staring at her. Compulsively, she offered an explanation. "He couldn't live with losing his job, that's what happened," she said.

The glassy expression on the other woman's face never changed. "Trade you for a cigarette," she said, offering her magazine.

Lisa shook her head and turned away, saying nothing. Instead she just stared fixedly at the "No Smoking" sign.

Back in Chicago, Kate stood alone once more in the hotel room, her hand clutching a dead telephone, the sound of Stark's voice still ringing in her head. "Mrs. Goodspeed," he had said with a touch of glee, "I know all about the abortion. Every detail. Let's talk."

She forced herself to breathe slowly and deeply, hung up the receiver, and began pacing the room. No, not this. Please, not this. Abby could not be exposed now, it would be too cruel. Lord, it was hard to think clearly when she was still absorbing Luke's betrayal. She was only making her pain worse, but she could not get out of her mind the image of Luke and Claire lying together naked. Luke's hands on another woman. What did he whisper to her? How did he touch her? Kate blinked, hard. It was easy to say someone was having "an affair," nice sterile word, it took out all the reality of physical intimacy. But to think of Luke pushing deep inside another woman, kissing her the same way. . . . Agonized, she rubbed her eyes, trying to wipe out the mental image. This charade of a campaign had to limp on, no matter what. She had to get tougher. Fast. For Abby. She needed a plan. There had to be a way of fighting Stark. A plan, a plan.

Suddenly she stopped pacing, gripped by an idea. She was deep in thought when the phone rang.

"Kate, we're leaving, are you ready?"

It was Luke.

"No," she said slowly. "I'm not."

He was silent. Then, "I won't insist."

"I need to be alone for a while," she said. "I'll come home tomorrow. I'll tell the kids myself. And, Luke—"

"Yes?"

"Abby and Nat do not have to go to school tomorrow. Please tell Mrs. Leonard."

By early evening, the children were back in Cleveland Park and Luke was back on F Street with Marty at campaign headquarters.

The reaction to Luke's press conference was now pouring heavily over the wires. It wasn't good.

"Goodspeed Dodges Rumors," read the Associated Press story.

"No Straight Answers from Goodspeed," reported Reuters.

Marty threw the stories aside and kept shuffling through a pile of wire copy, talking nonstop, an auctioneer selling his wares.

"I'm moving up that foreign policy speech, it'll get us some good press," he said, glancing up at the quiet figure standing at his office window. "Especially with the German prime minister in town. If his people get off their rear ends and nail down a time, we'll do a quick press availability for the two of you at the Capitol—just a quick handshake, good words, good visuals, over and out. We're also going to hit Enright hard with an ad on his ties to those failed Texas banks; we'll cream him. And I'm bagging the 'Nightline' interview. All Koppel wants is a smart-ass replay of the press conference. You'll dedicate that dam in Southern Illinois instead." An aide rushed in with the first hurried campaign-tracking polls. Marty skimmed fast and bit savagely on his cigarette.

"Not so good, right?" Luke said calmly from the window.

"Not so good."

"What's the gist?"

"People think you're dodging the rumors."

"I am."

"Shit, you have to."

Luke didn't reply.

Marty watched him closely. "Don't wimp out on me, Luke," he said. "Not if you want to win this election."

Luke said nothing. Marty, too, was silent. A single buzzing fly flew lazily from the window to his littered desk, crawled among the papers, and then took off on a slow, droning flight over Luke's head, dipping and arcing around a shiny brass light fixture that hung from the center of the ten-foot ceiling. By the time Marty spoke again, the buzzing of the single fly sounded like a full swarm.

"Quitters don't win," he said quietly. "You're no quitter."

"Stop worrying."

"You're down because of the kids, right? On the plane? So they wouldn't talk much—they'll come around. So will Kate. They always do."

Marty slowly pulled a red-circled piece of wire copy from the stack of papers in front of him, hesitating. "I've got some bad news," he said. "Don't get excited, all right?"

Luke turned from the window.

"It's Feldon. He tried to commit suicide this morning."

Luke blinked. "Steve?" he said, obviously stunned.

Marty was already reaching for the phone. "He's at George Washington Hospital. We'll get a condition report."

Luke said nothing, but the expression on his face was making Marty nervous. "Hold on," he repeated. "Don't get excited." In less than a minute, he had the hospital administrator on the line. He asked a few questions, listened, then covered the mouthpiece and looked up. "He's been pumped out, and he's holding his own. Took a helluva lot of sleeping pills."

"Poor devil."

"You got one word right."

"Why would he try to kill himself?"

"He's a weak guy; face it."

Luke thought. His face was grim. "He wasn't, once."

"People change. He wasn't up to the job."

"Yeah, but he's part of the reason I'm where I am today."

"You're forgetting something. You're forgetting he tried to destroy you with your wife."

Luke crunched a sheet of paper from Marty's desk into a tiny ball and pitched it savagely toward the wastebasket. It missed. "I haven't forgotten that for a minute, Marty."

"Good."

"Let's be plain about this, he was also telling the truth."

"Hold on," Marty protested. "You're losing perspective."

Luke allowed himself a small smile. "Is that it? Thanks, Marty, I've been wondering."

"You've lost me."

Luke shrugged. "Maybe I'll drop by the hospital."

"You want the entire press corps flying after you? We don't need more goddamn lurid headlines."

"I want to think about it."

"You've got a speech in Denver tomorrow, remember? We've rescheduled it three times. Luke, quit fooling around. The Black

Caucus has just denounced you, they've got that rally scheduled tomorrow at the Capitol. You want to make more trouble for yourself?" Marty suddenly remembered he was still holding an open phone line. He began speaking rapidly into the receiver, watching Luke.

"Look, Senator Goodspeed is deeply distressed, on the road right now with a killer schedule, so we need the best information you've got. What's that? You're talking to the doctor?" Marty paused, then smiled with relief. "Good. Great." He gave a thumbs-up to Luke. "Yes. Uh-huh. Senator Goodspeed wants to be sure he gets the best of care, the very best of care. Yes, wonderful. We'll stay in close touch. Goodbye."

Marty cradled the receiver and looked at Luke quizzically. "You aren't serious about blowing off your schedule for this, are you?"

"I can't ignore him."

"Just sit tight," Marty said. "Feldon's doing fine, he'll be home in a day or two. When he is, we'll get you there for a quiet visit with a loyal old friend, private, no press, maybe a shot or two consoling his ex-wife—hey!" Marty brightened with an idea. "We'll fix her up with a campaign job, anything to help out a friend. . . ."

"Cut the bullshit, Marty," Luke interrupted impatiently. "Steve's in that hospital because of us."

"Like hell he is," Marty shot back, his smile vanishing. "He's the asshole who tipped the press about you and Claire. Don't kid yourself."

"If he did, he wasn't sitting on an exclusive. It would have come out one way or another."

"After the election, who cares?"

"Yeah, who cares?" Luke smiled, showing a thin edge of teeth. "Maybe just my wife."

"Look, he's your old pal, okay, but he's also an incompetent bastard who settled for revenge when he couldn't do his job. If you rush over to the hospital, you look like you're feeling guilty about firing the guy. The press will jump all over you as the sonofabitch who drove him to try suicide. You want that? We haven't got enough problems right now?"

"You're a smart man, Marty." Luke's voice was quiet, but it carried an odd ring. "What would I do without your human touch?"

Marty paused. "Okay," he said slowly. "I'll call Kate and get her back; I don't know why she wants to stay in Chicago, anyway. The two of you will go together—later. That's the way to do it."

"Kate's not going to want to do anything with me."

"She has to, eventually. Sooner the better. This one brings the two of you together again." Marty was talking rapidly now. "The two of you, caring for an old friend, it could be good for the polls—look, we've got to get moving, you've got calls to make. Go make them; I'll call Kate."

Luke gazed at Marty as if seeing him for the first time.

"How do I know," he said agreeably, almost conversationally, "that you were really talking to the hospital administrator?"

The room was silent. The fly was still buzzing, but the noise was now reduced to an insistent whine. Marty picked up the receiver and thrust it toward Luke.

"Call him yourself," he said.

Luke contemplated the phone for a long moment, and then strode from the room.

The radio bulletin Kate heard in Chicago an hour later that afternoon was shocking. She stared out at the dull, accumulating fog of a rainy Chicago day. Stark's call. Now this.

Steve had tried to kill himself. How did someone reach that point of despair? Lisa's words in Kate's own living room returned, unbidden. Steve had given everything to Luke, and he'd never got much in return. Was it true? Had it always been true? And if it was, was his despair their fault? No. She had to resist this new burden of guilt. Steve was becoming more and more unstable, his judgment increasingly flawed. Why else would he have confronted her so cruelly?

You're forgetting something, she told herself. All he did was tell the truth. Involuntarily Kate covered her face, then stared around the hotel room. She was already feeling claustrophobic.

What would Luke's reaction be to this? Would he take a minute to remember his closest friend? Restless, she paced the room in her stocking feet, her head aching with unanswerable questions. She had to figure out what to do next. Where was her life going? I'm not ready to deal with that question, she told herself. I can't face thinking about the future. Not yet.

269

◆ ◆

The children. She must watch them closely; stay tuned to their feelings. If this damaged them, she would never forgive Luke. I will dream about that press conference, she thought. I know I will.

For long moments, she stared at nothing. The idea that had come to her after Stark's call was taking root in her brain. It could work; yes, it could, if she had the guts to follow through. She straightened slowly, feeling a sudden easing of the ache in her spine.

It was taking a chance, an awful chance.

She reached for the phone.

"Joan."

"God, your line's been busy all morning, it's been driving me crazy. How are you? Why aren't you home yet?"

"I think I'm going to be okay. Did you watch?"

"Watch!" She heard Joan's indignant snort. "I wanted to kill him."

"Funny. Me, too."

Joan laughed. "If you can make a joke, even a feeble one, I'm not so worried."

"I'm going to ask you to do something with me," Kate half whispered into the phone.

"Sure," Joan said. "Bet it's illegal."

Kate smiled into the phone. "No murder, I promise. But I need you, I really do." She tried to keep the shakiness out of her voice.

"Okay, you've got me. When? Where?"

"Here in Chicago, tomorrow morning."

"Why? Don't you want to come home? It's not good to sit alone in a hotel room, you and I can get drunk and cry for two hours at my place, isn't that better?"

"I want to do something here, something important. I want you to take a drive with me."

"Where?"

"To South Bend."

Joan considered that. Then, doubtfully, "I'm not really up for a trip down memory lane."

"It's much more than that."

The silence was brief.

"Okay, I'll be there. I'll get a flight out early in the morning. But what are you going to do between now and then?"

Kate thought about it. "I'm going to send for room service," she said. "I'm going to eat a thick steak, drink two pots of coffee, and pour hot fudge over a double order of ice cream."

"Wow. Wouldn't vodka be safer?"

In the twenty-four hours since the press conference, Kate had become increasingly calm. The tears were not coming so often. It was time to think clearly.

She glanced at the date below the masthead of the *Chicago Tribune* brought to her room with breakfast, and her heart thudded. The election was now only two weeks away. That was the relentless reality; she couldn't simply ask for a postponement and withdraw to hide. I'm going to have to march in lockstep, she thought, not knowing whether my marriage is over, whether it's salvageable, or whether it has become nothing more than a joke. No matter what was going on in her private life, there were demands ready to engulf her time. Speeches, appearances on the road, were piling up. The office had called three times; Mrs. Leonard reported the fax machine was belching out paper she should be reading. At least activity offered a form of anesthesia for her grief. It's what people were supposed to need when they experienced a crisis or a loss. Activity; lots of it. Maybe she was lucky to have it.

The *Tribune* had the breathless kind of story from Annie Marshall she had expected; no story by Peter. That seemed strange. Quickly she scanned the results of the CBS-*Washington Post* poll. Luke was down five points overnight, a scary plunge, and Enright was hammering away on the importance of electing "a president with character." She perused the faxed copy of the morning Hotline as she munched on a cold bagel. "Goodspeed Stonewalls Press" was the headline from the *Minneapolis Tribune*. "Goodspeed Does a Dodge as Clock Ticks," said the *Philadelphia Inquirer*. She suddenly stopped and stared at a roundup item:

"Goodspeed Aide in Apparent Suicide Attempt."

The item was brief and careful:

"Steve Feldon, former Senate administrative assistant to Luke Goodspeed, was hospitalized Monday night at George Washington University Hospital after swallowing an undisclosed number of sleeping pills. Sources say Feldon was despondent after Goodspeed ousted him from his presidential campaign."

That was all; nothing more. It wasn't even deemed important enough for the first page.

Joan slid behind the wheel of the rented red Camaro, inserted the ignition key, and gave a quick glance behind her. "Our friends?" she said, nodding toward the dusty black sedan in back of them.

"They'll keep their distance," Kate said, glancing casually back herself at the Secret Service agents.

"Do you ever think about what it'd be like living with them every day of your life?"

Kate shrugged. "I hardly notice them anymore," she said.

Joan laughed. "Then you're ready for the White House."

They drove south, weaving through Chicago's Michigan Avenue traffic, past the hotels and parks along the lake, through the deteriorating fringes of Hyde Park, and out onto the Skyway heading toward Indiana. Joan kept up a light running commentary on the declining quality of hotel food, the state of the roads, and the hulking, brooding presence of the Gary steel mills approaching on their left. With remarkable containment, her sister thought appreciatively, Joan didn't so much as mention the press conference. She was holding her tongue, waiting for Kate to take the lead.

"Remember what we thought when we saw those mills at night?" Kate said abruptly, nodding in the direction of the haze-filled sky.

"We thought the world was on fire," Joan replied.

"I used to think that must be what hell looked like."

Joan chuckled. "You believed in hell longer than I did," she said.

"I think I still do."

They drove on. Joan asked nothing, and Kate was grateful. She leaned back, opened the window a crack to allow in a thin stream of cold air, and closed her eyes. She hadn't been back to South Bend in many years. How many? Twenty? Fewer than that. The last trip was when Mother died. Joan had been in Europe on a honeymoon with one of her husbands. Which one? Kate couldn't remember. She smiled to herself. Probably Joan would pretend she didn't remember either.

"I've forgotten—when Mother died, who—?"

"Alfredo Mancini," Joan replied. "The one who always insisted he was a count. Mother hated him."

Kate laughed. "Good old Al," she said.

Joan didn't laugh back. "He wasn't half bad, I guess," she said. "If I hadn't been so intent on spending my way through Italy, we might have had something. Maybe even a kid."

"I've never heard you express regrets before," Kate said.

"Is that what I'm doing?" Joan waved a careless hand at the small neatly clipped lawns on the outskirts of South Bend, many of which displayed carefully enshrined statues of the Virgin Mary. "Maybe this stuff is triggering my old guilts."

Kate smiled. There never had been a shrine to the Virgin outside the old family home, the Dutch Colonial in Harter Heights. Mother had scorned this form of Midwest devoutness, treating it with the contempt she reserved for all things she decided were of a lower class—phony Italian counts included.

They were turning down a familiar street.

"Let's park," Kate said.

Joan pulled over, and the two sisters got out. In front of them, sitting on a slight rise of earth, was the house in which they had grown up. It stood silent, weary, a veteran of years of active families and minimal upkeep. The shutters on the bedroom windows were covered in faded green paint, and one of them still hung by a single hinge. What a strong hinge that must be, Kate marveled.

"It looks smaller than I remembered," Joan said.

"The places you go back to always do," said Kate.

"Kate."

"Yes?"

"Why are we here?"

Kate walked slowly down the block, looking around. "Remember those kick-the-can games at night?" she said. "And the fireflies we collected in bottles?"

"Come on, Kate."

"I had a phone call yesterday from Ernie Stark."

"*That* creep." Joan fairly spat out the words.

"He's found out about Abby."

Joan said nothing. She looked stricken.

"He said he knew all about the abortion," Kate continued. "Remember the woman at the clinic? The one I saw at Neiman Marcus? She must have got to Stark. I think that's what happened."

"That bitch." Joan's face grew very pale. "I can't believe this."

"I know. I can hardly believe it myself."

"Kate, this is awful. I'm sorry."

"You know what he wanted from me? A trade-off. Exclusive confirmation of Luke's affair in exchange for killing a column on the abortion." Kate let out a dry, sharp laugh. "I told him he had no conscience, and he said, 'I just *report*, Mrs. Goodspeed. The voters elect or destroy. Not me.' "

Joan drew a deep breath. "You *must* talk to Luke," she said. "As fast as you can."

Kate pushed at a dead branch with the tip of her shoe. It cracked and broke at her touch. "There's more," she said. She could sense her sister's wariness. "I want to tell you something, and I wanted to tell you here—because it still feels like home, I guess."

"I'm waiting."

Kate pulled her old down coat closer and turned up the collar against a stiffening wind. "I had an abortion, too," she said, "when I was nineteen."

Joan looked at her sister. She appeared genuinely shocked. "You?" she said.

Kate smiled wearily. "Surprise, surprise."

"That's incredible. I never would have thought—"

"You never would have thought your big sister actually had sex with anyone?"

"Not in those days," Joan said. "Not good girls. I, of course, was not a good girl. You were."

"Well, get ready for another shock." Kate drew a breath. "I'm going to announce it publicly."

"You're *what?*" Joan stopped dead on the sidewalk.

Kate pulled gently at her sister's elbow. "Let's keep walking," she said, glancing back at the Secret Service car following them at a discreet distance down the street. "I miss the old elm trees, you know?"

"Kate, you've been through too much," Joan said hurriedly, all teasing humor gone from her voice. "Don't go crazy."

"I'm not, believe me."

"Why would you do this?"

"I'm gambling," Kate said softly. "If I give the media this good a story, Stark's exposé of Abby looks like overkill. He's gotten in trouble before. The *Daily News* gets nervous when he gets too vicious; I think they'll want him to pull off." She took a deep breath. "Anyhow, I don't want to live with this anymore. One person convinced me. A woman who came up to me after the show I did with Eleanor Enright."

"Who?"

"A teacher, one of my history teachers. Back when this happened, she was the only person I could turn to. She lent me the money to go to Chicago for the abortion."

"So now she wants to blackmail you."

Kate emphatically shook her head. "No," she said. "Not at all; she's not like that. She didn't judge me then, and I don't think she's judging me now. But when she came up to speak to me after the show, I thought I would die." Kate briefly closed her eyes. "I didn't recognize her at first, and then I did, and I wanted to run, but there was nowhere to hide. There is never going to be anywhere to hide."

"You're telling me she didn't threaten you?"

"That's right. She told me she's rooting for us. She said some reporter came to the university to interview her a few months ago, and she told them I was a wonderful student—" Kate smiled. "All that stuff."

"Did she realize she frightened you?"

Kate nodded absently, gazing at a bump in the sidewalk near the curb. "This is where I fell over on my bicycle," she said. "When I was ten."

"Kate—"

"She realized. I started to move away, and she whispered to me not to worry. She whispered she would never say anything about my being—'sick,' as she put it." Kate shrugged her shoulders in a slow-motion, weary gesture. "Did she mean it? Was she real? I think so. I looked at her eyes, and I didn't see any double message there. But it only proves how crazy it is for me to try to keep anything secret. Our lives—there's nothing private anymore. Sooner or later, someone will find out about my abortion, and maybe Abby's, too. It will come out. And I know I can't live like this any longer. I can't live with this dread of exposure of myself, Luke, or the kids."

"Luke will think you're punishing him for screwing around with Claire—which I assume has been confirmed."

"Oh, Joan." Tears were running down Kate's cheeks. "It hurts."

Joan gently touched her sister's arm, saying nothing.

275

"I mean—did we work all these years for this?" Kate's tears flowed now, unchecked. "I used to just bounce along, enjoying, coping, taking everything for granted. Lisa Feldon said I have this sense of entitlement, and she's right. I've been some kind of golden girl, at least in my mind, with a great husband, two perfect kids, and an air pillow for long plane rides. Does this make any sense? All that's changed. Now it's as if I'm out on a ledge, high up, with a wind blowing and a blindfold on. One misstep and I'm gone. I'm angry, God, yes, I'm angry. I think of Luke with that woman, and it just hurts. He thinks all he has to do is say he's sorry, and it gets wiped off the books. It hurts."

"Maybe this is a time when you shouldn't do anything."

Kate, with great effort, dried her tears and shook her head. "First, I'll talk to Abby. Then Luke."

Joan frowned. "It'll be like going inside a nuclear reactor to prevent a meltdown," she said, half to herself. "You'd better be braced for anything."

Kate paused. "I hope I am," she said, picking her words carefully. "Look, this may sound unbelievable, but I'm not trying to get back at him. If I'm honest—and God, that's what I'm trying most to be—part of me has wondered if something like this wasn't inevitable at some point or other. Look at him. Who wouldn't be attracted? Somehow, I've got to absorb what's happened, and go on. What else do I do if I stay married?"

"If that's what you decide. I mean—" Joan paused—"it won't do any good to pretend to yourself you aren't angry."

Kate didn't answer immediately. They walked a few steps more as she stared hard at the sidewalk. "I can't see any other route clearly right now," she said finally. "Joan, this is my life. He's my life. We've been partners for a long, long time."

It was Joan's turn to be quiet for a moment. "I don't know," she said softly. "I don't think you've worked this through all the way."

"I know I haven't, but I can't afford to wait," Kate said. "What I can't put up with is what secrets have done to us and to our kids." She paused again. It hurt almost beyond endurance to say these things out loud. "I've been deliberately blind when it comes to Luke," she said. "He draws from a thousand people, and I'm only one of them, whether I like it or not. I've wanted him to be perfect on my terms, and I taught myself how to avoid the fact that

276

he isn't." She lifted her chin high. "I can't afford to delude myself anymore. Why *was* I so blind? Was I as set on winning the White House—regardless of cost—as Marty and Claire? Claire thinks so. Is she right? Was that why I went along with that awful press conference?"

Joan shook her head. "This is going to backfire, I know it."

"I want the heat off Abby, that's my bottom line."

"How will the kids react? How much are they supposed to be able to take?"

"I don't know," Kate said. "I've agonized over it, and I'll probably keep agonizing over it for years if this does them any harm. I'm going to talk to them both, explain everything, and hope they'll understand I'm doing what I have to do."

"I guess Luke could always practice law in Chicago. He'd love that."

Kate blinked back tears again. "Joan, I'm scared," she said.

Joan reached for her sister's hand and squeezed.

"Do you think I'm making a mistake?"

"I wish I knew," Joan said quietly. "I wish I could tell you, one way or the other. I guess it depends on what you want to accomplish."

"I'm trying to save my marriage—and my kids. I still want Luke to win this election, but we aren't able to be honest with ourselves or each other anymore, and that depresses me more than I can tell you."

"And that's more important to you than Luke becoming president."

"Yes."

"God, there's got to be a better way. This could blow your whole life off the map."

"I think it's blowing up now."

Joan frowned. "Luke could withdraw from the race, and that would save all of you."

"He couldn't do it. No—" she paused—"he shouldn't do it. He'd be a good president, I really believe that. Does that sound crazy?"

"No," said Joan, with a sigh. "Just ambivalent. I guess you have to do what you have to do. Nobody can decide for you."

Kate was silent, wishing for something else.

"I'm with you," Joan said gently. "I hope you know that."

277

This time, she put her arm around her sister and hugged—Joan, the one who never hugged.

They turned and slowly began walking back to the car. In back of them, trying to appear unobtrusive, the Secret Service agents executed a quick U-turn.

"I'm waiting for the obvious question," Kate said.

"I'm debating whether I should ask it."

"It's okay."

Joan glanced at her sister, then away, past the house. "So, who was the father?"

"Who do you think?"

"Luke."

Kate hesitated; an infinitesmal hesitation. "Yes," she said.

"And you never told him?"

Kate pushed a lock of heavy hair back from her face. "Hey, remember the era in which you and I grew up?" she said. "Luke was packing up to leave for law school, and not that interested in me anymore. I was ashamed, panicked, and desperate, so I decided to handle it on my own."

"You could have told me."

"Come on, Joan," Kate chided lightly. "Weren't you a bit young for that kind of confidence? Tell my little sister?" She paused. "Although I did try to talk to Mother." Kate briefly closed her eyes, remembering too vividly the frightened look on her mother's face, and found herself once again trying to forgive. How long until she could be sure she really meant it? "She pretended she didn't understand, so I knew I was on my own."

"Poor Mother," Joan said, her voice heavy. "The Church didn't prepare her for us. But later—when you and Luke got together again in Washington?"

Kate was looking somewhere else, somewhere far away and long ago. "I said nothing."

"Why?"

"What good would it have done?" she said, brushing a loose strand of hair back from her eyes. "When I realized I loved him, really loved him, that we were old enough and smart enough to make a go of marriage, it scared me to bring up the past. It was over, done. It might have poisoned what we had."

Joan rolled her eyes. "You mean he might not have believed it was his baby."

Kate did not hesitate before answering. "Maybe not," she said.

"Then you didn't really trust him, not even then."

This time, Kate was silent as they trudged farther down the block. "Maybe not, who knows?" she said thoughtfully. "I don't trust my memories. I only know I wanted to pretend it never happened." She glanced at her sister. "By the way," she said in a suddenly playful manner, "do you know denial can be a healthy psychological mechanism?"

"So I've heard."

They had reached the car.

"Well—" Joan dug into her pocket for the car keys and moved slowly around to the driver's side of the Camaro. "I know one thing," she said. "I'm not feeling nostalgic for the joys of marriage anymore."

12

"So Ernie Stark is going to do it, after all. My nightmare's coming true."

It was late that same night. Kate, spent from the trip back from South Bend and the flight home, sat close to her daughter on the old front-porch swing at the house in Cleveland Park. The hopelessness in Abby's voice tugged at her heart. There had been no easy way to break the news of Ernie Stark's plan. Kate put an arm around Abby as they sat together, rocking gently back and forth. "Maybe," she said. She would wait her out. Just hold her, try to stop the shivers, and wait her out.

"At least I don't have to worry about humiliating myself in front of Daddy anymore," Abby said. She rubbed her fist into her forehead with the vigor of an angry child. "He's taken care of that."

Kate said nothing. There was no way to tamp down Abby's anger and confusion with soothing little maternal noises; it was too late for that. The Chicago press conference would stay with all of them for a long time. We have to be honest with each other now, she thought. No pretense. No public smiles in private places.

The old swing, unused, unoiled, was making high-pitched protesting noises. Kate ran her finger over a thin powder of red rust on one of the chain links attaching it to the porch roof, making a note to look for some lubricating oil under the kitchen sink. There used to be a little can there, she was sure of it, or maybe it was in the basement. She absolutely had to oil this swing. But not now. Now she had to tell Abby her own secret, and it wasn't going to be easy.

"Abby—"

Her daughter looked at her warily. "Oh, shit, Mother. What else?" she whispered.

Luke walked through the bedroom door after midnight, his step tentative. He stopped. Kate was sitting, pale and quiet, propped up by pillows in their bed.

"Do you want me to leave?" he said.

"To go where?" she said in a low voice.

"To hell. To a hotel."

It was like Luke; a direct challenge. Establish the floor first. The pain in Kate's chest was unbearably sharp as she put down the magazine she had been mindlessly flipping through. This one she had to confront directly, even though she still felt herself groping for light in a dark room. She had rehearsed the words. "I'm not leaving you, Luke," she said. "If that's what you mean."

"Do you want a divorce?"

"I've thought of it, I won't deny that."

She saw the uncertainty in his face. "That's not an answer," he said.

No, it wasn't. Hearing the word spoken aloud was startling. Ugly, brutal—and, at the same time, mesmerizing, like a blazing fire. "I know what you're asking," she said after a moment's pause, "but I'm not sure I'm ready to answer. Do we love each other, Luke?" She gazed steadily into his eyes. "Or do we just need each other?" She shook her head slowly. "I don't know."

Luke leaned back against the doorframe, every muscle in his body tensed. "I know how I feel," he said. "I love you. *And* need you." He stood, waiting for something from her. Something she didn't know if she had the strength yet to give.

"We have a long road ahead of us," she began.

"Right," he said quietly. "And not much time."

"I'm not talking about the campaign."

"I know you're not," he said. "You know about Steve?"

"Yes," she said. The news had shocked him; she could see it in his eyes.

"We should visit him. Marty tried to reach you last night, but you never returned his message."

281

Kate blinked. "Message?" she said. "Marty never called me."

Luke cast a slightly edgy glance in her direction. "Come on, Kate. I know you're not in any hurry to spend time with me right now, but this is different."

Luke was so used to being in charge. She felt herself bristling. "I called the hospital," she said. "I didn't ignore this, Luke."

"I'm not saying you did."

This was ridiculous, they shouldn't be arguing about Steve. But she felt her suspicions rise. Did Luke really want to see him, or was it a maneuver to look good? Her mouth felt very dry.

"I owe Steve an apology," she said. "Maybe he owes me one, too, but it doesn't matter anymore. Luke—I'm not sure I'm ready to go with you. Not yet. I don't want another camera trained on my face to show the world how I'm holding up."

"We've got to be seen together; that's how we repair our image."

That was too much. She hurled the magazine across the room. "I don't care about repairing our image!" she said despairingly. "I care about repairing us!"

Luke turned quickly so she couldn't see his face, and moved toward the bathroom, leaving the door ajar. She heard the sink tap turn on, a swift flow of noisy water. The medicine-cabinet door squeaked open. Suddenly she could see his reflection in the cabinet mirror, and what she saw on his face was unreadable.

He caught her eye. "I'm not going to defend my motives," he said, staring steadily into the mirror. His voice was muffled for a second by the towel, then clear. "I've got a helluva lot of things to sort out, and Steve's only one of them. I hope you'll come anyway." He walked back into the bedroom and faced her. His face was stiff. He looked miserable.

"You think I'm a total shithead, don't you?" he said.

"Luke." Even before she started, it felt hopeless. There were no words for what she wanted to say; but she had to try, anyway. "The price is getting pretty high, isn't it?"

But Luke wasn't about to answer such a dangerous question directly; he had trained himself too well. "Everybody wants a piece of me," he said with a shrug and a stab at lightness.

"Marty's press conference made that worse."

"It wasn't Marty's press conference," Luke shot back. "It was mine. I was the one who put us in that debacle, let's get that straight."

She felt a touch of melancholy relief. At least Luke was taking the blame for the family's humiliation.

"Do you still want to be president?" she asked.

Luke straightened, a surprised look on his face. "Of course I do."

"We're paying a very high price," she said. "Is it worth it? I have to know."

Luke didn't respond immediately. His face seemed oddly out of focus, like a puzzle with a piece missing. He touched her shoulder with a habitual comforting gesture. "This may hurt you," he said. "And I don't want that. But my answer is yes."

She gazed at him without speaking.

"Look, honey, hear me. Please." His voice grew so quiet she could barely pick up his words. He sat down next to her on the bed, and cradled both her hands in his. "I'm sorry," he said. "There's no way I can convey with words how sorry I am. I was stupid and cruel, and the thing that scares me the most is that you may stop loving me." He tried a tentative smile. "I can't stand the idea of eight years of state dinners in the East Room without you."

Kate looked away. He was afraid, she could see it. He was afraid she would rob him of his prize. Even if there was more, even if Luke meant every word, or thought he did, it didn't matter. The pain was too piercing. She could not let him in too close. She could not even let him sit physically too close, because the familiar scent of his skin and hair still smelled of betrayal.

"I've wanted this too long," he said, his voice more urgent. "Honey, the White House! Don't tell me you don't want it every bit as much as I do, because I'm not sure I would believe you."

Kate slowly shook her head, feeling stunned. He actually thought she might try to force him out of the race. "I'm not asking you to quit, Luke," she said. "You should be president; I want you to be president. I asked you that because I had to hear you confirm what I really know—before I tell you something *you* need to know." She rose from the bed, pulled her robe close, and turned fully toward him. "Ernie Stark called me yesterday, after the press conference."

"What did he want?"

Kate took a deep breath. Hearing the words finally come out of her mouth felt like unloading forty pounds of stone from her chest. "Abby had an abortion two months ago," she said.

Luke's head jerked forward. He winced as if hit.

"We tried to keep it a secret," she said gently. "But Stark found out, and now he says he'll print the story before the election—unless, of course, you give him a better one, the only one he really wants." It was still hard to say it plain. "Confirmation about you and Claire."

Her words were greeted with shocked silence.

"An abortion?" he managed finally. "Abby?"

Kate saw the hurt, the disbelief. She'd tried to be gentle, but this was not the kind of blow that could be softened. Even now, even with all the pain inflicted on her, she wished she could make it easier, but she owed Luke the straight information.

"I wish it weren't true," she said. "But it is, and it's something she hoped you would never have to know."

"My little girl? I don't believe it."

"I know it's hard, Luke. Believe me, I do."

"Who did it to her?"

"A summer intern," Kate said. "No one we know. She won't talk about him."

"You let her have an abortion?" Luke's voice was shaking. "Why wasn't I told?"

"She didn't want you to know."

"That's not good enough, Kate. I'm her father!"

"How could I tell you?" she said, spreading her hands, palms up, in an unconsciously imploring gesture. "You've got the responsibilities of running for the most important job in the world—how can I pull your attention away from that? In the middle of a campaign?"

Hearing her own voice, Kate realized exactly what she was doing. She was voicing the essential trade-off of their lives—a trade-off that put his political agenda ahead of any personal one, no matter what it was. This was the way it had always been. But where and when had the decision been made? She'd never before asked the question of herself.

"What right did you have to decide without consulting me?" He was shaking with anger now.

Kate stood still. In her own bedroom, with her own husband, she was on the defensive. He was putting her on the defensive.

"Abby decided, not me."

"Oh, sure." His voice was mocking. "*You* let it happen, and you deceived me, maybe I could have helped her, done something for her—"

It was too much.

"Don't accuse me, Luke," she said, angry herself now; pushing back tears. "If you want to talk about family decisions, let me remind you I've made them mostly on my own for a long time because I've had to."

"I never asked to be protected from anything as serious as this."

"You didn't?" Kate said, stung. "You do, every day. You do it by being too busy to pay attention, by being too important to be disturbed. We defer to you—all the time. God, when I think about it! If there's blame here, you share it."

"You took away my right as a parent to know what was going on with my child! Do you think I'm such a bastard I wouldn't care? Do you think I would have deserted her?"

"Why are you angry right now? Because you weren't there to hold her hand and listen to her cry or because you weren't in control?"

The angry light faded from Luke's eyes, and for an instant she saw confusion. He sat heavily in a chair.

"Is she all right?"

Kate's body trembled with relief. "As all right as she can be, at the moment," she said. "If that terrible man makes this public, she won't be. She'll need us, Luke. More than ever."

"The poor kid." He lowered his head into his hands. "I'm not going to let that bastard drag her through the mud, Kate. There's some way to stop him, and I'll find it."

"I already have."

Luke looked up. Their eyes locked, and Kate felt her heart thumping deep and hard. She needed calm now. Total calm.

"There's something else I have to tell you, and you must listen. I need you to listen," she said.

"Why do you say that? Of course I'm listening."

"It won't be easy." She heard the anxious tone in her voice, but she couldn't pretend. "Can you hear something you won't like and still try, try to understand?"

There was a knock at the door.

"What is it?" Luke called, automatically tightening his tie.

Mrs. Leonard opened the door slightly, pulling a wrapper around her, her face worried. "There's a fax marked 'urgent' coming in," she said. "Three pages. Shall I bring it to you?"

"No, not now." Luke had hesitated, almost imperceptibly.

Mrs. Leonard retreated.

"All right, Kate," Luke said. "I'm listening."

A second knock on the door.

"What *is* it?"

Mrs. Leonard's gray head appeared once again. "A call from Mr. Apple," she said. "He said it's important."

Kate grabbed her head with her hands. "Not *now*," she said.

Mrs. Leonard retreated again, this time pulling the door firmly shut behind her.

Luke began to pace up and down, first kicking his shoes across the room.

"Please sit down, I need to be able to look at you," Kate said. Her stomach felt sick, and she couldn't stand another minute of waiting.

To her relief, Luke obeyed. This time, she took his hand in hers. "This is hard," she said. "But you have to know."

Awkwardly Luke patted her hand. He looked both wary and vulnerable.

"I had an abortion, Luke, back when we first dated in South Bend."

After all these years, she had finally said it. Her tongue felt thick with the truth as she saw the color drain from his face.

"You?"

"Yes."

Luke sat in total, shocked silence. Then he spoke. "Kate—how?"

"It only took once," she said. "That one time."

That one time. In the sheltering grass, by the Notre Dame lake, on that hot, humid August night filled with chirping cicadas when she knew he was going away and she would never see him again and the moon rose above the water. . . . Please, Luke, she prayed. Remember. Did he remember?

He said nothing. Two seconds; five.

"The summer before you left for Harvard."

Luke stirred. "I can't believe—"

"It's a shock, I know." Let there be no denial in his eyes, no skepticism.

"You and me. Kate, you're telling me you were pregnant with my baby." Luke's voice was low.

Kate could breathe again. "Yes," she said. "When we were kids who barely knew each other."

"Why didn't you tell me then?"

Kate countered with the question she had harbored for over twenty years. "If I had," she said, "what would you have done?"

Luke started to speak, and stopped.

"Well, I know," she said quietly. "You would have thought you had to marry me, but you wouldn't have wanted to. We would have been like all those poor kids back then who had sex and found themselves trapped. If you had married me, you would have resented me all our lives, I've always been convinced of that. It would have meant giving up law school. It would have ruined your life."

Luke found his voice. "I don't know what I would have done," he said. Tentatively, sadly, he smiled. In truth, neither of them would ever know.

"Honey—" he said.

She drew away slightly, forcing herself to ignore his outstretched hand, knowing she had to leave him room for what was to come.

"Luke, you aren't going to like what I'm about to tell you. But it's something I have to do." She breathed deeply. "I'm going to go public with this."

Luke blinked, and his mouth actually fell open. He froze so totally, she felt compelled to repeat herself.

"I'm going to announce I've had an abortion."

"My God," he managed. "On top of everything else? Why?"

Could she explain? Was it possible? "Because it will come out sooner or later anyway, I'm convinced of that now," she said. "I want to protect Abby, if I can. Maybe Ernie Stark won't think he has such a big story if I produce a bigger one." She paused. "Maybe he won't print it at all; I'm gambling on that. And I can't stand feeling like a liar anymore."

The struggle in Luke's face was terrible to watch. "You kept it a secret from me for twenty years and now you want to tell the whole world? You can't possibly be serious."

"I am."

"Kate, I don't care how clever your strategy is, I don't want this!"

"Luke, trust me, please." She worked to keep her voice firm but it was very hard. "There are people who know about it; the people who helped me back then. One of them came up to me after the show with Eleanor. She was trying to tell me her lips were sealed, but don't you see? It will hang out there, one more dirty little secret, and

I'll always be looking around the next corner, waiting to be exposed." She paused. "In fact, I have been waiting, I guess, all our lives."

"That's why you reversed course on my pro-choice statement, right?" Luke shot the question at her; a challenge.

She shook her head in the negative. "I changed my mind because of Abby. Not because of me."

He started to say something, then stopped. "What do you mean, 'one more dirty little secret'?" he said.

He knew what she meant—they had been married too long for him not to know. He wanted to force her to say it, to put her on the defensive. "That's no puzzle," she said. "I lied about myself, and you lied about Claire."

"And because I won't give a public confession," he said slowly, "you are going to force yours on me."

"No, that isn't true. Luke, listen. I want us to be able to live with what *is* true." Suddenly her agitation began to fade. This was indeed what she believed, and because of that, it was easier to say than she had expected. "I don't want us to have to live with lies and the fear of being exposed."

"Kate, how are you going to explain to the world the fact that you lied to me about this for our entire married lives?"

"I'll just tell the truth."

Savagely he punched the side of the chair. "I'll protect Abby, do you hear me? I'll do it. Okay, we've lived with lies, but we're not going to anymore. I don't want you throwing your body on this damn grenade!"

"Do you have a better idea? What do you want to do, put a contract out on Ernie Stark? Luke, be sensible. Listen to me, I'm trying to keep us from losing what we are!"

"God!" Luke strode back and forth across the room, pushing at his hair. He leaned against the wall. "I'm angry at myself, too, do you understand that? Will you grant me that much?"

For the first time, she felt a quiver in her defenses. "I want to believe that," she said. "It means more than hearing you tell me how sorry you are for Claire."

"I'm angry at myself, but if you want to hear truth—" he looked at her, a wary look in his eye— "I'm giving you truth, now. I can't absorb these—these deceptions, even if you didn't mean them to be. Not this fast. I'm trying, but not this fast."

"*You* can't," she said angrily. "Do you have any idea what I'm holding in?"

"Maybe the real name of the baby's father," Luke shot back.

Kate stepped back as if struck.

"If it were mine, why wouldn't you have told me?" he challenged.

"How could I do that?" she said, shocked into defiance. "You dumped me. You were this great campus hero on your way to law school, and who was I? A scared kid with nowhere to turn!"

Luke was digging in. "You're covering something up," he said. "Otherwise, you'd have told me long ago."

Kate stared at her husband. This wasn't Luke talking. This was a wounded man flailing for balance. Well, if she had to, she could lay out more truth. "You really want to believe that, don't you?" she said. "You don't want to think that Luke Goodspeed, the All-American Catholic boy, actually could have made love to a young woman and never admitted to himself the possibility he left her pregnant, do you? You've allowed yourself the luxury of disapproving of abortion on moral grounds all these years, because you never had to face what it meant. Not to that young girl, someone you hardly knew; not to me, your wife; and not to Abby, your daughter!" She was crying now.

"Kate—"

"I'm doing the one thing I have to do to save Abby, and it's the one thing that might save you!"

He seemed to be standing at a great distance, or was it she? "You and Marty have constructed this tight little dream world," she said, her voice trembling. "You think you can control everything, fend off problems, bend people to think the way you do—and I think if anything destroys you, it will be that, not me!"

Luke stared at his wife. His chin was thrust forward, and his face looked carved from stone. "I'm going to pretend you didn't say those things," he said, his voice hard with anger. "I'm going to try to remember you hate me right now for Claire, and that part of you is out for revenge. Sure, what you're proposing makes sense. I've got to hand it to you, Kate, you're a brilliant strategist. Risk it all on a throw of the dice, right? 'Honesty is the best policy,' right? The hell with that! I don't want the world to know about our private lives! I don't want them to know about the mistakes and the hurt and the pain—" He stopped, took a breath, and went on, his voice breaking. "Look,

I may not be the greatest father in the world, maybe I've tuned out on you and the kids, but I'm not going to stand by and see my kid eaten by wolves. There's got to be a better way than this, and I'm going to find it!"

"I wish there were, Luke. Believe me, there isn't."

He wheeled and strode for the door, which opened just as he reached it.

"Senator, the office again." Mrs. Leonard's face was pink and agonized, and Kate knew their voices had penetrated the house.

Luke shook his head, raising a hand as if to ward off something. He stood motionless, but it was only an instant of hesitancy. He abruptly turned on his heel, pushed past Mrs. Leonard, and left the room, leaving Kate to ponder on the fact that his outburst had been the truest emotional response she had got from her husband in a very long time.

Knowing she would never sleep, Kate turned off the light. Luke was gone. She had heard him talking to Marty on the phone; heard the car pull up; heard the front door slam. At this moment, she and her husband were strangers, and the thought made her tremble.

The bedroom door opened in the still house, and she saw a figure in a white cotton gown coming toward her. Abby was standing by her bed, her face pinched in the gloom. When she spoke, her tone was reluctantly admiring.

"You've got guts, Mother."

Kate sighed and reached for her daughter's hand. "Did you see your father leave?"

"He came into my room." Abby was trying not to cry. "He just sat on my bed and held my hand and didn't say anything. Then he hugged me and left."

"He's angry. He doesn't want me to do this."

"What did he say when you told him about me?"

"He wanted to know if you were all right. He loves you, you know that."

"I've been lying in bed awake a long time, wondering why he couldn't talk to me, and why I couldn't say anything to him," Abby whispered.

"Sometimes feelings hurt too much," Kate said softly. "You don't always need to talk."

"I wish you and Daddy felt that way."

"You heard us."

"Sure."

Kate couldn't suppress a moan.

"Not every word," Abby corrected quickly. "Enough, I guess. Have you told Nat what you're going to do? Just so he's ready?"

"Yes, I told him." It hadn't been easy. Nat had twisted and turned in his chair, refusing to look straight at Kate. What had she expected? How was an eleven-year-old boy supposed to handle something like this? "He knows what's coming, but I'm glad you're thinking about him."

"He's not so bad," Abby said, "for an eleven-year-old."

She pulled back the covers, hoisted the folds of soft muslin of her nightgown, and climbed into the bed next to her mother. Kate moved to the center, leaving a warm, concave space.

"I wish you had told me before," Abby said. "At first I was really mad. I thought I was such a terrible person when I had to tell you what happened to me, and here, all along, you'd gone through the same thing." She paused. "But then I thought, that means you know what it feels like, maybe more than anybody else."

"I couldn't tell you, honey," Kate said, almost whispering. "I had lived with it for so long—"

"It's okay, I'm over it." Abby was silent for an instant. Then, "Mother," she whispered as she settled in and pulled up the blankets, "I wish I had your guts, I really do."

"You're tougher than you think you are, baby."

"I dunno. I've never been through this before."

It was a true statement, and Kate could say nothing. Instead, she held Abby close.

"Were you scared?" Abby asked.

"When?"

"When you found out you were pregnant."

Kate faced the memory, but it took an effort. "Frightened to death," she said.

"You felt alone?"

"Yes, but that wasn't the worst part. The worst was, I felt I had

291

committed a mortal sin, and God would surely send me to hell."
Kate shifted the weight of her daughter's head, settling it into the
crook of her arm. "I was still very religious," she said. She kissed
Abby's hair.

"Did you try to tell your mother?"

"Yes, I did."

"Like I tried to tell you."

"Yes." Kate pursed her lips, expelling a breath. "But with less
luck, I guess."

Abby stirred. "Nobody's perfect," she said shyly, stirring the embers of an old family joke.

Kate's mind was on the past. "My mother didn't get hysterical or
scream or anything like that," she said. "She just wouldn't listen
when I tried to tell her. She stood in the kitchen and stared past me.
I remember she was holding a soapy dish over the dishpan in one
hand and a rag in the other, and I stood there and watched them drip
and felt completely alone."

"She pretended she didn't understand?"

"She started talking about how she had to clean out the refrigerator."

"Maybe she was scared, too."

Kate sighed and stroked her daughter's hair. "Maybe she was."
They lay together, contentedly.

"Mother?"

"Yes?"

"Could she ever have understood?"

Kate considered her reply in the darkness. "I don't know," she
said. "She was from a very different generation."

"That's not all of it, I'll bet."

"How come you're so curious, all of a sudden?"

"Come on. Tell."

"I guess you're old enough to know," Kate said. "Mother was
pregnant when she married your grandfather."

Abby lifted her head, her voice reflecting the astonishment of the
young for the sins of the old. "How do you know *that*?"

"I was the baby, that's how."

"She told you?"

"I learned to count, very early."

"So she thought you were making the same mistake."

Kate sighed. "I was the baby that trapped her in a bad marriage. And then I was the daughter who found a way out that had been denied to her. I think she resented me on both counts."

Abby was silent for a moment. "That's heavy," she finally said.

Kate kissed Abby's forehead. "Don't forget, abortion was illegal then. At least you don't have to feel like a criminal."

"I do, anyway," Abby said. Her voice was small and muffled.

Kate was silent.

"Mother?"

"Yes?"

"What's going to happen between you and Daddy?"

"Oh, honey." Kate felt a searing band of heat around her heart, and she hoped her voice sounded more confident than she felt. "I don't know right now. But we'll work our way through this."

"Lots of people get divorced."

"I know."

"Why shouldn't it happen to you?"

"We've been married a long time, Abby. And the bonds go deep, a lot deeper than anything that happens on this campaign." Kate stopped to hear the sound of her own words. Was it true, or was she repeating something she wanted to believe? Or thought she should believe? "Try not to worry. You're not saying you want us to, are you?"

"No." Abby was silent for an instant. "I was just wondering if you still loved each other."

Kate tried to keep the answer firm and with no silence between it and the question. "Loving somebody doesn't just end, honey," she said. She didn't know if it was the whole truth, but this was not something to discuss with her child.

"I'm wondering if you mean you're stuck."

"Why would you say that?"

"Presidents don't get divorced."

Kate considered this, tucking it into a corner of her mind. She would mull it over later. Right now she felt herself drifting, comforted by Abby's presence.

"Mother?"

"Hmm?"

"I'm glad you're telling me these things, but I'm angry, too."

"I'm not surprised."

"I want to yell at you and tell you that I'm still a kid. That I shouldn't have to know all this stuff, that it shouldn't be happening."

"But you do, and it is."

"Yeah, but it shouldn't be. I'm really pissed at Daddy. I'm just too tired to yell."

For a moment, both were silent. Then Abby spoke again.

"I'm scared about you going public," she whispered. "People will criticize you and try to humiliate you, and it's my fault. You're doing it for me."

"Not entirely, honey. I'm doing it for myself, too. I don't want that secret using up any more space in our lives."

"But if it isn't Ernie Stark, somebody'll come after me, sooner or later anyway, won't they? No matter what you do?"

"I don't know. I think it's very possible, I can't pretend otherwise."

"It's not fair to either of us."

"No, it's not, but nothing is. I wish I could say it won't happen. But sooner or later, it might."

Abby moved her face and Kate felt the wetness of her daughter's tears on her bare arm. "I'm sick of politics," Abby whispered. "When I grow up, I'm going to sell computers."

Kate squeezed her hand.

"Me, too," she said.

Wednesday morning. The phone shrieked to be answered, and Marty's voice poured forth, hot as the coffee scalding her lip.

"Why are you doing this?" he demanded.

"Because it's your best chance to kill the stories about Luke and Claire," Kate said. She needn't waste her breath talking about Abby—not to this man. All she wanted now was to get him off the phone.

"Nobody's going to change your mind, huh?" Marty said. "Not even Luke?"

"No," she said, nursing the burn in her mouth with her tongue.

"You should have told me about Abby, damn it. We don't need any more trouble, you know that."

"I'm trying to mop up the mess you and Luke already made, Marty."

"It's taking a helluva chance," he said in a musing tone, ignoring

294

her words. "You're the *wife*, that's tougher politically. Abby's a kid. Nobody can control kids, they have abortions and shoot drugs and do whatever they want, but a lot of voters out there think you should be perfect. And what about the cardinal? He'll have your neck. Risky. Very risky. How sure are you Stark's gonna do this?"

"Very sure. He left no doubt of his intentions."

There was a short silence at the other end of the line. Then a stunning surprise: a low, slow chuckle.

"Kate, I keep underestimating you," Marty said. "You've gone and come up with a scheme to take the heat off Luke and make yourself a heroine, and it just might work. Yep, it just might." His voice became more businesslike. "You better fill out the details carefully. I want to know the exact story before you go public. Luke wants to find another way, but I can't see anything we can do fast that would have the same impact. Now we've got to figure the right—"

"Marty, the story is true."

"Yeah, sure." Another chuckle. "As I was saying, we've got to figure the right way to drop this little bomb and do it at precisely the right time."

Kate's temples throbbed, tiny hammers in her head pulsating. She didn't know whether to laugh or to cry. Marty didn't believe her. He actually thought her plan was a total ruse, and he was impressed. His admiring tone brought a surge of nausea. My God, she had once actually wanted this man's respect. "Marty, you amaze me," she said. "I'm giving you the truth, and you don't recognize it when you see it. You want to believe everybody is like you."

"No, I believe everybody is *not* like me," he said swiftly. "That's how I win elections. Now *you*—you want your husband to win, and you'll do whatever the hell it is you have to do to bring it off for him, right? That I understand." It was said quite pleasantly, and Kate had to steel herself to swallow a sharp response. She forced herself to concentrate on watching the morning sun creep into the kitchen, touching the white cabinets with gold. It would be a beautiful day.

"Okay, you don't have to believe me," she said. "It doesn't matter whether you do or not, I guess. But you're not orchestrating how I do this, I am."

Silence. His tone became cool. "I'm the guy in charge of damage control," he said. "You come up with the ideas; I execute them. We cannot afford a fuck-up."

"Not this time. I'm in charge of my own story."

"Kate, you really are a—"

She hung up.

Kate sat at her desk in the library at home in the weak, haloed light of a fifty-watt bulb, unable to bestir herself to reach across to the lamp and turn up the light. The phone rang.

"Okay. It's arranged." Peter's voice was quiet and thin with tension.

"You'll do the interview?" she whispered. "No one else, Peter. That's non-negotiable."

"Yes," he said. She heard a faint whistling sigh over the line. "No problem. I'm a regular on their Sunday morning show. They're comfortable with that."

"No moderator; no other questions." This was important, she couldn't risk a slip.

"Right now they'd agree to anything."

"Thanks, Peter."

Peter heard the wobbly tone and tried to respond. "When do you tell me what this is about?" His voice, straining to be neutral, came out gruff and tense.

"At the studio. Before we go on the air."

"I hope you know what you're doing, whatever it is."

She waited a beat. A long beat. Final consideration. "I do," she said.

"All right," he said. "See you at five o'clock. Shall I ignore all these phone messages from Marty?"

"Yes."

Later, wrapped in an old olive green trench coat, Kate slipped from the house into the backseat of a waiting sedan.

"Let's go, Jerry," she said quietly. "ABC bureau, just off Connecticut."

"You bet." Jerry sniffed a couple of times but asked no questions. He knew something was up, but he would do anything she asked, and that gave Kate a second's glow of comfort. This wasn't going to be easy. Jerry maneuvered the car into a U-turn and headed down the hill toward Connecticut Avenue, a Secret Service detail following close behind. Kate stared at the familiar storefronts, wondering briefly if she would ever again lug a vacuum cleaner into the repair shop to be fixed. Or stop in with Luke at their neighborhood Italian restaurant for a winter supper of spaghetti and wine. Or do anything normal and simple that wouldn't end up on the evening news.

"Everything okay?" Jerry was watching her in the rearview mirror.

"You want the truth?" Kate inquired with a smile. "No."

"Can I help?"

"Just stand by me, Jerry."

He cleared his throat. "Yes, ma'am," he said.

They had crossed California Street. She turned to catch a quick glimpse of the graceful old Wyoming apartment house on Columbia Road, a favorite of hers—a building that symbolized a calmer time. Would there ever again be a calm time in her life? A few moments more, and they were turning off the broad boulevard and on to DeSales Street. Kate saw the ABC studio just ahead and felt a clutch of panic. Was she really ready for this? Could she trust Peter? And then an odd thought. If her mother were still alive, she wouldn't have the nerve to do what she was about to do.

Ten minutes later, Kate sat waiting in the station's holding room. Jerry emerged into the hall, looking around wildly, his face the color of gray ash. The ABC studio was heaving with activity. Staffers were whispering and hurrying back and forth, casting glances at Jerry. The news director was on the phone with the anchor desk in New York, and New York was demanding to know what was going on. Why was Bradford, a newspaper reporter, doing a segment for the evening news with Kate Goodspeed? Who the hell gave Washington the right to preempt time for some mystery campaign announcement?

"Peter!" Jerry said in relief, his nervous hands clutching at Peter's lapel as the taller man appeared before him. Jerry still didn't know what was happening, didn't know why Kate was here. All he knew was, Marty was furious, firing off calls to the studio, demanding Jerry put Kate on the phone. "She's got to coordinate this with me, you tell her that or you've got no job!" Marty had roared, but Jerry couldn't do that. And obscurely, through his fright, he realized

297

Marty couldn't control the situation either. All Jerry's timid soul could do now was ride the wave. In his confusion, he saw one amazing thing. Kate needed him, maybe for the first time. He was supposed to stand guard, in some impossible way, but if that's what she wanted, that's what he would try to do.

"Peter!" he repeated. Then, more calmly, "She wants to see you."

"Don't leave this doorway," Peter ordered, as he turned the knob.

"No, sir." Jerry stopped. He'd never called a reporter "sir" before.

Kate didn't try to hold back. As Peter came through the door, she faced him and buried her head in his shoulder.

"I'm glad you're here," she said simply.

Peter closed his eyes, inhaling the subtle floral scent of Kate's perfume. His arms briefly encircled her in a hug, her bones tiny under his large hands.

"What am I here for?" he asked. That was Peter, gruff and to the point when things got emotional. She stood before him, erect, dressed in a simple, high-necked dress of cherry red wool that made her pale skin almost translucent. Her mouth trembled.

"A confession," she said. She watched the muscles of his face stiffen, saw his eyes grow watchful.

"I don't know if I want to hear this," he said quietly.

"I'm not going to submit to political blackmail anymore," she said. "I'm tired of being afraid."

Peter sat down on a chair and put out his hand, palm upward, a classic plea.

"Kate, don't tell me anything you don't want made public, please," he said. "Don't tell me too much, because I care a lot and I want to know." He paused, adding in an almost inaudible voice, "And that scares me."

She had gone over this in her mind a thousand times. Should she tell Peter about Abby? Was it fair to him? "If I hold one fact back," she said slowly, "it changes nothing. But if you later find it out, you may feel manipulated, the way you did before, and I don't want that. But if I tell you what it is, I must have your promise not to divulge it."

"I'm supposed to decide?"

"You have to choose whether or not to make a leap of faith, I guess." She smiled weakly. "Faith in me. But if you don't, it's okay. Just so you understand that then I have to keep something from you."

Peter studied her for a long moment, his brow furrowed. "You're trying to protect someone else," he said.

"Yes."

"But not yourself. Or Luke."

"That's right."

His handsome face was immobile, and then she saw the deep creases in his brow ease. He seemed to have reached a decision.

"I trust you, Kate. I guess it's as simple as that."

"Peter, there's nothing more wonderful you could ever say to me." She looked at him blinking back quick tears, her hands shaking with relief. "I don't know where I'm headed," she said softly. "I don't know what's going to happen, and I need somebody who believes in me."

Peter stared, hesitated.

And then Kate had to say it. "Peter," she said, her voice shaking almost uncontrollably. "I don't know if Luke and I are going to make it."

In a single motion, Peter stood and put his arms around her, pulling her close in something more than an impulsive hug. She caught her breath and hugged him back, inhaling the warm smell of his skin. How good it felt! His lips briefly brushed her cheek before they both pulled away. Gently, Peter guided her into the chair opposite his and took her hand. Kate shivered in the heat of his powerful grasp. There was no turning back now.

"Okay, pal," he said gently. "So tell me."

The set was very quiet. Not a rustle; not a whisper. Peter and Kate sat side by side in two straight-backed swivel chairs at the anchor's desk, turned toward each other, a setting that gave them the patina of a news team. Kate was glad for the desk between her and the camera; it hid her trembling legs.

"Mrs. Goodspeed, you've said you want to tell a very painful story," Peter began.

"Yes, I do," she said, then hesitated.

"Something that happened to you when you were a young woman, a student at Indiana University—" Peter prompted.

"Yes. I find it very difficult to say, but I want people to understand that people in public life, like myself and my husband, are human and we make mistakes."

"What happened, Mrs. Goodspeed?"

This was harder than she had anticipated. My God, I'm telling fifteen million people, Kate thought suddenly. She licked her dry, caked lips. "I became pregnant," she said. "And, like so many young women, I was desperate. I had an abortion."

"What else do you want to tell us about this?" Peter was being very careful; not pressing too hard, leaving her a window to escape.

"I was too frightened to tell the young man—" She stopped.

"And who was he? Do you want to say?" This part was carefully scripted. There was no way of avoiding the question of who would have been the father, Kate knew that.

"Yes, I do. It was the man I later married, Luke Goodspeed. We were both very young, and I did not tell him."

"Did you seek help anywhere else?"

"It was very hard," she said. "I couldn't go to my family for help. I was too ashamed."

"And why was that?"

"Because I was a Catholic." There, Cardinal Kovach, she thought. Now you know why I was so mad.

"Who helped you?"

"One person. A kind woman who told me where to go for a safe abortion."

A few more questions, all of which Kate answered briefly, but as clearly and honestly as she could. She was struggling with exhaustion. How long would this go on? It felt like an eternity. But then her eyes caught a glimpse of the studio clock and she realized the interview had lasted less than three minutes.

Peter was finishing the carefully scripted set of questions they had decided on together. "Is there anything you want to add?" he asked finally.

"Yes." Kate looked directly into the camera. "I'm glad I've done this," she began. "It's important not to be afraid of the truth. There's too much political bullying in this country, too many ways of making people like us afraid, and we don't have to submit to it." She paused, hesitated, and decided, impulsively, to say more.

300

"I want to say a few words about what these past few months have been like," she said. "A presidential campaign is a challenge, a wonderful opportunity, and, I must tell you, a brutal experience. Families suffer. When nothing about your life feels private anymore, you begin to feel like a trapped animal, and that's hard to endure." She tried to smile. "It's not considered good form to admit this hurts," she said. "We're supposed to take anything that's dished out. That's because the job of the presidency is the most important one this country has to offer, and those of us who live with the man or woman who seeks it are expected to go through a particular crucible." Again she paused. "And you know what? That's fine. That's why I'm telling you the truth about a particularly painful time in my life. It's up to you to decide what you think of me. But I've got one last thing to say. Luke Goodspeed isn't perfect, and neither am I. But he's the most qualified person to run for the presidency in a long time, and he would make a great president."

She stopped.

"Cut!" yelled the director.

Kate sat, stunned. The crew was clapping.

Fifteen minutes later. Peter checked his watch, stepped to a pay phone, then quickly punched in a number.

"Hi."

Burt Barrows's voice roared forth. "Where the hell are you? What's going on? The Goodspeed campaign is going bananas, nobody over there's saying diddly-squat, and the rumors are wild. Have you got a story or not?"

"Yeah. I've got a story."

"I want copy! And I want it now!"

"I'm dictating right now," Peter said. "Fast. The basics you can pick up on the six-thirty news. Jennings will lead with it."

"Jesus, Peter!" Barrows was sputtering. It wasn't like him to sputter.

Peter smiled, a tired smile cut with a webbing of deep lines and creases that seemed to add ten years to his already weathered face.

"You told me to get something good, and here it is. Now, gimme rewrite." He chuckled. "I've always wanted to say that."

301

"Try a new joke next time," Barrows snapped. Peter heard the soft whirr of a computer clicking on. "Shoot. I'm taking it myself. And it better be more than Jennings got."

In New York, Ernie Stark, baffled and furious, sat slumped in his chair, staring at the television screen. Unbelievable. She had stolen his story, damn her. He leaned forward and picked up two sheets of paper he had just pulled from the printer. What a joy it had been to write this particular eight hundred words! He had been able to coax some marvelous detail out of that nurse from Chicago. She had been there; she remembered the frightened young woman from Indiana who years ago had sneaked into a dingy South Side doctor's office for an illegal abortion. Kate Goodspeed, of all people. Little Goody Two Shoes. And now Kate had told the story herself and preempted his column. Why? He directed a rancorous stare back to the television screen. The bitch was a real gambler. Was there something he didn't know?

Stark picked up the pages, still stripped with the perforated holes of computer bond, and ripped them to pieces. So much for a stale scoop. Then he stared out the window at the cold, twinkling lights of Manhattan and grinned suddenly to himself. Ah, he already had an idea for capitalizing on this turn of events. Turning swiftly, Stark dialed a Chicago number.

"Hello?" he said smoothly. "Cardinal Kovach's office?"

Thursday dawned, bloodshot and cold. Kate rolled over in bed, hugging the pillow close, more exhausted than she could ever remember. The phone was ringing, but she wasn't going to touch it. Mrs. Leonard could get it. Jerry had slept on the living-room sofa, something she had agreed to when she saw film crews gathering around the house when they arrived home after the broadcast. He was loyal, he was going to stay loyal, and she was grateful. She needed him. Kate kept her eyes closed, trying to think of something to do that would be normal. She burrowed her face deep, remembering Peter's gentle guidance during those harrowing few minutes, the touch of his steadying hand.

The phone was ringing again. Voices were rising from the kitchen.

302

The newspapers would be piled on the table. The Hotline would be waiting. She had to find out how Steve was doing.

Kate pulled herself up to a sitting position, hugging her knees, glancing at the other side of the bed. It was unrumpled. No call from Luke after the broadcast; no note. Nothing. Marty would try to take over now, put his spin on her announcement, but what would Luke do? Was he dead set on viewing what she had done as revenge? Was he that blind? And if he was—what was their future together worth, anyway? She rubbed her forehead. Exercises. That's what she would do, she would get down on the floor and do those stretching exercises Joan said were so good for aching backs.

The blue carpet felt springy and soft. Now, how did it go? Kate raised one bent leg to her chest and then thrust it into the air, holding for a count of ten. Her back sent out a protesting twinge of pain. Maybe she wasn't supposed to raise her leg so high. Gingerly she lowered it to the ground, then stretched both arms above her head, pushing out with her toes. She raised both legs to her chest and lifted her upper body from the ground, arms forward. That was better. It actually felt good.

"Ma'am?"

Mrs. Leonard, who seemed to wear a permanently anxious look lately, was staring at her from the partly opened door.

Kate hastily sat up, pulling her nightgown to her toes.

"What is it, Mrs. Leonard?"

"I'm sorry, but—well, we've got so many messages coming through. Mr. Spanos said maybe I should wake you up."

"Is Steve okay?"

"No change."

"What time is it?"

"Ten o'clock, Mrs. Goodspeed."

Kate blinked.

"I can't believe it," she said.

"Your sister brought over fresh pineapple, flown in from Hawaii. Nat and Abby didn't go to school. They said you told them they could stay home today." Mrs. Leonard was struggling between sympathy and disapproval. "Again."

"That's right," Kate said. She could sense the housekeeper's immediate relief; she hadn't been conned by the kids, after all. "Don't worry."

"Your sister and Mr. Spanos are doing the *New York Times* crossword puzzle on the kitchen table. They wondered if you knew where the big Webster's is."

Kate stood, feeling better. The world couldn't be crumbling too fast if Jerry and Joan had time for a crossword puzzle.

"In the living room, bottom shelf of the bookcase," she said. "I'll be right down."

She gathered fresh underclothes and went into the bathroom, where she pulled her nightgown over her hair and dumped it into the wicker laundry hamper by the tub. Carefully Kate adjusted the shower head. Luke liked the water to pulsate; she preferred a solid, drenching spray. She stepped into the tub and lifted her face to the water, giving herself up to its comforting warmth, thinking of what lay ahead.

"Kate, let me show you." Jerry was excited, yesterday's wrinkled shirt unbuttoned at the collar. He waved the Hotline as she walked into the kitchen combing her wet hair. "We're getting some great reaction, this is terrific, even Marty's gotta calm down now."

Kate began thumbing through the Hotline. Jerry usually overstated good news and downplayed bad news, but the first-day stories were pretty good. Reporters had scrambled fast for reactions, and their stories were peppered with declarations from pro-choice and feminist organizations. The National Abortion Rights Action League was jumping right in, adopting her as one of their own. "Like many women, the young Kate Goodspeed was forced to obtain a secret, potentially dangerous abortion because she was a victim of this nation's archaic customs and inadequate laws," the organization declared in *Newsday*. "That's why we need to keep abortion safe and legal."

The National Organization for Women was heralding her for her "stark courage and loyalty to feminist values." Kate Goodspeed, their statement declared, "should be elected president of the United States instead of her husband for her uncompromising support of a woman's right to control her own body and therefore her own destiny." Kate smiled wryly at that one. Would that she did feel "in control of her own destiny." At the moment, her destiny felt very much in flux.

She frowned, scanning the bottom half of the page. One statement, so far, from the Church—by the U.S. Catholic Conference, and reported in the *Miami Herald*. It was very cautious. "Mrs. Goodspeed broke a fundamental law of the Church," the statement read. "But she deserves our understanding for admitting her abortion was an emotionally devastating choice."

No denunciations; at least not yet. They would come soon, very soon. Kate bit her lip nervously.

"Pretty nice, huh?" said Jerry. "Everybody's casting what you said to favor themselves."

"I'll bet Marty talked to every organization before we got home last night, Jerry."

"Yeah," he said. "You're probably right."

She leafed curiously through the rest of the Hotline, then reached for the morning *Washington Post*. "What about Enright?"

"He's being real careful," said Jerry. "If he attacks, you're a full-fledged martyr. He's got trouble enough with women voters."

"Kate!"

Joan was standing in front of the television, laughing. "Look at this," she said, motioning toward the live cable news show on the screen.

Kate stared. At first, all she saw was an oddly tidy line of demonstrators marching back and forth on the sidewalk in front of the downtown Goodspeed headquarters. She looked more closely and saw a mix of women of all ages—teenagers in jeans, middle-aged women in flowered dresses, grandmother types in pastel suits wearing pearls—all carrying Goodspeed for President signs, cheering, and chanting her name.

Joan couldn't stop laughing. "My God, they're from Central Casting!" she said. "Marty doesn't miss a bet!"

Kate smiled. She felt a surge of relief. If the staged demonstration made the evening news, it would be good for the campaign. Marty was indeed doing his job, even if she felt oddly like a marketing device. Without Marty's handling, what would reality be? *I want to ask Luke that question*, she thought suddenly. *I want to sit down with him and talk with him for a long time, and maybe we'd be able to understand each other again. Maybe.*

Joan had wandered to the window, munching all the while on a dripping slice of pineapple, gazing out onto the sidewalk. "You've

305

got a horde out there," she said, pointing outside. Kate walked over and stood by her sister. Even for someone inured to constant media coverage, the sight was startling. The driveway was filled with a growing throng of reporters and camera crews, all milling, shouting, laughing, and jostling each other. Some were doing standup television reports on the Goodspeed lawn; others were wandering as close to the shrubbery surrounding the house as they dared.

Kate heard a sudden bang behind her and whirled around. Abby, startled, looked up from her seat at the kitchen table where she was reading the papers. The chair on which Nat had been sitting was sprawled backward on the kitchen floor.

"Nat!" Kate saw her son run from the room. She hurried after him, into the living room, and saw the boy, his arms filled with papers, bound onto one of the sofas and start slapping sheets of newsprint over the windows.

"Nat!" Kate said again.

"Gimme tape! Gimme tape!" Nat yelled, shaking off her hand.

"Nat, what are you doing?"

"I'm covering the windows so they can't see us!" He was crying now. "I don't want them to see us! They're moving closer, they were watching me eat my cereal!"

"No, son, no." Kate was crying too, wrestling Nat off the sofa, pulling him down beside her. "Listen, listen to me."

His heaving shoulders felt skinny and vulnerable under her hands, and Kate felt a sudden, wild yearning to hide her child from the whole damn world. She held him close, saying nothing until he stopped crying.

"Mom—"

"We don't have to hide from anybody," she said, her voice fierce. "We're not criminals. Don't worry, son, don't worry."

Nat struggled free of her hands. "You can't stop them," he said in a choked voice. "Nobody can." He ran from the room.

Kate started to follow him.

"No, let him go," Joan said gently from the doorway. "Let him calm down, talk to him later."

Kate hesitated, then strode back into the kitchen. "Jerry!" she commanded.

Jerry was beside her instantly, looking startled.

"Call those TV stations, get the news directors on the phone," she said, nodding at the crowd outside. Her voice was shaking with barely controlled anger. "Tell them to call off their animals and remind them they're human beings themselves. And tell them any-body peering through my windows gets a fist in the face!"

"Right away," Jerry said. He ran for the phone.

"Mr. Apple called," Mrs. Leonard interjected. "He's got a press conference set up for you and the senator and the children here at the house this afternoon and—"

It was too much.

"No!" shrieked Kate. "No!"

Kate knocked on the door of Nat's room. There was no response.

"Nat?" she said.

"I'm busy," came a muffled reply.

"Can I come in?"

"Not now, Mom."

She waited, considering.

"Did you get the Nintendo game you wanted?"

"They were out."

"If you let me know what it is, I'll send Mrs. Leonard to get it."

"Naw, that's okay."

"It must be interesting, Nintendo."

"Yeah."

Kate waited, but there was nothing more. She turned and began walking back down the hall to the stairs, her heart heavy. Then she heard Nat's door opening.

She turned around. He was studying the wallpaper in the hall with fierce concentration, looking very young.

"Nothing's like it used to be," he said.

"I know," she answered. "May I come in?"

He nodded. "If you don't yell about the dirty clothes on the floor," he said.

"Okay."

She followed him into his room almost on tiptoe, stumbling over clothes and books, and sat on the edge of his bed.

"Want to talk?" she said.

307

He sat down next to her, folding his arms protectively in front of him, tucking his hands into his armpits. A child's gesture. It was going to be up to her.

"Are you scared?" she asked.

He considered. "Yeah," he said.

"Of what?"

Nat looked down at his feet. "Of losing you guys."

Kate was momentarily taken aback. "You're not going to lose us," she said. "We're your family."

Nat sat silently, struggling with something, looking everywhere but at her. "Nobody talks normal anymore," he said. "You're all screaming, and Dad's always gone, and I'm sick of all this stuff about us on TV every night."

"I wish I could make everything work right, but I can't," she said. "We're going to have to ride this out, but we'll ride it out together."

"Everything's about sex. I hate sex."

Kate hid a sad smile. "Maybe you need a talk with your father," she said.

Violently, Nat shook his head. "No," he said.

"Are you lonely, son?"

He stopped again and considered. "No," he said. "I've got Harry."

"What do you and Harry talk about?"

"Sports, mostly." Nat was suddenly shy. "And girls."

Kate tried for an expression of studied indifference. "You and Harry talk about girls?"

"I ask him questions. He knows a lot of things because he grew up on a farm."

Kate remembered the *Playboy* magazines hidden under her son's mattress and decided he knew more about sex than he was letting on. But she wasn't supposed to know about them, so she said nothing. It was true, Nat got overlooked more than Abby did. It had been always true. She took his hand and squeezed. "I love you," she said simply.

"Me, too," Nat said, head down, awkwardly swinging his foot.

"Is there anything you want to talk about now?"

Nat was silent for a brief moment. "How come reporters go so crazy?" he said.

"They get scared they'll miss something somebody else might get," Kate said. "Especially when something big happens." She sighed. "I was one once, remember? They're mostly good guys, just trying to do their jobs."

"Harry hates them."

"That's because they make his job harder."

She waited to see if he would ask anything about the abortion. Should she press? I don't know, she thought wearily.

"Harry says all this stuff about you isn't important." Nat said the word "stuff" with an extra degree of scorn. "He says I should be proud of you."

Kate felt a rush of gratitude. "Tell Harry thanks."

Briefly, Nat flashed a grin. Then he slid off the bed and walked over to the television set. "Want to try Super Mario?" he asked.

"What is it? I'm flattered you ask. But I don't know how."

"It's a Nintendo game. I'll teach you," he said. He flicked on the set, sat down, and started a game as Kate pulled up a chair.

"Who's that?" she pointed to a red figure bouncing across the screen.

"That's Mario," Nat said. His tone was absorbed and authoritative. "He's got a brother named Luigi, he's green. And then there's Toad and Princess." He punched the remote control, guiding Mario down a cliff and away from danger.

"What's the point?"

"They have to go through seven worlds until they reach the monster they have to kill."

"That's tougher than real life."

"Easier." He punched the control again, and Kate watched the small, lurid figure on the screen jump a chasm. Nat handed her the control. "Watch out for the little red guys with masks," he ordered. "They'll kill you."

Kate fumbled almost instantly. Mario was hit and fell to the bottom of the screen and disappeared. Nat grabbed the control and Mario reappeared outside the door.

"Oh, I thought he was dead."

"You get three Marios before you die completely."

"That *is* easier than real life."

Nat thought about it. "It's more fun, most of the time," he ventured.

"Do the villains get theirs?"

309

"Sure." Nat was concentrating on the weaving, bobbing screen images. "Mario's going to kill the frog," he said.

"How?"

"By throwing vegetables at him and making him eat them."

"Brussels sprouts?"

"I guess." Nat smiled faintly.

"That would kill me, too."

"Ah, Mom."

This time they smiled together.

At headquarters, Marty worked the phones all day, periodically pacing, mumbling, his mouth moving. By five, after hours spent coaxing and wheedling reporters, he was sweating under the pitiless neon ceiling light. This was tough damage control. Too many layers. You got one thing nailed in place, another slipped away. Hell, walking a tightrope was his job. So far, a few lucky breaks. The first news cycle had been mostly good stuff, very important. The slapped-together demonstration in front of headquarters would be on both the NBC and CBS evening news shows—bingo for that one. He could thank Claire for putting it together. But Operation Rescue and the other anti-abortion groups were mobilizing. Kate shouldn't have vetoed the press conference; it would have been good for her to appear. At least, Luke's stand-up at the airport praising his wife's honesty came off okay. Jesus. Marty rubbed his head. Sometimes he felt he was trying to push a cooked noodle across a table with his nose.

Marty drained the final lukewarm drops of a Coke and threw the can into a trash basket by his desk where it joined half a dozen others. He reached for a bottle of aspirin and wrenched off the cap. Two, on the tongue. Marty swallowed, grimacing. They tasted like hell without water.

Now it was a matter of watching the polls. If they shifted disastrously, Marty was ready with a new strategy—one that would orchestrate sympathy for a good candidate with a crazy lady for a wife.

He glanced at the clock. The evening news shows were ready to go on the air.

"Where are the goddamn tracking polls?" he roared.

Aides rushed in to face an almost manic boss. They're almost ready, they assured him. Any minute.

"Any minute isn't good enough! Now! I want 'em now!"

Several times Marty started to yell for Claire. Several times he bit his lip savagely and pounded his desk instead. His demeanor was ferocious, except when he picked up the phone to talk to a reporter.

"Broder? Yeah, how are you? How are *we* doing? Hey—" Marty now had a big smile on his face, a lazy, gravelly tone in his voice. "Yeah, I knew. She's a strong woman. Courageous, that's the word. You bet. We support her. It only proves what I've told you guys all along—Luke can't be smeared; he's too good. Wait—"

An assistant with pages fresh out of the computer ran in, a triumphant grin on his face. "Here," he whispered.

"Hang on, Dave," Marty said, grabbing the sheets and scanning them. "You want to know what's happening? Our support is staying steady—okay, we had a bit of a dive before, but now basically we're holding firm. You bet! Hell, the polls will be shooting up tomorrow. You'll see."

Marty slammed down the phone and started punching in Tom Brokaw's number. "No plunge, no plunge," he whispered. "Just in time for the fucking news." Suddenly another piece of paper was shoved into his hands. Ernie Stark's column. Marty stared at the headline on the piece.

"Exclusive—Cardinal Threatens Excommunication for Kate Goodspeed."

"Shit," Marty breathed. His eyes looked slightly wild.

13

"You look beat," Marty said Friday morning as Luke strode into his office. "Why'd you cancel the layover in Colorado?"

Luke shrugged impatiently, threw his black leather travel bag into the chair facing Marty's desk and rubbed hard at the heavy stubble on his chin. Flying half of Thursday night without a razor had taken its toll.

"Too much happening," he said. "What's the play on Kovach?"

"See for yourself," Marty replied, tossing him a copy of the *Washington Post*. "Page one, lousy head, but below the fold. Page ten in *The Times*—'Cardinal May Employ Sanctions,' something like that. They dragged in his trouble with the unions last year. They don't like Ernie Stark much, I'll say that for them."

"What else?"

Marty waved a clutch of paper in his fist. "Endorsements, plenty of them," he said. "Gloria Steinem, a couple of congresswomen, Governor Lacey Hudson—I need some Catholics, but I'll get them. Got one." He grinned. "Your mother."

"My mother?" Luke's mouth literally fell open.

"Took a little cajoling," Marty said. "Just a one-sentence quote; the *L. A. Times* used it. 'My daughter-in-law, Kate Goodspeed, has demonstrated a rare kind of courage by revealing her long-ago abortion.'"

"Don't let anybody interview her."

"Are you kidding? I know when I'm ahead."

Luke walked over to the windowsill, stared out the window, and sat down. "If Kovach excommunicates Kate, he's going to have to excommunicate me," he said.

"Don't say that," Marty said quickly. "He's bluffing."

"Don't kid yourself, he's not a nice guy."

"Kate promised she'd keep her mouth shut, not make matters worse. You talked to her yet?"

Luke hesitated. "No," he said. He did not elaborate. "This isn't going to be easy for her."

Marty snorted. "She didn't sound too upset to me."

"Born a Catholic, die a Catholic. You don't know how deep it goes."

Marty stretched lazily, but his body bristled with controlled irritation. "Maybe not," he said. "But I know a lot about running a campaign. And I see Kovach as just one more politician who wants something. This guy wants to force you to make the Church the center of this campaign. He wants you to quit talking pro-choice and come flat out against abortion, no more, no less."

"Well, he isn't getting what he wants." Luke moved back to Marty's desk and this time picked up the morning *Wall Street Journal*, scanning the front page.

"He'll find that out pretty quick," Marty said. "And when he starts realizing his meddling could boomerang, he'll pull off. What are you looking for?"

"An update story on Texas Associated Life; they're sliding fast," Luke said.

"So they get bailed out, right?"

"I'm afraid the well is running dry." Luke glanced briefly at his campaign manager, then back at the paper. "Nothing today. It's a real mess."

"You know something I don't know?"

"There's trouble ahead for the whole damn industry, that's all."

Marty studied him closely. "Yeah, you know more," he said. "Gilmartin, right? Well, you'll be the guy in charge."

Luke flashed a quick grin. "Just in time for the Republicans to blame us." He tossed the paper down again and began pacing the room. "What about Palmer?"

"Your statement goes out Sunday morning; the press will claim we held back until after the debate, they're right; we'll deny it. Usual stuff. Norton knows what you're planning, and he's out of his head with anger."

"I know," Luke said. "He called me in Colorado."

"Then you know he's demanding a meeting with black leaders."

"Yep. Set it up. Invite all the heavyweights. We'll do it right after the debate."

"You'll all be wiped out, Luke. Better the next morning."

Luke considered. "Okay, the next morning, in Boston. Get them there, and keep it quiet." He resumed pacing, rubbing his chin. "What about Steve?"

"You and Kate hit the hospital in—" Marty checked his watch— "an hour. A volunteer will pick her up, drive by here and take you both to GW."

"I need a shave," Luke said, stretching. "Where's your razor?" Silently Marty pulled a scruffy leather pouch from his top drawer and tossed it to Luke. "Take it with you," Marty said. "You've got a speech in Connecticut this afternoon."

"Too damn much campaigning, Marty," Luke said suddenly. "I'm gone all the time. I haven't been home since Tuesday night."

"When you got the big news." Marty's laugh was not pleasant.

"Yeah, when I got the big news."

"Why did she kill that press conference yesterday?" Marty said, resentment in his voice. "For Christ's sake, people are asking why you haven't appeared together yet. What's the matter with her? Without the two of you holding hands for the cameras, all the nets have is the damn cardinal." Marty's irritation was growing. "Luke, I've gotta say this to you—Kate is too emotional. Too volatile. She'll screw you up yet."

Luke jammed his fists into his pockets and leaned against the door, facing Marty. "Hey," he said, "she didn't do the screwing around."

"Or so she tells you."

Luke stiffened. Instinctively, Marty moved to erase the words from the air. "When you get up on that stage tomorrow night," he said quickly, avoiding Luke's eyes, "don't let Enright goad you into anything rash. He'll try to throw the cardinal at you, the whole works, you can bet on it, so it's important to move it out to the general picture as fast as you can. Declare your support for your wife, but be detached. Don't make it personal. Let yourself be a little sad about the frailty of human nature; that kind of thing." A shadow of a smile crossed his face. "We've all been there, right?"

Still the offending words hung there, pushing Marty to talk faster. "Remember, strength and compassion; don't waste words," he said. "Then push the debate back to your message and—"

Luke's voice cut in, sharp as a stabbing pair of scissors. "Don't you dare judge my wife," he said coldly, opening the door and turning at the threshold. "I'll handle any questions that come up about her abortion. This you don't orchestrate. Understand?"

Marty nodded. Luke moved through the door, almost bumping headlong into Jackie, Marty's secretary.

"Senator—" she said, putting out a hand to stop him.

Luke shook his head and strode away. Jackie moved quickly into the office, approaching Marty, whispering urgently.

Marty's face turned suddenly pale. "Luke!" he called.

Luke stopped and turned. Marty's voice had filled the room. "What?"

"Come on back."

"No, I've got too much to do."

Marty's ample figure was now sagging against the doorway. "Forget the hospital," he said slowly.

Luke stared at Marty's expression. Slowly, he retraced his steps.

"GW hospital," Jackie hissed as Luke passed her once again. "On line two."

Marty had already picked up the phone. "Yeah?"

Luke stood very still.

"Yeah, Doctor. Yes, I understand," Marty said into the phone, his voice somber. His eyes never strayed from Luke's face. "Okay. Sure. God, that's awful. We'll—right. A real loss." A long pause. "Thanks, Doctor. He isn't here right now, but I'll tell him. He'll be devastated. Do me a favor, please?" He waited. "Don't talk to the press yet."

Marty replaced the receiver slowly and looked up at Luke.

"Don't say anything," Luke said.

For a long moment, the two men stared at each other.

"Look, it wasn't the pills, it was heart failure," Marty finally ventured. "His heart couldn't take it; he slipped into a coma."

Luke did not budge from where he stood in the center of the room, rigid as a sentry.

"This isn't your problem, Luke. The guy was weak, probably

depressed or psychotic or something. It's a rotten shame, but these things happen."

When Luke finally spoke, his voice was hoarse with shock. "Steve's dead," he said.

"Look, you did your best. You had no way of knowing what would happen."

Luke said nothing. Marty hunched across the top of his desk, curling his fingers over the edge, looking past Luke for the first time. "Flowers," he said, muttering to himself. "We'll send flowers. Gotta keep that doctor quiet for an hour, then we're ready." He focused again on Luke; the man's face was too damn gray-looking.

"Kate," Marty muttered again, reaching for the phone. "We need Kate."

Saturday morning. The black Honda carrying Kate and Luke crawled slowly to a stop in front of a nondescript building on Wisconsin Avenue on a block cluttered with busy shops. Motorists, usually honking and sliding through yellow lights at this juncture, were slowing down, watching curiously. They saw the camera crews in front of the funeral home; they knew this was a bit out of the ordinary. Being Washingtonians, they wasted little time. Unless the president was in attendance, it wasn't worth too much neck-craning.

Kate gazed at the shabby little funeral home. She had driven past this place many times and had never really seen it, and there was something disturbing about that. Funeral homes should be stately and dignified, not storefronts squeezed in by a video store and a grubby café. This made death seem less important.

She reached numbly for the door handle, still trying to accept the fact that Steve was dead. It had happened, it was done.

"Wait," Luke whispered.

She paused. It was the first word Luke had spoken in the car.

"I was so angry, I could've killed him," Luke said, his voice now only barely above a whisper. "My closest friend."

Kate couldn't bear to look directly into his haggard face. Was this her vindication? Did she want Luke to suffer? She bowed her head and pushed down on the handle, opening the door. He was struggling with guilt right now; and so was she. It didn't ease her sense of responsibility to dwell on Steve's desperate anger that afternoon in the Roma. She kept seeing in her mind's eye the laughing Steve, the man who had shared with them that great moment when Luke decided finally to run; the friend lost. She stole a quick glance at Luke. Through this wooden exercise in joint mourning, they had barely spoken. Here we are, she thought, her head swimming in pain, almost as dead as Steve.

"You must go," Marty had barked yesterday morning.

"Of course I'll go," Kate had responded angrily. "With or without Luke."

"With. And wear black."

She wore a navy suit.

Kate stepped out of the car and Luke followed, immediately lacing cold fingers through hers. They walked up the sidewalk past an array of clicking cameras and—for once—silent reporters, held together as if by rope. Luke made no further attempt to speak. She could feel the reverberations from the depth of his shock, but there was nothing she could say or do to break its hold. She decided to say nothing, to simply hold his hand. It was the only private communication that didn't have to be filtered through their public image. It was the acknowledgement of their joint suffering. It was not only appropriate, visual, and sympathetic—it was real.

Real.

She formed the word soundlessly as they made their way through the crowd. Heavy clouds were moving in as they reached the front door. There would be rain this afternoon. Kate spotted Jerry Spanos, nervously hitching up his trousers, standing with the funeral director just inside the darkened doorway.

"I thought you might need me," he said.

"You honor us," she whispered. Her words astonished both of them, and Jerry flushed.

"Senator and Mrs. Goodspeed, hello." A man with large ears, wearing a dark gray suit, stepped forward, smiling at them both with more than professional solicitousness. "I'm Mr. Radner, Alex Radner, the funeral director," he said. "It's certainly a pleasure to meet you both. Please, follow me."

Dully, Kate followed Luke through a narrow, faintly perfumed hall to a large empty room at the end of the corridor. The room was poorly lit, and she had to strain to see through the gloom. It wasn't empty; far from it. A huge spray of flowers dominated several smaller bouquets; she knew Marty's handiwork before looking at the card. In the center of the room was an open coffin gleaming with brass and polished wood, and suddenly Kate could barely breathe. She saw Steve's familiar profile—the strong, cleanly cut features she remembered so well, not the anxious, constantly moving eyes and nervous chin of the past year, but the strong Steve, and she suddenly felt all she and Luke had to do was walk up and say hello to him, and he would rise and greet them with a smile and all would be well.

"We do our best," murmured Radner, noting her reaction to his art.

Luke was clutching her hand tightly now, but she couldn't take her eyes off Steve as they moved closer to the casket. Her eerie sense of his presence vanished as they reached the box. This wasn't Steve. This was a statue carved out of something, and it was meant to look like him, but, close up, it didn't—it didn't look like anybody. She reached out impulsively and touched his face. It was so hard she could have knocked on it, as on a door, and she quickly withdrew her hand. She looked at Luke. He was gazing into the casket with an expression she had never seen before. She started to say something, anything, but a voice, mocking, almost laconic, cut through the quiet.

"I passed on the inner-spring mattress. Amazing, isn't it, what they try to sell you?"

Kate's eyes flew to the shadows beyond the coffin and saw Lisa Feldon. Lisa stood alone with an orange scarf of some flimsy, glittery fabric on her head, her cheeks blotched with what looked like hastily applied orange rouge. There was a small smile on her face. It took Kate a few seconds to see her rage.

"Yeah, Marty told the funeral director nothing but the best, but I figured Steve wouldn't need an inner-spring," Lisa said lightly. "Now the flowers—" she waved a hand at the huge spray of lilies and roses—"they make a Goodspeed statement people can *see*."

"Lisa, anything." Luke's voice was quiet. "Anything we can do—"

"You can leave, Luke, that's what I'd like," Lisa said, just as quietly. "That's what you should do."

It was said so calmly, Luke at first didn't react. Then he bent forward, as if hit in the stomach. "Please—" he began. Kate sensed a flurry of movement and whispering, and then the funeral director stepped forward, facing Lisa. He was holding something in his hand.

"Mrs. Feldon," he said nervously. With a lurch of her stomach, Kate recognized what he held—a gold ring with the seal of the state of Illinois, a gift from Luke to Steve after their first triumphant race for the Senate. Steve had treasured that ring. She saw Luke's eyes flicker.

"It's a little late—" the funeral director continued, hesitating delicately.

Lisa looked at him blankly. "You mean you can't get it on his finger?" she said

"Yes, that's right." Radner's tone was kind, but Lisa did not soften; instead she spoke with the emotion of a bus passenger asking for a transfer.

"Then please just pin it inside the jacket of his coat," she said. She moved closer, standing now on the other side of Steve's coffin, facing Luke and Kate. "Don't say anything nice to me," she said softly. "Please."

"Lisa—" Kate felt she had to try to say something.

"It's over, Kate," Lisa interrupted, not unkindly. "Completely over. Let it rest."

Luke stared straight ahead, his face cold with pain. Kate saw in his eyes for a fleeting second the look of an old man; quickly, urgently, she squeezed his hand. But he didn't respond.

"Let's go," she pressed.

Silently, with one last glance at Steve, they turned and walked slowly from the room.

By noontime Kate was back at the house, packing mechanically for the trip to Amherst. I don't want to go, she thought, as she rolled a fresh blouse in tissue paper and tucked it into her overnight bag. Lord, she wanted out. She checked her watch. Luke was in a debate prep session at headquarters, and Jerry would take her to the airport at two o'clock. Part of her yearned to crawl under the covers and fall asleep and think of nothing. But another part of her, well trained, could go through the motions, all the motions, whatever was required to get through a hard time. She thought of the children, remembering the relief on their faces this morning when she told them they would not have to attend the debate.

"It doesn't look good if we're not there, does it, Mother?" Abby asked.

"I don't care," Kate answered. "You don't have to go."

They looked at her, nonplused. It was as simple as that? Slowly, a smile spread over Nat's freckled face. He tugged at his good school sweater, pulling at a perilously loose thread, but Kate didn't have the heart to stop him.

"We're off the hook?" he said.

"You're off the hook."

"Thanks, Mom."

That had been the most gratifying thing she had heard in weeks. She, of course, was not off the hook. She stopped, her hand poised with a soft flannel nightgown over the bag, struck with another thought: neither was Luke. Especially Luke. Luke had to be campaigning, and no excessive depression or grief could show through; it would only raise questions. Luke was supposed to make a few caring, thoughtful statements about Steve and his contributions, then get back to the work at hand. Keep a low-key demeanor, that's what Marty was advising; contain the response, push the focus back onto the campaign. The mandate now was to make Steve's death a manageable issue.

Kate tried to concentrate on the task at hand, remembering to throw in an extra pair of stockings, but she felt too tired to continue. She sat on the side of the bed, staring at a small ragged hole in her jeans. She kept seeing the white, set face of her husband at the funeral home, his feelings stitched tight inside, and she with no way to reach him. None. Her mind turned to another threat. Would Kovach really go through with trying to excommunicate her? Could he do that? It sounded too drastic, too melodramatic. To be drummed from one's church, whether one took the punishment seriously or not—well, it was strange to contemplate. It made her feel oddly like a child again. Kate smiled to herself sadly. Like her mother's child, actually.

Outside, the media encampment around the Goodspeed home had dwindled to a few camera crews and a cluster of second-string reporters. The first string was on its way to Amherst for the debate, which meant the spotlight had shifted for the moment. Kate gazed out the bedroom window, staying back far enough where they couldn't see her. The men and women talking quietly among themselves looked listless and tired. Maybe it was the avalanche of complaints that had flooded into the networks and local news shows after the footage of Nat with his sweater pulled up to hide his face.

She asked herself, Were they seeing what she was seeing? The front of the house was a mess. Crumpled sandwich bags smeared with mustard and catsup; a discarded sweater on the battered lawn; pages ripped by the wind from a fluttering notebook; camera equipment everywhere.

A couple of cameramen began silently pulling their cameras back to the sidewalk. Others were eyeing the deep gouges in the trampled grass. As Kate watched, one woman in a tattered bomber jacket began gingerly tucking a torn piece of turf back into place.

Yes, they saw. She felt a sense of easing claustrophobia, but with it came a deepening melancholy.

Kate heard a soft knock on the door and opened it to the wary eyes of a Secret Service agent encamped on the porch.

"Some reporter wants to see you," he said. The word clearly left a bad taste in his mouth. "Peter Bradford, *Chicago Tribune*. He says you know him."

"Yes, that's okay." Kate brushed a long strand of hair out of her eyes and wished fleetingly, ridiculously, that she could take a moment to put on lipstick. She looked past the agent and saw Peter standing at the bottom of the steps. He looked so concerned, so calm, so real, she could barely keep from crying. "I'll see him," she said.

Peter stepped past the threshold; Kate closed the door.

"Peter," she said. Was she surprised? Could she be honest with herself? Peter didn't wait for her to move first. Gently, he tipped her face upward and kissed her hard and full on the mouth. Kate closed her eyes.

Then he pulled away. He was saying something, but she couldn't hear the words. She was thinking only of the feel of his lips against hers; she rested her cheek against the comforting, scratchy tweed of his coat.

"You asked me on the plane, what was the most daring thing I've

321

ever done," he said, "and now I can tell you." He tipped her face up again and gazed at her steadily, his eyes probing with tender persistence. "It's coming here. Today."

Reluctantly, Kate looked him full in the face. She didn't want to talk. A sudden lassitude was draining her energy; she wanted only to keep her eyes closed and rest again against his coat.

"Kate—" His eyes bore into her with unrelenting concentration. "You're not trapped, Kate."

She must pull out of her torpor, she must respond.

"I love you, Kate; that's it, plain and simple," Peter said. He spoke with quiet force. "I have loved you for a long time, and I can't stand by and watch any more of this without telling you. You've been put through too much, and you deserve better."

Her eyes filled with tears. She reached up and touched his lips, but she couldn't trust herself to speak.

"I think you should know something," he said. "I've asked for reassignment."

She paused, hand in midair. If Luke won the election, that meant Peter was cutting himself out of a prestigious White House beat. Peter wanted that job. Could he really mean this?

"Feeling what I feel, I can't cover your husband anymore, Kate," he said, seeing the question in her face. "You know that."

She had no claim on this man; she couldn't protest. No claim at all. "What will you do?" she asked.

"Go back to Chicago as an editor. It's all arranged."

"But, Peter—" And then she stopped. There was simply nowhere to go. He was her friend; she wanted him to stay. But it wasn't enough.

He looked at her, the tension in his face increasing, and Kate felt the rhythmic ticking of the grandfather clock beating in cadence with her heart.

"I'll say it once more," he said. "You're not trapped."

No, Kate thought immediately, of course not. She was hearing the word now, turning it over in her mind. What did it mean to be trapped? Caught with no exit? Endangered? She knew what it meant.

"I know," she said.

She stared at Peter and he stared back at her, the two of them locked in a mutual realization—the realization that they were stepping close to a line that could not be crossed. Should not be crossed.

But the temptation was so strong. Could she just stand close to him and try to talk? Could they kiss again, would it be so terrible? They *were* moving closer, without intending to, she had taken a step and so had he. . . .

A clatter of noise on the front steps. Suddenly Joan burst through the door, raincoat flying, tossing her sharply jangling keys on to the top of the hall console. She saw Peter and froze.

"Anything wrong?" she challenged, standing poised for action.

"You know Peter," Kate said quickly.

"Yeah, sure. Hi, Peter." Joan was still waiting for the scene to be defined, her eyes switching from her sister to Peter and back again.

"Hello, Joan," Peter said. He turned from Kate, but he did not step back. His voice was strong and matter-of-fact. "How are you doing?"

"Okay, I guess. You writing a story?"

"Just getting a quote for a first-edition debate piece." He made no attempt to elaborate, leaving Joan to accept or reject the reason as she so chose.

"All the news before it happens, right?" Joan smiled; but she didn't look directly at her sister.

The spell was broken. Peter waited for a fraction of a second, but something had happened. Kate felt it happening. Peter was clearly waiting for something from her, and she struggled to respond, but she could not trust herself to speak. Then she knew why, suddenly and totally. This was not what she wanted. She had stepped close to the edge of something both hopeful and perilous, drawn by her own pain and despair, but this wasn't the answer. Peter was a wonderful man. He had given her a gift, a renewed sense of her own empowerment, but the resolution she needed had to come from inside herself, not from him. Not from any man, she thought firmly. Only from me.

After a long, awkward instant, Peter glanced at his watch. "Well," he said, "I know you've got plenty to do, so I won't take up any more of your time."

Kate turned to him, her eyes conveying what she knew he didn't want to see. "I'm glad you came," she said warmly. "Will we see you tonight?"

"No," Peter said, searching her face. "I won't be there." She saw him give up. His face relaxed into a rueful smile, then he was out the door and striding rapidly down the steps.

Patricia O'Brien

Joan gazed after him thoughtfully. Then she turned her gaze directly on Kate. "What did I break up?" she asked. "And do I owe you an apology?"

Kate smiled and shook her head. "No," she said. "Peter came to tell me I'm not trapped." Just saying the words, listening to them as they rolled from her tongue into the air, was an interesting experience.

"He's right, you know," Joan said, watching her sister closely. "You don't have to throw yourself on some funeral pyre."

"Luke's not dead and he's not going up in flames, Joan." Kate was amused in spite of herself.

"Peter's still right."

"I know he is."

Joan began studiously unbuttoning her jacket, again not looking at her sister. "So what does that mean?" she asked finally.

"It means I'm coming out of all this with strength I can count on," Kate replied. "My own. It slipped away from me for a while, but I've got it back."

"That sounds very independent of you. Do I hear a decision in the making?"

It was a fair question. "I'm thinking things through better now," she said.

Joan looked unconvinced. "Kate, just because there's never been a divorced president of the United States doesn't mean there never will be," she said. "Are you thinking about that? Is it an option?"

"Of course it is."

The firmness in Kate's voice clearly surprised her sister. She jumped, fumbling the last button of her jacket before regaining her aplomb. She pulled it off and threw it with an uncharacteristically careless gesture over the back of a chair. "I *thought* you and Peter were standing a little close," she said with a sly, lopsided grin.

Kate laughed. Actually laughed. "You never miss anything," she said. But Peter wasn't the issue. She had to test this herself; explore the unthinkable.

"It could be done," she said calmly. "Quietly, of course. Very civil. Nat and Abby and I would stay through the inauguration and then simply not move to the White House. No one would know what

324

to make of it at first. I'd attend public events, naturally. And then I'd simply fade into the background, and the media could have another field day. But Luke would be president."

"I need a drink." Joan plopped onto the sofa and studied her sister. "You aren't serious. You can't possibly be serious."

"I'm saying, 'I'm not trapped, and I have options.' " Each time she heard herself saying the words, she felt better.

"Kate—" Joan was searching for the words she wanted, a small furrowed line deepening in her brow. "I'm afraid now I've been goading you on, and I don't want to do that. Your life is different from mine, from most women's. Maybe I'm daring you to do something I would do, because I'm angry at Luke." She paused, looking troubled. "Just don't do anything drastic, okay?"

Kate smiled. Something truly was relaxing inside. "My dear sister," she said, "a lot of people would consider that the funniest line of the whole campaign."

"Senator Goodspeed!"

Kate glanced out the window in surprise. It was Luke. He jumped from the car, dabbing at the tiny scar from Kate's ring—reopened by a hasty shave—and strode up the sidewalk through the surprised cluster of reporters staked out on the lawn. His arrival was unexpected, and they were scrambling to recover.

"Sir!" A reporter with red hair and bony hands managed to push his voice above the rest. "Do you have a comment on Steve Feldon's death?"

"It's a tragedy, and I'm devastated."

"You fired him, didn't you, Senator?"

"We reached a parting of the ways, if that's what you mean."

The reporter persisted. "But you were friends, right? For a long time? Was he depressed, Senator? Is that why he killed himself? Is it true he tried to blackmail you?"

Luke paused before mounting the steps of his home. "What?"

"That's one report, Senator," the reporter said, clearly pleased to have Luke's attention. "We hear he was reacting to the rumors about your having an affair—"

"Lay off," Luke said. "Don't malign the man. He's dead, and

that's not true." He looked up the steps, directly into the eyes of his waiting wife.

"Ready?" he said.

"I'm ready," Kate answered, looking directly at her husband as she handed her bag to an aide. She looked at the reporters. "No more questions," she said levelly. Together the two of them walked to the car and stepped inside.

"I thought I was meeting you at the airport," she said as the car swung into the street.

"I changed my mind," Luke replied in a low voice. "Is that okay?"

She nodded. It felt strange sitting next to him for the second time in one day, so close she could smell his skin, the way she had smelled Peter's, and still feel a chasm between them. She leaned back into the seat cushions and waited. Did he want to work out a media response with her for tonight? Was that it?

"I can't believe he's dead." His voice was so low she had to lean forward to hear.

"I can't either." Even though she had touched Steve's stone-cold face, she still couldn't believe it.

"No one else will ever be my friend in quite the same way," Luke said. "He's gone, and something's finished."

His voice held such queer finality, such total loneliness, Kate had to reach for his hand.

"You don't have to say anything," he said quickly. "You're the only person I can talk to about Steve, and I'm taking advantage of that. You owe me nothing on this one, Kate."

"I can still understand your loss."

"It didn't have to happen this way."

"We don't know that."

"You're being kind," he said quietly. "But I do. I've been thinking a lot about this. I've been thinking about what I did to Steve's ego. Where the hell did I get the idea that he could take the kind of humiliation I handed him? Could I take it?" He considered, staring out the window for a long moment and then answered his own question. "I don't know if I could. I don't know if any man could. I could have handled this better. I could have thought about my friend as a friend, and not as—" he paused, as if giving plenty of time for the self-accusation to sink in— "not as a liability. You know that's true."

Yes, she did know. There was no denying it. Again the memory of Steve's worried face, his ravaged eyes, came back, unbidden. We both knew he was being destroyed, and we did nothing, she thought. Or at least, not enough.

Luke turned then, looking straight into his wife's eyes. "I'm not just thinking about Steve, Kate. I'm thinking about you. I'm asking myself some questions, and I'm having a tough time figuring out the answers." He took a deep breath. "Steve was a liability, right? Not you. You've always been an asset." He pronounced the word slowly, as if it felt foreign on his tongue. "You've been the right kind of wife, the right kind of mother, photogenic, smart, a good campaigner, all that stuff. Yeah, I've viewed you as an asset. My asset. I'm asking myself, Isn't that almost as bad as viewing Steve as a liability?"

Kate caught her breath in surprise.

"It all reflects off me, doesn't it?" he went on. The questions were coming with an obvious, painful effort. "How good you make *me* look?"

"Yes," she managed. "I guess it does."

"I don't know if I can stop it, and that scares me."

"Knowing you're doing it is a first step." It was more than that, much more than that.

"Yeah." His smile twisted tiredly at the corners of his mouth. "The world is full of first steps." He dived suddenly for his briefcase tucked beneath the seat in front of him, and pulled out a magazine. "Seen this?" he said, laying it gently on his wife's lap.

Kate stared. There she was, in full color, looking somber, on the cover of *Newsweek*. The picture had been taken the morning of Luke's press conference, and the effects of her lack of sleep the night before showed in meticulous detail.

"A New Kind of Candidate's Wife," read the banner across the top of the special election edition. Underneath, in bright red, the question: "Is the Country Ready for Honesty in the White House?"

"Will I want to read it?" she asked.

"Yes, you will," Luke replied. "You've been elevated to sainthood, or close to it."

Was there an edge in his voice? She looked at him closely, and saw nothing but a kind of weary amusement. She glanced down again at the magazine. So this was the payoff. It felt strange, seeing the result of her morning of utter humiliation staring back at her, defined by

Patricia O'Brien

Newsweek as strength. I know exactly what I was thinking when that photograph was taken, she thought. The world is truly bizarre.

"You have guts," he said quietly.

"Thank you." She couldn't risk anything more; her voice was too shaky. She had to make sure the ground beneath her, the strength inside her, was truly firm. She looked out the window. Traffic was moving quickly; they would make it to National Airport faster than usual.

"Luke, do you think you'll really win?" she whispered.

"Yes. Believe it or not, I do." He glanced at her, his fingers working idly with the edges of his tie. He had something else to say, but he couldn't seem to get it out.

"I'm talking to some people about starting a Capitol Hill intern program in Steve's name," he finally said. "It won't have my stamp on it; I don't want to hurt Lisa anymore than she already has been."

"That's a good idea."

"Don't waste your praise, babe. It's part of what I owe." He stole another quick glance at her, then turned his head so she couldn't see his eyes.

"Where did you go?" he asked.

"When?" She was momentarily confused.

"For the abortion."

Her heart began hammering. She could not bear another challenge, another bitter accusation. "Chicago," she said.

"Did anybody go with you?"

"No." She had been utterly alone, holding a scrap of paper in her hand, trying to find an address on a strange street on the South Side, afraid to ask directions, sweating in the brutal heat of a Chicago summer day—oh, yes, Luke. I was alone.

"Is that when you stopped going to Mass?"

"Yes." He could never understand what it had been like to kneel in the back pew of a darkened church, staring at a line of quiet penitents waiting outside the confessional, knowing she could never join them to confess to an act which the Church considered a sin, because she was not sorry. But how strange it had felt to be on the outside of her church, looking in.

"I used to wonder why," he said. "But I never asked." He sighed almost imperceptibly. "I can't believe I never asked."

328

"Senator, we're here." The driver's voice cut through, sharp and oddly cheerful. "Good luck at the debate."

The car was pulling onto the tarmac of the general aviation terminal, and Kate swallowed back an answer. Ahead of her was the plane. She wasn't sure she had the strength to climb those bloody steps one more time.

The familiar acrid combination of sweat and steaminess that marks a basketball game permeated the gym of the Amherst campus of the University of Massachusetts. The faint locker-room aroma actually added to the aura of tension building in the room. Over a hundred reporters, crammed together on makeshift benches, sat ready to watch the final Enright-Goodspeed debate on a huge screen that covered one wall of the gym. They were the ones with early deadlines, and they had elected to give up the highly prized press seats in the debate hall. They had sacrificed the immediacy of being on the scene for the advantage of pounding early-edition stories into their laptops and transmitting before the debate was wrapped up.

"Not enough phone lines," complained a reporter for the *Boston Globe* as she waited for a telephone so she could hook up the rubber cups of her computer to the receiver and send her story.

"There never are." A reedy-looking man from the *Tampa Tribune* smiled. "It's a campaign rule because they hate us."

"Where's Bradford?" a reporter from the *Philadelphia Inquirer*, never taking his eyes off the screen, asked Annie Marshall.

"I don't know." Annie acted puzzled, but she had noted Peter's absence an hour ago and was putting together her own explanation. She was remembering the look on Peter's face when he first saw Kate at Luke's press conference. What had *that* been all about? And why had he been so pissed at her for nailing Kate with a question? Barrows hadn't said it straight out, but she knew what was happening. She knew why he had sent her here tonight for what could be the biggest story of the year. Peter was off the campaign. That was heavy stuff, and Annie wanted to know why. Two and two, she told herself, could add up to a whole lot more than four.

"Come on." The reporter's attention was now riveted.

"No, really." Annie opened her eyes wide and gave a helpless shrug. The *Post* reporter next to him was looking interested. Annie chose discretion. "I think one of his kids was sick, or something."

Luke stood with one hand on thick gold velvet curtains, poised to walk out on the stage and take his seat. Kate stood beside him; she would watch the debate on a television monitor in a backstage room, a decision decreed by Marty. "If you're in the audience, the cameras will keep focusing on you," he said. "You're here for the pictures tonight, that's enough." That was fine with Kate. She found herself wishing again she had been able to stay home.

"Good luck," she whispered.

Luke flashed her an awkward smile. "Thanks," he said, and was gone.

Kate stepped back from the curtains and turned, only then seeing a waiting figure emerge from the shadows. She froze at the sound of the familiar, throaty voice.

"You really grabbed him by the balls, didn't you?" Claire spoke in a light, conversational tone, but her eyes crackled with hostility.

"What are you doing here?"

"Just watching things play out, Kate. You amaze me, you know? I've got to tell you, I thought you were too soft before. But I was wrong; you're one tough cookie. Smart, very smart. You may pull this election off and get your revenge at the same time."

"You don't know what you're talking about," Kate shot back. "What gives you the right to criticize?"

"Nothing." Claire's voice was matter-of-fact. "I stand here with no credentials, that's understood, so don't waste your breath declaring I haven't any." She took a step closer, and Kate could see the faint glow of a lit cigarette, forbidden in this area of the auditorium, in the fingers of her right hand. Claire was not one to abide by anyone's rules—not now, not at any time—but it struck Kate that there was something forlorn about the gesture.

"All I'm here to say is, you don't fool me," Claire said. "You're punishing Luke, that's what you're doing with this abortion story. And you know what? I care that you're hurting him. You want to know why I fell in love with him?" She laughed when she saw Kate's face. "Yes, Kate, you heard me right. Tough, cold Claire Lorenzo really fell in love with your husband, which probably makes me easier to hate, I guess. I knew what he needed, he could look at me, and I knew what was bothering him. I was more the wife than you were! Surprised?" She took a breath. "I'm not going to pretend I didn't do everything I could to bring him to me, because I did." Her eyes flashed with something deeper now. "But you win. You had to win, I knew that all the time, you're the long-suffering wife, and he needs you. Women like you—" She shook her head violently. "What makes you think Luke Goodspeed can be an ordinary man? Why should he be?"

Kate felt her hands begin to shake, but her head and heart were strangely calm. Why, indeed? What was "ordinary"? And she knew that wasn't what she wanted from Luke. Claire had it wrong. There was no way to explain, to force her to understand, because it would never work. The kind of life she wanted was alien to Claire, and probably always had been. But it wasn't alien to Luke.

"You won't like this," Kate said, "but I have to say it anyway." She took a breath, marveling at her own ability to finally put the words together. "You live in a dream world and I'm just realizing that, and I'm realizing I'm the one threatening you—not the other way around." She threw her hands in the air. "I can't believe I'm saying this! You think you know Luke, and you think I'm just one more political wife who lives on the sidelines, while you live at the core of what it's all about. But you know something? *That's* the illusion." Kate took one step forward and was only peripherally aware that Claire took one step back. "You don't know Luke," she said. "You've been with him at the most intense time of his life, but you don't know who he is or what he wants, not in the same way I do."

Claire started to speak, but Kate raised her hand. "Wait," she said. "I'm not telling you I know how all this will shake out. I'm not telling you Luke and I are going to be reunited and live happily ever after. What I'm telling you is, you were *never* his wife. You don't know how he feels when his little girl gets sick and you don't know what he says when your mother dies and you don't know—" She stopped suddenly. It was the expression on Claire's face. She looked like an angry child.

Suddenly a man's voice cut through the gloom like a blast from a gun. "Claire! What the hell are you doing here?" Marty stepped forward, his face dark with anger.

"I'm leaving." Claire's voice had taken on a slow, affected drawl.

She took a deep drag off the cigarette, dropped it to the wooden floor, and crushed it with a slow, rotating motion of her right foot. She tossed a glance at Marty. "You know where to find me when you need me," she said. "And you will. Mrs. Goodspeed here will make sure of that." She walked away.

Marty stood rigidly still, and Kate barely glanced at him. She simply brushed past without comment and made her way to the room with the television monitor. She was trembling, but it wasn't with tension or fear. An old dream, a dream of a fear of the dark, was running through her mind, and she was feeling what she had felt when she used to awake from that dream and switch on a light. She had a sudden impulse to run back to the stage and do something, maybe squeeze Luke's hand or say something—no. It was too late.

The room was hushed. The debate was about to begin.

"Shut up, you guys. Listen!"

The reporters in the pressroom were restless. So far, the debate was tame, nothing juicy, no fireworks. Issues, issues. A question from a debate-panel member on Enright's environmental record. If he was so pro-environment, why was he in favor of removing the restrictions on offshore drilling? A question for Luke. Should the federal government buckle under to New York's demands for more funds for its collapsing bridges? Then some sharp jousting with Luke on David Palmer. Was he supporting the Liberian's admission into the country? If not, why not? "Tomorrow," Luke said calmly, "I will announce my decision."

Finally, the last panel question. The reporters tensed. The panelist from the *Atlanta Constitution*, a forthright, dark-haired woman, was leaning forward.

"Senator Enright," she said.

Enright's oversized, noble head loomed large on the screen. He looked fully energized, totally presidential, standing tall on his hidden riser—a man ready to fight for a cause.

"Senator, I know you have said you will not comment on the charges of the past week which involve your opponent and Miss Lorenzo," the woman began in a strong alto voice. "But can you comment, if you will, on Mrs. Goodspeed's confession to having had an abortion? Would you say this raises the issue of character in this presidential race?"

Enright turned directly toward Luke as he answered, executing the maneuver slowly enough for the television cameras to catch its weighty import.

"My sympathies are with Mrs. Goodspeed, although the more cynical in politics will probably not believe me," he said. He raised his hand in a supplicating gesture. Then he delivered his well-rehearsed attack in a gentle, almost ruminative tone.

"But even more, my sympathy goes to the unborn child who was deprived of the opportunity to live." The words rang forth, stopping the slightest murmurs in the hall. This was Enright at his best. He paused, letting his words sink in. The reporters pounded furiously on their computers. "Abortion," he went on, drawing the liquid middle syllable out as far as possible, "is the crime of killing; an irresponsible anti-human act. We need a government that is pro-life." Supporters scattered in strategic clusters through the studio audience broke into energetic applause.

Luke stood ramrod-straight in an overly starched shirt and his bright orange tie. "There are good people on both sides of that issue, Senator," he said. "Neither side has a monopoly on morality."

Enright shook his head with an almost imperceptible gesture, a masterful conveyance of sadness and weary disgust. "I think it's time to know how you stand on this," he said. He articulated every syllable, carefully. "Cardinal Kovach has defined this as an issue where waffling is not a tolerable position. And he's right." Enright was carefully avoiding direct comment on the threat to excommunicate Kate; that was too thorny, especially with the latest polls. A sympathy backlash was stirring.

Luke drew himself up to his full height. "Plenty of women are desperate and alone, and feel they have no alternative to abortion," he replied.

Backstage, staring at the television set, Kate curled herself tight onto a plastic-covered sofa, pulling her knees up in what she knew was an absurd action of self-protection. She wished she could have her arm around Abby right now; she hoped Nat was in bed. Watching closely, she recognized the slight throb of a tic under Luke's right eye.

"You're being very cautious," Enright said with a small, tight smile. "This was your *wife*, Senator. What are the voters of this country to conclude about the two of you? There is such a—" he paused for maximum effect—"such a volatility to your lives. Your aide, that poor unfortunate man, committing suicide—but that's another issue. How can you not expect questions about your character?"

Luke turned full toward his adversary, eyes blazing. "I doubt if there is a family watching us now, Senator, perhaps including yours, that doesn't include a sister, a daughter, a cousin, or someone else close who hasn't had, or wishes she had, or wants to have, an abortion," he said. "It's the most personal decision a woman can make, and thank God we've become enlightened enough to permit her that decision. You wanted my stand on this issue? You've got it. And if Cardinal Kovach plans to excommunicate my wife for telling the truth, then he brings pain to Catholic women everywhere and shame on himself. But not on my wife."

It had all come forth in a burst.

The room grew unnaturally still. The smile on the face of the moderator froze.

Luke paused. His voice became slower and stronger. "My wife has shown the importance of honesty in the most public way possible," he said. "That took courage, Senator. She stood by me, and I stand by her. And I think the American people understand what it means to make mistakes."

"What time is it? What time is it?" Frantic, the reporters were yelling at each other, lunging to rewrite their stories. "Why the hell didn't they do this before deadline?" The exchange had not been planned, but no one on the panel was daring to interrupt.

Annie's fingers trembled on the computer keys as she tried to formulate a lead. Thank God she worked for a newspaper on central time.

"Jesus, he's admitting the affair," breathed Houston.

"Don't be ridiculous," snapped Buffalo, who couldn't stand Houston. "That's an old lead."

"Is he?" asked Wichita, looking down the table at the ABC correspondent.

ABC shook his head in the negative. "He's stopped waffling on abortion, that's the news."

Network confirmation. That did it. The reporters in the room began tapping furiously into their computers.

Enright grabbed the floor. "Americans deserve leaders who don't make such mistakes," he said sharply.

Luke shook his head. "Americans want the strength in their leaders that comes from being tested," he said. "You're not born with it—you develop it. I have that strength, and my wife has that strength. And I have the strength to govern this country, not as some infallible god, but as a human being." He paused, as if contemplating a course of action, then turned full toward Enright.

"You've dragged in my late colleague and friend, Steve Feldon, and I'm not going to let that pass," he said in a strong, deliberate voice. "Steve doesn't need a eulogy. His friends and his colleagues know he was a good man. But he deserves one from me, and this is as good a time as any to give it."

Luke paused to give his words more emphasis.

"I owe him a profound debt—for his friendship and his professional guidance," he said. "Without Steve Feldon, I wouldn't be here."

"Then why did you fire him?" Enright shot back.

"Because I lost sight for a while of what I was in this race for," Luke said. He stopped for a millisecond. There was not a sound in the auditorium.

"We're not running for sainthood here," Luke went on, his voice even stronger and more deliberate. "Just for president. We'll only be *voted* on in this life, Senator—later on, we'll be judged."

An instant passed. Enright opened his mouth to speak, but a burst of applause from the studio audience interrupted him, spreading rapidly through the hall. Soon it was resonating, ricocheting off the walls.

Kate uncurled her legs and sat straight, tears streaming down her face. "Luke," she said, speaking out loud to her husband's image on the screen in the empty room. "You're talking to me. This time, you're really talking to me."

Then the debate was over and the applause rose again as Luke strode from the podium.

"You were terrific," Marty said, rushing forward onto the stage. He surveyed the clamoring crowd of reporters and supporters surging onto the stage with the triumphal expression of a victorious general, calculating quickly which reporters should be steered immediately to Luke.

"You did it, Luke," he said. "You really did it."

"Thanks," Luke said hoarsely. It was the voice of a man who had forgotten to speak from the diaphragm. But he was smiling, although it wasn't quite his usual grin.

In the Amherst gym, all was chaos.

"Hit that answer in the lead, goddamn it!" screamed editors from Los Angeles, Denver, Miami, and Washington as they turned from their television sets and punched in the temporary numbers of the phone lines in the Amherst gym. In two minutes, the phone lines were overloaded. Reporters cursed as they wrote; cursed as they transmitted their stories, loudly declaiming the rigors of their insane jobs.

None of them meant a word of it because they loved what they did. This was what there was, what it was all about. They were euphoric.

That night, mute with more than exhaustion, Kate and Luke collapsed into bed in a Boston airport hotel.

"Let me hold you," Luke whispered. "Please."

Kate turned toward the middle of the bed where the warmth was and lay in her husband's arms. Neither had energy for a shared word. Together, they slept.

The next morning came brutally fast.

"They're waiting," Marty said, as Luke opened the door to his knock at seven in the morning. A thin-faced aide hovered anxiously behind him.

"They're in the meeting room downstairs, Senator," he said, nodding toward the elevators. "And they look like they're ready to tear you apart."

"I want to be there," Kate said quickly.

"Hey, get some rest," Marty said. "This'll be messy."

"All the more reason, Marty."

But Marty had turned his attention to Luke, his face set for battle. "These guys have been on the outside for a long time," he said. "If you can't convince them, offer them jobs. Tell them half the federal judges you appoint will be black until there's a balance. They're hungry."

"I'd rather tell them I'm right," Luke shot back. "They don't want to be bribed."

Marty shook his head. "Yeah, but you can't give them any evidence now. You can't even be specific about what Palmer is doing. Why should they believe you? And remember, Maurice Norton is the guy in the crowd who decides whether there's a lynching or not."

Luke looked at Kate, the veil of tiredness lifting slightly from his eyes. "You sure you want to be there?" he said.

She nodded.

Together they went down in the elevator, walked down the hall, opened the door to the meeting room, and entered. Kate looked around the room—crowded with about twenty of the most prominent black leaders in the country, seated on either side of a long boardroom table—and her heart sank. Maurice Norton was glowering with the ominous presence of an avenging judge, while Amanda Boynton—the new mayor of Los Angeles, frequently mentioned for a Cabinet post in a Goodspeed administration—turned in her seat and stared at them coldly. We should have met with them sooner, Kate thought. This is late. Very late.

"Senator, we've read your statement refusing support for David Palmer's entry into this country," Norton began without preamble. "And we want an explanation."

"I'll do the best I can," Luke said, as he moved to a vacant chair. Kate hesitated, then decided to remain at the door where Luke could see her, but away from the others.

"David Palmer is trying to get into this country under false pretenses," Luke began. "I'm convinced he's involved in major illegal activities."

"Where's your proof?" exploded a voice from the far end of the table.

"I would have had it for you today," Luke said calmly. "But the man who brought all this to my attention has been killed. I don't know who killed him, but I do know the people who have the information you want are too afraid to come forward now."

"That's all you've got for us?" asked Mayor Boynton in angry astonishment. "It's not enough!"

"Get this straight," said a portly Baptist minister from New Orleans, his voice rumbling through the room. "We want Palmer. More to the point, we need him. He's an important symbol of achievement for us, as important as Nelson Mandela, and we're not opposing him without absolute, solid proof of what you claim."

A murmur of assent rippled through the crowd.

"I'm not asking you to oppose him," Luke said. "I'm asking you not to attack *me* when I oppose letting him in—which, ladies and gentlemen, you might as well know, gets announced today."

The minister let out a snort of disgust. "You're expecting pure faith?" he said. "We're not automatically tied to you Democrats, Senator, remember that."

"You're telling me, Reverend, if I do this, you may throw your support to the Republicans?" challenged Luke.

"That's what he's saying," said the voice from the back of the room.

There was a short, total silence. This was a gauntlet Luke had to pick up.

"I've never let you down," he said, eyes flashing. "I cast my first vote in the Senate to make police brutality a federal crime. Voting rights, affirmative action—I've backed you to the hilt, because I believe in the same principles you believe in. And now, when I tell you I can't support this man because he isn't what he seems, you tell me you just might support Enright—who hasn't stood with you for five minutes in his whole career?"

"You run that risk." It was Norton's voice rumbling authoritatively through the room.

"Maurice, you of all people should know what I'm saying," Luke said angrily. "What good is a symbol if it's a weak symbol? What message do you send to young people if you offer them cardboard instead of truth? You mock your own values and your own goals if

338

you do that." He leaned toward them, face intense. "Palmer is dangerous," he said. "I tell you, that is the truth."

"Why can't you give us any solid facts?"

"I know the details of what he's done, and details of the lives he's ruined," Luke said. "I know he's involved in some elaborate and illegal schemes, and I believe I know how they work. But I can't give you the names of the people who know, because their lives wouldn't be worth a damn thing if I did." A ripple of sound moved through the room. Luke stood straighter, looking each person straight in the eye. "Yeah," he said softly, "I know what I'm asking. You know the agenda. I need your support in this election, and I can't win without it. But I'm not going to pass on this one. Palmer is a sham; the worst kind of anti-hero. He's not a worthy symbol for any of us. The man who died had great courage; he tried to get us the hard evidence we need, and he paid with his life. We're going to get that evidence, no matter how long it takes. But right now, I've got to ask you to trust me."

Norton slammed his fist down with sudden force. "Senator," he said, "we're tired of electing men to office who say 'trust us,' because they can't win a majority of the white vote. We're tired of electing men who need us, and then leave us when the voting is over. Maybe if black voters supported a few Republicans, you people would pay more attention." Norton was standing now. "I've heard enough," he said, and stalked to the door, brushing past Kate, slamming it behind him.

The speed with which he left took Kate's breath away. She hesitated, then impulsively slipped out the door and ran down the corridor after Norton's retreating figure.

"Wait!" she called. "Don't do this!"

Norton kept walking.

"Where's your courage?" she yelled, ignoring a startled waiter carrying a tray of coffee and breakfast rolls down the hall.

Norton stopped and turned. "I have no quarrel with you, Mrs. Goodspeed," he said coldly. "What do you want from me?"

Breathless, Kate drew close. "I'm asking you to go back into that room," she said, as calmly as she could. "You know Luke's never let you down. You know that!"

"He insults us," he said, just as coldly. "I'm not buying this kind of 'trust me' crap, not ever again. Do you understand, Mrs. Goodspeed?"

"So you'll ignore the truth for a grandstand play, whether it's for the right cause or not?" she said. "I don't believe it. That's not you. That's not your reputation." She had to challenge him; she had to get him to pay attention.

"Look, I'm telling you this because I have to," she said. "Luke is convinced Palmer is the head of a major drug cartel and that he's coming here to establish a base in this country. Oh, it'll all come out eventually. When Luke is elected, he'll get this guy. But right now—" she looked at him imploringly—"please, go back. Listen to him, just listen. He doesn't have to risk losing your support, you know. He doesn't have to come out against Palmer; nobody else is, not even the people who know something is very wrong. They're too afraid; they figure they can get him later. Are you afraid?" Her voice was growing stronger. "Luke isn't; you can see that. He's convinced he's right, that's why he's doing this. Think about it!"

She waited, holding her breath. Would Norton pay attention? Was it too late?

He hesitated. "Do you understand what you're asking?" he said. "Young blacks here think Palmer is this generation's Martin Luther King. Do you know how few heroes they have? Why should we sit by and say nothing when this happens?"

"If one of your heroes ends up destroying the pride you feel in yourselves, you've betrayed your own people," she said. "That's why."

He stared at her silently, curiously. "You really believe in your husband, don't you?" She saw the question in his eyes. Maurice Norton knew what was going on. He knew he wasn't the only one forced to think about betrayal.

Slowly, she let out her breath. "Yes," she said. "I do."

"Palmer will get in anyway, Mrs. Goodspeed," Norton said. "If Luke can't make a case against him, the die is cast."

"Maybe so. But he'll be exposed sooner or later. People will remember what Luke did. And they'll remember what you did, too."

Norton's eyes narrowed. "I'll deal with that when I come to it, Mrs. Goodspeed."

"Fine. All I'm asking now is, go back and listen."

Norton stared hard at her. Unflinchingly Kate stared back. A matter of seconds, but it felt like hours before he spoke.

"All right," he said. "I'll go back in that room and hear what he has to say. But I'm warning you, Mrs. Goodspeed, we've taken a lot."

"I know that."

The next salvo was totally unexpected. "Your sister has trouble balancing wine in a crowded room, Mrs. Goodspeed," he said. "Do you know that?"

"I understand there was a problem," Kate said, holding her breath again.

"Yes, indeed there was."

She decided to take a chance. She looked him straight in the eye. "Red or white?" she asked.

"Red."

"Oh, shit."

The expression on Norton's face didn't change. "I understand guerrilla tactics," he said. "Sometimes they're the only ones that work."

Slowly, they walked back to the room together.

One hour later, it was over. Luke, perspiring profusely, offered his hand to each person as they left the meeting room. Most took it, some silently, some with a few words.

"Okay, Luke," said Norton, solemnly shaking his hand. "You've got what you wanted. You'd better be right."

And then they were gone. Luke turned to Kate, and took her hand. "You turned that around, Kate," he said quietly. "Thanks."

She looked him straight in the eye. "You know why."

"Will you come upstairs with me now?"

Wordlessly she nodded agreement. As Luke took her hand and they headed together for the elevators, Kate noted Marty had the sense to step aside and say nothing. Finally.

"Kate."

They were in the room; the door was closed. Luke stood slumped against it, deep hollows carved beneath his eyes. He didn't pace, he didn't talk, he simply gazed at his wife.

Kate felt a stillness enveloping them both; not a tense, questioning stillness, no, it was something calmer and better. What mattered now was what they could draw from themselves, what they could offer each other. If there was to be anything, she realized with calm certainty, they had to find it now.

"Is there a chance for us?" he asked quietly.

"There is if we both want there to be," she said. They were only words strung together, but in her heart, this time, they constituted a prayer.

"Kate, Kate." He shook his head wearily, back and forth, as if its weight were almost too great a burden on his shoulders. "I'm not whole without you, I know that in a way I've never known it before. But do you know that?"

"I'm beginning to believe it," she said. The tears were coming, she could feel them building, ready to spill forth. There was no need to protect herself, no need to hold her feelings back. I'm not going to have to play a role, she thought, and that realization gave her strength.

"Can you forgive me? Can you love me? Can it ever be the way it was before?"

"It won't be the way it was before, it can't be," she said gently. "But, Luke, I don't want that. I would never be able to go back to that. I want something better, something stronger, and you do, too. I'm right, aren't I?"

He studied her face with an expression of unguarded tenderness. "Yes, you're right," he said. "But, honey, the more I try to be honest with myself, the more scared I get."

"Tell me why."

Luke moved slowly from the door, stretching the muscles of his neck, rubbing it with his hands. "I'm thinking about why you would stick with me after what I've done," he said. "I'm trying to figure it out. You haven't much of a choice, have you? We've spent so long not knowing the truth of what we're seeing or hearing when we're alone together, how do we know what we've got? What does it mean?" He shook his head again. "I'm not sure what I'd see if I held a mirror up to my own face right now. Am I making any sense?"

"Of course you are," Kate said, her heart skipping a beat. He had to look into that mirror; he had to see what was there. "That's the way we've both been living for too long," she said. "That's why it can't be the same, ever again. I do have choices, Luke. I'm not trapped just because you may become president. I know that now."

342

"Then why would you stay with me?" he said. "Maybe I've gotten too good at this game, Kate." He turned away, but Kate swiftly raised both her hands, encircled his neck, and pulled him toward her.

"No," she said, her voice suddenly impassioned. "It's not going to keep happening like this, I'm not putting up with any more of us avoiding each other. Luke, I'm staying. Believe it, damn it. But I'm staying for a payoff, and it's not the one you think it is. You say you knew I would because there was no choice. But you're wrong, there *is* a choice—if I want it. Don't you see? I'm not staying because I'm trapped." She swept one hand into the air in a flinging gesture. "I know I can't expect you to put aside a collapsing insurance industry or a confrontation with Israel or a fight with Congress—you sell us both short if you think that!"

He was reaching now, his hands groping for her.

"Look, this isn't going to be easy," she said, moving into his embrace. "I'm not trying to drag you down into a smaller world—that never was an option for us. I'm not married to a man who's going to scramble eggs for Sunday brunch, ever."

His voice was muffled in her hair. "I don't want a wife who sacrifices herself," he said fiercely. "I don't want a political asset."

"You never will have only that." She wasn't going to allow an instant of deflection, not until she had said all she had to say, not until she had told him all that was within her heart. Was she getting through? Would he stop being so bloody afraid?

"I'm ready to let part of you go, don't you see?" she said. "But I'm not willing to let go of the private Luke, the man I love. That's the payoff I want. That's the payoff I demand. I should be your haven, and you should be mine." She was crying openly now. "It's trust, Luke. Not a photo op at the seashore. Trust. Without it, there would be no use going on. You think just because there's never been a divorced president, I'm trapped? You're wrong, dead wrong. You could be the first."

Luke gazed at her. "Yeah," he said. "And without you, I'd be the one who was trapped. Lost is more like it." His grip on her tightened. And then it was as if a dam had burst. "God, Kate," he said, the words pouring forth. "I don't want that. I don't want that at all. I don't want there to be a life without you, no matter what I do, or where I do it. I love you with all my heart, you're at the core of what

I am all about, and without you, I understand nothing. That is the bottom-line truth."

For a long moment, wordless, they clung to each other. They were tasting something new, something infinitely more hopeful than what had been before. They would not know, could not know, what lay ahead. But they needed each other, that was what they both knew now, and they knew it in a way different from any time before. Kate trembled, kissing her husband's cheek. I will do all I can to keep this together, she vowed to herself. But I'll not do it alone. That's the pact we have now.

"Kate."

"Yes, Luke?"

"I know it was our baby. Forgive me."

She closed her eyes, and felt the healing begin.

Epilogue

. . . Kate raised herself slowly from her chair as an excited network anchor called California for Luke Goodspeed. Only two electoral votes to go. The next state would take Luke over the top.

Her heart began racing. It was done.

She flicked off the set and looked around her hotel room, listening for reaction from the hundreds of campaign supporters and workers packed in the ballroom downstairs. The walls in the hotel were thin, the corridors wide, and the elevator shafts were wonderful conduits of sound.

Any second now.

With her right hand she reached for a brush on the dresser and began to run it through her hair. There would be no time for fast fix-ups later, no time for a touch of fresh lipstick or for checking her panty hose or for looking into her own heart or for deep breathing or for thinking.

She stopped still when she saw herself in the mirror. She actually looked serene, a joke which Joan would love. She looked like a woman collected, contained, and forged in fire for the job she was about to undertake. She looked—well, not young, but strong and beautiful, or at least so Luke had told her only an hour ago, in this very room, when he held her close and kissed her before descending to the crowd below.

Kate listened again. Had it happened yet? Was it official? She heard the undulating murmurs of voices and an occasional happy

345

shout reverberating up from the crowded room one floor down, but it hadn't happened yet.

Mother, she said silently to the mirror. I've done my best, I've found strength I wish I had been wise enough and old enough to give you when you needed it. If you had had that strength, you could have helped me. I wish you were with me at this moment, here, in this room, so I could tell you that, finally, I understand. And I love you.

Kate blinked back a tear. This would not do, there was no time to repair her eye makeup now. She smiled at her image. So what? The world could live with her streaked eyeliner on election night, and so could she.

Soon.

The woman in the mirror looked taller somehow. Her dress was a deep, rich blue wool, cut simply with long, tapering sleeves and a soft cowl neck. She looked thinner, too. But what really mattered was what Kate saw on her face. "Hey, you're me," she said out loud, pointing to the mirror. "I don't have to hide from you."

Kate smiled then. The impact was sinking in, finally, and she felt—was it happy? Not quite; something else. I will never have a certain kind of life I wanted with the man I love, she thought. It will be a different kind of life, and there is no going back. Some things are lost, and they are lost forever, but Luke and I are going to embrace what we have. A shadow flickered across her face. Would it work? Yes, she assured herself—we will make it work.

Suddenly, the floor beneath her feet seemed to vibrate. She closed her eyes. Thank you, Luke, she thought, for understanding that I wanted to spend this one moment alone.

And then it came. An explosion of sound. She could sense it coming toward her, a wave of acoustical energy, surging up through the elevator shafts, through the corridor, through the door, into the room, curling around her body. Slowly she raised her arms over her head in a gesture of acceptance.

At this very instant, in towns and cities across the nation, and in the capitals of the nations of the world, the news was out. Luke Goodspeed had been elected President of the United States.

The door behind her burst open. She looked into the mirror and saw the figure of her husband filling the doorway.

"Are you ready, sweetheart?" he asked. She couldn't see his eyes very well through the shadowed light, but his hand was reaching for her, and she shivered at the touch of his warm skin. "Are you ready?" he asked again, excitement vibrating in his voice.

Was she? What lay ahead? Kate turned, her shoulders straight.

"Luke," she said, with a smile on her face and a strength in her voice she hadn't expected to muster, "I'm as ready as I'll ever be."